THE
CHINESE
EMPEROR

THE CHINESE EMPEROR

Jean Lévi

TRANSLATED FROM THE FRENCH
BY BARBARA BRAY

VINTAGE BOOKS
A DIVISION OF RANDOM HOUSE
NEW YORK

FOR AGATHE

FIRST VINTAGE BOOKS EDITION, FEBRUARY 1989

English translation copyright © 1987 by Harcourt Brace Jovanovich, Inc.

All rights reserved under International and Pan-American Copyright Conventions. Published in the United States by Random House, Inc., New York. Originally published in French as *Le Grand Empereur et ses Automates* by Editions Albin Michel S.A. in 1985. Copyright © 1985 by Editions Albin Michel S.A. This English translation was originally published, in hardcover, by Harcourt Brace Jovanovich, Inc., in 1987.

Library of Congress Cataloging-in-Publication Data
Lévi, Jean.
  The Chinese emperor.
  Translation of: Le grand empereur et ses automates.
  1. Ch'in Shih-huang, Emperor of China, 259–210 B.C.—
Fiction. 2. China—History—Ch'in dynasty,
221–207 B.C.—Fiction. I. Title.
PQ2672.E942G7313 1989   843'.914   88-40175
ISBN 0-394-75996-6 (pbk.)

Manufactured in the United States of America
10 9 8 7 6 5 4 3 2 1

No tyrant's power can compare with that of a poor wretch ready to kill himself.

CIORAN

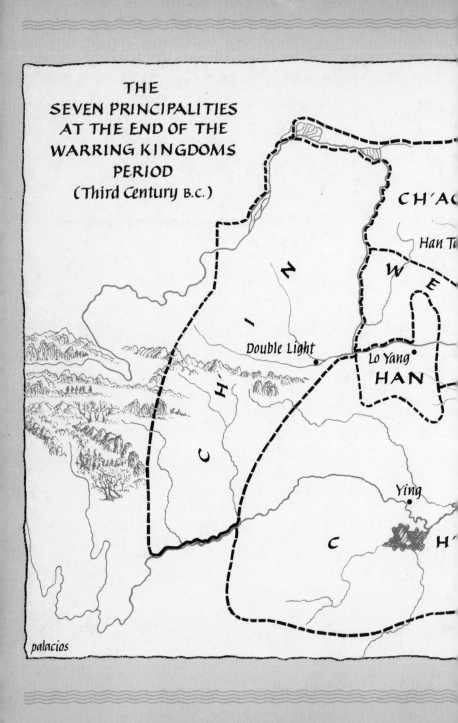

THE
SEVEN PRINCIPALITIES
AT THE END OF THE
WARRING KINGDOMS
PERIOD
(Third Century B.C.)

CH'AO

Han Ta

W E

Double Light

Lo Yang

HAN

Ying

C

H'

C H I N

C

palacios

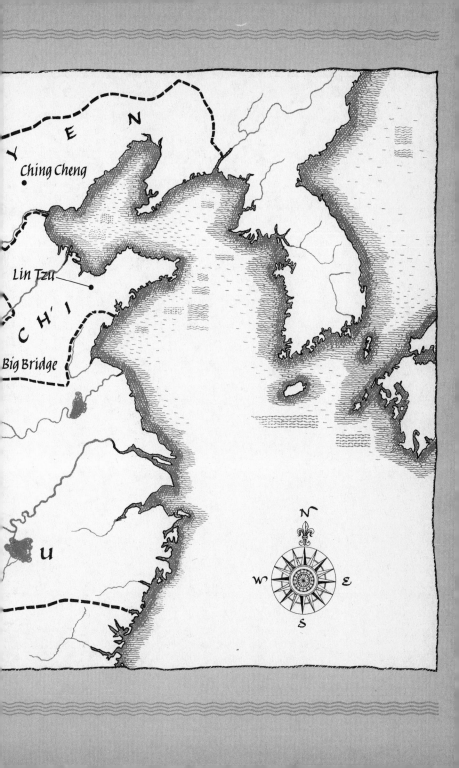

CONTENTS

BOOK ONE

*Lü Pu-wei,
or the Age
of Guile*

CHAPTER I

THE PETITION

The fat man heaved a dejected sigh and glanced absently out the fretted window of the study. He had come here to write. But he could smell the scents of the garden, and the broad leaves of the cacao trees quivered under the caress of the morning sun. A peal of feminine laughter rang out near the duck pond. Concubines in light robes were pelting one another with petals and many-colored silk streamers as they danced around the clear waters. He felt like going out and chasing them through the trees—and catching them, too! But what was he thinking of? He had to toil away at the petition. His future and perhaps his head depended on it.

A plaintive song rose into the warm air:

In heaven there is a holy couple,
But between them lies the Milky Way.
The shuttle clicks,
But nothing is woven.
Goad in hand,
He urges the steer.
Every night parted,
And reunited but once a year,
Today they are one again....

How could he have forgotten? It was the seventh day of the seventh month, the fast of matrimony and women's work. He thought about his wife, the brave and loyal companion of his early days as a merchant—and the disapproving witness of his rising career as a minister. For three years now she had been living on the Hill of Wild Grasses west of Lo Yang, no longer present to see her gloomy prophecies come true. Yet it was as if her warnings had saved him from the fate she predicted for him. Who could tell, though, whether the letter he was writing on the day when the Wagoner and the Weaver were in conjunction might not bring them together again—in the underground abodes of the Yellow Springs!

He turned back to the sheafs of bamboo and applied himself to his writing:

> I find it most difficult to address my sovereign. I stick at every word and rewrite every expression, not because it is hard for me to summon up phrases or compose a text, but because I am afraid of being misunderstood. I dread your reactions, I am paralyzed at the thought of displeasing you....

He frowned, read over what he had written, grunted crossly, and scratched out the last sentence angrily with the scraper. No, that wasn't the way. He was writing not as someone who wished to please his sovereign but as a sincere man, a slandered minister proclaiming his innocence. But the worst of it was that it was true: he *was* afraid of this prince whom he had dandled on his knee and who might even be his own . . . But about that he wasn't sure. If, as some people maintained, that *had* been one of his "investments," it was the most disastrous investment he had ever made.

If I festoon my sentences as finely as the embroideries that come from the slender hands of the weaver maidens of Chiang Nan, you will exclaim, "How literary!" If my style is rigorous and direct and I nail down my thoughts tersely, you will shrug your shoulders and say, "How dull!" If I employ all the devices of rhetoric and pile up similes, parables, hyperboles, and allusions, you will think it merely a collection of empty formulas. If I denounce the intrigues and ulterior motives of your entourage, you will think me motivated by spite and scandal-mongering. If I expound deep-laid schemes long pondered in my retirement and reveal to you the most distant future, you will accuse me of boasting. I confine myself to practical matters and go into the minutest detail, and you see it as proof of a mean and limited intelligence. I follow the fashion and am indulgent toward the little failings of the great, and I'm a toady. My opinions conflict with those of the common herd and I castigate the feebleness of the age I live in—and that's a pose. My brush is full of energy and my style brilliant—mere convention. I avoid all literary artifice and go straight to the point like a surgeon—and I'm a boor. . . .

And *that* wasn't just rhetoric, he thought as he inscribed his angular ideograms: the problem was not so much finding sound arguments as making them convincing. One couldn't always guess the thoughts of the person one spoke to, and words often missed their mark. If you speak of gain to a prince who believes only in virtue, he'll accuse you of greed; but if you mention virtue to another, who thinks only of profit, you'll be called naive.

If you praise the integrity of a master who, while pretending to follow the path of virtue, is really only seeking efficiency, he will drop you while seeming to promote you. If you openly take account of his secret purposes, he will make use of your advice and put you down anyway.

He had had daily experience of this when his fame was at its height. . . .

Alas, however sensible your words may be and however sound your advice, will your prince listen to them? A trifle is enough to arouse his suspicions or wound his feelings. And once the poison of doubt has been dropped into his heart, a slander, a malicious word from a courtier, a mere coincidence of circumstances may bring about the fall of the reckless one who has thus laid himself open to danger. Did not Wu Tzu-hsü, wily as he was, have his head cut off? His body was sewn up in a leather bottle and thrown to the fishes in the Great River. The birds pecked out his eyes, the wind withered his cheeks, and the hot sun whitened his bones. Fan Su had his ribs broken and his teeth knocked out. Mei Po was made mincemeat of, pickled and sold in the market place. Shang Yang was quartered, and all his relations were destroyed. Such has been the fate of loyal servants and honest subjects of the state.

Far away from court, where my high office made me the object of much hatred, I feel even more vulnerable than a courtier making his trembling request: I cannot justify my actions in person. Certain things cannot be satisfactorily consigned to writing. If someone jealous of me should have my prince's ear, my words will be misinterpreted. The noblest of intentions and the loftiest of goals will be set down to base self-interest. The more blameless my conduct, the more heinous the designs that will be attributed to me. . . .

The former minister mopped his brow. Was it so hot that he was perspiring here, where even in the height of summer the walls gave off a cellarlike chill, or was it anxiety that made his hands so clammy?

After this rather abstract passage, a few anecdotes were called for by way of illustration and entertainment. That was always the technique of the great philosopher Hsün Tzu. He checked through his heap of notes and copied out with renewed energy:

Chi-fu Wen-po died and sixteen of his wives were so grieved they killed themselves upon his dead body. But his mother was unmoved. When her people expressed surprise, she said sourly: "Confucius was a sage and my son did not see fit to follow him into exile when he was banished from the principality of Lu. If his sixteen wives died with him, it only shows they thought more of him than he did of the sage." No doubt she sincerely believed that she was speaking the language of virtue, but how was she to prevent malicious minds from seeing it as spite? For words, like deeds, mean different things according to the angle they are seen from. I am afraid that, as in the case of Chi-fu Wen-po's mother, anything I say in my own defense may be turned against me, and that now that I am out of favor my own integrity will be turned into cause for complaint.

Flaw in Jade, when he enjoyed the favor of the prince of Wei, made use of the royal chariot to get to his mother's death-bed as quickly as possible. According to the law, any official who used the prince's chariot without permission was supposed to have his feet cut off. But instead of punishing him the prince exclaimed: "What a dutiful son! To help his mother through her last moments, Flaw in Jade was not afraid to risk the most dreadful torment." Another day, when he was walking with his sovereign in the orchard of the royal palace, he picked a peach, took a bite, and, finding it to be ripe and sweet, held it out to the prince. The prince cried, "How he loves me! He forgoes a great pleasure so that I might enjoy it instead!" But when the favorite's beauty declined and the prince's love faded, everything Flaw in Jade did was wrong. Thinking back over the past, the prince grumbled, "To think that this creature dared to take my carriage without my permission, and offered me a peach defiled by his breath!" The same deeds that once seemed signs of virtue and love were transformed into terrible crimes. Delight was succeeded by disgust.

The words of a favorite always bear the hallmark of wisdom, he muttered as he went on writing. But once a man has incurred a ruler's displeasure, everything he says or does only increases the ruler's dislike.

As you know, a dragon has a scale under its neck which must never be touched; if it is, this peaceful creature, which makes such a marvelous mount, goes raving mad and tears its rider to pieces. A prince, too, has such a scale, and anyone who lives with him may count himself lucky if he never strokes it the wrong way.

The story goes that when Cheng Ts'en was in Fei, a namesake of his committed a murder. A neighbor lost no time in informing his mother, "Cheng Ts'en has just killed a man!" But his mother calmly went on spinning. A few minutes later, someone else came and told her, "Your son has committed a murder!" Still she continued as if nothing had happened. But when a third person came with the same story, she dropped her spindle, jumped over the wall, and ran away as fast as her legs would carry her. So it took the reports of only three people to sow doubt in the mind of a woman as certain of her son's virtue as Cheng Ts'en's mother. I don't possess Cheng Ts'en's virtue, you don't believe in me as Cheng Ts'en's mother believed in him, and there are more than three courtiers ready to slander me. So, my prince, I fear that you may drop your spindle!

The ex-minister laid down his brush and read over his notes with a critical eye. Three examples were rather a lot. Should he leave one of them out? It would be a pity—they were his favorite anecdotes. He thought he remembered having read them in a treatise on oratory by Han Negation. . . . To hell with moderation! He'd keep all three.

Might not the king find the bit about the scale of the dragon rather impertinent? Still, he liked tweaking the tiger's whiskers, and one had to know how to take risks occasionally. And hadn't that metaphor won a certain famous orator the position of prime minister?

At this point a young eunuch broke the thread of his thoughts by bringing in the light collation he had ordered when he got up: millet wine, dried fish, fruit, and—his favorite dish—fried beans.

How time flew! He'd been laboring over this letter for five days now, and still it was far from correct. He could talk, yes. He could get around anyone. Perhaps it was being in trade that had developed the gift of gab in him. One of his enemies had called him a barker. . . . What had become of the insolent wretch? Had he had the man cut up in pieces and pickled? No, not that one—he'd merely laughed at him. . . . Still, he did sometimes regret not having had a scholarly education. As soon as it came to writing them down, his ideas, which a moment before were all neatly and accurately organized, took off in all directions like a flight of wild ducks shot at by an archer. And here, in his retirement, he had no one to advise him or arrange his arguments for him into fine parallel phrases with examples from the classics and apt quotations. No, unfortunately, he had no Li Ssu with him, only second-rate scholars, conscientious but mediocre brush-pushers.

Luckily, he could fall back on the dissertations his retainers had written in the days of his glory. He could remember something from the oratorical contests he once organized at his court, so the money he'd spent feeding that army of empty-bellied talkers hadn't been entirely thrown away.

He picked absent-mindedly at the dishes set out on the tray, but didn't feel hungry. He put down his ivory chopsticks and went back to his epistle:

> I want to demonstrate my sincerity and the importance I attach to the greatness of your house, not so much to save my unworthy self as to save you from the base flatterers and intriguers with whom you are surrounded.

And to think it was the people who were once his most enthusiastic supporters who were now howling for his blood! He gave a wry smile as he remembered Li Ssu, whom he had raised from a minor provincial official to a privy councilor, and who was now his worst enemy and most formidable opponent.

> No, I am not afraid of death. Is it not the natural end of all things and the conclusion of every human life? Even the greatest sages of antiquity had to die. I know I am subject to the inescapable laws of the universe, which decree that autumn must follow summer, the moon wax and wane, and day give way to night. If I thought that my death was necessary to the preservation of the state, and that I must give my life in order to save yours, I would go forth to execution gladly.

Gladly? He shuddered, and looked around with satisfaction at the pleasing array of galleries, summerhouses, terraces, and gardens. His glance rested lovingly on the sinuous curves of walls standing in the shade of ancient trees, then ranged over the rich carvings on beams painted bright vermilion and blue. Through the shifting screen made by a copse of speckled bamboo he could see slender white shapes disporting themselves in the pool. He could hear ripples and chuckles. Fans of spray pitted the smooth surface of the water; some of his women had removed their clothes and were splashing about like great white swans.

The sight of those pearly bodies brought the blood to his face. He had been wool-gathering. If he wanted to go on enjoying the pleasures of life, he must buckle down to his petition. The chore had already been postponed too often.

> But I fear my death would tarnish your reputation and cast a slur on a prince I love. For while a fair punishment adds to a ruler's prestige, inflicting one that is undeserved only harms his good name. I care more for your glory than for my own life, and would rather lay myself open to calumny and risk your wrath than say nothing and live cravenly in gilded exile. Life would be hateful to me if I knew I owed it to an ignoble silence.

Every phrase must now be carefully weighed. One word out of place and he was done for. The *Book of Odes* described his situation exactly: "I edge forward shivering and shaking, walking on thin ice." Why didn't he have the virtuosity of the sophists he used to keep at his court when he was prime minister? Although he had fostered the love of art and literature so successfully in this barbarous country that its capital had outshone the Chi Hsia Academy in Wei, and although he had gathered together in his palace more scientists and military experts than the prince of P'ing Yüan and Prince Spring Awakening, he remained, when everything was said and done, a man of action. It was by deeds, not words, that he had climbed to the highest of honors.

> So I will tell you what is in my heart quite plainly, setting aside all the empty flourishes of rhetoric.

Sire, I have been atrociously slandered, the victim of an odious intrigue. It is true that anyone in high office should be able to detect the wicked schemes of great dignitaries and nip rebellion in the bud. But I was Lao Ai's dupe, not his accomplice.

No doubt this fault calls for some exemplary punishment, and you must think me bold to beg for clemency when in your infinite goodness you already declined to inflict the ultimate penalty on an old servant of the state, merely sending him into exile on his own property. But I should like to say in my defense that my negligence was caused by the very diligence with which I tended the affairs of our country.

With my mind full of many vast projects, waging war on your enemies so as to widen Ch'in's borders, endeavoring to spread your fame abroad and bring the whole world under your sway—preoccupied by all these things, I forgot that danger might arise in the heart of the palace itself. I thought your throne was established beyond a doubt. But, alas, the queen your mother was harboring evil designs. When a rat hides under the mound of the god of the earth, it cannot be driven out. You cannot smoke it out for fear of burning down the sacred tree; you cannot drown it without destroying the mound. Lao Ai had become a rat under the altar of the god of the earth. He hid in the shadow of the throne. In handing him over to justice, might I not have undermined the king's authority? Am I to be blamed for having relied on your own firmness and perspicacity?

He put down his brush and reread the passage anxiously. Wasn't he admitting that it was he who once pulled all the strings? But, by the shades of his ancestors, he had to remind this brat that it was thanks to *his* contrivances that the kingdom of Ch'in had imposed its rule on all the nobles!

The fable of the rat was from one of Negation's speeches. The king, fond of Negation, would not mind frequent borrowings from his favorite philosopher. But perhaps, on such a thorny subject, the image wasn't in the best of taste. Lao Ai hadn't just been hiding in the shadow of the throne: it was from under the queen mother's skirts that the former minister had flushed him out.

Old memories brought a dreamy smile to his square and forceful face, but then he came back to earth. No, the young king was a prude, he would not have allowed himself to make such associations. Carried along by the rhythm of the writing, he would be grateful to the writer for his frankness.

> I scented out their intrigues early, but chose to say nothing. "He's in league with them!" people hastened to say. But it's not true. I wanted him to give himself away. And, indeed, emboldened by what he took to be his immunity, he broke cover, and my king showed his wisdom by striking him down at once and without mercy.

He had to admit he'd been incredibly foolish to introduce the scoundrel into the queen's apartments. But was that blunder enough to make the king forget the part his minister had played in the king's own rise to power? And it was on the minister's orders that his spies warned the king of what was going on. What else could the minister have done? Made a frontal attack on one who enjoyed the support of the regent, the queen mother? That would have been courting disaster. . . .

He was bathed in perspiration; there were great damp stains under his armpits. The calligraphy wasn't coming easy.

Now he needed to anticipate criticism—the classical rhetorical device of "taking possession." He had to exploit to the full the sophists' skill in the dialectical turning of tables, so as to trap the king in his own intransigence. He had to transfer the battle to the enemy's own ground, make the enemy turn his weapons against himself.

Of course, this part of the letter referred especially to Li Ssu.

> Perhaps you will criticize me for not having chosen my associates more wisely, for not having foreseen what would occur. But do not let this human failing blot out the services I rendered your father. I raised him from the position of a son of

a second rank to that of prince of one of the most powerful states in the confederation of nobles. I linked my fate to his, and with him endured many trials. Together we triumphed over all difficulties. I helped him in Han Tan and rescued him from an ignominious death. I used my wealth, my credit, and my connections to protect you and your mother when the people, reduced to starvation by your army, were ready to murder you.

I know very well that past virtues do not cancel out present offenses. It is one of the chief laws of the kingdom of Ch'in that men should be judged by their current success and not by their former glory. You have managed to conciliate public opinion by pardoning your mother, and you have won a reputation for magnanimity by not punishing your humble servant. But in fact you have confined yourself to half-measures. If I am really guilty, my crime deserves death, and some will wonder at your doing such violence to the law. Careerists who hide their greed beneath the guise of morality will have no difficulty persuading you that my death is necessary to preserve the security of the state. And so your clemency will have been both fleeting and useless.

But if I have committed no crime, and the tragic ordeal we have just gone through is only an accident, remember the services I rendered our country, call me back from my exile, and see if you cannot still make use of my talents. . . .

The golden light of a late afternoon in summer shone through the pillars and silhouetted the massive shoulders of the merchant as he pored over his notes.

The light showed him taking up a square of silk and copying out his letter, with many erasures. It showed him taking another square of silk and copying his letter out all over again, while graceful figures filled a summerhouse with bowls of fruit and other delicacies in honor of the two stars reunited for a night.

The sun sank behind the hills of Lo Yang. The twisted shapes of ancient pine trees stood out for a moment, black on crimson, before fading into the mist. The former minister drew the last character on the red-striped writing material, put his wolf-hair brush away in its case, impatiently shoved aside the unavailing scraper, and gazed thoughtfully at the slips of bamboo, the wooden tablets, and the pieces of fabric piled up on the low table and scattered over the flower-patterned terra-cotta tiles. The time he'd wasted writing this wretched petition! He could, of course, have dictated it to one of his scribes, but he wanted it to bear his personal imprint. A former prime minister ought to be an expert calligrapher. He hadn't managed too badly in the end, he thought. It sounded impressive. The arguments were properly marshaled. The various sections hung together just as in the writings of Master Negation, Su Tai, and Ts'ai the Benefactor.

He reread his stirring final appeal one last time, not without a certain satisfaction:

> My king, here on my estate in Honan I watch for a sign from you. When I think of the tasks still to be done and the snares lying in wait for you, I weep and sigh as I look toward the west. How I wish I could find the words to open the gates of your heart! How I should love to talk with you face to face about the great plans I cherish that cannot be committed to silk! My prince, I blush before my ancestors at the thought of enjoying privileges and emoluments without being of use to the community.
>
> If he has been importunate, your loyal vassal begs humbly, on his knees, the favor of being allowed to put an end to himself!

Now all he had to do was attach his seal. He rummaged among the jade signets with hieratic symbols, which hung on silken cords from his belt. But his hand came slowly away, empty. Of course it wasn't there anymore, the pale jade signet inscribed with a dragon and a tiger. Should he, then, use the seigneurial seal he was entitled to as marquis of Faith in Learning? He still had that one. But the king might think it in bad taste. What about the family seal? That smacked too much of trade; it was on all the goods turned out in his workshops. No, better put nothing but his signature: Lü Pu-wei— the signature of an ordinary individual writing to a prince.

And now to work out the most auspicious time to send it. . . .

He took his geomantic dial from its case and adjusted the rings that represented the terrestrial branches and celestial trunks in relation to the animals symbolizing the points of the compass—the white tiger, the green dragon, the firebird, and the dark tortoise. The constellations revolved around the fixed center of the Great Bear. A remarkable instrument—its shiny bronze surface contained the whole universe. Generations of merchants had used it in making their cunning calculations and determining auspicious moments. Men like Fan Li and Pai K'uei owed their fortunes to it. It was much better than divination by tortoise—that was too elaborate and old-fashioned. Besides, no one used tortoises now except a few princely families with pretensions to antiquity.

He didn't really understand the *Book of Changes*. He didn't trust those hexagrams; they even made him a little uneasy. They were too abstract. It was a system for scholars and scribes. He was faithful to the tradition of his caste—in this, at any rate. . . .

His mind had wandered again. He was getting old. Before, all his attention used to be concentrated on the object in view, but now he found himself daydreaming at the most inopportune moments. He must get back to reality.

He began calculating the stages of the journey. The courier would take a week to get from Lo Yang to Double Light. An eternity. When he was prime minister he had been entitled to use the mail service, and his letters went like lightning. But what difference did it make? The signs were unfavorable for the whole of the current period. Yet he couldn't put off doing anything for a year! . . . Time was short—so to hell with the signs!

He stood up, moved the lacquer screen aside, and told his page to call a messenger and give him the slim scroll of beribboned silk.

———

The young king let the costly scroll of painstakingly written silk fall from his grasp.

He could feel an attack of migraine coming on. He had laid aside his court dress—the snow-white silk robe painted with many-colored dragons and phoenixes, under a heavy fox cloak with gold-embroidered facings—and had hoped to use this brief interval of leisure to study a couple of legal texts and get to the bottom of some dubious accounts that one of his higher officials handed him during the morning audience, when he started to get the familiar dull buzzing in the ears, along with a pain at the base of his skull and at the roots of his teeth. It was not his ex-minister's letter that brought these symptoms on, but the letter had come at a bad moment, spoiling one of the few times of the day when he could relax. The short lull between the morning reception of dignitaries and lunch was—apart from night, of course—his best and most productive period, when his mind was clear and he felt as if there was nothing he couldn't understand.

But he'd known very well that this would happen, that sooner or later he would have to settle the matter of Lü Pu-wei once and for all. But he didn't like people or things to bring themselves to his attention in this way. He himself must be free to choose the moment to summon them to judgment. He ought to put off reading the letter until tonight.

No, that was unworthy of an enlightened prince: a master of men never procrastinated. Now he wouldn't be able to get this business off his mind until he came to some decision about it. The image of his ex-minister's pudgy face would plague him day and night, coming between him and his favorite reading, infiltrating his beloved criminal codes.

He could feel a nausea coming over him. The migraine was

taking hold. Could he make a wise decision while in this state? Was he sure of arriving at a sound judgment when he had a heavy head and a dry mouth? He sighed dejectedly and massaged his temples underneath his cap. Yes, he would have to give in and send for a doctor. He made an imperious wave with his hand and a young page sped forward. The king grunted with satisfaction as he noted the formal perfection with which the page moved: feet gliding rapidly in tiny steps, arms held slightly from the body and flapping like the wings of a bird, head stretched forward and focusing on a point neither above his master's chin nor below his master's waist. Ordinance liked everything, even the smallest detail, to be done exactly.

After ascertaining the king's wish, the servant flew to find a doctor; there was always one at hand. As he waited for the physician to come, Ordinance started thinking again. That very morning some former clients of Lü Pu-wei had asked for an interview, probably to plead the fallen minister's cause.

The doctor was announced: it was Hsia Wu-chüeh. When the eunuch asked him to enter, he prostrated himself twice, then took the pulse of the young king's eleven upper and lower veins. The trouble was caused by the main lower yang vein, the one linking the heels, through the spine, to the top of the head, then going down again through the temples to the cheekbones and thence to the eyes. When that vein is affected it vibrates, causing stiffness in the neck, migraines, and tightness of the chest.

Yes, that was it—he felt uneasy in his mind again, and heavy-hearted. Hsia Wu-chüeh ferreted about in the capacious bag where he kept his drugs and instruments. The young king recoiled slightly at the gleam of the long acupuncture needles, and was relieved when the doctor only took out some little white pills smelling of honey and *fu ling*. He swallowed them under the watchful gaze of the man who bore the crushing responsibility for the royal health. When the doctor withdrew, he began thinking again, a little more calmly now, about his former prime minister.

Should he get rid of him? For some obscure reason the idea of punishment did not appeal to him this time. Perhaps because it went against his sense of justice. Lü Pu-wei had managed to touch a sensitive cord. Ordinance had just recalled his mother to court; was he now to be harsh toward someone whose guilt had never been clearly established? Should he let him return to Double Light, then? No, not for the world—the king shuddered at the very thought. Let him stay on his estate in Honan? But Ordinance would not be able to sleep in peace while that large fat spider spun a web around him, plotting and fidgeting and keeping up secret communications everywhere. At this very moment he might be hatching a plot in which this petition was a key factor.

Ordinance would have to consider the letter in the light of the references made to Lü Pu-wei's virtues that morning. . . . He was becoming mistrustful—too mistrustful. But could a ruler ever be suspicious enough? Suspicion was part of the job of a master of men.

He had to admit, though, that he admired the letter's firm tone and easy style. Some passages were really excellent, and the arguments were convincingly phrased. The former minister managed to stress, without too much self-advertisement, the outstanding services he had rendered the king's father and the country. And could he be held responsible for the misdeeds of the king's mother? Wasn't it really thanks to him that Lao Ai had been eliminated? True, he had managed to profit from all the affairs he was involved in, but as a shrewd politician he anticipated that objection:

> People will tell you, if they have not already done so, that in all this I have worked as much for my own aggrandizement as for that of your house. I confess that that is so. But is it not human nature to seek one's own advantage? The whole world worships profit. Maidens of Chao and damsels of Cheng, with their white-painted faces, damask cheeks, and high heels, careless of their husbands' looks so long as the men have plenty of hard cash; merchants lost to shame; soldiers ready to face forests of spears and swords; honest government officials whose stomachs

are weary with continual fasting; thieves who snap their fingers at the law; tiger hunters; inveterate gamesters who spend every night in gambling dens—are not they one and all driven by the same desire for gain? Without the thirst for riches and glory, mankind would be ungovernable: greed is the surest guarantee of loyalty. Duke Hsiao knew this, and so did King Ch'in the Resplendent and your late father. That is why they were able to raise the Ch'in dynasty to its present height.

The king could only agree. Didn't his favorite authors, Shang Yang and Han Negation, say there was no greater threat to a state than men of integrity? And integrity was one thing the merchant could not be accused of. He had been honest enough, also, not to try to make use of his former finery.

So what was the reason for the uneasiness, this faint feeling of irritation with a letter in which every expression had been chosen to please the recipient? Was that itself the reason? No, for the letter also had a certain breeziness: the fables about the dragon's scale and about Cheng Ts'en's mother were almost impertinent. That was the supreme skill of the courtier—to combine a hint of offense with flattery. No, the source of his dissatisfaction lay in the profusion of images, the verbal extravagance, the ostentation and excess that betrayed someone not really at home in the world of literature. Why three anecdotes to illustrate a figure of rhetoric when one would have sufficed? Lü Pu-wei knew he, the king, valued conciseness. Clearly, the former minister had learned something from the rhetoricians he used to keep at his court like a string of thoroughbreds, but there was one thing they couldn't teach him, and that was elegance. Whatever a person does, what's bred in the bone will come out in the flesh. The young king reread, with a curl of the lip:

> Some will no doubt seize upon my expensive way of life as a means of turning you against me. They pretend to be shocked at the size of my estates, the splendor of my palaces, the sump-

tuous clothes I wear, my fine stable. But should not representatives of the state contribute, through their own luxury, to the fame of the country they serve? What would people say of a prince whose ministers went about in oxcarts and dressed in rags? Especially since, unlike the marquis of Abundance and the parents of the late Empress Hsüan, the wife of your glorious great-grandfather, I have been able to amass a fortune through the wise use of my official earnings and gratuities and by means of prudent commercial dealings—and not through bribery or corruption. My opulence, far from injuring the royal family, only adds to its luster.

There was something grotesque about mentioning such trifles when one was in danger of beng charged with high treason. And the merchant's wealth *did* offend the king. Lü Pu-wei's insolent display of luxury irritated him—the man was usurping the royal prerogatives! When a minister's style of living is as sumptuous as the king's, there is a confusion of rank and an infringement of power. For society to be properly run, hierarchy needs to be reflected in every detail of life, to be seen in concrete form—in such things as clothes and carriages. And what audacity, to refer to the relations between his mother and Lao Ai! Admittedly the affair was common knowledge, but he might have had the tact not to dwell on so painful an episode.

No question about it, the king hated him. He raised unpleasant memories. Memories were always unpleasant. But what was the king to do?

His headache was no better, but he had to make a decision, and quickly, too—the decisions of an educated prince were always swift. He recalled the maxim of Prince Shang: "The ruler of a country where decisions are made in a day will rule the world; the ruler of a country where they take a day and a night will be strong; but where decisions take two days, the country will be destroyed."

He had no one to advise him. He felt so lost and alone. Kings called themselves orphans, and they were quite right: a man who was the father and mother of a people *was* an orphan. Who was there in his entourage whom he could trust? They were all hand in glove with Lü Pu-wei or with Lü Pu-wei's enemies, if not both. The rest were base flatterers, toadies whose bland smiles and slimy obsequiousness revolted him. Not a single honest, upright man, not one duke of Chou or Kuan Tzu.

Well, yes, there was Li Ssu. But the king didn't feel up to an interview with him. His words were always so difficult to understand. Not that his thinking was confused or obscure—on the contrary, it was lucid and almost too cogent, as if language interposed no obstacle between his mind and the listener. The king had to make a great effort not to lose the thread, though he never wearied of listening. Li Ssu cast a spell over him. It was only afterward that he realized how profound his views were and how sound his judgment. All very exhausting.

But he must come to some decision.

Yes! He would ask the acting minister to provide him with a report on Lü Pu-wei. He loved reports, and Li Ssu would know what was expected of him. Not a long disquisition full of advice—the king already had more advisers than he knew what to do with—but a well-researched file with useful comments, written in a terse, unambiguous style.

After all, the king knew nothing of the events that had taken place just prior to his birth or while he was still a child; he had only a few vague impressions of unconnected, insubstantial scenes, nothing solid or reliable. What he needed was information, and clever Li Ssu was the man to provide it. It would also give him something to read during his long sleepless nights.

His brow cleared. He straightened his robe, smoothed his cuffs, called a page, and told him to prepare his writing materials. Sitting down, he made the brush fly over the silk.

Li Ssu gave a sinister chuckle as he unrolled the prince's letter, which came accompanied by the fallen minister's petition. At last he had an opportunity to eliminate once and for all someone who, despite his fall from favor, was still the only obstacle to his own success. If he was really clever, he could simultaneously rid himself of a rival and win the complete confidence of a suspicious king. He would spread his wings and rise upward like a phoenix. He'd waited years for this moment. As soon as he'd become Lü Pu-wei's secretary, he'd started collecting papers and other evidence concerning all the politicians, building up a regular archive. The archive not only taught him the history that lay behind the present but also provided him with ammunition against his enemies.

It had proved its usefulness at the time of the inquiry into Lao Ai's failed coup, and now it was going to come in handy again. The secret of success lay in the presentation of the material: not as a mere criminal brief but, rather, as an evaluation of a period of history.

The silver seal he wielded as honorary minister tinkled against the jade pendants hanging from his belt as he took out his brush and poised it over the square of silk. He remained like that for some time, staring motionless into space, then lowered the brush and began to ply it boldly and smoothly:

> Prince, I am at once delighted at being chosen from among all the wise and virtuous advisers at your court and fearful lest I fail to show myself worthy of this favor. I rejoice at enjoying your confidence but tremble already at the thought of losing it.
>
> For a stranger who, despite his lack of merit, has recently been made an acting minister, it is indeed a dangerous task to try to advise his sovereign in so delicate a matter. You say you find yourself in a quandary over the petition sent to you by the merchant Lü Pu-wei, and you ask me to suggest a solution. But how dare I offer an opinion when you yourself are undecided? In judging affairs of state or any other highly important matter, one hesitates to express a clear and precise opinion for fear of

being accused of partiality. And it is true that when we think we are making a perfectly just decision, we may not really be acting as evenhandedly as we should like other people, and even ourselves, to think. Some personal feeling or vested interest often comes into it. Even when this is not so and no ulterior motive distorts our judgment, the prince himself has only to suspect that it does and any relationship of trust and friendship between a devoted servant and his sovereign is destroyed.

Then jealous onlookers lose no time in detecting this chink in their mutual understanding and doing all they can, patiently and insidiously, to widen it, now with an ambiguous word, now with the grossest slander. It is thus that princes lose their most loyal subjects.

If I advise you to rid yourself of Lü Pu-wei, everyone will say that I am motivated by envy. If I plead for him to be pardoned, people will point out his liberality toward me and the gratitude I owe him for introducing me at court. You place me in the cruel dilemma of having to appear either a traitor or an accomplice!

But what in fact deters me is not so much the fear of tittle-tattle—I know you are too wise to heed that—as my contempt for the lengthy bombast our orators indulge in to justify decisions dictated by interests they are careful to conceal.

There are as many reasons for condemning Lü Pu-wei to death as there are for pardoning him, and I can easily imagine a sophist making his arguments oscillate between the two extremes, so that the man you are ready to throw into boiling oil one minute is fit, the next, to be put at the head of your government.

Such is always the way when one judges only by the surface of things, but in a case like the one we are dealing with here, we must rise above contingency, widen our purview, and appraise not individuals themselves but their historical significance. My prince must concern himself with great political trends rather than with the wretched individuals who thrash about feebly below him.

You know how I hate the sophists' long tirades about history, and it would be against my principles to expound my personal views on politics. For it is mere deception to give one's prince advice not founded on concrete facts.

Facts, nothing but facts properly verified—that is what an honest servant of the state should offer his master. Truth is derived from comparing as many sources of information as possible. So, instead of a labored academic dissertation, here is a file, the Lü Pu-wei file, which will show you the plain, down-to-earth reality. Gossip, letters, police and secret agents' reports, conversations overheard and written down by the spies of various princes—these are what your humble servant proposes to offer to your perspicacity. In choosing these particular pieces of evidence from among the thousands that have been gathered by our services, I have sought to give an idea of an age rather than to describe the behavior of one man. These notes, whether official or clandestine, will reveal a world of intrigues, betrayals, and abused authority, but also of devotion and self-sacrifice: the world of a prime minister whom you never really knew.

I have not thought it necessary to repeat what is already familiar to you. Most of the evidence concerning recent events was brought to your attention at the time of the first inquiry. But I have included a few new documents that throw light on some points that previously remained obscure. Not every item is of equal value. While I have no doubts as to the veracity of the spies and secret agents and the writers of the official records, I am dubious about some of the rumors they report. Truth, however, sometimes hides behind hearsay. I have adopted Han Negation's method of investigation; I agree with him that one needs to consult every possible source in order to arrive at a proper assessment.

I admit that I have sometimes been tempted to leave out

certain items for fear of shocking you, but, at the risk of your disapproval, I have not given way to that cowardly impulse. Not everything you read here will be pleasant, but is it not said that "As a thousand sheepskins are not worth one fox-belly muff, so the praises of a thousand flatterers do less good than one word from an honest man"? Also, "Honeyed words are a poison, sharp criticism is a cure." So, instead of giving you an expurgated version of the facts, I inform you even of that which may seem offensive.

I would rather incur your anger than conceal something on the pretext of good taste but really out of base sycophancy. Nothing must escape the eye of the master, so nothing must be left unsaid. A prince who discourages frankness sets foot upon a slippery slope: henceforth he hears only what is likely to please him. Surrounded by a servile court anxious to anticipate his wishes and minister to his worst proclivities, he is cut off from reality. When he notices this, it will be too late: there isn't always a Fan Sui around to set him right. But I know my king's wisdom too well to be afraid of upsetting him with material that may be painful.

One more point. I will send you the last writings of Master Negation, which will show you Lü Pu-wei's indebtedness to him in his piece about the difficulties of discourse. Unfortunately, he understood the letter rather than the spirit.

CHAPTER II

THE LÜ PU-WEI FILE

The young prince put down the letter and smiled. That was Li Ssu all over.

Meditatively, he opened the casket containing the documents that made up the file. They had been divided into four sheafs of different sizes, each marked with a number and title indicating its contents. Ordinance marveled at his minister's thoroughness. He picked up the first sheaf, a scroll containing entries of various lengths, undid it, and began to read.

AUTOBIOGRAPHICAL FRAGMENTS

Preliminary observation by Li Ssu

In the course of a house search carried out by palace agents at the time of the first inquiry, we found various writings from the brush of the prime minister. Although the official in charge of the investigation considered them irrelevant, they were copied down and placed in the archives. I do not know what Lü Pu-wei intended to do with this motley collection of jottings. Some might be drafts for a treatise on trade that he meant to add to the one on agriculture in his *Springs and Autumns*; or they might be sections of a preface intended for the same work. Though he often spoke of it, no one ever actually read it. But the style and tone are appropriate to a composition of that kind; of course, a merchant can have only the vaguest ideas about literature. The other items are notes by the minister himself on the outstanding events in his life. That is rather strange; it would make him his own historian.

But the form is of little importance. What I wish to give you is Lü Pu-wei's own point of view. Take these fragments as a sort of confession—or as answers to an interrogation of which the questions have been lost.

Autobiographical notes by Lü Pu-wei

According to the Theory of the Five Elements, wood corresponds to the east. And yet we find mountains rich in copper in Tan Shang. The south is supposed to mean fire, but in Yüeh there are rivers as wide as oceans. The west is meant to indicate metal, yet it is the provinces of Shu and Lung whose forests produce the most valuable wood. North means water, and the gloomy capital of Yü Tu is surrounded by sandy deserts. Thus does the world remedy excess by the redistribution of wealth.

In our own day, west of the mountains the earth produces huge trees and slender bamboos, while ox hair, precious stones, and hemp are still to be found. East of the passes is the area for fish, salt, lacquer, and silk goods, and music and the arts flourish there. The region south of the Blue River is full of all sorts of useful trees and spices: oak, catalpa, ginger, and cinnamon are plentiful. So are gold, silver, lead, and cinnabar, and while sharks and rhinoceroses provide material for armor, elephants supply ivory and giant tortoises their shells. To the north of the Dragon and the Stele Passes stretch great grasslands supporting herds of horses, cattle, and sheep. This region produces the finest furs, and it is from here that nerves, tendons, gut, and horns are imported.

Those are the great natural regions of the Empire. But the merchants, so that things may be fairly distributed, send into these parts the various riches of mountains, lakes, jungles, deserts, and oceans. Without the merchants, the juicy oranges and mandarins from the Blue River would not be for sale in our city streets; the salt of Chü Yen would not be mined; our market places would not be bright with fleecy rugs and blankets from the steppes; and the rich timber from the Blue River would be wasted!

I myself, Lü Pu-wei, am a merchant, from a family of merchants, the Lü, in Po Yang, former capital of the princes of Wei. From earliest childhood I was initiated by my father into trade. "Follow the example of Fan Li," he would say to me. "After helping the princedom of Wu to rise again out of its own ashes and making its ruler wealthy, he set out on a barge and journeyed over rivers and lakes. He traded in Ch'i under the name of Owl Skin and became immensely rich, then gave all he had to the poor and left everything to go to T'ao. T'ao was the hub of the Empire, a transit center for all the produce of the seas and mountains. There he assumed the name of Red Duke and built up another fortune before departing this life. The property he had amassed allowed his descendants to live in luxury for generations."

So I read Fan Li's *Principles of Accountancy*, studied the laws of supply and demand, and learned the rules governing the periodical changes that take place in the world, since astrology enables us to forecast plenty and dearth. According to Fan Li's theory, when the planet T'ai Sui is in the part of the sky corresponding to metal, the harvest will be a good one; if it is in the quarter of wood, there will be famine; and if it is in the quarter of fire, we shall have a drought.

My father also told me: "To become rich you must use your capital and not let it lie idle. You must exchange one kind of merchandise for another. Even if you have to sell them off cheap, get rid of perishable goods as soon as possible. At the peak of a rise there is always a fall; the trough of a wave is followed by a crest. At the top of a rise, sell as if you were throwing away dung; in the trough of a wave, buy as if you were gathering jade and pearls. Never forget that goods and money ought to circulate as freely as running water."

The person he most admired was Pai K'uei. "Pai K'uei," he used to say, "was the greatest merchant of all time. He invented modern commerce. He would buy anything everyone else rejected and sell anything everyone else was fighting over." He, too, had worked out an astronomical system, but one with much more scientific rules, for as time went by, Owl Skin's method had become widely known, and whereas Fan Li's forecasts covered only the annual cycle, Pai K'uei's dealt with a sequence of two or three years.

And so I learned that in order to manage capital one needed the political subtlety of an I Yin, the military strategy of a Sun Shu, and the legal rigor of a Shang Yang.

The secret is to recognize the right moment. A good merchant swoops down on opportunity like a tiger or a hawk on its prey. He never haggles—haggling is for hucksters.

So I bought cheap and sold dear. My passionate study of astrology had taught me to forecast the main market trends. Permanent warfare between states made communication difficult and supplies uncertain, which only furthered the schemes of a bold and enterprising young man.

I went all over the Empire, setting up a network of connections. I was entrusted with several missions and managed to acquire friends at the seigneurial courts. Thanks to secret contacts, I was kept informed of all military operations and diplomatic maneuvers. I knew exactly what goods to buy and sell, and where. I speculated in fodder during the wars between Ch'in and Chao. Later on, when the other merchants were rushing to buy luxuries, I bought basic necessities, which I stored and then sold for twenty times what I had paid for them, when the war-devastated fields could not produce a grain of millet or an ounce of silk. I went to Tai, on the edge of the steppe, and exchanged the silks and jades I'd bought out of my profits for horses and oxen, which I then took to market in the Central States. There, because of the war, animals for draft and slaughter were worth their weight in gold. I made a fortune in just a few days.

I then ventured into Ssuchuan and set up foundries and salt mines. I pushed on south to the lakes and rivers of Ch'u, land of elephants, rhinoceroses, and turtles, where all is abundant and the women are immodest and the men licentious because of the damp air and lush vegetation. There I bought lacquer ware patterned in red and black, pearls bright as stars, fiery-red corals, iridescent mother-of-pearl, fragrant woods for making chests, and pale, gray-veined bamboos.

From the region of Ch'i, where the people are honest and parsimonious, I brought back a cargo of dried fish, cloth made from vine and hemp, stiff silks, and staid lacquer ware.

Mandarin oranges from Chiang Nan, pears from northern Shan T'ung, persimmons, cinnabar, ginger, cardamom, ox and buffalo hides, sharkskin, slaves from the tribes in Yün Nan, tortoise shells, heady-scented flowers, building timber, chariots, bronze, pig iron—there isn't anything I haven't sold or bartered. I amassed hundreds of thousands of gold ingots, bought estates, built houses vast as palaces with many courtyards and winding galleries. Elegant four-story pavilions rose up from them to pierce the sky, and in these I crammed treasures that had once belonged to princes, singing girls, and concubines bedecked with jewels. The melodious accents of my female musicians echoed the trills from my aviaries. The many-colored plumes my wives wore in their hair, and the pheasants depicted on their gold-brocaded robes, cinched at the waist with belts whose fringed ends swung down to the hem, were bright as the tails of the peacocks in my poultry yards. And the animals in my menageries were groomed, beringed, and beribboned like brides. For was I not a prince of trade, one of those uncrowned kings whose industry earned them an income putting them on a level with nobles owning a fief of ten thousand souls?

I loved the smell of the markets, where the sharp musky scent of ginger mingles with the sweeter odor of cinnamon bark, and the smooth aroma of jasmine is countered by the mustiness of cattle and rancid whiffs from quarters of mutton. I visited the towns of the Northwest, where men are quarrelsome and the air rings with guttural sounds from barbarous throats and with the thin impatient whinnying of full-rumped, long-legged horses. I knew the luxury of the towns of the South, whose soft scents make one dizzy. I met the most important merchants: those who soar like the great *p'eng* bird above the mob of sellers of rice water, soy sauce, and dried fish, and who will have nothing to do with the big market gardeners and producers of lacquer ware, even though these make a profit of five to one and have an income equal to that of a high official. I was among the wealthiest.

I became friends with Wu Lao, who dealt in livestock. He bred horses and bartered them for luxury goods, which in turn he exchanged for ten times their value in herds from the khans of the steppes. He owned so many beasts that they blocked the valleys. In Pa, I made the acquaintance of the widow Ch'ing, a woman both energetic and chaste. She did not hesitate to draw a sword against brigands if her caravans were attacked and no one ever dared make dishonorable propositions to her. She ran some foundries and applied the family industry to the making of bronze weapons and iron tools. I also met Tao the Peaceful, of Ch'i, a clever fellow who had made a fortune from dealing in slaves. He bought the most difficult and impertinent ones, those whose owners were anxious to be rid of them at any price, and used them to run his various businesses. People said it was more profitable to be Tao's slave than a nobleman's steward.

I used to entertain and be entertained by these men. I dealt with them as equals, and my style of living overshadowed that of a prince.

But although I had friends among the loftiest members of the nobility and was involved in the affairs of several princes (some of whom even owed me money), I was still only a commoner, and part of my wealth had to remain hidden. I could not display all my luxury without trespassing on the prerogatives of the aristocracy. I had often seen people of my own class arouse the jealousy of the nobles through their prodigality, and the lords did not fail to put them in their place.

Business had taken me several times to Han Tan, capital of Chao, one of the main trade centers of the kingdom. The people there were so addicted to trade that even in the most squalid alleys they carried on all kinds of commerce, not so much for gain as out of habit. I set up one of my many residences there and was introduced to the highest dignitaries in the land. I frequented the court of Chao the Victorious, prince of P'ing Yüan and brother of the king. But it sometimes happened that I was reminded of my origins, and I began to dream of rising above the clouds and outstripping Kuan Tzu and Fan Li in both fame and fortune. All I had to do was wait. I was sure some new and impressive enterprise would soon present itself.

In the forty-third year of King Ch'in the Resplendent, I met White Crow. He was being held hostage in Han Tan after the states of Ch'in and Chao had signed a pact of nonaggression. His carriage was very shabby—a patched-up leather body with the clumsiest harness and a pitiful peal of bells. The four broken-winded creatures that drew this strange conveyance looked ready to drop. And the young man's appearance matched theirs. He wore a plain cap of lacquered linen, leather boots that had seen better days, and a fox-lined coat worn at the cuffs, beneath which could be glimpsed a robe scarcely fit for a minor official. Everything about him showed that he was in difficulty, and it struck me that here was my chance, an opportunity I must seize with both hands.

I made inquiries. He was living in a wretched mansion on the outskirts of the city. No doubt his allowance for clothes, board, and lodging was very meager; Ch'in did not bother about him. I learned that he was ill-used by Chao, too, because of the continual attacks and encroachments on its territory by his grandfather's army. Yes, the investment I had dreamed of was within my grasp—the secret jewel, the buried pearl to keep shut up in my coffers until the right moment came.

After taking advantage of a visit to my home town to ask my father's advice, I went back to the capital of Chao, sold some lacquer ware and Wei pottery that I'd bought in P'u Yang, and called on White Crow, the prince of Ch'in, who lived a few leagues from the city in a district inhabited by peddlers, rice-water vendors, artisans, and poor scholars. His house was even more squalid than I had expected. It had only two courtyards, and these were separated by a small one-story dwelling that had whitewashed walls but no other attempt at improvement. The ancient roof was extended by a simple lean-to supported on thin lacquered wooden posts. Weeds choked the unpaved courtyard, the paintwork was flaking, the outhouses were falling down, and the undecorated window frames did not fit.

I sent my name in by an unkempt page and, once admitted, wasted no time on elaborate greetings. When my host offered me a mat, I came straight to the point.

"I should like to widen your gate," I said.

"Start with your own before bothering about mine," answered the prince, smiling.

"My gate needs yours in order to be widened itself," I replied.

White Crow understood. He led me into a small antechamber and made sure no one was listening, then had me sit beside him so that we might discuss our plans freely.

"The King of Ch'in grows old," said I without more ado, "and the prince your father, Family Peace, has just been chosen heir apparent. Now, it is no secret that the lady of Hua Yang is the prince's favorite and has him completely under her thumb. The choice of his lawful successor rests entirely with her, and she has no children of her own. You are one of the youngest of the princes; your mother is only a second-class wife and has been deserted into the bargain. You live a long way from court and don't enjoy the support of any coterie. I fear you have been forgotten since you have been held hostage here. If King Ch'in the Resplendent should die, which he is bound to do soon, Prince Family Peace will succeed him on the throne, and you will be unable to compete with Tzu Hsi, the eldest son, or with any of the other better-placed children. They are present, on the spot— already spreading their nets and trying to get into their father's good graces."

"You seem to enjoy rubbing salt in the wound!" exclaimed the prince with some impatience. "I know all this. But what can I do?"

"You are poor and living in exile," I went on, undeterred. "You have nothing to offer your relations, nor any means of winning friends who might form a party and secure the notice and approval of the feudatory princes. Now, although your humble servant does not possess unlimited capital, I should have enough to be of service to you with the lady of Hua Yang and your father. I will do my best to see that you are named rightful successor to the throne."

White Crow bowed to the ground and exclaimed, "I put myself in your hands. If your plan succeeds, you shall have half of Ch'in!"

I gave him more than five hundred pieces of gold so that he might cut a suitable figure among the princes and acquire a following. For my part, I made several trips to the various states of the Empire and, not stinting, bought the finest goods I could find, to offer them in due course to the lady of Hua Yang, as gifts from the young exile. I was careful to choose things from Ch'u—pearls, ivory, lacquer ware, ornaments made of kingfisher feathers, and mandarin oranges, of which she was very fond, as she was of everything from her native country. After completing these preparations, I went to Ch'in and sought an introduction to the sister of the princess.

I put up at the inn where I usually stayed on my business trips, and pretended to be busy with my own affairs.

I sent one of my pages, laden with gifts, to pay my respects to the princess's sister and ask her to pass on a few expensive trifles to the favorite. It took me no more than a week to obtain an interview with the lady of Hua Yang. I presented her with some fine pieces of jade, some gossamer silks, some lengths of cloth sewn with pearls and gold thread, and various specialties from her own country. She was particularly delighted with the mandarins, sweet and juicy and red as the sun at dawn. In Double Light there are no mandarins to be had in the markets, and they appear very rarely even at princely tables.

It seemed to me that my best plan was to press on and win the princess over in one grand strategic maneuver. I got in touch with her brother, Prince Source of Light, and lavished gifts on him: chariots drawn by four Tai horses, cloaks of sable and arctic fox. I soon became quite friendly with him, and persuaded him to speak of my jewel in flattering terms to his sister. He did his job well, and I learned that she had taken advantage of a leisurely moment to say a few words to Family Peace about White Crow's reputation for wisdom and intelligence: everyone was singing his praises, she said.

Seeing the prince take an interest in the son whose very existence he had forgotten, she burst into tears.

"I have had the signal honor," she sobbed, "of being chosen for your gynaeceum and of enjoying your favors. But, alas, heaven has not been pleased to give me children. I should be so glad, so happy, if in your goodness you would grant me what heaven has denied. Name White Crow as your successor so that he may care for me in my old age like the dutiful son I am sure he is."

The prince, surprised, accepted, and had a contract drawn up in cinnabar characters on a green jade seal, providing for White Crow to succeed him on the throne.

Comment by Li Ssu

Some of the facts in Lü Pu-wei's notes are corroborated by other evidence, but they leave much unexplained and contain numerous inaccuracies. Lü Pu-wei had long been active politically. No matter what he says, this idea of setting a prince up on a throne was not a spur-of-the-moment thing. What I heard from an old servant of his father's when I was on close terms with the latter leads me to believe that Lü Pu-wei had had the idea in mind for a long time. The man claimed to have overheard the following conversation between his master and Lü Pu-wei, then twelve years old.

"What profit does agriculture bring in?" asked the boy.

"Twice the original investment."

"And dealing in precious stones?"

"A hundred times the amount."

"And setting a prince up on a throne?"

"Impossible to put a figure on that!"

"Then that's the profession for me. Slaving behind a plow doesn't even bring in enough to eat. But if you deal in princes, you can feed your descendants to the hundredth generation!"

There is other evidence to back up this suspicion. I have it on sound authority that Lü Pu-wei "turned" a man called Purity of Jade, whose name was the only pure thing about him. The Lü family employed him as an accountant, but in fact he worked as a commercial spy for Wu Lao, a dealer in livestock on a large scale who ran an intelligence network for Ch'in. Purity of Jade must have been very useful to Lü Pu-wei and his schemes, as the following shows.

The king paused for a moment. Gazing pensively out the window, he could see the roofs of the city, red in the setting sun. One last ray lit up the agate inlay on the lofty towers of Lü Pu-wei's palace. The sound of a clapper announced the closing of the tollhouses.

The king tried to imagine what his father's life must have been like in Han Tan as an impecunious exile. He felt a mixture of pity and scorn. His grandfather had reigned for scarcely a year, his father for only three. From these autobiographical notes it was clear that Lü Pu-wei had been on very close terms with the family of the heir apparent's favorite. And his relations with the king's mother herself were well known. Had the farsighted merchant's long-term plans included a normal life expectancy for his "investment," or had he intended from the start to eliminate two kings—in order to be free to do as he liked? The king seemed to remember some mysterious whisperings when his father died. The word "poison" still echoed in his mind. But he had been so young at the time—perhaps his memories were confused? Still, he had been sufficiently impressed to arrange immediately for his food to be tasted by servants before he ate it, and had had spies posted in his kitchens.

Perhaps the following part of the file would explain everything. He tore the silken cords off the next sheaf of evidence.

THE WAR BETWEEN CH'IN AND CHAO

Preliminary note by Li Ssu

The material assembled here concerns the struggle between the Tu Ts'an party, which favored Prince Tzu Hsi, and that of Lü Pu-wei, which supported White Crow, held as hostage in Chao.

Although I have done my best to arrange these documents so that their main outlines emerge clearly, it seemed best to preface them with some explanation—not because I doubt your perspicacity, but because I am not sure of my own ability to organize such disparate material intelligibly. I should be afflicted indeed if you were to blame your own inadequacy for what is due to my own lack of skill. But I know you are so quick, a word or two will enable you to decipher these devious motives and elaborate schemes.

In the tortuous manner of the day, all the characters involved in the drama made use of the indirect approach. The prize at stake—Prince White Crow, your father—was being held hostage in Chao, and his enemies decided to eliminate him in a roundabout manner by forcing the king of Chao to put him to death. All that was needed was for the Ch'in army to pose a serious threat to Chao's provinces.

This policy was inspired by a personal grudge that the then prime minister, Fan Sui, bore against Wei the Assembler, who was related by marriage to the king of Chao's brother, the prince of P'ing Yüan. Because of the complicated web of alliances, other countries were soon drawn into the struggle.

Meanwhile, Lü Pu-wei's room for maneuvering was very limited: his only hope lay in backing Chao against Ch'in and bringing pressure to bear at the Ch'in court in support of the peace party. And so it came about that the war that set the whole Empire aflame arose out of hole-and-corner factional intrigues.

Confidential report from Purity of Jade to Lü Pu-wei
on the subject of events at the Ch'in court

Sensation in Ch'in! Prime Minister Shang Gratification is none other than the orator Fan Sui, who, after being denounced as a traitor by the eminent official Hsü Chia, was beaten on the orders of the prime minister of Wei and left for dead.

Wei, worried about the political reversal that had taken place in Ch'in after this so-called Gratification's accession to the post of prime minister, sent Hsü Chia as ambassador to try to persuade Ch'in to maintain the alliance between the two countries.

When he reached his inn, the ambassador was surprised to encounter his former subordinate, the orator, poorly clad and on foot. Hsü Chia invited him in for a meal and gave him a warm cloak.

But when Hsü Chia presented himself for his audience with the Ch'in prime minister, he went white, then green, and opened and shut his mouth like a fish—he had recognized Fan Sui once again in the dignitary before him, who wore a tall cap of office and was surrounded by a brilliant entourage.

Inspired by the shades of his ancestors, Hsü Chia at once bared his bosom and banged his head against every one of the steps of the prime minister's dais.

"I was entertaining a phoenix unawares!" he cried. "I didn't recognize you! Have me slowly boiled alive, exile me to barbarous climes that never see the sun, to cleanse me of the injury I have done you. . . ."

"What crimes have you committed to deserve such punishments?" said the minister impassively.

"Alas, they are so many that the hairs of my wretched head could not number them," lamented the ambassador, forgetting in his terror that he was bald.

"You committed three," thundered Fan Sui. "The first is that without proof you accused me of being an agent in the pay of the enemy, when you knew very well where the tombs of my ancestors were! Your second crime is that you did nothing to help me when the unspeakable Wei the Assembler had his henchmen kick my teeth in and throw me into the latrine pit! The third is that you looked on while drunkards peed on me! Those are your three crimes. But I shall spare your life because of your friendly act just now."

Before the ambassador from Wei went home, Fan Sui invited all the important people in the capital to a banquet. Hsü Chia had to sit at the bottom step on a threadbare mat, with only scraps to eat. All through the meal, the minister glared at him and reminded him: "Don't forget to give my message to your king. If he doesn't send me Wei the Assembler's head, and soon, I shall slaughter every single person in his capital—do you hear?"

The first thing that that fool of a Hsü Chia did when he got back to Wei was to go and warn Wei the Assembler, who fled in a panic to Han Tan, where he found refuge in the house of the prince of P'ing Yüan. His presence there was meant to be kept secret, but somehow it has reached the ears of the king of Ch'in. Fan Sui is implacable, and King Ch'in the Resplendent is ready to do anything to please his prime minister.

Your humble servant thought it best to let you know of these developments so that you might take the necessary precautions.

In answer to your request, I have gathered the following information.

The king learned Wei the Assembler's location from a letter written to Chao by a Ch'in spy. I discovered that a cripple living in a house next to the palace in Han Tan has contacts with a man suspected of being in Fan Sui's pay. The cripple admits working for Ch'in—not for money but because he hates the prince of P'ing Yüan, who refused to decapitate one of his concubines for making fun of the man's infirmity.

From his door this person can see the comings and goings of the prince and his court. And the palace employs him to do odd jobs, so he can gather information from the servants, male and female, without arousing suspicion. Ch'in, which was setting up an intelligence network among the princes, was soon able to win him over and make him one of its own spies.

For the moment we have spared his life. He might be useful. We await your orders.

To Lü Pu-wei from Purity of Jade

It is a pity that the price of P'ing Yüan could not be persuaded. I myself have only limited freedom of action in Ch'in. I can look on as a spectator and inform you of developments, but I have no influence on the course of events.

King Ch'in the Resplendent is readying a trap for the prince of P'ing Yüan. He means to invite him to his court and then hold him prisoner, to blackmail the king of Chao. It will be difficult for the prince to refuse an invitation couched in the friendliest terms; so he will go, and become a pawn. If the king of Chao gives in, that will be the end of it, but if he does not, things may not go well for your precious jewel.

In any case, the marquis of Ying's policy is to bring pressure to bear on the bordering states while making friends with the outlying ones. There can be no doubt that, after Han and Wei, Ch'in will attack Chao. So arrange to have your goods sent home!

From Lü Pu-wei to an informer in Ch'in

What we feared has happened. The prince of P'ing Yüan has received an invitation from King Ch'in the Resplendent that is very much like a summons. If he resists, refusing to send the head of the prime minister's sworn enemy, things could turn nasty. As you know, I have urged the favorite to press the heir apparent to expedite the return of my jewel. The king of Chao will not listen. I shall do what I can to make the prince of P'ing Yüan rid himself of the prince of Wei, but I do not have much hope of success. A misplaced sense of honor prevents him from turning out a friend who has sought refuge with him. Continue to keep me informed.

To Lü Pu-wei from Purity of Jade

The king of Ch'in and the prince of P'ing Yüan have been carousing: they haven't been sober for ten days. But the king of Ch'in has nevertheless managed to convey his wishes to his guest. "King Wen of Chou," he told him, "once made Lü Shang his tutor and his father-in-law. Kuan Chung, minister to Duke Huan of Ch'in, became the duke's uncle. I myself look upon the marquis of Ying, my prime minister, as a father. It so happens that his mortal enemy is living under your roof, and I should be greatly obliged if you would send me that person's head. Otherwise you will not leave here alive!"

The prince of P'ing Yüan turned pale, then rose and said: "Is it right to abandon in misfortune someone who became your friend when he enjoyed the highest honors? If you have known someone when he lived in luxury, should you not help him in adversity? Wei the Assembler was my friend. If he was under my roof, I would refuse to hand him over. But he is not!"

From King Ch'in the Resplendent to the king of Chao

Your younger brother is in my hands. The sworn enemy of my minister Fan Sui has been given refuge in your brother's palace in Han Tan. Send me his head *immediately*, or you will feel the steel of my soldiers. As for your brother, he is in danger of nevermore setting eye on his native country!

To Lü Pu-wei from his cousin Lü Li, in Wei

The matter you mentioned has been resolved here in Wei, and what I have to tell you should put an end to your anxieties.

When the king of Chao's guards attacked the prince of P'ing Yüan's residence, Wei the Assembler managed to escape and take refuge with the prime minister, Yü Ch'ing. Yü Ch'ing was ashamed of his master's behavior, and since he did not think he could change it, he abandoned his post and fled with Wei. They had nowhere to go, so they ended up at Big Bridge, where with the help of Prince Bulwark of Faith they hoped to cross over into Ch'u. But Prince Bulwark of Faith, fearing reprisals by Ch'in, was not eager to take them in.

"Yü Ch'ing? Who is he?" he asked his servants.

Then Master Hou the Bony, keeper of the city toll, revered by the prince for his wisdom, exclaimed ironically: "Yü Ch'ing, in his clogs and straw hat, managed to gain access to the king of Chao. At his first audience he was given a hundred gold ingots, at the second he was made a councilor, and at the third he became prime minister. In those days everyone knew him. But as soon as he throws away his cap and seal of office and forsakes his rich emoluments to accompany a fugitive friend into exile, you suddenly wonder, 'Who is Yü Ch'ing?' "

Prince Bulwark of Faith, red with embarrassment, called for his chariot and drove as fast as he could to the hut where the runaways had taken shelter.

Unfortunately or otherwise, he arrived too late. I had already sent to warn Wei the Assembler that the prince was making difficulties about receiving him, and he had had the good taste to cut his throat.

The people of Wei lost no time in delivering his head to the king of Ch'in, and no doubt the prince of P'ing Yüan will soon be set free.

To the prince Tzu Hsi from one of his agents

You asked me to keep the merchant Lü Pu-wei from Han Tan under surveillance after he entered into communication with the favorite's party. Here is the latest news.

One of our people, who has infiltrated the entourage of Prince Source of Light, the brother of the princess of Hua Yang, overheard the following conversation between the two men.

"Do you know you have committed a crime that could cost you your head?" said Lü Pu-wei.

The prince turned pale. "What?" he exclaimed.

The merchant nodded toward the prince's entourage and brought his mat so close that their knees almost touched.

"Yes," continued the merchant in a low voice, "your supporters monopolize the highest government posts, and Tzu Hsi's friends have to be content with the minor ones. Your chests and storerooms are crammed with precious stones; your apartments overflow with jade ornaments, fine furniture, and rare fabrics; thoroughbreds from Central Asia paw the ground in your stables, and your private quarters are bright with the costly headdresses of your wives. The king is old. I have it on sound authority that he might die at any moment. And if Prince Tzu Hsi should be chosen as successor to the heir apparent, your position would be about as safe as a basketful of eggs, and your life as vulnerable as early-morning flowers in the first rays of the sun.

"But I know a way out. If you heed my advice, you can go on enjoying the wealth and honors you owe to your sister's favor, without having to worry about being cut off in your prime. Yes, you can be as strong as the four pillars of T'ai Shan, and nothing will ever shake you!"

Prince Source of Light got up off his mat and came closer still. He made a low bow. "Your servant begs you to enlighten him," he said.

"Your sister enjoys the favor of the heir apparent," said Lü Pu-wei. "He is madly in love with her. But she has no son. So Tzu Hsi will be his successor. Now, Tu Ts'an is Tzu Hsi's right-hand man and has a great influence over him. If Tzu Hsi comes to the throne on the heir apparent's death—and you know he is very delicate—Tu Ts'an will rule the country, and I fear that in that case your charming sister's house will be invaded by weeds.

"White Crow is a very gifted young man, and as virtuous as he is wise. Unfortunately, he is vegetating in Chao, forgotten by everyone. And his mother is not in a position to advance him at court. The poor fellow is always gazing to the west and yearning for his native land. It's heartbreaking. Yet, if only the princess of Hua Yang would urge her honorable spouse to set him up as his lawful successor, White Crow would gain a country and your sister a son to be a prop to her."

From the same to the same

Lü Pu-wei has just had an interview with the princess.

I tried to eavesdrop on their conversation, but the wily merchant spoke in the dialect of Ch'u (which he learned in the course of his frequent visits there) and I could not understand what plots they were hatching. All I can tell you is that afterwards the favorite asked the heir apparent to try to persuade his father, King Ch'in the Resplendent, to insist on Prince White Crow's return.

I later found out that the heir apparent gave the princess of Hua Yang a contract engraved in cinnabar letters on green jade, and although I could not discover what it said, I have good reason to suppose that she wheedled out of him a promise to make White Crow his heir.

The favorite's party is all-powerful, and we cannot expect much help from the marquis of Ying—he is on very bad terms with Tu Ts'an, who would replace him as head of the government if you succeeded the heir apparent upon the death of Ch'in the Resplendent. And you know how the prime minister hates quarrels about the succession. If we told him of the favorite's schemes, he would just put it all down to sordid family squabbles. Our only chance is to send him an eloquent messenger who can convince him that he ought to attack Chao, in the hope that our army's continual encroachments will make Chao decide to put White Crow to death. You would then be rid of that obstacle.

This plan has some chance of success. The marquis of Ying's policy is to conquer Han, whose territory overlaps Ch'in's. Let us go along with that and urge him to ask Han to take command of Shang Tang. Han is bound to agree, and when that province, which it is impossible for him to defend, has been cut off and is about to fall into the hands of Ch'in, we shall then force it into the arms of Chao. The people of Shang Tang hate Ch'in and will welcome Chao as their savior. I know the governor of Shang Tang, and it won't be difficult to bring him into our scheme. In that way we shall deflect the anger of Ch'in to Chao, and put the life of the hostage in jeopardy. But you must act quickly, because Lü Pu-wei is bringing all sorts of pressure to bear on the king of Chao, to make him release what he calls his "precious jewel."

To Lü Pu-wei from Purity of Jade

Pai Ch'i, General Peace of Arms, has just launched an offensive against Han. After seizing Ching Ch'eng, he encircled five fortified towns and killed fifty thousand enemy soldiers.

Then he advanced on Nan Yang and blocked the T'ai Hang road. The town of Yeh Wang has capitulated and Shang Tang is completely cut off. Cereals are worth their weight in gold there, and I don't think you'd be sorry if you sent a consignment.

From Tu Ts'an to Prince Tzu Hsi

As we planned, the king of Han, in order to make peace with Ch'in, has surrendered the command of Shang Tang to the marquis of Ying. The prince of Tang Ch'eng was requested to ask the governor to leave and hand over his command to Ch'in. The governor refused. He has just been dismissed.

To Tu Ts'an from one of Tzu Hsi's agents

We have done our work well. When the governor refused to relinquish command, we had him replaced by Feng T'ing. He advocates a strong policy against Ch'in and will certainly not want to let the province fall into its hands. But, being a realist, he knows that Han can do nothing to keep it, and will seek an alliance with Chao.

From Chao the Panther to Lü Pu-wei

An envoy from the governor of Shang Tang has just arrived in Han Tan. The inhabitants of Shang Tang refuse to become subject to Ch'in, and want to be allowed to hand the place over to Chao instead. I tried to convince the king of the complications such an allegiance would entail, but my arguments only annoyed him.

"What?" he said. "Refuse a province that's being handed to us on a plate, when we've kept a million men under arms for years without ever taking a single fort?"

The prince of P'ing Yüan, General Lien Po, and Minister Lin Whatever-You-Say backed him up, and I withdrew, very disappointed to have failed in my mission despite all my efforts.

Master, we've been betrayed! That scoundrel Chao the Panther, who claimed to be your friend and to support our cause, was really working for Tzu Hsi. Our services have intercepted a report the two-faced wretch addressed to his master. This is what it said:

"You ought to be pleased with me! I pretended to defend the pacifists' point of view, but I did it so clumsily I completely undermined the argument I seemed to be putting forward. The king is now convinced that he would be a coward not to accept Shang Tang. So, by appearing to preach conciliation, I threw him into the arms of the war party, and thanks to me the views of P'ing Yüan and the others have prevailed."

We must be careful of this man. I hope you have not entrusted him with any other missions, for he could be fatal to us.

From Lü Pu-wei to Purity of Jade

Don't worry, my friend, I have never entrusted Chao the Panther with any mission whatsoever. He is one of those non-entities who attend the council only because of their family connection to the king. He's a puppet trying to impress himself and others with an importance that he does not have. Rest assured, my little Purity of Jade; I only use men whom I can buy. But money is of no use with Chao the Panther—not because he is rich already, but because you do not try to buy a man who would gladly pay to be bought. In reality, he did belong to the peace party, but could not bear to see his advice scorned by the king, and, rather than lose face, he affected this role of a minor Su Ch'in. But I fear nonetheless that Ch'in may use this to make him serve their ends. And you know how closely their purposes correspond to ours at the moment! So we must keep an eye on him.

But that is not why I am writing to you. The situation between Ch'in and Chao is going to get worse, and the war looks as if it will be long and cruel. It could cost me my finest jewel. So I want you to buy up cereals on as large a scale as you can without attracting attention and send them to my warehouses in Han Tan. I've given similar orders to all my stewards.

Account of the campaign by the Chao army historian

The news from the front is as follows:

After the attack on Shang Tang by Wang Ch'i, leader of the Multitude of the Left, the inhabitants fled to Chao, and we sent a garrison to Eternal Rest to protect them. In the fourth month, the Ch'in army crossed the frontier and attacked the Chao forces. Lien Po became our commander in chief. Also in the fourth month, an attack was launched against the enemy's outposts and was repulsed; the general in charge of the operation was killed. Sixth month: the Ch'in army broke through our lines, captured two forts, and took their four commanding officers prisoner.

Seventh month: we constructed strong fortifications.

Seventh month: general offensive by Ch'in against the outer line of our fortifications in the west. Two commanding officers taken prisoner, our troops scattered, and the wall completely destroyed.

Seventh month: General Lien Po has prepared for the Ch'in attack by strengthening his defenses. Our orders are to leave the initiative to Ch'in, avoiding action outside our own lines. Any officer responding to enemy provocation will be punished by death.

To Lü Pu-wei from his chief steward

The price of grain and perishable goods is shooting up. All the men in Chao have been enlisted in the army. The harvest is ruined, the fertile plain of Eternal Rest ransacked. The barns are already half empty and the cereal merchants have been caught unawares. If the war continues, we shall hold all the stocks left in Chao, and I know Ch'in is having provisioning difficulties, too.

From Chao the Panther to the marquis of Ying

The money you sent by your envoy got here safely and has been distributed among various members of the king of Chao's entourage and administration. There's a rumor that Lien Po is about to capitulate. We have also arranged for Chao's counter-espionage to intercept a sham letter saying the only war chief Ch'in feared was Chao Kuo, son of the glorious tamer of horses, and that we could only rejoice that Lien Po had been made general in chief.

We have entered into contact with Yü Ch'eng, one of the king's favorites. He is jealous of Lien Po's military valor and hates him. He could be of use to us in slandering Lien Po and ridiculing him for cowardice.

Lü Pu-wei to Purity of Jade

The situation is becoming critical. The king of Chao suspects Lien Po of ulterior motives: he is very angry about all his retreats. He doesn't realize that it's a miracle that Chao is resisting Ch'in as well as it is. From what I hear, every defeat has been as good as a victory. Although we have given ground, the price the generals of Ch'in have paid has not been compensated for by the territory they have gained. A few more of such "victories" and Ch'in will be suing Chao for peace.

There is talk of Lien Po's being replaced, and if he is I fear Chao's army will be wiped out and the way to Han Tan laid open to Ch'in's generals. That would be a serious blow to my ambitions. Try to find out if the rumors about Lien Po are coming from Ch'in's agents. If you secure proof that they are, we might manage to make the king of Chao change his mind.

From a Ch'in agent to the marquis of Ying

The trap worked. Chao Kuo has just been made general in chief in place of Lien Po. The Chao army is in complete disarray. The soldiers are complaining and ready to revolt—Lien Po was very popular with them. He shared their food, let them come to see him in his tent, and listened to their grievances. They regarded him as a father. We've gained more from his removal, without striking a blow, than we have from all our victories so far!

From Chao Kuo to the king

Prince, a few hours from now I shall have the pleasure of informing you of a great victory. Ch'in is retreating in disorder and its lines of defense have been penetrated. I must stop now— the war calls me away.

To the king of Chao from the instructor general of the Chao army

Prince, we have been betrayed! Ch'in has sent Peace of Arms to relieve Wang Ch'i of his command.

Chao Kuo, after turning the regulations issued by his predecessor upside down and reappointing a whole new general staff, launched a frontal attack against the Ch'in army with the intention of breaking through the enemy positions in depth, as laid down in his treatise on strategy. The Ch'in army appeared to give way, and fled in the utmost disorder. But just as we seemed to have victory in our grasp, they turned around and, with the help of previously prepared entrenchments, contained our attack. Meanwhile, twenty thousand men belonging to Peace of Arms' flying columns executed a flanking movement and cut off our rear. Five thousand well-armored crack troops blockaded the rest of our force inside the camp fortifications. So our army is cut in three and without logistical support. Our men have dug themselves in to resist enemy attack and are waiting for reinforcements.

Send help quickly, for more than two hundred thousand men are caught in a vise and I don't know how long we can hold out without supplies.

From the Chao instructor general

All Ch'in youths aged fifteen and over have been sent to Chao in an attempt to cut off our supplies completely. They are constructing extensive earthworks.

The king of Ch'in has paid a personal visit to Eternal Rest and addressed the army. Everyone was promoted one rank and invited to a huge banquet. We could hear the sound of the drums and fifes, and our men's stomachs were tortured by the smell of roast meat and white rice. Instances of cannibalism have been reported.

From the Chao instructor general

There have been more instances of cannibalism. We carried out several summary executions in order to restore some semblance of discipline. All the horses have been eaten except the mounts of the highest officers. Several attempted sorties turned out to be costly failures. We dug galleries under our fortifications, but enemy action caused them to cave in and thousands of our men were buried alive. As soon as one of our soldiers shows his nose in the open, he is shot down by the enemy's crack crossbowmen.

From the Chao instructor general

(Forty-sixth day of the siege.)

Desperate attempt at a sortie by the general in chief at the head of his last company of shock troops.

Before attacking the enemy defenses, General Chao Kuo

exclaimed: "Even if history sets me down as Chao's worst general, at least let me not be its most craven! I have only my life left to offer my prince in expiation."

He raised his cup of wine, drank once, and poured the rest on the ground, saying: "Spirit of my father, I fear that not even my blood can remove the shame with which I have stained your name!"

Then he climbed into his chariot, whipped up his horses, and flew fast as a thunderbolt out of the fortifications, yelling like a tiger. His teeth ground together, his eyes flashed, and his hair stood on end so furiously that it lifted up his cap. All the army shouted "Hurrah, hurrah," and waited motionless. The Ch'in archers watched him from behind their palisades.

He hadn't gone twenty paces when an arrow pierced his throat and sent him rolling in the dust.

Peace of Arms counterattacked and captured most of our lines. As I send you this report, we are negotiating our surrender.

From the prince of P'ing Yüan's wife
to her brother Prince Bulwark of Faith

My dear brother, the situation is desperate, and we await your help as a thirsty man begs a drink of cold water.

Peace of Arms is a butcher! Of our fine, brave army of five hundred thousand heroes, nothing remains. Yours is the hard heart that has delivered us over to this bloodthirsty tiger, and so I send you this account of the slaughter as I heard it from the lips of one of the few survivors of a glorious army, in the hope that it will move you!

"We surrendered when, famished after forty-six days of siege and having lost our general in chief and all our best officers, we judged any further resistance useless. Our leaders raised banners of truce and parleyed with the Ch'in army. We were told that we would be sent back to Chao as soon as hostilities ended and peace was signed. We surrendered our arms to the victors.

"To lull our suspicions, Peace of Arms invited us all to a banquet, and after renewing our strength with some food at last, we set about digging ditches to strengthen the Ch'in defenses. It was then, while we were busy ramming earth, that the Ch'in archers and crossbowmen sent a shower of arrows down on us from the towers on which they had been posted. Then armored troops and crack infantry charged with their spears, swords, and halberds.

"There was a frightful commotion, blades of bronze and steel slashing down ceaselessly until they were covered with blood. The air rang with the cries of the dying, and earth was drenched in crimson. A sickly warm haze hung over the plain, and the Ch'in soldiers, drunk with the reek of blood that covered them from head to foot, hacked and hewed and mangled without mercy. They trampled the wounded underfoot, trudged through blood and mire, over the hearts and livers and lungs protruding from disemboweled corpses. Then they piled earth into the ditches containing dead and wounded alike. Of the four hundred thousand men who surrendered, only two hundred and forty of the youngest were spared to bear witness to what it means to oppose Peace of Arms!"

To the king of Wei from a Wei agent

Lü Pu-wei has given presents to the sophist Su Tai, to get him to go to Ch'in and persuade the prime minister to agree to a peace between his country and Chao. Su Tai is hesitant, but if you were to back Lü Pu-wei it might incline him to speak in our favor.

Let him try to sow dissension between the prime minister and his general in chief by making the former believe that the latter means to supplant him!

Your humble servant went to Ch'in as requested and said the following to the prince of Ying:

"If Chao is destroyed, Ch'in will rule the Empire. And it will all be due to General Peace of Arms. For hasn't he conquered more than seventy cities and forts for his prince, and completely destroyed Chao Kuo's army of five hundred thousand men, thus outdoing the exploits of the greatest ministers of antiquity?

"Yes, the fall of Chao will mean that Peace of Arms will become the highest in the land. And are you sure you can tolerate having to obey him?

"You know, moreover, that Ch'in is now hated by everyone in the Empire. Didn't the people of Shang Tang throw themselves into the arms of Chao rather than fall into your power? And the carnage at Eternal Rest isn't likely to make them change their minds.

"If Ch'in destroys Chao, northern Chao will turn to Yen, eastern Chao to Ch'i, and the southern part of the country to Han and Wei. And all your efforts will have been for nothing.

"The best thing would be to put a stop to the present campaign as soon as possible and accept some territory from Chao and Han in exchange for peace, as their rulers suggest. This would give you the dual advantage of advancing your borders and at the same time depriving Peace of Arms of part of his success."

Report from Purity of Jade to Lü Pu-wei

The king of Ch'in, at the suggestion of his minister, has just accepted the peace offers of the kings of Han and Chao, in exchange for six cities in Chao and the region of Yüan Yung. Chao and Han agents have sown discord between the general in chief and the prime minister by telling Peace of Arms how

Fan Sui, jealous of his success, had his campaign halted. Peace of Arms was so upset that he took to his bed and refused to appear at court.

From Chao the Panther to Tzu Hsi

(Third month of the forty-seventh year of King Ch'in the Resplendent.)

After the treaty was signed between Ch'in and Chao, Lü Pu-wei gave a great banquet in honor of White Crow. It was a sumptuous meal, and all the greatest noblemen were there. The guests were entertained with dancing and acrobatics, and as they watched they drank deep. White Crow succumbed to the attractions of one of the dancers, the most beautiful and accomplished performer in the capital. What man could resist her voluptuous singing, her languorous dancing, those long silk sleeves sweeping through the air like the wings of a bird, that willowy waist, those eyes as liquid as a lake under an autumn sky?

When all the others were raising their glasses to wish one another a long and happy life, the prince, red with excitement and very tipsy, raised his to the fair one and asked Lü Pu-wei to give her to him. She is Lü Pu-wei's favorite, and at first he turned pale, but after a moment's hesitation he agreed. No doubt he did not want to ruin months of long and patient effort just because of a woman.

Announcement of the birth of Ordinance, son of White Crow, addressed to the heir presumptive, Family Peace

At the eighth hour of the first month, a son was born to one of the wives of your humble son White Crow. Left alone on the bed, he yelled for three days without stopping. On the third day, arrows of thorn wood were shot in the four directions. Since he was born in the first month, the time of official proclamations and annual decrees, and because his crying was so imperious, he was given the name of Ordinance. As his father,

I, White Crow, performed the ritual sacrifice to the ancestors and informed them of the birth of a son. Lü Pu-wei was chosen by the auguries to be the sponsor, and, having purified himself and put on his ceremonial vestments, he carried the child in his arms throughout the solemnities. Then the infant was handed over to its nurse.

In the third month, as is the custom, he was given his personal name. And since I, your devoted son White Crow, am far away from you, I hasten to inform you of the happy event.

From Chao the Panther to Tzu Hsi

Prince White Crow has just had a son. The child cried so terribly that the nurse appointed to look after him refused to take him, saying she could not bring up one who would be the ruin of his family. She was beaten and dismissed.

In ancient times, before manners grew corrupt, princesses used to be careful to eat correctly when they were pregnant, and to listen to nothing but sacred music. They were especially strict about their language, keeping it moderate and dignified so that the child in the womb should not be exposed to any harmful influence. This used to be called "the education of the fetus." But the fetal life of Ordinance—that's the name of White Crow's offspring—was surrounded by soldiers' oaths, the banging of war drums, and the lewd songs of Cheng and Chao, and fed on roughly hacked meat and other injurious victuals. No wonder the baby frightens the nurses away!

There are rumors that Lü Pu-wei is really the father. The mother was Lü Pu-wei's concubine before she married White Crow.

This rumor might be used to create trouble between the two men. But I cannot guarantee that such a ploy would be successful. The prince is bewitched by the woman.

I expect you will find the latest political developments quite encouraging. After a respite lasting several months, Wang Ch'i is again at the gates of the capital, and the people of Han Tan are very hostile to Ch'in. I wouldn't give much for the prince's chances if the situation becomes critical. Lü Pu-wei must be expecting the worst: he has been buying up grain and other foodstuffs in great quantities and storing them in his warehouses in preparation for a lengthy siege. If he loses his "precious jewel" he can always fall back on business.

From the princess of P'ing Yüan to her brother Bulwark of Faith

Brother, we are greatly troubled. The city of Han Tan has been under siege for months—to me it feels like centuries. Every day I go to the top of the tallest tower and strain my eyes scanning the horizon in the hope of seeing the clouds of dust sent up by your chariots. But, alas, all I see in that vast plain is the gleaming black breastplates of the Ch'in legions.

What are the king of Wei and his general Ching Ping doing? We are running short of food. Famine cannot be far off; already we are eating the husks as well as the grain. The soldiers are exhausted, and the women have to see to the defense of the city. Do you think of us? Do you think of your sister? Do you want to see her a slave of Ch'in?

From Bulwark of Faith to his sister

I send you this letter in the hope that the souls of our ancestors will allow it to reach you. The man who brings it is utterly devoted to me: either he will get through, or he will die and the words I am setting down on this silk will be destroyed forever. This message must not fall into the hands of our enemies.

Do not imagine that I am indifferent to your misfortune, or that I do not gnash my teeth when I think of what you are enduring. Do you think me so base that I could still lift my head if Chao was ruined and my sister a captive of the infamous enemy?

Our king did agree to send an army to help Chao, but the

ruler of Ch'in, informed of this by his agents, wrote him a threatening letter that so alarmed him, he sent a message to his general in chief telling him to halt and set up camp at I, on the frontier. Our king means to be only a spectator, while giving the impression that he is doing something.

I am thinking of taking my own three thousand loyal followers and attacking Ch'in myself, to avoid the shame that will sully the prince of Wei!

From the prince of P'ing Yüan to Prince Bulwark of Faith

If I, Chao the Victorious, prince of P'ing Yüan, married into your family and became your kinsman, it was because of my admiration for the innate sense of justice that made you come to the aid of the widow and the orphan.

Han Tan, reduced to the last extremity, is on the verge of capitulating, yet still we do not see the dust of your chariots on the horizon. Is this how you help those in distress? Was I taken in by a groundless reputation?

If you despise Chao so much that you do not care if it falls into the hands of bloodthirsty barbarians, at least think of your sister!

From Prince Bulwark of Faith to his sister

Sister, dry your tears. Summon up your last remaining energies and hold out a little longer against the fury of Ch'in. I am flying to your aid, though it makes me a traitor to my king, a rebel. If only I can save Chao!

Seeing as nothing could move the king and dispel the terror inspired in him by the fierce prince of the West, I gathered the boldest of my men and prepared to engage in a hopeless battle against the Ch'in executioners. As I passed through the Barbarians' Gate I met Hou the Bony, a sage who prefers to live far away from official splendor but whose great designs build empires. When I dismounted from my chariot and told him of my plan, he answered coldly:

"Your humble servant will not go with you!

"You entertain knights and good men at your table, and you have an excellent reputation. Yet when the Empire is in mortal danger all you can think of doing to help it is engage in a battle that is lost in advance. But that is just what the Ch'in army wants! It throws raw meat to a hungry tiger! Is this how you expect to cover yourself with glory? And to think that you have the impudence to open your door to good men!"

"What do you advise me to do?" I asked, bowing low twice.

He came up close. "I have my spies," he whispered. "The seals of military command are in the king's bedroom. You know that So-Be-It is the great favorite, and comes and goes freely in the royal apartments. Well, her father died in a feud against a rival clan, and for three years she has been secretly plotting revenge against the murderer. She will move heaven and earth to have someone bring her his head, and will steal the general in chief's seals without hesitation for anyone who does as she wishes. Once you have the tiger seals, you can wrest command of his army from King Ping and fly to the aid of Chao. Now, there is a deed worthy of a hero of antiquity!"

It did not take me long to bring the favorite the head of her father's murderer, and she as promptly handed over the royal seals. I asked a friend of mine, Shu Hai the butcher, a stouthearted fellow of enormous strength, to come with me. As I was going out again through the Barbarians' Gate, I met Master Hou once more. He was waiting to bid me farewell. I began to weep.

"Why do you weep?" he asked. "Are you afraid to die?"

"Certainly not," I replied. "But General Ching Ping is suspicious. I am sure he will refuse to relinquish command. So I shall have to kill him. It is his death I weep for, not my own!"

Then Hou the Bony bowed and said, "I am too old to come with you on this venture. Will you let me count the stages of your journey, so that on the day when you enter the camp as its leader I may turn to the north and cut my throat to help you?"

We parted with tears in our eyes.

When I reached the general's camp, I asked to see him and went into his tent brandishing my seals.

"I am in charge of several hundred thousand men," said Ching Ping. "That is a great responsibility. And here you come in your chariot saying that you are supposed to replace me! It must be a joke!"

And he refused point-blank.

Then Shu Hai drew from his sleeve an iron cudgel weighing forty pounds and brought it down on Ching Ping's head. The bones cracked and the brain spurted out on the ground.

And that is how, unknown to the king, I took command of the army.

We are swooping down on Han Tan, and I have no doubt of our victory.

We shall soon meet in the liberated city.

To Prince Bulwark of Faith from his sister

I send you this letter to tell you how glad I was to receive yours, and at the same time to give you an idea of the distress that we are in. The city is starving and exhausted after a year of siege. The dead and wounded number in the tens of thousands. The Ch'in soldiers, infuriated by our fierce and resolute resistance, have paraded their Chao prisoners, horribly maimed, outside the city walls; they have also profaned our tombs and mutilated the sacred remains of our ancestors.

Cannibalism is commonplace in the city. People exchange their own children and eat them, and everywhere you can hear the sound of bones being cracked open to extract the marrow.

The prince my husband, fearing the city might not be able

to hold out until your army arrived, threw open his barns and arsenals. We can only thank our stars for the farsightedness of the merchant Lü Pu-wei, who built up stocks before the siege. He has handed out food on a large scale, and this has helped a little.

All the ladies of the household tear up linen for the wounded. Everything made of metal, however valuable—bells, bronze vases, plate, tripods, and cauldrons—has been melted down to make arrows and spearheads. We haven't a single padded garment or piece of jewelry left: the prince has distributed them all among the soldiers and the neediest citizens.

He therefore formed a small force of men on whom he could rely and led them in a sortie that took the Ch'in army by surprise and made them withdraw several leagues. The women and children took advantage of this to go collect edible leaves and plants and anything the enemy might be able to use in the siege.

But we cannot hold out much longer. I hope this letter will be superfluous, and that you will already be within the walls of Han Tan by the time the messenger reaches your camp.

One last word. The inhabitants of the city are so outraged by the acts of sacrilege committed by the Ch'in army that they want to put the hostage, White Crow, to death. The king has yielded to their pressure and had him arrested, and he is soon to be executed. I have taken in his wife and little son, for I pity both them and the unfortunate prince. Why should a son pay for a crime for which he is not responsible? And the young prince did so much to help us in our distress!

The flame burned quietly in the bronze cresset, and in the distance Ordinance could hear the sounding of the third watch. The shrill of crickets was magnified by the silence of the night, and a muffled clink of weapons told of the changing of the guard. The headache and nausea that had plagued him in the afternoon had gone, and he felt alert and clearheaded.

He began to reflect on the futility of all the maneuvering he had just been reading about. These people thought that they were playing tricks with time, but in fact they were only the dupes of history. Ordinance himself meant to usher in the reign of the inevitable.

A shadow passed across his broad brow; he crumpled up the letter from Chao the Panther. How dare anyone utter such blasphemies about the birth of the most powerful monarch in the confederation—the being who bore the thirty-six stigmata of royalty on his left thigh? He would have liked to erase the past, to push it back into the void—but he had no power over it. The most he could do was root it out of people's memories. He promised himself that when he had conquered Chao he would burn down Han Tan and slay all its inhabitants, or at least all who were old enough to remember his father.

Then he sat up straight, adjusted his robe, and with his long, strong fingers undid the cords of the third bundle of documents.

DISSENSION IN CH'IN

Preliminary note by Li Ssu

Lü Pu-wei, being a man who knows how to seize an opportunity, decamps and sets about removing the main obstacles between himself and the premiership.

From Chao the Panther to Tzu Hsi

My dear prince, life is certainly strange. Just when your enemy's fate seemed to be sealed, chance smiled on him. The bird has flown! I admit I was partly responsible. Convinced that I should soon be reaping the reward of my patient efforts, I allowed my vigilance to relax, forgetting that Lü Pu-wei could buy anything he wanted, especially officials.

The mob, ravenous with hunger and enraged by the profaning of their tombs, surrounded White Crow's palace and demanded his head. Agitators whom I had placed among them started to attack his residence, but the king got word of it from some of his officers and ordered the crowd to be dispersed and the prince taken to prison under escort. To placate the people, he promised that the prince would be executed at dawn the next day. But when they came to fetch him, the prisoner and his guards had vanished. White Crow's wife and son have disappeared, too. She has acquaintances among the wives of the highest court dignitaries, and before her family fell on evil days it was one of the most brilliant in all Chao.

So you have lost every means of bringing pressure to bear.

To Tzu Hsi from one of his agents

White Crow and Lü Pu-wei have eluded their guards and arrived in our lines disguised as dried-fish merchants. Lü Pu-wei has many friends here, acquired by means of handsome presents, and many officers look to White Crow for promotion. So we are powerless.

To Fan Sui from one of his spies
at the court of the princess of Hua Yang

Lü Pu-wei has arrived in Double Light, accompanied by White Crow, until recently a hostage in Chao. They went to see the lady of Hua Yang. White Crow, on the advice of Lü Pu-wei, dressed in the Ch'u manner in order to please the young favorite. She was delighted with his fancy clothes and hat covered with mythological beasts. She laughed and clapped her hands and called him "her little boy from Ch'u." She fell for him completely, and her one idea now is to adopt him and have him made heir to the throne. Everyone at court calls him Boy from Ch'u.

The heir presumptive saw White Crow and asked him to

recite a relevant poem from the *Book of Odes*. Boy from Ch'u bowed low twice and declined. "Since childhood," he said, "I have lived alone, far from my parents, and I did not have good teachers to see to my education. I do not know how to recite poetry." This was quite a clever ruse, and the prince dismissed him, assigning him an apartment in the palace.

The next day, when his father had a free moment, White Crow said to him: "While I was in Han Tan, I met some of the friends you made when you were there. Now that I am home, I think many of them would be hurt if you did not trouble to inquire what had become of them. You need only mention a few names, and it would gain you the reputation of being a good friend and add to your renown. News travels fast from one principality to another. Your son humbly begs you to consider it."

The prince was pleased with this advice, and the princess of Hua Yang seized the opportunity to get him to give her Boy an honorary title.

From White Crow to his wife

Do not doubt that I feel for you in your trouble: I turn my face to the east and sigh and weep at the thought of my dear wife and my son exposed to all kinds of dangers in a foreign land.

The news from court is fairly encouraging. The way things are going, Ch'in should make peace quickly, and you should soon be home, reunited with your husband, who misses you, and enjoying in Ch'in honors more worthy of your rank than the secluded life in a hostile city forced on you by the vagaries of politics.

To the prince of P'ing Yüan from one of his agents

As you know, relations between Peace of Arms and the marquis of Ying have become very bad, thanks to our efforts. So bad, in fact, that Peace of Arms has taken to his bed, no longer attends audiences, and refuses to take command of the army despite the urgent requests of the king of Ch'in.

It is partly because of this quarrel that Han Tan is still standing and White Crow still in this world. To repay Lü Pu-wei and his protégé for the part they played in the imbroglio, the king allowed the hostage to escape: their efforts to set the general and the marquis at odds must have seemed an adequate guarantee of their loyalty to Chao. The king also thought it prudent to have a pretender to the throne in Ch'in who was sympathetic to him and might help to reconcile the two countries. After Wang Ling's lack of success—he lost five instructors in a skirmish against our troops—Cheng An-p'ing and Wang Ch'i have scarcely done better. Exhausted by an eight-month siege of our glorious Han Tan, they have beaten a pitiful retreat with the armies of the league at their heels.

Despite the pressure brought to bear on him by the king and the prime minister, Peace of Arms, the butcher of Chao, still refuses to take command. Resentment isn't the whole explanation: Ch'in lost more than half its men in the battle of Eternal Rest, and the country has been bled white. The army now consists of boys of fifteen. But the bloodshed, far from causing panic, has only increased our determination. General Peace of Arms made a monumental error, thinking that he would wipe out one of the most experienced armies in existence, made up of veterans who thought nothing of marching twenty or thirty leagues with full packs, and he found himself face to face with a whole people in arms, fiercely determined to sell their lives dear. No wonder he preferred to let others burn in the fire he had lit.

Peace of Arms was jubilant when he heard of Wang Ch'i's defeat. "I told you so!" he exclaimed. "Once again the facts have borne me out. And see what a situation we're in just because no one would listen to the voice of wisdom."

These words, reported to the king, added to the exasperation he had been feeling for some time toward his general in chief. Asked one last time to assume command of the army and defend the homeland against the irresistible advance of the league of princes, Peace of Arms again categorically refused. Thereupon he was reduced to the rank of sergeant and requested to go and live in exile as far away as possible from the capital.

But for six months, on the pretext of illness, he has remained in his house in Double Light. The king's patience is exhausted, the prime minister is like a bear with a sore head, and the alarming reports that keep coming in about the military situation do nothing to help. Lü Pu-wei is taking advantage of the situation to advance his pawns and pour oil on the flames. He takes great delight in informing each of the two adversaries of what the other is saying about him.

To conclude, the situation is as follows: Peace of Arms' position is most precarious, but, paradoxically, his fall would very probably bring about the fall of the prime minister, who cannot easily do without his best strategist. And in the end he is one the king will hold responsible for Ch'in's misfortunes.

To Prince Spring Awakening of Ch'u from one of his agents

King Ch'in the Resplendent sent an envoy to ask Peace of Arms, Pai Ch'i, to set out at once for the place of residence assigned to him, since his further presence in the capital would be prejudicial to the king's authority.

But after the general's departure the king and his minister were obliged to go into conference, because Peace of Arms had calmly gone and settled only ten leagues from the capital!

"Pai Ch'i is just snapping his fingers at you!" said the prime minister, who had sworn to destroy the general. "He refuses to obey the order of banishment. It's intolerable, it can't be allowed to go on!"

The king decided to act. He sent a messenger to hand Peace of Arms a sword and request him to do away with himself.

Witnesses have reported that before he cut his throat the general raised his eyes to heaven and cried, "What crime have I committed against the gods that I should have to suffer this punishment?" He remained like that, with his head thrown back, for a while, then murmured: "But of course . . . I do deserve death. I have committed a great crime. At the battle of Eternal Rest I failed to keep my word: I let four hundred thousand men die an ignoble death when I had promised them they would survive."

Then he seized the sword and cut his throat.

To the prince of P'ing Yüan from one of his agents

The king of Ch'in now regrets what he did, reproaching himself for punishing unjustly a general who did nothing but great deeds. An official sacrifice to his spirit has just been arranged in every town and district in the country.

We shall probably soon be rid of the prime minister. Things are going badly for him. The protégés he recommended to King Ch'in the Resplendent have all turned out to be quite incapable. Cheng An-p'ing, whom he made general in chief of the army instead of Peace of Arms, got himself and twenty thousand men encircled, and surrendered with the whole of his force. The law of Ch'in requires that any official who promotes an incompetent to a post of responsibility should be punished as if he himself were guilty of his nominee's deficiencies. So the prime minister is liable to capital punishment, plus the extermination of all his kin up to and including the third degree of consanguinity!

Second report from the prince of P'ing Yüan's agent

The king must be very fond of the marquis of Ying! He has just issued a decree saying that anyone who refers to the Cheng An-p'ing affair will be liable to the same punishment as Cheng An-p'ing himself! And, to put a stop to any rumors about disgrace, he has increased the marquis's emoluments and given him more land.

But the poor marquis is unfortunate in his choice of subordinates. Wang Chi, whom he made a governor in return for his help in difficult times, has just been convicted of high treason. He was about to hand his city over to the league, having embezzled three years' taxes.

The king cannot conceal his dismay, and the minister is very downcast. During their last audience the marquis said: "When a prince is worried, his prime minister is shamed; when the prince is shamed, his prime minister commits suicide. I can see you are weighed down with cares. Might I ask why?"

The king answered: "Is it not said that sharp swords call for brave soldiers, and devious politicians for subtle stratagems? The blades of Ch'u are sharper than wasp stings, and their generals more secretive than carp. I fear that through the valor of its army and the duplicity of its politicians Ch'u may get the better of Ch'in. We have not enough weaponry to meet Ch'u on equal terms. My best general is dead. Cheng An-p'ing and his followers have betrayed me. I am alone, bereft of my best soldiers and surrounded by enemies. Do you expect me to look carefree?"

The king thought that by appealing to his minister's dignity he might get the man to pull himself together, but his speech had the opposite effect. The marquis of Ying spends hours brooding. He looks distraught, and in my opinion will soon fall like a ripe fruit. But the king is too fond of him to let him go, and could easily be persuaded by a skillful orator to refuse his resignation.

From the prince of P'ing Yüan to Lü Pu-wei

I am sending you an orator from Chao who will, I hope, work wonders. We have managed to throw him out of Chao, where he intended to settle, and have pointed him in the direction of Ch'in and told him what is expected of him. There's no one like him for catching people in the toils of his eloquence. I think he's a match for Fan Sui!

From Lü Pu-wei to the prince of P'ing Yüan

I had no trouble obtaining an interview for our sophist, Ts'ai the Benefactor. I put it about that he was the best dialectician in the whole Empire, and he himself bragged that at his first audience with the king he'd overthrow the marquis of Ying and take his place as prime minister.

When he heard this, the marquis, stung, exclaimed disdainfully: "The political theories of the Five Emperors and the Three Kings hold no secrets for me. I know the teachings of the Hundred Schools of philosophers by heart—Moists, Taoists, legalists, Confucians, cosmologists, soothsayers, the lot of them. I have studied the cynicism of Master Yang, the paradoxes of Master K'ung Sun-lung, the sophistry of Master Hui Shih and so on. I can cut the ground from under the feet of any orator, and I don't see this ranter getting the better of me in debate and taking my job!"

He nevertheless summoned Ts'ai the Benefactor to see him. "The sun declines after reaching its zenith," said Ts'ai, "and the full moon starts to wane. When anything reaches its apogee, it descends. There is a time for everything—for growth and for decay, for promotion and for downfall. It's an inescapable law, and the wise man submits to it. And so we find him in the post of an official in peacetime, and hidden in some cave when the government is in trouble. As someone once said, 'When the phoenix soars through the sky, the man of talent emerges from the shadows.' And remember the aphorism 'In a world at odds a great man is but a wandering cloud.'

"Your vengeance has been fulfilled and your merits

rewarded. Can it not be said that your career is complete? The shrewdness and intelligence of men like Su Ch'in and Shih Po ought to have taught them to avoid pitfalls and escape disgrace, but they were blinded by greed for riches and honors. A wise man, however, abides by tradition and moderates his desires. He takes from the people, but with discretion; he makes use of others, but at the right moment; he is not intoxicated by pride or success. He models himself on the norm and becomes indistinguishable from it. And thus he is able to leave an empire to his descendants.

"Consider the fate of four great men—Shang Yang, Wu Ch'i, Ta Fu-chung, and Peace of Arms. They all had misfortune fall upon them when their heads were still wreathed with their exploits—because they knew how to put themselves forward but not when to withdraw. Fan Li did know, and chose to disappear on a boat one fine day and be reborn in T'ao as the Red Duke, merchant and millionaire.

"You are a good *po* player. Some like to go for double or nothing, whereas wiser players count points. But you know all this. As prime minister of Ch'in you have, without leaving your mat or going beyond the colonnades of your house, established your position above that of the feudatory princes. And you have made your prince's name so formidable that the Empire itself is within his reach. Have you not accomplished what you had to do, and is not now the time to settle up and have done with the prince? If you don't do so immediately, you will meet with a fate even more terrible than that of Shang Yang, Wu Ch'i, or Ta Fu-chung.

"You know the proverb 'Look in water and you will see your reflection; look in men and you will see your fate.' The *Book of Documents* tells us that we must not stay long in the shadow of our achievements. Instead of courting a tragic end, hand in your seals of office and suggest a wise man to succeed you. Then you can retire to some wild mountaintop retreat, or to a lofty dwelling overhanging a quiet river. You will have the chance, unusual in our history, of following a brilliant political career with a peaceful old age.

"Why seek martyrdom by clinging to your position? Is it because you cannot forgo honors and have to be forced to leave, or is it, rather, that you don't know how to set about leaving? The fate of Shang Yang hangs over you. One of the hexagrammatic sayings in the *Book of Changes* is 'The great dragon has regrets,' and this applies to those who know how to rise but not to fall, to spread out but not to pull back, to advance but not to retreat. You would do well to think about it."

"Yes," conceded the marquis of Ying, "anyone who cannot restrain his desires loses what he aims for. Anyone who always wants more than he has loses what he already possesses. Thank you for your advice. I intend to follow it."

He had Ts'ai stay for dinner and honored him with a sumptuous banquet, and he has just introduced him to the king with enthusiasm.

"I have among my guests," he cried, "a certain Ts'ai the Benefactor from east of the mountains. He is a scholar of the highest distinction. He has understood the essence of the politics of the Three Kings and the Five Emperors. The laws of long- and short-term historical change hold no secrets for him. If I had to entrust the government of a country to anyone, he is the man I would choose. I have had the opportunity of meeting all sorts of people in my life, but I have never seen his equal. I ask you as a favor to grant him an audience, so that you may judge for yourself."

After his interview with the king, Ts'ai the Benefactor was made an acting minister, and it cannot be long now till our common enemy resigns. Another few weeks at the most, so as not to arouse the king's suspicions.

From Lü Pu-wei to the prince of P'ing Yüan

As I led you to hope, the marquis of Ying resigned from his post and was replaced by Ts'ai the orator, from whom I intend to get whatever I want.

King Resplendent has just died, in the fifty-sixth year of his reign. Prince Family Peace has suceeded him on the throne, and his son Boy from Ch'u has been named heir presumptive. So the mortal enemies of the princes of Wei and Chao are either dead or retired. Peace of Arms is at peace in his grave, and the new king has still to strengthen his position. Of a delicate constitution, he is said to be seriously ill. He may well die before long, and then Boy from Ch'u would come to the throne. He has lived in Chao, where he still has friends despite the suffering and dangers he endured there. And I know he is too good-hearted to deny old friendships.

Don't forget he will know how to show his gratitude if you send him his wife and son: he faces east and sighs for them every day. By this friendly gesture you will ensure peace and sympathy between your two countries, and for yourself many years of good will from the king of Ch'in.

To Spring Awakening from one of his agents

The marquis of Ying did not survive his retirement long. Was it sorrow at being ousted that brought him to a premature end? Whatever the reason, he did not have much time to enjoy his freedom.

Gossip has it that his death was not natural, and the name of Lü Pu-wei is whispered. But when I saw the marquis a few months before he resigned, he was already haggard, absent, and hollow-cheeked, like someone mortally ill, and I don't think any wickedness on the part of the merchant is needed to explain his death. Inaction kills statesmen more surely than poison.

Please forgive these philosophical reflections on what must for you be a piece of good news. One of our most formidable enemies is now out of the way for good and all.

The king put down the last item with some disappointment. Nothing about the poisoning of his father and grandfather! Not so much as a rumor or a bit of tittle-tattle. Unless . . . But no—Li Ssu wasn't the sort of man to spare him. Yet this third section did end on the questionableness of the marquis of Ying's death. . . .

What did the acting minister mean to suggest? He never left anything to chance. He had chosen and arranged the documents with a definite purpose. Wasn't this his way of hinting that it was by no means impossible that Lü Pu-wei had committed such a crime? But the Ch'u agent no sooner expressed the theory than he dismissed it.

It was quite possible for Ordinance to imagine his father having poisoned his grandfather Family Peace before being murdered, in turn, by his own wife. Unless the whole thing was a ruse on the part of Li Ssu to make him, Ordinance, suspect Lü Pu-wei, although there wasn't a shadow of proof. . . .

No, that was crazy—such an approach wasn't at all like Li Ssu. He always set himself above moral questions. The world of intrigue, betrayal, and murder in which Ordinance had always lived was making him unduly suspicious. Things were probably infinitely more simple: Family Peace had been entirely under the spell of the lady of Hua Yang, and Lü Pu-wei had enjoyed her favors. He could count on White Crow's gratitude and on the support of White Crow's wife, while his wealth had won him good will at the Ch'in court and among the nobles. He was influential enough not to have to fear the resentment of a prince who owed him everything and was nothing without him. He had no reason to commit murder to guarantee his power. Whatever the turn of events, the merchant was sure to profit.

Ordinance had to admit it—the whole thing had been engineered in a masterly manner.

There were still the rumors he thought he'd overheard. But had he mixed up two quite different events? His memories were all so vague from before the day he put on the cap of manhood.

He could hear the snarls of the rutting tigers in the Shang Lin gardens, and a bright white light was coming through the slats of the shutters. It was the fourth watch, the time he liked best, when his mind spread its huge wings and soared like a great nocturnal bird of prey above individual contingencies, up where moral problems and family affection seemed like the vain and foolish preoccupations of mosquitoes.

Wasn't it weak of him to rack his brains over his parents' morality? Even if his present position *was* due to a few murders, that didn't make it any the less commanding. He was the final and perfect result of a concatenation of deeds that were elevated and sanctified by their common end. Some philosopher—he couldn't remember which—once said, "What does it matter where you come from? What counts is where you're going." Instead of passing judgment on the past, he should be searching it to find the shape of the future.

Now he saw his minister's purpose more clearly: these documents were a test, an examination he had to put himself through.

With renewed determination, he quickly untied the fourth and last bundle.

THE LAO AI AFFAIR

Note by Li Ssu

Here we have all the items in the painful dossier concerning the relationship between Lü Pu-wei and your mother, and the consequences thereof.

All political matters in Ch'in are in the hands of the prime minister, Lü Pu-wei. King Civilization-Through-Filial-Piety reigned for only a year, and his successor owed Lü Pu-wei such a debt of gratitude that he relied on him blindly. The minister's influence has become even greater since the king died, for the new ruler is only twelve years old and cannot assume control of the country's affairs.

The merchant has been given the former royal estate that once belonged to the Chou—a prebend of a hundred thousand families. His talents are such that it brings him in as much as a principality of a thousand war chariots. His territorial ambitions are insatiable. All he thinks of is campaigning against the other states so as to increase his possessions at the prince's expense.

And the wars indeed benefit his own fief more than the country he is supposed to be serving. Every time he wins land, nine-tenths goes to him and only one-tenth to the royal estates! His palace in the capital puts the royal palaces in the shade; his coaches and carriages are the most sumptuous in the Empire. Thousands of horses paw the ground in his stables; armies of girls decked out like princesses fill his private apartments. His sheds and storehouses are crammed to overflowing with silks and jades.

The towers of his palaces reach the clouds, and their covered walks wind in labyrinths over thousands of leagues. The beams in his reception rooms are outrageously decorated, and the ornate balustrades of his balconies are set with countless flashing jewels. Everywhere there are elaborate rafters, fretted window frames, pavilions with three or four roofs, panes of transparent jade on which dragons writhe and tigers gambol, so cleverly painted that they look ready to leap into the sky or pounce on their prey!

The horses that draw his coach have their manes braided and their hoofs varnished. They wear iridescent blue-green plumes. Their bits are of silver inlaid with enamel or gold inlaid with jet. The jade pendants that hang from their harness are heavier than those worn by princesses.

The canopied beds in his palace are protected by thick hangings of checkered silk; the screens are inlaid with mother-of-pearl, jade, or kingfisher feathers; low lacquer tables and chests delight the eyes with their delicate patterns and colors. The visitor is greeted with mats of supple reeds or finely woven bamboo, and carpets make bright patches on terra-cotta tiles enlivened with embossed circles, hunting scenes, or fabulous animals. Long-necked jars of silver picked out with gold, pitchers fashioned from rare woods by the best craftsmen in the Empire, cups of agate or K'un Shan jade, services of red-and-black lacquer from Yeh Wang—all hold the best wines and rarest foods in the kingdom.

The former merchant has more than ten thousand slaves and maidservants to wait on him. They are richly fed and warmly dressed, and more arrogant than government ministers. It's said Lü Pu-wei uses them as ambassadors in his communications with the nobles.

The inner palaces house hundreds of concubines, and elegant pavilions are overlooked by belvederes and tiered towers whose roofs of gleaming tiles rise skyward out of sight.

His singing and dancing girls are the most talented, his acrobats the most agile, his jesters the most amusing. His menageries contain birds of shimmering plumage and melodious song, huge tigers, enormous elephants, and all sorts of other strange beasts. There is one tawny animal with a reddish mane, more formidable than a tiger, that he has had brought here from the uncivilized lands of the Far West.

One anecdote will illustrate the incredible luxury in which he lives. The prince of P'ing Yüan sent one of his clients on a mission to Lü Pu-wei, who received him with great courtesy and lodged him in one of his best apartments. To show the sumptuousness of his prince and make an impression on the Ch'in dignitaries, the envoy from Chao gave a great banquet, at which he appeared wearing a pin of precious jade in his hair, and at his waist a sword with a jeweled hilt and a scabbard made of scales of jade set in gold and decorated with clusters of pearls. But what was his embarrassment when he saw that the least of the prime minister's servants wore slippers completely covered in pearls from Ch'u!

Jealous of the renown that Prince Bulwark of Faith in Wei, Prince P'ing Yüan in Chao, and Prince Meng Ch'ang in Ch'i had acquired by keeping thousands of scholars and sages at their courts, Lü Pu-wei decided he, too, would be known as a protector of literature and the arts. So he became a patron, that it might not be said that one of the most powerful realms in the Empire was also the most uncultivated.

After bestowing on himself the title of Marquis of Faith in Learning, he played host to all the itinerant scholars and sages in search of patrons, and treated them more generously than any nobleman before him. He regaled them with the choicest food, the clearest wines and tenderest meats, entertained them with songs and ballets performed by his troop of dancing girls, and smothered them in silks and gold. In this way he brought together three thousand of the most distinguished minds under the sun.

And, in order to outshine the Chi Hsia Gate Academy in the city of Big Bridge, he brought out a book containing the debates he had organized between the sophists and scholars at his court, and named it after himself. "It contains all the knowledge of our day," he said. "It includes an exposition by Li Ssu, one of my most brilliant protégés, of the legal theories of the school of Shang Yang; the nominalism of the neo-Moists; the sophistry inherited from Master K'ung Sun-lung;

the cosmological theories of Tzu Yen; the teachings of Confucius; the thought of the school of yin and yang; and calculations based on the almanac. Everything is contained in the Six Discourses and Twelve Annals of my *Springs and Autumns*: heaven, earth, the ten thousand beings, past and present, being and nonbeing, life and death, the permanent and the fleeting."

He is so proud of it that he has had it posted on the gate of the main market in Double Light, with a notice informing the populace that he will give a thousand gold coins to any scholar who can find a single word in it that needs changing. I leave you to guess if anyone has applied so far!

The above details are to give you some idea of the most important person in Ch'in—the man who exercises regal authority without the title of king. But he has yet another claim to the office, for not only does he wield a king's power—he also shares a king's bed. He is the queen's husband in fact though not in name.

As you know, King Ordinance's mother used to be Lü Puwei's concubine. He gave her to the young pretender, and she became queen when he succeeded to the throne. But after the king died they resumed their old liaison. I have this from the palace servants and from people close to the prime minister. The queen is still in the flower of her youth, and her passionate nature will not allow her to renounce all pleasure. Her son is still too young to understand certain things, and is anyway strictly supervised by his tutors in his own apartments. But, despite all the precautions, the affair is common knowledge, and the merchant's incognito visits to the palace are the subject of jest in all the alleys of the city. Urchins sing songs about it and mime the transports of the queen and the prime minister. People say that Lü Pu-wei, instead of having the honorary title of "king's uncle," ought to be called his father, alleging that the mother was already pregnant by the merchant when he gave her to White Crow. Lü Pu-wei is supposed to have told a friend one evening when he was in his cups that the queen's womb was probably his best investment ever.

I do not know if all these rumors are to be taken seriously, for from Lü Pu-wei's point of view it would be best to keep such pleasures to himself. Some day the king might be none too pleased to hear that he has dubious antecedents. I sometimes suspect that Lü Pu-wei may have created these stories about himself in order to kill any possible rumors of a coup d'état. For, in all the course of our history, what father ever dethroned his son?

To describe the situation in a nutshell, all decisions are made by the prime minister and the queen mother, with the result that to be in their good books is to enjoy the good will of mighty Ch'in itself. That is why, despite all its successes, the Western Kingdom has not yet been able to conquer the Empire: its prime minister is more interested in advancing his own house than in strengthening his country.

To Lü Pu-wei from one of his agents

Prince, your humble servant has been observing the young king's behavior, as instructed, and I cannot advise you too strongly to be careful.

He shows a precocious interest in affairs of state and is always interrogating his teachers and courtiers about the military situation. An avid reader of legal codes and treatises, he has recently asked to be kept informed of the trials in progress throughout the kingdom, to be given reports on the administration of the provinces, and to see the accounts of the prefects and provincial governors. He now goes through all the records with an eagle eye, uncovering any falsifications.

He expresses astonishment at your style of living, your emoluments, and the size of your estates. And some of his remarks make me fear that he is beginning to suspect something about your relationship with his mother. You should do all you can to nip this in the bud. One day you will have to resign yourself to handing him the scepter. A palace revolution would be madness: all the princes would be in league against you, and the question of the succession would become even more delicate. You know how hostile the princes of the blood are toward you. So, rather than making an enemy of the young king, try to win his good will. Sooner or later he will assume the cap of manhood and you will have to let him rule.

Conversation between Lü Pu-wei and one of his associates
(Evidence from Lao Ai's trial)

ASSOCIATE: The young king asked me what the punishment was for adultery between a male subject and a royal consort, and I was obliged to tell him that it was a crime of *lèse-majesté* and the guilty parties would be liable to the death penalty. He thought about this, then asked me if this would apply if the queen was a widow, and I told him that a subject was not responsible for the depravity of his ruler. This answer did not satisfy him. Ordinance is growing up and beginning to realize what is going on around him. Put a stop to your liaison as soon as possible if you do not wish to incur his displeasure. His anger could be terrible: he has a very imperious disposition. Is it wise to keep up a connection that is likely to deliver more pain in the future than pleasure in the present?

LÜ PU-WEI: I know that, but it would be very difficult for me to break things off without hurting the queen's feelings. You don't know what she's capable of when she's angry.

ASSOCIATE: Find a substitute, then, to satisfy her overwhelming passions. She'll soon be obsessed with her new lover and forget all about you. Then, if the king ever comes to know about it, his anger will fall on the queen's new favorite, and you will go on quietly enjoying the honors and wealth belonging to your position.

LÜ PU-WEI: Good advice! I already thought of it myself! As a matter of fact, there is a man named Lao Ai in Double Light, a frequenter of haunts of pleasure and debauchery, whose prowess has already been brought to my attention. I shall take him into my service.

Deposition of the royal governess
(From the preliminary investigation into the Lao Ai affair)

GOVERNESS: It is difficult for a woman who is entrusted with the education of girls, and whose one care is to instruct the royal princesses and consorts in good manners and morality, to speak about such things. Sou Lu refused to go through the village of the Scorned Mother because the mere name was offensive to her. How can your humble servant, who endeavors to follow the path laid down by the sages, bring herself to mention things too horrible to think of?

EXAMINING OFFICIAL: According to certain witnesses, it would seem you were paid by Lü Pu-wei to turn a blind eye to the things your virtue will not allow you to name. Have we not found in your quarters certain costly trifles form the storehouses of the prime minister? Don't say he gave them to you out of sheer gallantry!

GOVERNESS: It was the queen, my mistress, who gave them to me. It's all quite untrue. . . .

OFFICIAL: We have proof. If you persist in not telling us anything, we shall be in the unfortunate position of having to apply the bastinado. You'd do much better to confess. I don't think the king would be too hard on you. . . .

GOVERNESS: I didn't want to take the presents, but I was only a teacher, and, with all the other palace staff appointed by the queen and the prime minister, how could I have stood against them and explained things to the king, who is still a mere boy? No doubt I ought to have sacrificed my wretched life rather than become even a reluctant accomplice to the crime. But it is difficult to serve two masters. Do you know the story of the maidservant and the unfaithful wife? The husband went on a long journey and the wife took a lover. They lived together without a care for two years; then one day a messenger arrived with the news that the husband would soon be back. The lovers took fright and decided to murder him. The faithless wife put poison in a cup of old wine and told the maid to offer it to the master of the house to greet his return. The poor slave was afraid: if she said nothing she would lose her lord and master, but if she denounced the guilty party she would be left without a mistress. Then she had a bright idea: she pretended to stumble as she was bringing in the wine, and spilled it on the floor. The master, angry, had her whipped. That's the reward an honest and faithful servant received for her presence of mind.

I am in the same situation—punished for my dual allegiance. For, although it is true that I saved the queen, I never did the king harm, either. I could not have refused the gifts without putting my life in danger, and that would have served no purpose. What maidservant in the palace, what dignitary, be he ever so eminent, has not tucked away some presents with the seal of Lü Pu-wei's storehouses on them?

I have indeed, on occasion, let the prime minister into the queen's apartments, to be received in audience. It is no secret to anyone that they decided affairs of state between them. But I never noticed anything untoward during their conversations; everything was done in accordance with etiquette.

Sometimes, at night, by the uncertain light of the moon, I have seen a shadow slipping furtively out of the queen's palace. But I was never able to make out who her visitor was. The girls in the women's quarters used to laugh about the sighs and groans that came from the west wing, but I rebuked them and told them to keep quiet: it was my job to cool the imaginations of idle young women. I did all I could to teach them the four virtues. . . .

OFFICIAL: We don't want a treatise on the education of women! Get down to the facts!

GOVERNESS: But to understand this business properly you have to know how a royal gynaeceum functions. The ladies who live in the palace have been trained in the arts of pleasing, not in the four feminine virtues. They all believe they can rise above the rest if they use their charms and willingness to please to win the favor of the master of men. Whether they are "official" or "secondary wives," "splendid" or "lovely young women," musicians or dancers—whatever their rank and social position, all the ladies in all the six palaces have but one ambition: to be noticed by the august presence, and then to be honored by his favor and bear him a son.

Unfortunately, out of the three thousand girls who live in the palace, very few succeed in attracting the monarch's attention. They sigh, powder their faces, dye their cheeks red, and make their lips redder than cherries, but most of them wear themselves out waiting for favors that never come. Some fade away with grief, others with frustration. Shut up in the confines of the palace, they pace the winding galleries, lean out of their lofty windows, and dream of the simple life of merchants' wives, free to come and go in uncurtained coaches.

Their hearts beat faster at the prospect of a banquet: perhaps while they are dancing or singing they will attract the royal attention! Night fans their desires: stifled sighs can be heard from their rooms. Some indulge in solitary pleasures, others in forbidden relationships. And, while the languorous songs both of Chao and of Cheng can be heard in the banqueting halls, the eunuchs trouble their senses with suggestive gestures.

A governess can't be everywhere at once. I try to fill their long idleness with lessons, feminine occupations—the cultivation of silkworms and the weaving of ceremonial garments. I organize religious feasts and make them observe the various rituals. But they dote on sorcery. Concubines chosen to spend the night with the king go to the Hill of the Great Mediator and pray him to grant them offspring. Afterward they give a cup of wine to any who show the first signs of pregnancy, and put a quiver around their waist to ensure that they produce a male heir. They dance and sing and make music. But these are merely substitutes. . . .

Such has been the situation in all the royal harems ever since the decline in morals and the love of luxury put great men into the baneful habit of filling their palaces with women. In the old days the rule was that one nobleman—

OFFICIAL: Madame, please get to the facts! We don't want to go back to the days of the duke of Ch'u!

GOVERNESS: I will get to the facts in a minute!

That's how it is in every gynaeceum when the king is in the prime of life and can honor his wives with his favors. But what about the situation in a palace where the king departs, not halfway through his life, leaving a son too young to rule, a queen still young and fresh, with passions not yet cooled by time, and thousands of other forsaken consorts, all left to grieve over beauty withering away unused? Many of them enter into relationships with members of the court, or with foreign guests met at receptions given in honor of the young king or the regent. That is how disorder comes to reign in the innermost apartments and spreads to the western pavilion. . . .

OFFICIAL: What we want is specific facts. Do you know how Lao Ai got into the palace?

GOVERNESS: I heard some of the dancers and concubines chattering and laughing about it, but I was shocked and they wouldn't really talk about it in front of me. So I'm the last person to tell you anything about that. . . .

Deposition of "Lovely Girl" Full-blown Peony
(Item from the record of the first inquiry about Lao Ai)

FULL-BLOWN PEONY: The humble servant kneeling before you is innocent of any crime. She has never done anything wrong and
has always been sober and respectable. Anything I know I have
picked up from the whispered conversations of my companions.
They said they'd been told—by a concubine who was having an
affair with one of the pages of His Excellency the prime minister—that Lü Pu-wei had acquired a new crony named Lao Ai,
known to everyone in the city, with the object of . . . No, I
cannot say it—there are words that should never cross the lips
of any self-respecting woman. . . .

OFFICIAL: According to some of your friends, they crossed your lips
all right when you were in the palace! Take care: if you conceal
the least thing from the law, you could be charged as an accomplice.

FULL-BLOWN PEONY: Your humble servant's only desire is to serve
the cause of justice at all costs. . . .

Lao Ai was known all over the city for the size of his sexual
organ. To amuse his friends, Lü Pu-wei would often get him to
dance to the sound of fifes and tambourines with his member
erect through the hub of a wheel made of catalpa wood. To help
him maintain his ardor, he would be surrounded by naked female
musicians, and he was capable of cavorting thus several times
around the huge room. This entertainment would be followed
by orgies in which Lao Ai was said to equal the exploits of the
Yellow Emperor. He was supposed to have been initiated into
the arts of the Bedchamber by both the Dark Girl and the Girl
of Whiteness, and to be able to satisfy more than twelve hundred
women in one night without any fatigue.

The gynaeceum, duly informed of all this by Lü Pu-wei's
companions, seethed with excitement. The queen, always on the

lookout for gossip, soon knew all about her prime minister's latest recruit and made anyone, male or female, who had been present at the scene describe it to her. Finally she could contain herself no longer and asked Lü Pu-wei to introduce Lao Ai to her. He refused. But possibly her object had been to make him jealous, for we had noticed that his visits to her had been less frequent lately.

Then, like a thunderbolt, came the news that Lü Pu-wei, catching Lao Ai committing adultery with one of his wives, had had him castrated.

Thus it came about that Lao Ai entered the palace as a eunuch. The queen insisted on having him on her staff in the western palace. We all noticed how extremely fond she was of him, and there was a lot of talk, but I was only a concubine of the second rank, and all I heard of their secrets was the story that was being bruited about throughout the six palaces.

Evidence of one of the queen's mistresses of the robes
(Item from the record of the second inquiry into the Lao Ai affair)

I overheard a conversation between the queen and Lü Pu-wei in which he reassured her about Lao Ai's fate. She had been smitten with him on hearing about his good looks and skill in the arts of love. Lü Pu-wei told her that every official could be bought, and that for a small sum she could have her Lao Ai entirely to herself: the punishment that was supposed to have been inflicted on him was only a trick to smuggle him into her private apartments without arousing suspicion.

And that was how Lao Ai entered the service of the queen. The judges merely had his beard and eyebrows shaved off.

It must be supposed that she was satisfied with the way he discharged his duties, for the whole palace resounded with her cries of pleasure, and their revels went on day and night without stopping. Everyone knew about the queen's affair; she scarcely bothered to hide it. But she managed to keep the people in the palace silent and the king himself in the dark. It wasn't difficult for her to buy the complicity of her own entourage or of the rest of the court, and it would have been a bold man who dared to enlighten the king: his life would have been in danger, so great was the power of the queen and the false eunuch.

Lao Ai went everywhere with the queen, who lavished gifts and honorary titles upon him. Lü Pu-wei, the prime minister, turned a blind eye. It didn't take Lao Ai long to install henchmen of his in the six palaces. He had a whole army of young eunuchs, pages, and servants at his beck and call. He became an important personage, the real wielder of power. Didn't everyone have to pay a fee to him to arrange an audience or an interview, to secure a job, or to be introduced to the queen? He got extremely rich. The queen, whose passion for him grew all the time, was completely under his influence, and his fame came to eclipse that of the prime minister. Many careerists, and strangers who came to Ch'in to seek their fortune, had themselves castrated in order to enter his service. But in fact they were not all genuine eunuchs, and the palace became one of the worst places of debauchery in the whole capital. In the streets of Double Light people used to say, "The best way to obtain it is to have lost it."

Deposition of surgeons and superintendents
responsible for judicial punishment
(Reports on interrogations)

The surgeons and superintendents responsible for carrying out the punishment confessed, without recourse to torture, that they had taken money from an agent of the queen to perform a sham operation. All they did was pluck the subject's eyebrows and beard. Then they gave him the clothes and badges of office of a steward to the queen mother, together with a salary of two thousand *shih* of grain.

Extract from the conclusion of the second inquiry about Lao Ai

It has been established that the queen mother has had two sons by Lao Ai. Each time she became pregnant, she bribed a soothsayer to prescribe a visit to her palace in Yung for the sake of her health. Lü Pu-wei's complicity in the matter could not be authenticated, for by then he no longer had any dealings with her. The births were kept secret, and when the king went to Yung the two children were sent to another palace. (The queen had agents informing her of her son's movements.)

To Lao Ai from one of his agents

Prince, I believe I have done your cause some good with the king of Wei. This is what I said to him:

As you know, it is harder to keep something than to give it up, and harder to give something up than to lose it. Most princes give things up because they do not know how to keep them, and lose them because they do not know how to give them up. It is a very common error. Look at your own case: Ch'in has just taken ten of your cities and a hundred leagues of your territory. Is it not true that you had to yield what you could not keep? Today Ch'in is so strong that no country under the sun can challenge it. Yet you persist in trying to fight it, though Wei is bled dry and half ruined. Isn't this a case where you will lose because you do not know how to yield?

If you listen to the advice of your humble servant, the amount of territory you yield will not be large enough to endanger your country, and your humiliation will not be great enough to harm you. And by doing as I suggest, you will put an end to your people's sufferings at the same time you deal a blow to your mortal enemy.

You must know that throughout Ch'in, among the

highest government officials and the lowest street-porters, in palaces and in muddy alleys, the same question is on everyone's lips: "For Lao Ai or for Lü Pu-wei?" There are only the two factions. Whoever is not for the one is of necessity for the other. And since I can see only one way out for you—letting part of your country go and bowing to Ch'in's conditions—at least manage it so that all the credit reflects on Lao Ai. Negotiate with him and not with the prime minister. By adding to his reputation, you will be increasing your own influence.

For this policy will bring you the queen mother's goodwill. She will feel toward you as if you were her own flesh and blood, and through her you will enter into the good graces of Ch'in itself. And with the support of one of the most powerful countries between the four seas, you will be able to win over and ally yourself with all the princes in the Empire.

True, in the past Ch'in and Wei have signed treaties of friendship a hundred times, and a hundred times have broken them. But when the Empire sees that through Lao Ai it is possible to win Ch'in's goodwill and become one of the countries most sought after by the nobles, it is bound to turn away from Lü Pu-wei and swell the ranks supporting his rival. In this way you will get your revenge on your enemy by making everyone abandon him, and at the same time gain a strong ally.

To Prince Spring Awakening from one of his agents

The way things are going in Ch'in may well weaken its military power. According to reliable sources, the throne is in serious danger. Lü Pu-wei placed one of his own creatures in the queen mother's bed, thinking he would be able to make him do as he wished. But as soon as his protégé gained the queen's affections and the connivance of everyone else in the palace, he threw off the prime minister's yoke. He had himself named "prince of Everlasting Trust" and installed his own men in every branch of the palace administration. It may be true, as some say, that Lü Pu-wei's secret investment is the present king of Ch'in, but I have found out from some of the maidservants in the palace at Yung that Lao Ai has a couple of investments up his sleeve, too. And the feudatory princes, betrayed and humiliated by the prime minister, are turning toward Everlasting Trust.

Lü Pu-wei has recently learned through his agents that his position is threatened. I don't know yet what he intends to do. He has strengthened the king's and his own guard and summoned all his shrewdest advisers.

The king is growing up. Though reserved and inflexible, he has managed to surround himself with a group of loyal servants and upright officials. He is in contact with the officers of the shock troops. Everything is poised for a power struggle. We must contrive to take advantage of it. Is it not said, "When tigers fight, mangy dogs make the most of it"? Since we are too weak to be tigers, at least let us be mangy dogs!

From Hsieh Tiao, a Chao agent,
to the important official Ssu-ma Shang

Things are moving fast. Ch'in is heading for trouble. The queen has indulged in the worst excesses with a false eunuch by whom she has had two sons. Double Light is full of gossip, and street urchins imitate the goings-on of Lao Ai and the queen mother. The male organ is now known as a "Lao Ai," and to fornicate is to "Lao Ai." Adulteresses or loose women are called "queen mother," and their lovers "Lao Ai." It wouldn't surprise me if all this mud was stirred up by Lü Pu-wei: he is doing his best to undermine the position of his former protégé, who he fears may supplant him. It's now a fight to the death between the two of them.

The king is the only person in the whole city who seems to

know nothing about his mother's escapades. He spends all his time in his palace, reading legal texts and handbooks on government, but I'm afraid that sort of knowledge won't be much use to him, the way things are going. How can he be so blind as not to see what is going on under his own roof? Only the other day, Lao Ai made himself impossibly conspicuous. In the course of one of the carousals with which the palace has grown all too familiar, the guests, overexcited with gaming and wine, became rowdy, and one dignitary picked a quarrel with Lao Ai. Whereupon the latter, red in the face with rage, leaped up and cried, "I am the king's stepfather—how dare a nobody like you defy me!" The other man turned pale and slunk away with his tail between his legs.

But that wasn't the end of it. He went and told the king.

Some say the false eunuch has fallen into a trap deliberately set by Lü Pu-wei.

That's all I can tell you for the moment. I shall keep you informed of further developments.

Conversation between Lü Pu-wei and one of his agents
(Evidence gathered by Li Ssu)

AGENT: Prince, your position is threatened. I know for certain that Lao Ai has had two sons by the queen. On the two occasions when she was unwell and, on the soothsayer's advice, went to the palace at Yung, it was not to recover from an indisposition resulting from unhealthy odors but to give birth to the vile brood issuing from her copulation with Lao Ai. The dates had already made me smell a rat, and my suspicions were confirmed by some of the female attendants in the palace at Yung.

Lao Ai is preparing to overthrow the king and install his elder son in his place; the queen is his accomplice. If they should succeed, your life would be in worse danger than an autumn leaf threatened by frost. Your supporters already desert you, and the princes no longer make much of you!

LÜ PU-WEI: As you know very well, I have been trying for a long time to get rid of that stinking cur! But what can I do now that he's in the palace and hiding behind the skirts of the queen mother? Tell the king? The king is still very young and might do something rash—and in any case I don't fancy getting mixed up in an inquiry.

AGENT: Make use of the king to hit out at your enemy; it's your last chance. Better a possible catastrophe than an inevitable disaster! I see only one course of action open to you: to provoke Lao Ai publicly and make him say something to give himself away. It will be quite easy—success has made the man vain and above himself. Then denounce him to King Ordinance. King Ordinance will institute an inquiry, and with a bit of luck you can steer clear. It's unlikely that the investigation would involve you.

Note

Here I close the file. You, sire, being the leading actor in it, know the rest as well as I do. You put the villa into confusion.

Warned by his creatures—Chieh, the chief of the palace police; Ch'i, the director of the Senior Officers of the Center; the head of the queen's guard of honor; and several others—the rebel took fright and decided to forestall you by burning his boats. But you struck mercilessly and attacked him just as he thought to take you by surprise. The dragon mustered his scales, spread his wings, and rose into the sky with a clamor like thunder. His enemies were reduced to ashes and order was restored. The Western Kingdom is ruled by a steady hand.

I am sure that after reading this page of our history you will arrive at a firm and wise decision.

THE DECISION

When he finished reading the last of the firm, precise lines inscribed by his acting minister, the king sighed and with a sweep of his sleeve pushed aside the pile of documents that had accumulated on the red lacquer table. The gilded bronze lamp cast strange shadows over it. Whether embodied in the silk scrolls of princely missives, in the jade seals with cinnabar engravings, in the wooden tablets, or in the strips of bamboo covered with the angular signs of cursive *li* and the rounded ideograms of regular *Chuang*, history was there before his very eyes, set down on all those different materials darkly striped with words that were also pictures.

The golden dragon of the water clock had spat out almost all its liquid, and the bronze, jasper-inlaid hand showed that the hour was late. A wooden clapper in the distance sounded the fifth watch.

Beyond the door of the antechamber, Ordinance could hear the reassuring breathing of a guard. The last vibrations of a wistful lyre and the languorous refrain of a Cheng song faintly reached his ear. He also thought he could detect the weary sighs of the concubines hoping for an august visit as they lay on their brocade couches. Then a tinkling female voice disturbed the silence of the night, the last echo of a banquet approaching its end in one of the palaces in the city.

More than two thousand wives awaited him—proffered white flowers, their hearts heavy with unfulfilled desires—in the little cells opening out of the winding galleries. But he didn't want women. He preferred to spend his nights reading legal and administrative reports, far from the greedy, inquisitive eyes of the gaudy crowd of courtiers, in the secluded peace of one small room, cut off from the world and the cycle of days and nights, yet conscious of the passage of time through the crystal sound of the drops of water that marked the flight of the hours. It seemed to him then that his mind, detached from contingency, took on a singular sharpness. Freed from the bonds of everyday life, it moved in the realm of pure necessity; his intelligence frolicked in the absolute, the only place where great principles could find their application. His gaze wandered amid the clouds of smoke rising from the perfume burner, then he saw them as bronze mountains, contorted slopes, vertiginous gorges.

He felt a sudden pang and thought of death. Then, to drive away these somber reflections, he concentrated on the pile of documents. Yes, it was one of the forms of his past, more accurate and precise than his own memories and—for all he knew—more real.

He could only vaguely remember his childhood and the people who had watched over it. A few disconnected and incomprehensible scenes, some faces, a few gestures, a tone of voice—that was all. From the time he was shut away in the prince of P'ing Yüan's palace in Han Tan he could recall the coarse face of a nurse bending over him, and a woman, his mother, whose slanting, moth-antenna eyebrows, white forehead with a beauty spot, and scent of musk used to make him squall. He had a great fright at the age of two or three, when his father was sent to prison and the family had to flee. He could still remember the din, the shouting, the houses trembling to the roll of drums, the glare from the fires, and the rough arms of the man who bore him to safety. Next came a huge house, the prince of P'ing Yüan's palace, in a remote wing of which he lived among the women and children. He could remember the wall of ice between him and them.

The merry, fearless smile and the two curved black beribboned pigtails of the little girl who lived next door, the daughter of a lame neighbor, brought a few rays of sunshine into his dreary childhood. He had been fascinated by her peach-pit necklace, the yellow mark on her forehead, and the tigers painted on her clothes. She told him solemnly that they protected children from the demons of fever. Her mother, who came from southern Ch'u, went in for strange beliefs and peculiar practices.

The two children often played together in the courts and alleys adjoining the palace. He could remember one dinner party for dolls. Dust in little vessels of bamboo served for rice; the soup was mud and water in tiny shells; shavings stood for fried meat and slices of marinated deer; bits of wood represented, according to their shape, mutton, pork, or grilled steak. He and she sat side by side and ate in a dignified and grown-up manner. She made him offer up the liver and lungs to the ancestors and pour a libation of water. They enjoyed themselves hugely. But later, when he had to go home, he felt anger, that he had been cheated. The mud soup, dust rice, and meat made out of shavings were not a real meal. He was filled with the same anger now when he listened to the speeches of the sophists.

Piebald Cloud—that was her name, he remembered now—had not understood why he was so furious. To her their pastime was not silly or useless. She liked pretending, transforming reality through the power of words and imagination. She knew all sorts of games, grown-up games whose rules she made up herself. Although she irritated him, Piebald Cloud was the only person for whom he'd ever felt real affection.

One day he heard shrieks from the lame man's house. Guards with tiger mustaches and wolf eyes had come to fetch the cripple and put him to death: someone had denounced him. He was found guilty of high treason and had his throat cut. The whole family was massacred. And so Ordinance lost his only playmate.

But he didn't cry. His heart just grew hard with hatred against the princes, against the politics of leagues, against the whole chaotic world—and against dolls' dinner parties that left one hungry. Factional warfare had hurt him through his only friend: she was the lame man's daughter referred to in Li Ssu's reports. The merchant's intrigues had been the cause of his first and greatest sorrow.

But then, didn't he have to lose Piebald Cloud in order to win a throne?

He could also see, in the dim light of recollection, the bustling, bulky figure of Lü Pu-wei, his arms full of toys and sweets.

Then came the return to Ch'in, and the strange customs he had to get used to. That coincided with the coming of his permanent teeth and his not being allowed to sit any more on the same mat as the girls. On the accession of the king his father, a slight, pale man with an expression of suffering and disillusionment whose staid and deliberate gestures contrasted with Lü Pu-wei's exuberance, Ordinance was brought out of the women's apartments and put in the palace school, to begin learning the noble arts. Almost immediately afterward he was proclaimed heir to the throne: here, a vision of courtiers' bloated faces drinking his health and wishing him long life. He was given his own tutor and another teacher, though all that remained of them was a musty taste of Confucian homilies—long-winded sermons on magnanimity and justice in a world that trembled to the rumble of war drums and the tread of soldiers' boots.

He hardly ever saw his mother, and his father was too busy with affairs of state to take much interest in him. Lü Pu-wei made him presents of horses, jewelry, furs, and toys, but he bestowed them absentmindedly, as if preoccupied. Of his father's death and his own accession there was nothing to remember—only ritual tears, genuflexions, and sacrifices to the ancestors.

He gave audiences, semblances of audiences. More dinner parties for dolls. Power was in the hands of his minister, and decisions were made over his head. The secret understanding between Lü Pu-wei and his mother, reflected in knowing smiles and lewd touches, pained him like a physical wound.

When he was sixteen, the age at which the interaction of the yang and the yin caused the seminal fluid to flow, Lü Pu-wei gave him some pretty maidservants. But he was not in the least attracted to them. This worried Lü Pu-wei. Ordinance forced himself to have relations with the maidservants, to avoid the questions of the man who called himself his "uncle." He got no pleasure from it.

He preferred the loud voices of generals and the barking of military commands to the sensual songs and provocative laughter of dancing girls. He developed a passion for the writings of the philosophers from the school of law and administration. He longed to take over the reins of government, and silently champed at the bit. But they kept a tight rein on him. They used him like a dummy, a piece of wood painted to look like a king, an effigy in a tomb. It was Lü Pu-wei who pulled the strings. The secret agents, the envoys from the princes, the army officers, and the couriers all went to him. It was him people asked for audiences, to him that they applied for jobs, to his house that talented scholars went to offer their services.

Every effort was made to confine Ordinance himself to the empty pleasures of an idle young nobleman: hunting, women, drinking, games of chance, cockfighting, and horse racing. He liked hunting, which made him think of the excitement of military campaigns. The splendid horses and chariots, the streamers and banners flapping in the wind, the long pursuit across country, the arrows raining down on the victim, the danger from an angry tiger, the smell of blood, and the dying snarls of wounded beasts—all this he found intoxicating. Other pleasures left him weary and unsatisfied.

But he managed to gather a small group of talented scholars chosen from among Lü Pu-wei's entourage, and they initiated him into the techniques of administration. They believed in government by law, not by intrigue. It was around this time that he developed the habit of sitting up at night to read police reports and go through prefects' and governors' accounts.

The ceremony of the assumption of the cap of manhood was postponed because the omens were pronounced unfavorable. But now he suspected Lü Pu-wei of having bribed the soothsayers. The ceremony finally took place, at Lü Pu-wei's instigation, in Ordinance's twenty-first year—but he was still being manipulated. During the last two years before his coming of age, the minister changed his tactics. He began to introduce Ordinance to the competent men and outstanding officials in his own retinue, and even initiated him into the mysteries of diplomacy and intrigue. He taught him how to make use of agents and how to spread false rumors, letting the young man into the secrets of his own network of conspiracy and collusion. Ordinance was grateful, though slightly apprehensive.

In the light of the documents assembled by Li Ssu, he now realized that even then he had been a pawn in the struggle for influence between his mother's two lovers.

As a matter of fact, the accusation against Lao Ai had taken him by surprise. The image he had always tried to bury in the depths of his consciousness, not daring to look it in the face, had leaped out at him in all its hideousness. He knew the queen was shallow and given to intrigue. She never bothered about him, never showed him any affection, and he resented her coldness. But to learn that he was the son of a woman who was loose and depraved filled him with shame, rage, and disgust.

His first impulse had been to kill the slanderer, but then common sense prevailed. He thought it over and realized that if he yielded to impulse he would never again be able to learn the truth, to plumb the hearts and minds of his subjects. Their lips would be half closed and whisper nothing but flattering words.

So he instituted an inquiry, carried out by the most competent of his advisers. Even they had difficulty overcoming people's resistance and gathering irrefutable proof. So many had been bribed!

But he found out that not only had his mother been living in debauchery with a wretch who pretended to be castrated, but also that she had two sons by him, and lavished on them all the affection her legitimate son missed.

He went unannounced to Yung, meaning to catch his two brothers unawares, but the queen had been warned by her spies, and their father sent them to safety in the castle at Shen Yang. The castle was given to them by his mother, along with the rest of the prefecture, just before Ordinance received the sword and cap of manhood.

His agents informed him that Lao Ai was strengthening his guard in Double Light and raising troops in the commandery of T'ai Yüan, renamed Land of Ai. Ordinance was so furious, he wanted to strike at once, but Li Ssu advised him to let his enemy show his hand. To pretend to be taken by surprise in order to take the other by surprise—that was the best way of ensnaring all of them and destroying the whole faction. Moreover, public opinion would then view his severity as entirely justified, the reasonable reaction of a king who was the victim of a dastardly plot, not a tyrannical stroke by a ruler jealous of a vassal's power. The rebels must be made an example of.

Ordinance was helped by Lao Ai's own clumsiness. The only stratagem Lao Ai could think of was to counterfeit the seals of the king and the queen mother and use them to mobilize the police of the prefecture, the men from the royal guard, the government officials' mounted escort, the foreign cavalry, and the household troops. He then prepared to march on the Palace of First Fruits, where Ordinance had set up his headquarters and from which, warned by his agents, he at once launched all the forces he had secretly mustered—front-line troops recalled from the Wei front, officers of the royal guard, government officials, and palace eunuchs.

Ordinance could still feel the pent-up excitement of the moment when he ordered the princes of Shang P'ing and Shang Wen to attack—his first real act as king. He had looked on with pride as the long cohort set off in perfect order: in the middle was the infantry regiment, flanked by its cavalry; in front, the crack crossbowmen in their short tunics and puttees; then the flying columns in light armor, swift as the wind and bloodthirsty as wolves, known as the "headsmen," in nine companies marching five abreast. The bronze rivets gave off a greenish gleam in the clear sunlight of the cool spring morning. The shiny hats of the officers stood out from among the black topknots of the men. Huge chariot wheels creaked over the dusty road. Ominous flashes came from spears, swords, and pikes, and the long black mottled caterpillar formed by the royal guard and the eunuchs in their gaudy uniforms advanced at a swift and regular pace. The ground shook to the tread of clogs and wooden-soled boots.

The confident and well-disciplined army exuded a quiet strength. Was it not firm as a mountain, majestic as a forest, swift as the wind, destructive as fire?

The roll of the drums, the tinkle of the bells and chimes from the chariots, the whinnying horses and groaning wheels, the proud array of standards and banners filled his heart with gladness. He drove his own chariot forward to overtake all the rest and, when he had reached the head of the army, turned and addressed his men proudly.

"My loyal soldiers," he cried, "you know the laws of Ch'in. Any brigade that brings back more than thirty-three heads as trophies will be promoted one rank. Any soldier who retreats or fails to bring back an enemy head will be punished as if he were a traitor. All merit will be rewarded, any deficiency severely chastised. And now, my brave lads, fall on the enemy like tigers, like wolves hungry for raw flesh and reeking blood. There is no doubt of victory, for we are the law."

Then the hurrahs rang out, and the terrifying war cry of the headsmen: "Kill! kill! kill!" And then he slew the sacrificial victims and anointed the drums with their blood in honor of the Yellow Emperor, the god of war, and his minister Ch'e Yu.

Next was a blank, the anxious waiting, the mask of impassiveness. He controlled his limbs, calmed his blood, and concentrated his mind.

At last came news of the battle at the gates of Double Light. The mechanical precision of the Ch'in war machine, with its disciplined regular soldiers stiffening the ranks of the eunuchs of court officials, had overcome the ardor of Lao Ai's army. They brought back more than a thousand heads as trophies. The rebels retreated in disorder. Lao Ai and his accomplices were on the run.

Ordinance hurtled off to meet his army and, surrounded by all the severed heads, presided over the handing out of rewards and decorations.

Then he issued a proclamation setting a price on the head of the false eunuch: "A hundred thousand pieces of silver for Lao Ai alive, and fifty thousand for him dead!"

Not one of the rebels escaped: not Chieh, the captain of the guard; or Ssu, the officer in charge of palace affairs; or Ch'ieh, the assistant huntsman; or Ch'i, the director of the officers' training school; or many others. They were all decapitated, their heads exposed on pikes in the market place. Lao Ai was quartered, and his two sons sewn up in leather bags and beaten to death. His whole clique was exterminated.

The lightest sentence passed on any of his associates was three years' hard labor. Four thousand families were deported to Ssuchuan.

It had been a terribly cold month, with severe frosts, although it was summer. A pale sun hung over a bare and dreary landscape. A comet appeared in the western sky, and some people whispered that heaven was angry at Ordinance's severity. He had to take stern measures to silence the grumblers.

He could have left it at that, but he wanted to get to the bottom of the whole thing. Li Ssu was instructed to hold an inquiry. And that was how Lü Pu-wei became involved.

He had no qualms about ordering his mother into exile in Yung. Or, rather, he regretted not being able to punish her more harshly. He did not say goodbye to her when she left, though some of the queen's friends had begged him to, with doleful accounts of her tears and sighs and sorrow at the thought of being parted from her beloved son.

They begged him to forgive her in the name of the sacred principles of filial piety. Shouldn't a prince set an example of virtue, and wasn't filial piety the quintessence of benevolence? But that sort of talk only sickened him. Pity a depraved woman who nearly brought ruin on her country? Didn't she try to have him murdered, to replace him by a couple of vile bastards whose father had been dragged out of the stews of Double Light by a shady merchant? He was doing violence enough to his principles by merely banishing the queen, when her flesh ought to have been pickled in brine—without being asked to pardon her in the name of empty ideals.

Unfortunately—came the reply—he lived in a world where prejudice was strong and old habits died hard. To strike at the royal family at all was to strike at the king himself.

To put a stop to talk that made him blush and brought back unpleasant memories, he issued a decree: "Anyone who utters a remark or reproach to an orphan about a punishment inflicted on his mother will be considered to have committed a crime and be subjected to the cruelest torture. I will break his back and make mincemeat of his flesh. His arms and legs will be hung up to shrivel at the palace gates."

Even so, twenty-seven people had the audacity to brave his wrath: a procession of faces young and old, with postures and gestures, blustering, waving of sleeves, genuflexions, respectful shuffling of feet, disapproving rolling of eyes. And, inevitably, the terrible order—the cries of agony drowned by the sound of chopping, the dull thud of beaten flesh, the arms and legs hung over the gate. You could smell the stench even in the audience chamber.

It was said in secret that he was merciless. But it was not he— it was the law. He decided to proceed with the inquiry into Lü Pu-wei, and that was how he was confronted with the revelation about the merchant's relations with his mother. In the tenth month of the tenth year of his reign, in the season of punishments and severity, he made up his mind to dismiss Lü Pu-wei and ordered him to return his seals of office.

Even his own advisers asked him to make concessions in the case of his mother. His power wasn't strongly enough established yet, they said, for him to trample popular sentiment underfoot. Later, perhaps. . . .

It was at this point that a stranger appeared on the scene, one Mao Ch'iao from Ch'i. He asked permission to present the king with a complaint about his severity to the queen. Ordinance was overcome with uncontrollable rage. His face went scarlet, his eyes flashed, and the hair stood up on his head. But he managed to swallow his wrath, realizing how he might profit from a change of attitude brought about by a "fair objection." Still affecting to be angry, he said to his herald, "Ask him if he has seen the heaps of bones outside the palace gates."

The newcomer insolently replied that, indeed, he wished to take his place among them so that they might equal the twenty-eight constellations. The king, feigning exasperation, cried, "I won't give him even that satisfaction! Get the great cauldron ready!"

A tall, broad-browed man came forward, with the nose of a dragon and a square mouth. Mao Ch'iao walked slowly, not in the hasty shuffle that tradition prescribed. Ordinance heard what he said to the guard when the guard tried to hurry him: "I am a dead man when I reach the foot of the dais. Let me have a few more seconds."

At the bottom of the steps, he bowed twice and delivered his petition. Ordinance could remember every word:

"Life should not prevent you from thinking of death, and

wielding power should not make you forget the possibility of losing it. The fact that certain words have been forbidden does not mean that you will live and reign forever. On the contrary—an enlightened prince wants to know everything, both life and death, both greatness and decline. But I think you are not interested in such things."

"What do you mean?" asked Ordinance, pretending to be surprised.

"Your behavior has been wild and senseless."

"How so?" said the king, restraining himself with difficulty.

"You had your stepfather quartered."

The fool! His stepfather! Ordinance grew even more furious—he would have loved to tear the man to pieces. But this was a test. The parent of his people must stifle all personal feelings.

"You did this because his fame offended you. By having your brothers put in sacks and beaten to death, you showed that you have a pitiless heart. In banishing your mother to the palace of Fu Yang, you behaved like an undutiful son. In breaking the backs of good men who criticized you, you emerged as the worst of tyrants. Do you not see that everyone under the sun is turning away from Ch'in, and that all its former alliances are crumbling? I fear that if misfortune ever befell Ch'in you would bear a heavy responsibility."

Ordinance could see him now: the man, stripping off his clothes after he had finished his speech, advanced upon the executioner bare to the waist. Insolent—he was insolent and reckless. The king hated useless courage. Self-control! He could still feel in his muscles and bones the enormous effort he had made to control himself.

He saluted Mao Ch'iao with his left hand, and with his right signaled to the guards to let him go.

"For this great lesson," he cried, "I appoint you to a post of responsibility!"

And, to everyone's amazement, he made him a senior minister and gave him the title of "uncle," an irony probably lost on all but himself. His fate was sealed.

At the head of a brilliant procession of ten thousand horsemen and chariots, he rode to the palace at Yung to meet his mother and bring her back to Double Light. She was delighted, radiant with joy. Probably, knowing his vindictive disposition, she had expected her banishment to last forever. Her glee exasperated him. Was she going to take advantage of his clemency to continue her life of debauchery? He would see to it that she didn't. He mastered his feelings and seemed to act like a dutiful son happy to be reunited with his mother. He was beginning to learn his job. He even managed a faint smile, like a naughty child sorry for what he has done, when, at a banquet she gave in honor of Mao Ch'iao, she raised her glass and wished long life and happiness to "the man who was bold enough to defy an unjust decree, bring a ruined country back to life, and restore the altars of the god of the earth and harvests by reconciling a son with his mother!"

———

The inquiry into the machinations of the former prime minister took its course, and the king was kept informed of its progress by summaries from his legal officers. The part played by Lü Pu-wei in the Lao Ai affair began to emerge, and Ordinance couldn't bear to think of the queen and her former lover both in the same city.

The ex-prime minister's presence obtruded itself everywhere: in the splendor of his horses and carriages, in his ostentatious attendants tearing all over the capital. From the balconies of his palace on the southern slope of the hill above Double Light, the king could look out over the city as it lay lapped around by the river. Below, to the east, stretched a maze of covered walks over which jutted proud pavilions with tiled roofs glittering in the sun: the palace of Lü Pu-wei.

———

To be rid of his irksome presence, the king had requested him to withdraw to his estate in Honan.

The file put together by Li Ssu held no real surprises; Ordinance had already had some idea of everything it contained. But the mere act of reading it filled him with disgust—disgust with the people concerned, disgust with the overingenious traps that all too often trapped those who set them. What did it really matter if Lü Pu-wei was his father? It was the social factor, not the biological one, that counted. Lü Pu-wei was a stranger to Ordinance, whose true father could only be King Chuang Hsiang.

Lü Pu-wei was not without merit. He had put Ordinance's father on the throne and increased Ch'in's power and influence. If Ordinance himself was alive now and ruling over millions of subjects, he owed it to the calculations of the merchant.

A series of single high-pitched notes from a lute died away in the half-light of dawn. Ordinance felt a pang, a vague longing, and looked at the little table covered with opened scrolls.

Li Ssu was right. What he had to judge was not so much a man as an age. His task was not to mete out justice like some legal official applying a code, but to arrive at a political decision.

He opened his writing desk and took out the heavy inkstone, the stick of lampblack, and the wolf-hair brush. He beckoned a servant. Then he changed his mind. Given what he had to say, he should prepare the ink himself. Thinning the black mixture on the dragon-decked stone, he dipped his brush in the liquid and sent the tip of it flying over the square of silk.

———

The royal messenger dismounted in front of the huge porch of the guardhouse, showed the small tokens that served as his credentials, and headed for the great audience chamber. Lü Pu-wei, forewarned by his herald, hurried to meet the messengers, accepting respectfully the scroll that bore the royal seal of Ch'in. Once alone, he unfurled it with feverish haste; he had been waiting for days for the king's answer. Neither his wives nor his musicians nor his singers had been able to soothe his impatience.

And now his fate was here in his hands, set down in a few square inches. He had spent a long time trying to engineer his return to favor, sending loyal messengers to speak in his defense—not overtly, but by letting fall a word here, a word there. Yet he didn't really understand the younger man, whose reactions always took him by surprise. He was beginning now to doubt the wisdom of his policy. He drew a deep breath and forced himself to look at the letter. There were only a few lines.

What have you done for Ch'in that you should be allowed to enjoy a fief of a hundred thousand families in Honan? And what kinship is there between us that you should arrogate to yourself the title of "king's uncle"?
Leave at once, you and your family, for Ssuchuan!

He had risked everything, as in a game of *po*, and he had lost. He should have withdrawn his stakes! But he had not been clever enough to get out in time and lead a quiet life in some pleasant retreat. He would not have been able to stand inactivity, however. Once you have tasted the intoxication of power, once you have given orders to an entire kingdom, once you have benefited from the wealth of an entire country and your name has been on everyone's lips, how can you resign yourself to the affluent mediocrity of a provincial notable?

He could make a fortune in Ssuchuan. It was a rich but under-populated region whose resources had not yet been exploited. There were fabulous salt mines and large deposits of copper, tin, and iron. He had kept in touch with the merchants there. And, with all these wars, trading in bronze and iron was very profitable. He could see himself amassing another fortune, setting up new factories and foundries, flooding the Empire with his products. . . . But no—it was too late. He had been so powerful, climbed so high, that those who once fawned on him in his prosperity were bound to trample him in his misfortune. Such is the lot of deposed kings and fallen ministers: "A rich man has a hundred friends, a poor man doesn't even have a cousin."

A coup? Not to be thought of. His fief, vast as it was, could not challenge the most powerful country on earth. The king had the best troops in the Empire, the best generals.

But would Ordinance be satisfied with banishing him to a remote province? No, he still regarded him as a threat, a thorn in the tiger's paw. Sooner or later, Lü Pu-wei would be eliminated. . . .

He sighed, called a page, and ordered a great feast to be prepared. It must consist of the finest dishes to be found between the four seas: stuffed fetus of leopard; ant-egg pâté; stewed pads of bear's foot; thin slivers of doe in citronella sauce; slices of dried deer; lamprey pie; piglet stuffed with jujubes and baked in clay, then braised for two days; minced snail meat pickled in vinegar; stuffed boar marinated with minced meat and sorrel; bouillon of pheasant and hare, made with herbs; plus water chestnuts, mushrooms, and bamboo shoots.

He went and supervised the preparations himself, in the huge kitchen housed in a separate pavilion. A hundred servants bustled about the ovens, drawing water, cutting up meat in thin slices, grilling things on spits. The butchers stunned cattle and pigs with mallets, then cut their throats; bled goats by means of a slit below the ear; dismembered dogs. Maidservants plucked geese, ducks, and pullets, first plunging them into boiling water. Dried meat and tenderized quarters of beef gave off sweetish smells that mixed with the damp tang of carp and pike suspended from metal hooks. Turtles still jerked convulsively on the sticks on which they were transfixed.

In the middle of it all the master cook, red-faced and loud-voiced, gave rapid orders, with shouts and shoves, above the clatter of the choppers, the barking, bleating, and bellowing of the expiring animals, and the spluttering of the ovens. Sweating scullions collided in their haste; butchers and turnspits threatened one another with mallets and skewers. In one corner a buxom maid smacked an impertinent young slave with a ladle.

Steam from various boiling liquids mingled with the pungent smell of roasting lamb. A vinegary scent from the marinades in which raw meat steeped clashed with the caramel aroma from brochettes of pork. Ginger, cinnamon, and the tart savor of chives were dominant notes in that olfactory chorus. Old sensations that Lü Pu-wei had thought he'd completely forgotten came back to him. The strong whiff of markets where smells of dried fish, smoked meat, and frying fat mingled and merged with the sweet odors of honey: was this a moment from his youth, a fragment from the days of illusion and hope, escaping from time to come back and taunt him? He was seized with a sudden sadness. A fierce longing for the past joined with a pang of self-pity. He hurried from the kitchen.

He went and gave the final orders to his dancers and acrobats for their performances at the banquet. He summoned his treasurer and had him open the chests in his storehouses, and together they counted up the rolls of silk, coins, jades, pearls, and valuable vases.

Then he sent for his friends and relations and the rest of his entourage—some thousand or so people who had shared his good fortune but would desert when they learned of his downfall. He didn't blame them. It was only natural for everyone to do the best he could for himself. He'd have done the same in their place. Life was like a market: in the morning people jostled one another to be first, but in the evening they went by without even looking—not because they preferred to shop in the morning but because in the afternoon there was nothing left worth buying.

He must accept the idea that death was the natural end of life, just as autumn followed summer, just as apogee was succeeded by decline, yin by yang, and night by day. He had known fame and prosperity, his name had made the world tremble, and he had fulfilled his ambition of putting a prince on a throne and ruling a kingdom. Shouldn't he be satisfied? Master Chuang said death was a return. It was time for him to retrace his steps and find the origin of things. There was a time to put oneself forward and a time to stand aside, and the latter time had now come for him.

Seated on his mat on the dais in the main reception room, beneath the complex web of beams and rafters, he was moved as he looked down on the multicolored pattern made by his guests and the silent ballet of the slaves serving food and pouring wine at the little tables.

For the last time he listened to the melodious and disturbing music of Chao, as his dancing girls swirled their sleeves and fluttered their broad silk sashes. Their hair was as light as clouds in a spring sky, their teeth as bright as jade, their eyebrows long and arched like moths' antennae, and the perfume sachets hanging from their waists kindled his senses, still hungry for life and pleasure.

In the midst of the ribald laughter of the men heated with wine, and the shrill giggles of the women, two tears sprang from his eyes and ran down his cheeks. Everyone fell silent. His companions were astonished. The fallen minister stood up, raised his cup to his lips, and drank to the long life and happiness of them all. Then he spoke.

"The king, alas, has ordered me to leave for Ssuchuan. And who will go with me in my misfortune? No one! After the brilliant life I have been used to, how can I resign myself to vegetating in dreary and undistinguished exile? I already see my house deserted, and weeds growing over its threshold. You yourselves, who have just been chatting with me so merrily, will go offer your services to new favorites, for it is in the nature of things that every man should seek his own advantage, just as water flows down the steepest slope. . . .

"But even if I acquiesced in this humble retirement, I am afraid the king would still be suspicious and send me the sword of chastisement, that I might rid him of my inconvenient presence. Or he might accuse me of some crime and condemn me to degrading torture. I would rather receive death at my own hand than at another's, and the thought of cold metal piercing my sensitive flesh and still-vigorous heart is painful to me. So I have chosen to go surrounded by friends, and in the warmth and merriment of a feast.

"But before I leave you, and so that you may remember Lü Pu-wei with affection and tell the princes that he knew how to treat wise and good men, I have thrown open my storehouses. Let my wealth be divided among you. . . ."

His voice was drowned by the sobs of his thousand henchmen. Tears trickled down their cheeks like pearls and soaked their gold-embroidered tunics. With an imperious gesture Lü Pu-wei bade them be silent.

"No!" he cried. "I want to die in the midst of rejoicing."

Then he began to parcel out his treasures. When he had given away the last jewel, he drew a small vial from his sleeve and emptied it into his carved jade cup. He raised the goblet, wished his guests long life, and drank.

To the king from the governor of Honan

> Lü Pu-wei has been buried in secret by his thousand clients and followers on the Hill of Wild Grasses, beside his wife. In accordance with your instructions, all the foreigners who took part in the funeral have been expelled from the kingdom.

BOOK TWO

Li Ssu, or the
Absoluteness
of the Law

CHAPTER I

THE GRANARY RATS

Report from the official in charge of the chief town of the district

 In conformity with the instructions of the secretary of the prefecture of Shang Ts'ai, to inventory and sequester all the possessions—houses, wives and children, slaves, clothes (summer and winter), plate and utensils, livestock and crops—of the accused Shang Hua from the village of Drowsy Tiger, the following list has been compiled:

—One main dwelling, consisting of a large living room and two
 bedrooms, each with windows and a tiled roof. Good-sized
 beams in justified good condition.

—Ten mulberry bushes planted near the door.

—Various outbuildings.

—The wife, having fled, could not be inventoried.

—Children, consisting of a tall unmarried girl at the age of puberty, Wild Orchid by name, and a young boy, five feet five inches, called Morning Light.

—A slave of mature years called Tu the Pockmarked.

—A young unmarried female slave at the age of puberty, named Hawthorn.

—A brown dog, male.

The village elders, including Fu, a local notable, certified on their honor that there was no other article, utensil, or person to be added to the inventory. The headman of the village has been ordered to see that the goods seized are kept safe pending further decisions.

Li Ssu shivered with cold in the little closet that served him as an office; an icy draft came through the chinks in the poorly caulked windows and froze him to the marrow. He dropped his brush, blew on his numbed fingers in their silk mittens, and held them out in front of the chafing dish. Before returning to his tedious and thankless task, he looked gloomily around at the dilapidated walls that shut him in. For a moment he contemplated the cracks and blisters in the flyblown whitewash discolored with damp.

Depressed, he went back to copying the reports, duplicates of which had to be deposited in the archives of the district office before they were sent to the prefecture.

Deposition of Officer of the Watch Lu I of the northern quarter of the subprefecture of Shang Ts'ai. The body of an unknown man with disheveled hair was found in the third house on Barn Street. The police inspector was sent to conduct an inquiry, assisted by the prison superintendent, the slave Yü Chieh. The body lay propped against the wall in a shed, its head turned toward the south. On the left temple it bore the marks of a wound delivered by a blunt instrument.

On the back were two more wounds—vertical, four inches long and one inch wide, with flattened edges. It is possible the blows were struck with an ax or a halberd. Blood from the wound in the temple had formed a black scab on the head, stained the tunic, and dripped onto the floor. There were no other wounds on the body. The man was dressed in a short tunic and unlined canvas trousers. To the west of the body lay a pair of woven hemp sandals like those from Wei, one at a distance of six and the other at a distance of ten paces. The shoes exactly fitted the feet of the corpse. The earth all around being dry and hard, no footprints were found.

The man is fair-skinned and tall (over six feet), with long hair. There are two cauterization scars on the abdomen. The body was found a hundred paces from the watchman's post and two hundred paces from the hut of a market gardener named Li Yang. No one in the neighborhood knows the man or heard any cries for help or sounds of a struggle. The time of death cannot be exactly determined.

Permission to bury the body having been granted, it was wrapped in straw and interred in the wasteland to the northwest of the town, pending departmental instructions. The clothes and shoes have been sent to the court of justice.

And Li Ssu noted, with a sense of enormous futility, "Check districts and commanderies to see if anyone resembling the description of the victim has been reported missing."

Always the same curtain of silence. The affair in question was a settling of old scores between the faction of T'ien Chieh and a swashbuckler from Big Bridge, the capital of Wei. Some time ago T'ien Chieh's nephew had his throat cut by a guest. He had tried to force the guest to drink by seizing him by the hair and shoving the rim of the goblet into his mouth. The guest, enraged, thrust his sword into his host's throat and fled.

T'ien Chieh was a power in the land. A former client of Spring Awakening, the king's minister, he maintained a veritable army in Shang Ts'ai, recruited from the thieves, murderers, forgers, and tomb robbers in the province. His house served as a refuge for every kind of outlaw, and when he went out, people made way and bowed to the ground as if he were the prefect himself. He knew how to be openhanded, and was popular among both the workers and the notables.

The sister of the murdered man, angry with her other brother for not having struck down the murderer yet, left the corpse on the main road, vowing that it would stay there to shame him until it was avenged.

Avenged it had been, apparently, because a few days ago the body was removed. This happened at the same time that the corpse on Barn Street was discovered, wearing, by a strange coincidence, the sort of shoes that were worn in Wei. But no one would trace the matter back to T'ien Chieh.

Li Ssu turned now to a complaint lodged by Lord Shang Lo of the northern quarter of the town of P'ing Yü, concerning the theft of a long cloak padded with silk floss. The police officer in charge of the inquiry recognized typical Ch'in patterns in the footprints left by the thieves, who had dug their way in under the house.

Li Ssu gave a derisive laugh. For the last twenty years, ever since the king of Ch'u had been helped to escape from Ch'in, where he was held hostage, by a housebreaker, a dog-skin thief (so called because his fraternity broke into houses wearing dog skins, to throw the guard dogs off the scent), all the brigands in the country had enjoyed a strange immunity! To find the culprits, all you had to do was search T'ien Chieh's estate: he had taken in a whole band of fugitives from Ch'in who were experts in housebreaking. They were said to be capable of tunneling under the royal palace and filching the imperial seals. But who was going to bother T'ien Chieh or ask his clients to give an account of themselves?

The country was being plagued to death by bravos on the one hand and Confucians on the other—gentlemen who, under the guise of magnanimity, aimed only at flouting the Law. The authority of the state was set at nought; its officials were incompetent or hopelessly corrupt. The reports Li Ssu was copying were circumstantial and precise, but they would serve no other purpose than to wear out the eyes of hundreds of others like him, toiling away pointlessly in dusty, evil-smelling cages.

He looked at his long cloak lined with sheepskin. The silk was worn; the wool had turned yellow. By dint of some sacrifice, he had saved up enough money to have a new pelisse made. He was thrifty not by nature but by necessity. His income permitted no more than a modest style of living: he had only four slaves. And his job in the chief town of the district offered no hope of promotion, no chance of making a name for himself. He was in a dead end, a cul-de-sac, a cage with walls that smelled of dog urine. In Ch'u, anyone who worked for the government hoped to get into his superior's good books through flattery and bribes, not by doing his duty. It was the greediest who succeeded and not the most deserving.

The pickings available to government officials were by no means negligible. The regulations about pay said that those who traveled should be paid according to the area they were sent to and not the office they came from. If their salary had already been paid by the latter, the prefecture for which they were temporarily working had to reimburse the amount it received for that purpose. In practice, the officials arranged things so that they were paid twice. Any discrepancies in the accounts were made up by levies on the wages of junior clerks, or by special or illicit taxes. Minor officials were obliged to recoup by exacting bribes from the people. All the measures used in the granaries were falsified, all the accounts fiddled. One section of the population was exempt from forced labor or wasn't even listed in the records.

Li Ssu yawned. That was enough for today! There was still a long list of things to be done: a sale to the government of slaves guilty of impertinence; a request by someone to have his children deported for consistent lack of filial piety; charges of assault—of noses and ears and topknots cut off; cases of rape, adultery, and so on and so forth. The miscarriages and hangings could wait. He had to go to the granary to take a sample of rice for his superior.

Li Ssu closed his files and wrote the dates on the backs of the various items to be dispatched, along with notes saying whether they should be sent by mail or by courier. Then he left his closet, slipped on his shoes in the vestibule, and went out into a courtyard surrounded by other tiny cells occupied by an army of antlike scribblers. He crossed an unpaved esplanade, passed a flaking wall, and entered a huge enclosure in the middle of which stood an imposing building surrounded by a covered walk. At regular intervals along the whole of this gallery, doors in the bamboo fencing opened into stores of grain: corn, millet, glutinous millet for making wine, long-grain rice, round rice, green and white and red varieties. Every door led into one *amas*, and every *amas* represented ten thousand *shih*.

Li Ssu proceeded along the gallery with his ledger and his measures until he reached the seventh door, which led to the personal store of the assistant head of the district. He undid the padlock and went in. Then, in the half-light of the huge room, he saw it, bloated and enormous. Its dark hairs shone as if it had been dipped in oil. The animal looked at him out of cunning round eyes; its red nose was slightly damp. Suddenly it sat up straight, swished its ringed, wormlike tail around, and put its two front paws together in a sort of bow.

Li Ssu couldn't help declaiming a passage from the *Book of Odes:* "Behold the rat, how he bows with his paws, as if he knew the ritual!" Then he advanced upon it. The rat, not budging, stared at Li Ssu insolently. Was it the brother of those gaunt creatures that fled at the sound of a footstep or the bark of a dog? The ones that fed on refuse, the ones that Li Ssu cornered in the latrines and killed with a kick? He lifted his foot now, ready to strike, but his adversary bared its front teeth, let out a piercing cry, and attacked. Li Ssu jumped out of the way just in time, and they were face to face again.

As he edged around, to try to take it from the rear, Li Ssu recited the "Song of the Fat Rat" from the *Book of Odes:*

> *Fat rat, fat rat, my brother . . .*
> *Ever since we had dealings,*
> *You never took pity on my woe.*

He feinted, sprang to the left, and aimed a kick with his clog at the rat's belly. The rat, faster than he, avoided the blow. It leaped at his throat. He barely had time to protect himself with his sleeve.

> *Fat rat, fat rat, my friend,*
> *With you there's no respite. . . .*

Four more pairs of eyes now shone wickedly in the dark. So as not to lose face completely, Li Ssu sang out mockingly:

> *But now it's time to set out*
> *For a glorious future.*
> *In a rich country, you'll see,*
> *I'll live fat as a rat!*

He made a careful detour and began to measure out the grain. As he went back along the broad gallery around the building, he saw a whole family of rats stuffed with corn and coolly returning to their nest.

"Men are like rats," thought Li Ssu with a sigh. "They're the product of their environment. I've had enough of being a latrine rat. I mean to become a granary rat in future!"

CHAPTER 11

A HUNTING PARTY

It was a morning in late autumn. The earth still gleamed from yesterday's rain, giving off a scent of cool grasses and dead leaves. The
whorls of white vapor rising from the ground hung a gray halo around
the blue-green spotted tops of the thujas and cypresses. The big brown
dog tugged at the leash as little Hsieh trotted along, clinging to his
father's hand.

Before them rose the bare mountain peaks, their folds blood-
red with cinnabar and spangled with yellow like dragon scales in the
first rays of the pale sun. The path they were taking was damp, and
their leather boots crushed asarum, eupatorium, angelica, and alpinia.
The sharp, peppery smell of ginger made their noses tingle.

They went through a series of marshy depressions full of reeds
and rushes, past pools covered with a warm mantle of lotus, wild

rice, and bubbles. Then they took cover in a small blind and waited.

There was a rustle of wings, and a pair of wild ducks rose above the calm surface of the water. Li Ssu shot two arrows, one after the other, and both birds fell, sending up little plumes of spray. The dog dived in and soon brought back the small bundles of feathers, green and black like autumn leaves.

The boy hung them by their necks from a string tied around his waist, and the hunters walked on. The path sloped upward and grew steeper, and they emerged on an arid, gently undulating landscape covered with scrub—sedge and galingale, intermingled with wild oats. The dog sniffed at the dry grass, then grew excited and strained at the leash, his ears erect. Released by Li Ssu, away he sped, then pointed and flushed a hare. The hare made off like the wind, its huge ears laid back. All there could be seen of it was a white tail bobbing through russet grass dotted with the red berries of the wild eglantine. The dog drove its prey back toward the hunters, and Li Ssu, fitting an arrow into his powerful bow, took aim, let the string fly with a twang, and hit the hare in the eye. It fell, gave one or two convulsive jerks, and lay still. The little boy clapped his hands, danced for joy, then went to pick it up, the dog capering at his heels.

It was broad daylight now, and the sun cast a bronze light over the plain.

"Can I have the next one?"

"Not if it's a hare. You can if it's a rabbit. And don't forget what I told you—keep calm and concentrate. When you aim, remember to be like Lieh Yü-k'ou. He could hold his left arm so still that a cup of water on it didn't spill when he loosed the arrow, and his right hand was so swift that no sooner was the first arrow gone than another was fitted to the bow, and his whole body was like a statue. . . ."

"As yours?"

"No, that is only the beginning. It is the ritual way of shooting, the one used on ceremonial occasions. After that, you have to practice inner meditation and forget that you're aiming. Hung Ch'ao, P'eng

Jeng's pupil, spent three years contemplating a fly, until he knew it to the last detail, to the least vein on its wings. He could see the hairs on its legs, and nothing made him blink. Such was his skill that he could shoot arrows one after another so fast and accurately that the head of each fitted into the feathered notch of the one before, to form a continuous line that went from the string of the bow to the target. He made K'ung Sun-lung's paradox come true—the arrow that flies yet does not fly! Even more extraordinary, after a quarrel with his wife he drew his bow and loosed an arrow so that it grazed the pupils of her eyes without making her blink, and fell to the ground without raising so much as a puff of dust."

"Is that true?"

"Of course not! It's just one of the Taoists' tall tales. But there is truth in them if you take them for what they are—parables. Unfortunately, people these days take words for realities and metaphors for facts. . . . When you aim, concentrate on the target. Forget that you're aiming, don't think about what you're doing. It must become second nature. The movements and attitudes used in official archery at great aristocratic banquets were originally intended to help concentration. Gradually, form replaced effectiveness, and style became an end in itself. The Taoists wanted to return to the sources of archery, but with them, too, because they expressed themselves in images, the symbol eventually came to be more important than the reality it stood for. There's only one thing to remember: concentrate on the target and learn to be unconscious of your limbs and your movements. Become both archer and target. Then you score every time."

A hen pheasant rose heavily out of an artemisia bush.

"Shoot, Hsieh—shoot!"

The boy fitted a first arrow, missed the bird, instantly fitted another, shot again. This time the bird fell. Meanwhile, Li Ssu had killed three. Then they set off walking again, the big brown dog frisking along beside them. When they reached a wooded hill surrounded by high walls, Li Ssu called the dog and put its bronze-studded leather leash back on.

"Why are you doing that, Father?" said Hsieh in surprise. "Isn't there game here?"

There were magnolias with big white open flowers, cinnamon trees, eleoccocas, cork oaks, red osiers. You could hear the chatter of thousands of birds. A big hare bounded away, and a deer started out of a scented thicket of camphor trees.

"Why didn't you shoot them?"

"We're near a royal park."

"Yes, but we're not in it."

"The keepers often shoot dogs outside the parks, and I don't want to give them an excuse to shoot ours, then eat his flesh and sell his skin. Come, let's go."

"It's very beautiful. Are there tigers and stags?"

"No, there weren't any tigers—that's higher up, in the really dense forests."

They skirted the wall of the park, noisy with birds. You could tell that there were stags and boars and foxes. Every so often a monkey would swing through the branches. Then they went back down toward the river.

The boy was thinking again.

"Are you really going away?" he asked.

"Yes."

"Why?"

"So that one day you'll be able to hunt in a finer park than the one up there. You'll see—we'll ride in a chariot inlaid with jade and covered with clusters of pearls, with a canopy of crimson silk and drawn by tiger-eating horses. We'll hunt unicorns and shoot down black-and-white-striped tigers, tawny panthers, long-tusked elephants and gazelles. The gold-rimmed wheels of our chariots will run down *ch'iung-ch'iung*s and *chü-chü*s. Our slaves and other domestics will slay the terrified beasts—all we'll have to do is collect them, all the hares and silver foxes, the bears and stags, the wild asses, yaks, and boars. Then we'll go on lakes in sandalwood boats and catch king-fishers and golden pheasants. A winged arrow will draw a silver line across the blue of the sky, and a white swan will fall mortally wounded. Wild geese will rain down, together with black cranes, blue ducks, and gray herons."

"How wonderful! But we'll still have our brown dog, won't we?"

"No, he'll be dead. But we'll have *chiao*s, tall as young bulls, with black coats shiny as silk and purple tongues hanging out of their huge jaws. They pounce like panthers, they can bring a roe deer to bay, and they're bold enough to attack the white tigers of the steppes. They're the dogs of the khans—part of the tribute the barbarians send to the Emperor. And we'll have slim, long-haired pedigree greyhounds, too, which can run faster than lightning. And we'll have hawks and falcons, and panthers trained to fight *hsing-hsing*s."

"Oh no! Not *hsing-hsing*s!"

"Why not?"

"They're too fierce. Great black monkeys with long teeth! And people say they can talk!"

As father and son chatted, they came to a meadow of short thick grass with a spring in the middle. They set down mats, and while the boy collected dead wood, Li Ssu took some tow from his belt and kindled a fire. He wrapped a fat pheasant in clay and set it to cook in the embers, put some wine to warm, and placed in front of each of them a red lacquer box containing slices of dried meat spiced with cinnamon, star aniseed, ginger, and honey, along with jujubes, salted mustard leaves, and rice cakes. When the clay turned brown and started to crack, Li Ssu took it carefully from the embers and broke it open. The rainbow-colored feathers came away with the earth, revealing crisped golden flesh. He put the bird on a plate, and they helped themselves to the hot meat with their chopsticks. It was delicate and slightly wild, with a scent of angelica and mallow and the faint sweet taste of magnolia flowers.

He poured his son a drop of warm golden wine, and offered him a dish of preserved apricots and jujubes, whose bittersweetness brings out the flavor of game.

As they devoured the tender bird, they talked about all the wonderful dishes served at the tables of princes. Li Ssu had the lively imagination typical of the people of Ch'u. He loved describing the fantastic beasts and mythical beings that inhabited the corners of the universe, not because he believed in them but because he liked the sound itself of fancy's brilliant inventions. Now he told his son about some fabulous banquets. The guests were served lips of *hsing-hsing*—the man-eating monkey with a human head, the body of a dog, and a long tail. There were also brochettes of *huan-huan*. No one had even seen the *huan-huan*, and the ancient books were vague about it, but the long, repeated syllables conjured up a large badger with a striped coat and bushy tail. And of course there was also parson's nose of kingfisher from Huai, yak tail and elephant feet, the eggs that the phoenix buried in the quicksand south of Red Mountain, sturgeon roe from the northern sea, shark fins from the oceans of the South, and belly of tench from Wine River.

They made a list of all the creatures in the world: the great nine-coiled serpent inside the holy mountains, the white fox with nine tails, the dancing imp of the hills with a bull's head, which sounds like a drum and can be driven away only by the crackle of burning bamboo.

Hsieh was fascinated and kept asking for more stories: about I the archer, who had the grass of immortality stolen from him by his treacherous wife, Ch'ang O, whom the gods punished by banishing her to the moon. About the queen mother of the West, mistress of the western countries; about the daughters of Ching Chün, who were changed into striped bamboos; about Princess Ch'ing Wei, who was drowned and turned into a bird and tried to avenge herself by filling in the sea. And many others.

The day was now far advanced. They piled up the empty dishes, covered the fire with dirt, put the bowls back in the lacquer boxes and the boxes away in a canvas bag, and resumed the hunt. They scoured the countryside, and the brown dog started water fowl, partridges, rabbits, pheasants, and wild geese. Their bags, hanging on strings from their belts, reached to the ground, and activity and fresh air made their cheeks glow and their eyes shine.

It was late when they returned home. A reddish moon with a white halo cast a ghostly light over the town, and the boy was sad to think this was the last time in a long while that he would go out hunting with his father.

STUDYING WITH
A MASTER

When Li Ssu arrived in Lan Ling, in the northeastern part of the principality of Ch'u, in the middle of the winter of the ninth year of the reign of King K'ao Lieh of Ch'u, Master Hsün Tzu had just left the department to go to Chao. Prince Spring Awakening had dismissed him from his post as prefect on the advice of one of his entourage, who, it was said, had told him that the master wanted to take the prince's place as prime minister. Many people thought the whole thing was a plot on the part of Chao to attract the teacher there. Admittedly, the slander against him did coincide with the transfer of a large amount of money from Chao to Ch'u. And when he arrived in Chao, Hsün Tzu was received with the marks of highest esteem. Everything seemed to have been ready beforehand.

Li Ssu wrote a letter to Prince Spring Awakening telling him he had made a mistake. He was losing a sage and making Chao a present of one. But the letter remained unanswered. Li Ssu sighed, shrugged, and said, "The stupidity of princes will cost me a few hundred more leagues."

At his inn in Lan Ling, he made friends with a tall, gaunt young man with shining eyes and a large straight nose. The man was related to the royal family. His name was Han Negation. He, too, had come to Ch'u to study under Hsün Tzu, hoping that, since the Confucian master's reputation was very high in Han, he himself would afterward be able to get a job as a minister and control his prince's policies.

Because he had a stammer, others did not immediately become aware of his power with words. His thought always outstripped his speech, which probably accounted for his impediment. It made him shy, and since speaking was an ordeal, for he had to make a great effort not to stutter, he used very brief and elliptical phrases, initiating comparisons that he didn't develop, so that, although his arguments were extremely lucid, he sometimes seemed obscure.

The two men shared the same opinion about the age they lived in and the blindness of princes. They had similar tastes. They took a liking to each other, and set off together for Han Tan, where the master was now teaching.

Hsün Tzu, the only survivor of his generation, presided over the philosophers' banquets and was in charge of libations to the shades of the ancestors. But he owed his fame more to his longevity than to his eloquence.

He claimed to belong to the tradition of Confucius, but like Mencius, who, without acknowledging it, merely took over the cosmogonic theories then in vogue, Master Hsün had been influenced by Shang Yang.

Too intelligent to deceive himself but too obstinate to abandon his chosen doctrine, he grew bitter. His mouth turned down at the corners. Like his own prose, he was stiff and lacking in grace. He had a thick neck, short arms and legs, and a big nose. But at sixty-seven he was still hale and hearty, and his robust, stubborn manner inspired something resembling respect.

The king of Chao installed him in luxurious quarters and conferred on him the title of "honorary minister." Everyone treated him with deference, and his disciples swaggered, already taking themselves for important dignitaries.

It was to this man that our two friends sent pieces of silk and white jade to obtain the honor of an interview. Hsün Tzu graciously agreed to see them. They dismounted from their chariot laden with the customary presents, Han Negation going first and Li Ssu following. Negation bowed gracefully and would have delivered a well-turned compliment, but he was overcome with shyness and all he could manage to bring out was "I . . . I . . . Mmm . . . Mmmm . . . Mmmmmaster . . ." One of the master's followers, tall and well built, with a nose like a dragon, burst out laughing.

"A fine pair of recruits!" he sneered. "One stammers and the other's as lean as a wolf! You can read their miserable fates in their faces! Look at that hooked nose and those eyes too close together, and that tiger's body and those bearlike shoulders!"

Li Ssu, beside himself with fury, half-drew his sword and was ready to cut off the ears, nose, and topknot of the author of this outrage, when he thought better of it. He was not in Ch'u now, among the bravos, but in Chao, surrounded by orators. It was with his tongue and not his sword that he must avenge the insult. So he sheathed his weapon, went and stood before the master, and said in a loud, clear voice:

"Is that really one of your followers? When did Confucius ever bother about physiognomy? What does a man's appearance matter, as long as his mind is right? As far as I know, the ancients never mentioned such trifles. Can the study of appearances match the study of the heart? Can the study of the heart match the quest for virtue? If you knew the least thing about antiquity, you would know that in those days, however different from one another the sages might look, they all had pure hearts. If you who listen to me now were ministers, would you select men to serve you on the grounds of their appearance? If so, you would make poor advisers!"

Hsün Tzu smiled and shook out his sleeves.

"The voice of wisdom! Come, listen to me, you who call yourselves my followers!

"I know no better augury of happiness than being a good man, nor a worse one than having inclinations to evil. Height and figure and beauty have little influence upon a man's fate. If we look at antiquity, all the heroes and sages looked different. Yao was extremely tall and thin, Chün short and squat. Ching Wen was tall and fat, while his brother Duke Chou was small and dumpy. I can easily go on. King Hsü Yu had such large and prominent eyes that he could see his own forehead. Confucius was supposed to look like an exorcist's mask. Duke Chou resembled a dead tree stump. Hao T'ao was as green as a peeled cucumber. You couldn't see Hung Yao's face for his beard and whiskers. Fu Yüeh was as stiff as the dorsal fin of a hog fish. I Yin was as bald as an egg. Yao limped. T'ang the Victorious was paralyzed on one side. Chün's eyes had three pupils.

"My students, we are here to discuss virtue and integrity, not to measure heights or have beauty contests or vie with and scorn one another. If men were judged by what they look like, not many of the sages could have competed with the tyrants Chieh and Chou, who were so great and powerful they could hold the multitude in awe. And yet they lost both their kingdoms and their lives, met with an ignominious death, and will be remembered with loathing until the end of time.

"Looks and features provide only a superficial clue to human beings as they really are. And to use these trivialities as evidence against a man is the lowest form of argument!

"I do not wish to see people who claim to be my followers showing that they have been influenced by the pernicious and corrupt age we live in. Everyone nowadays, from princes to country bumpkins, thinks only of powder and pomade, of finery and display. Little village roosters strut about in far-fetched fashions, made up like courtesans and mincing like maidens from Cheng. And at the sight of these fine dandies, the girls lose their heads and leave their mothers, fathers, husbands, and children to run away with them. Then after a little while these good-for-nothings, rejected by their princes and outlawed from respectable society, are dragged off to some gloomy provincial prison and executed in the market place. They spend their last moments weeping and sobbing and wringing their hands, imploring forgiveness and regretting their misdeeds. But, alas, it's too late, and the executioner's knife severs the young swan's delicate neck! That's where appearances get you.

"As it says in the *Book of Odes:*

> *The snow that but this morning*
> *Covered the garden,*
> *When the sun appears*
> *Instantly vanishes. . . ."*

The sermon was over. Hsün Tzu always ended with a quotation from the *Book of Odes*, as if driving in a final nail.

Li Ssu and Han Negation were accepted as pupils, and by the next day, the man who had insulted them left in search of another master.

Hsün Tzu was lecturing on study. Some fifty students sat respectfully before him, facing north, with styluses deferentially poised in their right hands and wooden or jade writing tablets in their left, ready to take down the master's words.

"Study," said Hsün Tzu, "develops a man's abilities. Human beings are flexible. They are the only living creatures who can be molded by education. And it is education alone that enables man to make up for his natural inferiority. An hour of study under a master is more rewarding than a lifetime of solitary meditation. Study multiplies our faculties; it's like a vehicle that enables us to travel without walking, like a boat that crosses the stormy wave without danger or weariness, like a mountain from which we may scan a vast plain. Environment and situation play a more important part than innate qualities in the development of our abilities and aptitudes: a weed grows up straight in a field of hemp; white sand mixed with coal turns black; sweet-smelling cinnamon bark stinks horribly if you throw it into a sewer. A wise man, like plants and other creatures, must choose the places he lives in and the people he frequents. That is sure way of remaining unsullied by common or vulgar habits, and it enables the sage to purify and perfect his virtue.

"This does not mean, however, that the things that happen to us do not originate within us: our fate depends on ourselves and not on external factors. Glory or woe reflect our own actions, and our destiny is what we are, just as worms and maggots grow spontaneously out of rotten meat or carrion."

A pupil bowed and asked respectfully, "Where does study begin and where does it end?"

The idiot, thought Li Ssu. Now we'll be here for another hour.

"If you look at it externally," came the reply, "that is to say, in terms of curriculum, it begins with mechanical recitation of the classics and ends with the reading of ritual texts. But if we look at the deeper significance of study, then I would say it begins with the good man and ends with the sage. Lessons and lectures have definite objects in view, but their real meaning is unlimited. For it is study that makes man what he is, and anyone who turns his back on knowledge ceases to be anything but a beast. . . ."

Li Ssu was nodding and beginning to drowse. He jerked himself upright and glanced at Han Negation. Hang Negation's eyelids were half shut and there was a smile on his lips. He sat straight, but swayed gently as he breathed in and out. He was dozing, too! Li Ssu touched him lightly on the elbow and whispered, "Are you asleep?"

"Let's say I'm in a state of inner nothingness," answered Han.

Hsün Tzu now was talking about the classics.

"The *Book of Odes* sets standards and the ritual texts provide a framework for classifying different kinds of behavior. That is why study ends with the rites, which are the perfection of virtue. The respectfulness and moderation taught by them, the harmony imparted by music, the knowledge conferred by the *Book of Documents* and the *Canon of Poems*, and the subtlety and shrewdness contained in the Annals of *Springs and Autumns*—these teach a good man all he needs to know about the universe. . . ."

——

A few days later, Li Ssu and Han Negation were talking together in the little living room of the house Han Negation had rented. They were discussing the troubles of the day and the teaching of the master. After a moment's hesitation, Han Negation blushed and said, "I've written something about divination. It's somewhat like what our master says, but I treat the question more generally. The defect of the divinatory sciences is not so much that they are full of exceptions and negative examples as that they do not deal in empirical experience, and thus are not a true instrument of knowledge."

He held out a few strips of bamboo covered with writing:

Prescience is the name given to knowledge of the future actions of things, living creatures, and people. But in my opinion it is mere lucubration, useless conjecture devoid of any concrete foundation. My reason for saying this can be seen in the following anecdote:

Yen Ho, the famous soothsayer of Ch'u, was sitting beside his disciple when they heard the lowing of a cow. The disciple shut his eyes, concentrated, and said, "It's a black cow with a white patch." The master said, "Yes, it's a black cow, and the white patch is on its horns." They sent a slave boy out to check. It was a black cow with strips of white linen wound around its horns.

The art of Master Yen Ho is fit only to dazzle fools—it's the mere ostentation of knowledge. To verify what the disciple had said, they had to send the little urchin out to see. Only then did they know for certain that the cow was black and had strips of linen around its horns. After the master had refined his senses and strained his intellectual faculties to the breaking point, all his perspicacity achieved no more than a brat's two eyes! As the *Lao Tzu* says, "Prescience is but a tumor on the body of knowledge, an antechamber to stupidity."

"Quite right!" said Li Ssu. "Exactly what I think, though I could not have expressed it so clearly." He was silent for a moment. "But why did you come to study under Hsün Tzu?" he asked. "What can he teach you?"

"Nothing," was the reply. "But he can help me. He can give me the right to say that I've studied under a great master."

"Isn't the fact that you're a prince enough to get you a post? Surely a man in your position doesn't need to leave his family and go on a long journey just to . . ."

"My position is not as brilliant as you think. A prince is surrounded by dogs. It's because of dogs that I left Han."

"Dogs? With me it was a rat!"

"The rat under the altar of the god of the earth?"

"Not exactly . . . But tell me about the dogs."

Han Negation answered, in his hesitant voice, with a fable that he'd written.

Once upon a time, in Sung, there was a wine merchant. His measures were fair, he was attentive to his customers, his wine smelled good and did not grate on the palate, and his shop sign was bright enough to be seen from a distance. Yet his wine did not sell. The poor man could not figure it out. One day, at his wits' end, he went and asked the chief merchant in his street what was wrong.

"It is because of your dog," said the man.

"What does my dog have to do with my business?"

"People are afraid, because once it bit a boy who had been sent for a jug of wine. That is why your sales are so bad."

"Is that a parable?" asked Li Ssu.

"The government of Han has its dogs," said his friend. "And when honest scholars who know how to rule efficiently come to give the princes advice, a whole pack of officials swarms around them, barking ferociously. I've been bitten by the dogs at the court of Han."

"What did you mean about the rat under the altar?"

"In the country, a big tree is often worshipped as the god of the earth, and rats make their nests in the bank beneath it. Impossible either to smoke or to flood them out. A prince has his own kind of rats—the members of the royal family, the minions and favorites who grow and prosper in the shadow of his throne."

"What *I* was talking about," said Li Ssu, "was the granary rats and the latrine rats that you have in government offices in the provinces. Granary rats, fat and full, fear neither man nor dog. Other rats are thin and nervous and live on filth. And this made me think: Just as huge pine trees become puny and stunted if you transplant them from the top of a mountain down to some stony scree, so a man of talent loses his dash and ability if he has to vegetate in a minor post. People, like animals, are the product of their situation and environment. I thought: Here I am a latrine rat, and nowadays the only way to become a granary rat is to learn to be an orator. So I decided to go and study under a master. Now, even if you're progressive yourself, it's fashionable to be (or to have been) taught by a master who stands for the past. Princes hanker after the past. Hsün Tzu is nearly seventy and will soon die, and even if he doesn't—he's as strong as an ox—he'll be revered like a saint for his longevity. In either case, it will be a great advantage to have been the pupil of one of the oldest teachers in the Empire. That was how I reasoned, and why I chose him."

"So you want to be a fat rat!" said Han Negation. "I hope you won't eat all the grain in the public granaries!"

"Everyone wants to be fat," answered Li Ssu. "The only difference is that some are born fat and others have to struggle and scheme to become so. But ambition is the one thing that's evenly distributed in this world—and a good thing, too, say I, for social order is based on greed." Li Ssu spoke with passion, his eyes shining.

"You are right," said Han Negation apologetically. "I am still sometimes influenced by the prejudices of my class and have not completely rid myself of the old reflexes. Yes, ambition is a virtue and disinterestedness a weakness. And it's because people don't understand this great truth that the world is in such straits. Li Ssu, you have just taught me a lesson, and I shall put it to good use."

———

A few days later, Han Negation produced a treatise based on this conversation. And so the days and months went by: they listened to the master's teachings, then met afterward, to talk about how to bring order into a world disorganized, torn by war, and incapable of turning its back on the past.

Hsün Tzu was weary. Every passing day tore one more silken thread from the web of illusion he had woven around reality. Various orators challenged the master, and he defended himself inch by inch, obstinate, unwavering, and sometimes devious. Han Negation listened to him hold forth, then discussed it all with Li Ssu in his little study as they drank wine and nibbled at jujubes, fruit, slices of dried meat, and watermelon seeds—and all the time he was writing feverishly, covering whole scrolls of silk and bundles of bamboo with his rounded, elegant script. His brush was as quick and fluent as his tongue was inarticulate.

Li Ssu admired this facility. He himself had great difficulty setting his thoughts down, but, on the other hand, he had a ready tongue and was swift at repartee. He could speak impromptu, and had learned from Hsün Tzu how to argue convincingly: how to seem to yield to the reasoning of an opponent only to advance his own ideas; how to make the weaker line of thought seem the stronger; and how to dazzle an interlocutor with false logic. He searched religious texts and music for similes and metaphors. He learned how the effective use of association and parallel could make black pass for white, high for low, and true for false. They also served to vary the rhythm of a speech, to introduce pauses in a close-knit argument—necessary halts, and as welcome as green meadows with cool springs which one encountered while climbing a difficult mountain. They rested, amused, and delighted the listener. You could flash a thousand jades, trinkets, and dream horses before his eyes, and when, dazzled by the treasures vouchsafed him by the power of words, he tried to commit these marvels to memory, he missed the weak link in your argument or the fault in your logic.

Li Ssu's compositions lost their administrative dryness and became as glossy, supple, and scintillating as watered silk. The sentences unfurled smoothly, like the coils of a great serpent.

He now listened intently to the oratorical contests between the master and other speakers, in order to soak up their methods and see through their stratagems. In one debate that he found particularly edifying false reasoning triumphed over true. His master, who had never held a sword in his life, reduced a general to silence on the subject of war!

Afterward, the victor gathered his pupils together to expound the argument further.

But a brilliant student named Ch'en Hsiao asked an embarrassing question. "In your discourse on war," he said, "you talk of kindness and generosity, of justice and respect for religion. For me, kindness consists in loving one's neighbor, and religion, in following reason. How can reason and loving one's neighbor play any part in an activity that aims at extermination and conquest?"

"You do not understand," answered the orator. "Kindness certainly does mean loving one's neighbor. But does not loving one's neighbor also—and above all—mean hating what may harm and therefore destroy him? I agree that justice consists in following reason.

But does that not include the elimination of whatever conflicts with it?"

Li Ssu reflected that Shang Yang had said all this a hundred years ago, and said it better. He had also drawn the consequences: "If you must use the sword to put an end to killing, do not hesitate to kill! If you must resort to worse cruelty to put an end to torture, do not hesitate to use the most terrible tortures!"

Li Ssu asked a question of his own. "For four generations, Ch'in has won one victory after another over the feudatory princes," he said. "Its army is about to become master of all the earth. Yet it does not seem to me that Ch'in has shown more kindness or justice than any other country. Isn't the explanation, rather, that it has been good at profiting from circumstances?"

"Li Ssu," replied the master, "there is one thing you will never understand. What you call profit is only illusory. There is only one true profit—that which comes from the practice of justice and generosity. Although Ch'in has been victorious for four generations, it has always been haunted by the thought that the eastern provinces might revive their alliance. Despite its successes, Ch'in's army remains the product of an age of decadence, incapable of applying great principles. Only religion makes possible the establishment of distinctions among classes. Religion is the foundation of society, the source of all authority and respect for superiors, the guarantee of success and glory, the royal road to dominion over the Empire.

"In the past, the people were made use of only when necessary. The rulers showed them love and affection. Inferiors were the shadows of their superiors, subjects the echo of their masters. One judgment was enough to make the whole Empire tremble, and the guilty, knowing that they deserved their punishment, would bless the hand that smote them. There was no need for outright repression—fear of the king's majesty spread over the whole society like the calm waters of a great river.

"Rewards and punishments, guile and duplicity will never be

enough in themselves to get men to put their energies at the service of their sovereign. If the master of men does no more than confine the rapacity of his subjects within the bonds of rewards and punishments, the slightest upset may bring him face to face with disobedience and rebellion. Widespread informing is a poor expedient, worthy only of porters and rice-water vendors. It will never help to unify the masses or civilize the nation. The men of antiquity blushed to speak of it. They revered virtue and religion."

Li Ssu bowed to his master and said nothing. But he couldn't help smiling ironically. He was sure that history would prove him right.

Hsün Tzu also spoke at length about religion and music, but whenever he embarked on these subjects Li Ssu and Han Negation both felt that he was speaking of something dead.

"Ritual," he would say, launching into a discourse on religion, "is the highest perfection, the supreme expression and the sublime fulfillment of humanity. Nothing can be added to it, nothing can be taken away. It enables us to distinguish among classes and establish a hierarchy, while imparting an exquisite pleasure to superior and inferior alike."

Li Ssu used to half-close his eyes and let his mind go blank, so as not to be influenced by this nonsense.

On other occasions Hsün Tzu would talk of human nature, which he considered to be bad. "Man is vile by nature," he said. "Without someone to guide him, he is motivated only by the basest interests." But, uttering this truth, discovered long before by Shang Yang, he would fall back into the old Confucian groove again. "The innate perversity of man can only be overcome," he went on, "by a favorable environment, and above all by a master or a guide to act as a model. The sages of old established the rites of religion as a safeguard against human folly and depravity. By the position they occupy in society, these rites serve to educate the masses and elevate the conscience of mankind."

In the view of Li Ssu and Han Negation, who often discussed

this matter, it was because of man's evil instincts that he was a social animal.

"A society is formed," maintained Li Ssu, "not by taking exceptional people as a model but by reducing exceptional people to the norm."

And Han Negation read aloud some passages from his latest treatise, *On Regicide:*

When a man who has learned the techniques of manipulation finds himself at the head of a country, he does not try to win the people's affection but seeks, rather, to force them to serve their master out of necessity. Anyone who relies on the love he inspires in his subjects to make them obey him is doomed, but he who uses methods that leave them no alternative but to sacrifice their lives for him will rule the world.

A prince never has extraordinary qualities. He does not have the piercing sight of a Li Lu or the keen hearing of a Shih Kuang. He sees to it that the whole Empire is his eyes and ears. Although he lives outside the world, hidden away in a labyrinth of galleries, nothing and no one escapes his vigilance.

Li Ssu nodded. "Precisely. In a system like that it's of no importance whether citizens are honest or deceitful. The techniques of government make it possible to do without intelligence and wisdom. Most princes are no better than ordinary mortals as regards either virtue or behavior, knowledge or courage; and yet no one, however bad or bold, dares lift a hand against them. Such is the strength of social position."

Han Negation took up the argument. "A wise prince doesn't ask his subjects to behave well—he uses methods that prevent them from behaving badly. He must never forget this truth: that in his whole kingdom he won't find ten men ready to do what he wishes or follow the path of virtue of their own accord. Therefore, he must employ the whip, to see that everyone obeys his orders.

"A good craftsman doesn't care if his pieces of wood are not perfectly straight or round—he has tools to smooth what is uneven or straighten what is crooked, and these tools enable him to produce the uniform goods required by the people. Similarly, a king worthy of the title has no time for men who follow the right path of their own free will. He knows that philosophy insists on the application of repressive laws: government is concerned not with the individuals but with the multitude. He uses methods that eliminate chance and render men of destiny superfluous. By virtue of his position, a prince is master of every kind of wealth; he also possesses the terrifying thunderbolts of the law; as long as he applies the techniques of manipulation skillfully, he will have an intimate knowledge of the thoughts and deeds of every one of his subjects."

It was as if time were suspended. A great calm hung over the Empire, as though all the world were holding its breath before some dreadful hurricane. Important diplomatic maneuvers were going on in the background, but the war had abated. The princes were recouping their strength after the grim struggles of the previous decades. Even Ch'in had put its army "at ease."

But the calm was deceptive, for everyone knew that the fate of the Empire would soon be decided, and decided by force of arms.

CHAPTER IV

CONVERSATIONS
WITH A FRIEND

Negation and Li Ssu had been in Chao for three years when Prince
Spring Awakening wrote a letter to Hsün Tzu asking him to resume
his post as prefect of Lan Ling. The person who slandered him had
been unmasked, and one of the members of the prime minister's
entourage strongly advocated his return. People scented some sinister
intrigue behind all this, but no one really knew now who was responsible for what, so subtle and complex was the web of alliance
and intrigue. These were uncertain times, when princes were always
trying out different schemes, feeling their way rather than proceeding
in any definite direction.

Hsün Tzu accepted his former protector's offer. His prestige
had waned in Chao, where he enjoyed many honors but very little
influence. He felt rather like one of the sacrificial urns exhibited in

palaces because of their great age but never put to use. He didn't want to be a relic—he considered himself a man of his time. The honors, titles, and dignities lavished on him had the wry taste of a funeral panegyric.

So the orator and his band of followers went to live in Ch'u, where Li Ssu encountered a familiar language, a well-known landscape, and a way of life that he abhorred. From Lan Ling, already a long way from Shang Ts'ai, his native village could only be reached over very bad roads. But he did make several trips there to see his wife and sons. Hsieh had grown, was nearly old enough to wear the cap of manhood, and attended classes at the local school.

As the years went by, the master grew more pessimistic and morose. He talked less of ritual now; his teaching centered on the wickedness of human nature. He began to take an interest in rhetoric, in the rules of eloquence and how to cajole princes with dazzling words. The sense of his own failure had somehow made him aware of the difficulties of rhetoric. He felt that he had neglected the art of pleasing. Or perhaps he was unconsciously influenced by the age he lived in and the preoccupations of his contemporaries. It was now that he gave his best lessons ever: Han Negation and Li Ssu were astonished to find him almost brilliant.

"When the noblest and purest of beings," he said, "meets the vilest and most immoral of men, he cannot go straight to the point. He must weigh each word and consider each expression. If he takes remotest antiquity for his model, he is called a braggart. If he speaks of recent times, he is vulgar. What untold skill it takes to talk to a prince—even just to choose the moment when he is most likely to listen! And so a wise man, when he addresses a nobleman, talks about antiquity without seeming to mention bygone things, thus following the fashion without falling into triviality. Sometimes a sentence is slow, sometimes it is swift and staccato. The tone may be lively to begin with, like the joyous sound of a stream running over stones, then become broader and more restful, like a majestic river flowing across a great plain. Discourse is like a channel that guides a river between the desired banks, the pattern that enables a carpenter to straighten a misshapen piece of wood. Through many detours it reaches its goal by the quickest way. It may be summed up thus: gravity captures the attention, truth retains it, logic fascinates, brilliance persuades, and comparisons illustrate. The listener is so dazzled and enchanted that he will accept anything, even if what you have said would otherwise be displeasing to him. Thus you can bring around to your own point of view even those who seem most hostile to it."

These teachings made a great impression on Han Negation. Rhetoric fascinated him. He showed his friend several attempts at essays on the subject, but was not satisfied with them. Like all students of oratory at that time, he and Li Ssu did exercises that consisted in writing addresses to some dead king in the name of a famous sophist like Shang I or Tzu Ch'in. The pair of them became extremely good at this, and even Hsün Tzu, who was sparing of praise, could not conceal his admiration.

Meanwhile, King Chuang Hsiang had come to the throne in Ch'in and, on the advice of Lü Pu-wei, was threatening Han. His armies had already taken the cities of Ch'ang Hao and Jung Yang, and were marching on Shang Tang.

War broke out again, and Han Negation thought his time had come. The king of Han, confused and worried by the Ch'in army's advance, was looking for a man to fit the moment and would probably be ready to listen to Han Negation and give him a job. Han Negation prepared to take leave of his teacher and of his fellow pupil Li Ssu. The two friends had one last passionate debate about the techniques of government and the present situation in the kingdoms.

"To bring about perfect order," said Li Ssu, "you must introduce merciless laws and terrifying punishments, to force people to do willingly what they hate and gladly what they fear. A prince must use violence to combat guile, deceit, and sloth. By means of rewards and punishments he bends his subjects' energies toward one end: agriculture. When men are employed in productive tasks, they are in fact rustics. But if you restrict people's activity and ensure that they remain stupid without giving their rusticity something to do, their unused strength will breed corruption. That is why any prince worthy of the title, after concentrating his subjects' energies on a single goal, will make it a rule to destroy the surpluses that result from a war of destruction. The wealth of a country is in direct proportion to the stultification of its people; its power is in direct proportion to their degradation. Individuals must at all costs be prevented from becoming masters of their own time and lives. Exceptional people, sages and eccentrics, must be done away with. Citizens who are not stimulated by the lure of reward or checked by the threat of punishment are ungovernable. Anything that stands out from the normal must be sawed or hacked off."

"That's the meaning of the *Book of the Way and of Virtue*," interposed Han, "for anyone who really understands it." He quoted thoughtfully:

> The rule of a saint
> Fills bellies
> But empties hearts,
> Weakening wills
> While it strengthens bones.

After a pause he went on: "But, assuming one does introduce collective responsibility and widespread denunciation, tell me, Li Ssu, how is one to tell true allegations of wrongdoing from false?"

"By cultivating solidarity on the one hand and dissociation on the other," came the reply. "Because of the solidarity that comes from collective responsibility, men inform on one another. Then, by taking each witness separately and confronting him with his own informer, you break up any collusion or conspiracy that might let the men join together against authority."

"I've thought about this," said Negation, "and it's not so simple as all that. Investigation, verification, and confrontation—in short, finding out the truth about everything and everyone in a society— call for a central stock of facts handled by a staff specially charged with the management of the masses and chosen from those who raised themselves above the rest by their aptitude for this sort of task. But they mustn't be completely stupid, or they won't be able to do their job properly—that is, to see that brutishness prevails among the majority. Do you see what I mean?"

"Yes, it *is* a problem."

"So intelligence cannot be dispensed with altogether. But, that being so, it must be turned against itself. A way must be found of neutralizing it. In a word, the sovereign should concern himself not with the people but with the administration."

"How so?"

"When you want fruit to fall from a tree, you shake the trunk, not the separate leaves."

Li Ssu was silent, thinking. "Yes," he said slowly. "Now I understand. To lift a heavy weight you use a lever. But to do so, you must concentrate on the lever rather than on the weight."

"Exactly. The law applies to the people. Officials are responsible for applying it. A prince must provide himself with the means of controlling the administration, for his subordinates' one idea is to usurp his place. The art of politics lies in detecting the thoughts of one's executives and finding out all about them—to be able to terrorize them. Officials must also be chosen for their abilities, and given an appropriate place in the hierarchy. That calls for much skill— Shang Yang's method, which involved promoting officials in proportion to the number of heads they cut off, was too crude. Does a man who cuts off heads make a good carpenter? No. Still less does he make a good administrator.

"Politics is the hidden face of the law. The latter concerns everyone; the former is the exclusive property of the prince. Politics is secret and impenetrable, whereas the law is public and universal. . . . I've written a little piece about it. Would you care to read it?"

He took a bundle of bamboo strips from his sleeve. This is what Li Ssu read:

> *Neither change nor alter.*
> *Move with the Two*
> *Without ceasing.*
> *Follow the reason of things:*
> *Everything is in its place.*
> *Nonaction*
> *From top to bottom:*
> *Let the rooster watch over the night,*
> *The cat catch the rats,*
> *Each to his own task,*
> *And the Master remains unruffled.*
>
> *Names are double,*
> *Things are troubled.*
> *The Sage, doing nothing, possesses the One,*
> *And names are named,*
> *Things are given.*
>
> *The Master acts through the Name.*
> *If he does not know it, he turns to the Form.*
> *Of their equalization Usage is born.*
> *The Two are worthy of belief,*
> *Inferiors do not lie.*
> *He looks to what should be.*
>
> *The Prince understands the Name.*
> *His subjects answer with the Form.*
> *When the two coincide*
> *Prince and subject are in harmony.*
> *Method of examination:*
> *I feel strange, as if I were drunk.*
> *The barrier of lips—the barrier of teeth.*

I do not begin.
Lips and teeth.
I am more and more in the dark.
They speak separately.
I see through them.
All opinions converge toward them
Though He has not brought them together.

Empty and calm—that is the way of the Tao.
Matched and classified,
By three, by five,
That is the form of things.
I classify—things.
I match—the void.
The trunk remains strong. Not a flaw.
He moves, He frolics, and without acting
He rules.

Pleasure causes trouble.
Hate creates resentment.
Banish pleasure, banish hatred,
And make the Tao your dwelling
By emptying your heart.

"Very fine," said Li Ssu. Then, "Are the Two the forms of punishment?"

"Yes."

"And Usage is the use of rewards and punishments through the adjustment of Name to Form?"

"That's right—you've got it."

"So a prince must master language in order to make names and things identical and to deal out punishments correctly. In other words, if every name has a single corresponding meaning that is accurate from the social point of view, language becomes an effective means of control, making it possible to apprehend reality and categorize actions."

"Exactly," agreed Han Negation. "If a son doesn't inform on his father when his father has stolen a sheep, he isn't a dutiful son, as Confucius would have it, but the accomplice of a thief. This is his *penal description*, and as such he must be tried and sentenced; he must not be praised for his filial virtue—that is a moral judgment, irrelevant to the state. Worse than irrelevant, for, as you yourself have taught me, morality is fundamentally antisocial."

"And since his subordinates are always trying to deceive him, a ruler must discover the reality that lies beyond words: hence 'The barrier of lips—the barrier of teeth.' So there must be investigations and checks, spying, comparison of evidence, traps, torture, and so on, in order to establish the purity of language that is the manifestation and guarantee of the purity of society."

"Names are also functions in the hierarchy," explained Han Negation, pouring himself a bowl of millet wine as he began to chew some watermelon seeds. "Every post conferred corresponds to a form of work. And the forms must coincide with the names."

Li Ssu sipped at his wine, took a few jujubes, bowed to his friend, and said with a sigh: "It's very good. But, alas, you'll always be far beyond me. Why, after creating a Li Ssu, did heaven have to go and produce a Han Negation!"

It was Han Negation's turn to bow.

"Make no mistake," he cried, "you are better than I am! There has to be a Li Ssu to put the theories of a Han Negation into practice. And let us thank heaven that, having created a Han Negation, it also produced a Li Ssu! I don't have your force of character, or your authority and ambition. I'm hesitant, indecisive, shy. I have no talent for repartee and am still riddled with prejudices about morality, loyalty, and suchlike. I may succeed in banishing these from my writing, but they hang over me and oppress me within myself. I'm at my best only when I'm sitting cross-legged alone in a room, with a brush in my hand and some strips of bamboo in front of me. Then it's as if I'm inhabited by the gods. Perhaps—even probably—I am a great theoretician, but I fear I am an indifferent statesman."

With these words, the two friends parted.

———

Lü Pu-wei, having managed to put his creature at the head of the most powerful state in the Empire, was now prime minister of Ch'in. But rumors of conspiracy were in the air. Orators swarmed all over the provinces. The kingdoms were being ravaged by the armies. All society writhed in the convulsions of a world that refused to die. It seemed to Li Ssu a propitious moment. Hsün Tzu, that old Confucian windbag, had no more to teach him, and Han Negation had gone away. Lü Pu-wei was letting it be known everywhere that he needed men of talent to give Ch'in a fresh start.

So, one fine day in the fifth month of the third year of the reign of King Chuang Hsiang, Li Ssu said goodbye to his old master. But before he left he bowed and asked, "You know Ch'in. What sort of country is it? How did it strike you?"

Hsün Tzu replied somewhat brusquely. "I can only repeat what I used to say to Fan Sui, the marquis of Ying, when he was minister to King Resplendent and asked me for my opinion as to how he should rule."

Li Ssu, irritated, burst out in a tone that he regretted later: "Come, master—I've always been told one ought to seize one's opportunities. You know the present political situation: the great states are at one another's throats. This creates unprecedented openings for itinerant counselors of all kinds and opinions. Ch'in is getting ready to roll up all China under its arm like a mat, and I don't doubt it will succeed.

"The golden age has come for orators, but it can't last long. People who are content with their lot and make no attempt to rise in the hierarchy are mere beasts with human faces, further removed from true mankind than the orangutang. I know of no worse shame than to be a commoner, and of no worse misery than to be poor. It is too easy to resign oneself to mediocrity and cry out against decadence and corruption; to deck oneself in the tatters of integrity and virtue and cast scorn on contemporary affairs through the broken window of one's hovel. That is why, venerable master, I find myself reluctantly obliged to leave you, to go try my luck in Ch'in."

CHAPTER V

THE RISE OF LI SSU

In the late spring of the first year of the reign of King Ordinance of Ch'in, a traveler in the long coat of a scholar, driving a modest-looking chariot, presented himself at the gates of the frontier post at Han Ku K'ou. A long line of merchants, peddlers, vendors of salted fish and rice-water, swashbucklers, bravos, orators, laborers, and ambassadors crowded around the tall towers. Guards were examining passes and safe-conducts, recording merchandise, interrogating returning Ch'in citizens to make sure they weren't fugitives of one kind or another. Medical officials were fumigating all harness and saddlery and leather coach fittings to get rid of parasites, for the people of Ch'in believed that the princes of the eastern provinces neglected their horses, and they didn't want infection to spread to Ch'in, which had an excellent system of disease diagnosis and prevention. Our traveler was impressed.

As he passed through the barrier, Li Ssu noticed a large crowd of men bound hand and foot. They were peasants who had tried to escape forced labor and been either caught or informed against. Some of them had even given themselves up at the critical moment, so effective was the vigilance of the guards and so powerful the fear of punishment.

Li Ssu took a deep breath, enjoying the clear and already warm air. He felt elated. What order, what organization! As he made his way toward the capital, he was struck by the regularity of the plots of land, their boundaries as straight as bowstrings. The dikes were in excellent repair; not a weed or a bramble was to be seen on the embankments. The irrigation channels spread a shining and orderly grid over the yellow earth, an endless checkerboard on which plows drawn by sturdy oxen left rows of darker stripes.

Going through the small towns and district centers dotting the road that flanked the Yellow River, Li Ssu noted how well the granaries were kept, how new the thatch looked on the roofs, and how the administrators' accommodations, unlike those in Chao and Ch'u, were always built some distance away from the storehouses.

He saw none of the long lines of convicts so often encountered in the towns of the eastern provinces: the authorities here had banned their passage through urban areas, villages, and markets, lest the sight of them cause unrest. But he did from time to time catch sight of innumerable red patches, which turned out to be prisoners engaged in ramming earth, building dikes and walls and roads, or pounding rice, all in time to a voice that set the rhythm.

Li Ssu's mood was light and joyful, and he looked around at this land, this country, as if it were already his. He gazed with pride on the wooded hills, the silt-laden rivers, the great herds grazing the lush grass. And he admired the accuracy of Hsün Tzu's description: since he had left him, he felt a vague affection, even respect, for his former teacher.

What this well-lubricated machine, this smoothly functioning organization needed was a purpose, and above all someone who could point out that purpose. Li Ssu felt that he himself was capable of channeling all this energy, and of unleashing it on the world at large. Like a horse pawing the ground in its stall, Ch'in was waiting only for a coachman to grasp the reins with a firm hand, brandish the whip, and let it hurtle forth over infinite space.

———

Li Ssu managed to get into Lü Pu-wei's good graces and become one of his entourage. He carried out some difficult missions successfully; the minister got used to his services and came to value his skill. He collaborated in the compilation of the great encyclopedia that the merchant sponsored, having become a statesman and a patron of the arts. Li Ssu's advice was shrewd and his point of view discerning. He was a good speaker, but could also make himself feared. He acquired horses and carriages. He wore a robe patterned with crossed axes and figures of multicolored brocade, all in the finest silk. He lived in spacious apartments and ruled over quantities of slaves.

He took advantage of one of the young king's free moments to tell him of his aims.

"A man of little worth," he said, "is unable to seize his opportunity and strike through the chink in his enemy's armor. Great things are achieved only by turning your adversary's weaknesses to your own account and then mercilessly exploiting your advantage. Duke Mu was supreme ruler of Ch'in, but he never succeeded in annexing the kingdoms beyond the eastern mountains. That wasn't because he lacked political sense, but because of the historical situation. The central plain was divided among many princedoms, and there were still flames among the Chou dynasty's dying embers. And so the Five Rulers, each in his turn, lit up the Empire with glory, but they never had standing enough to supplant the Chou and refuse to do them homage.

"But things have changed since Duke Hiao ruled Ch'in. The house of Chou is at its last gasp, and the princes are at such furious odds that there are no more than six powerful countries left in the central plain. With the formidable strength of your own realm and the keenness of your intellect, you could bring all the princes into subjection as easily as a cook scours a pot. You would thus unify the Empire and fulfill the great imperial design. You would win eternal glory for yourself and hand your name down to posterity.

"But if you cannot take your chance quickly, I fear the princes will pull themselves together, join forces, and form an indestructible alliance. And once the opportunity has been allowed to slip, even if you were as great a captain as the Yellow Emperor, you would struggle in vain to overcome them."

This speech made a great impression on the king. He was grateful to the prime minister's protégé for taking an interest in him, and for treating him as if he were in charge. Li Ssu was made officer of the royal decrees and wore the bronze seal hanging from his belt on a dark-green cord. His emoluments added up to a thousand *shih* of grain.

The princedoms were once again ravaged by war, and the princes sought to patch up new alliances. Li Ssu sent men from Ch'in to recruit secret agents among the intimates of all the princes and their ministers. Those who accepted his proposals were handsomely rewarded; those who refused were murdered.

But this policy was not entirely successful. Lü Pu-wei was playing a game of his own, aimed at increasing both his influence and his property. Seeing this, the feudatory princes began to gain a hold over him. Li Ssu drew closer to the king. They shared a passion for laws and regulations, and Li Ssu initiated the king into the workings of the administration of prefectures and subprefectures. He explained the necessity of having an absolute authority imposed by means of ruthless punishments. He dictated the great maxims a prince needed to know and practice if he did not wish to put his throne in peril, such as "A great prince does things lesser princes would be ashamed of" and "A ruler governs not through men but through laws, and these must be severe to be obeyed."

Their discussions often continued far into the night. Sitting on a mat in the privacy of the king's study, they would talk about how to rule men and administer things. Li Ssu became animated as he expounded the ideas he had once debated so passionately with his friend Han Negation in the austere little room in Han Tan.

"A country is governed," he would say in his firm, precise voice, "when punishments are eliminated by virtue of their very brutality; a country becomes disturbed when punishments are resorted to because they are so mild. For punishment is the expression of authority, authority fosters power, power begets fear, and fear authorizes clemency. Thus mercy is born of the immoderate use of force."

Sometimes he would go on like this till dawn, repeating the most striking assertions of his former fellow student: "A sovereign guided by ministers applying the techniques of manipulation will not be taken in by fashionable sophistries. He will make forms and names identical, will settle what is true and what is false, and will judge words by the yardstick of results. For if the paths that lead to glory or to death are clearly demarcated, what minister will dare deceive his prince, what official will try to do violence to the law? When a country is a prey to troubles, it is not because of the sins of inferiors but because the leaders themselves have failed to use the means that would give them a proper hold over the people. Instead they adopt methods bound to cause dissension, and neglect the techniques that would guarantee peace and order."

———

In the ninth year of Ordinance's reign, the rebellion led by Lao Ai broke out. Lü Pu-wei, from whom Li Ssu had managed to distance himself, was implicated. Ordinance put Li Ssu in charge of the inquiry.

He was made honorary minister and wore the red cord bearing the silver seal. His income rose to two thousand *shih* of grain. He and his sons, whom he had sent for to join him in Double Light along with his wife, were habitual guests at the royal hunting parties. He already imagined himself at the utmost height of success when, like a bolt from the blue, there came the news of a decree expelling all foreigners from Ch'in.

Taking advantage of the stir caused by Lü Pu-wei's dubious role in the sham eunuch's rebellion, the old Ch'in aristocracy and part of the royal family had presented the king with a report on Sheng Kuo, a hydraulic engineer from Han. He had been commissioned to build a huge irrigation canal three hundred leagues long to take water from the river Ch'ing and channel it eastward to enter the river Lo at its confluence with the Yellow River. A million prisoners sentenced to forced labor, together with slaves and conscripts, had already spent five years working on the project. But the lengthy dossier compiled by the services of General Piao K'ung proved that Sheng Kuo was a spy working for Han, and the construction of the canal a gigantic act of sabotage designed to ruin Ch'in, or at least distract it from the conquest of the countries east of the mountains.

The king nearly went mad with rage, and the xenophobe party took advantage of his fury to get him to sign the decree. All foreigners had to leave the country within a week on pain of death. Lists were drawn up, houses searched. The air rang with the sobs of wives and children. Guards were everywhere, ordering foreigners to leave at once. The mob, egged on by the aristocratic party, stoned the first groups of deportees as they left.

A legal official, accompanied by two palace guards who wore the panther tails over their caps, which distinguished the crack units, came to give Li Ssu his expulsion order; from outside, all the beggars and idlers of Double Light could be heard yelling: "Death to the foreigners! Traitors! Worse than locusts! You despoil our country! Go home! Go home!"

The noise grew louder and more menacing. Stones hit the walls and the fretted windows. One window was broken. The children began to cry. Li Ssu's wife, pale and trembling, tried to hurry up the slaves and servant girls, while some impudent lackeys, delighted at this turning of the tables, made no attempt to conceal their mirth.

Li Ssu and his family finished packing, stowed their trunks into carts, and crept out the back way like thieves. Soon they joined the ever-increasing flood of deportees escorted by the royal guards, whose main concern was not to protect them but to make sure they didn't escape and hide somewhere in the capital.

So Li Ssu retraced the road he had traveled so cheerfully ten years before, in the days when he thought the world was his oyster. Sitting upright in his chariot beside his silent wife, while his sons, Yu and Hsieh, gritted their teeth to keep from crying and his daughters dried their tears on their sleeves, he felt stunned. The blow had been so sudden and unexpected, he hadn't even thought to ask for an audience with the king.

The party advanced slowly, halting about fifteen leagues from the capital. At the inn where they stopped, Li Ssu threw off the apathy that had at first descended upon him. He couldn't leave Ch'in like this—as if he was a failure; driven away like a beggar; expelled as one of a crowd! Since it was all over anyway, he had nothing to lose by sending Ordinance a petition. Wasn't this precisely the moment to test the power of words, to put into practice the lessons he had learned under Hsün Tzu? He opened his writing desk and sent his brush flying over the silk.

"Nothing could be more inept than the measures your ministers have just decided upon," he wrote.

If the wise princes who formerly ruled Ch'in had refused to employ men of talent because they were foreigners, do you think your country would be basking in its present wealth and military might?

Is it consistent in you, prince, to issue this decree and at the same time collect jades from Mount K'un, egg-shaped pearls from Sui, and jewelry from Ho? You do not scorn to wear these foreign gems, which seem to have stolen their light from the stars. And do we not see you proudly buckling on the great sword Fine Blade, forged by Mo Yeh and Kan Ch'iang for the king of Ch'u?

Are not your carriages drawn mettlesome by steeds from the steppes? Are not your wives adorned and your vases filled with the rainbow feathers of the kingfisher and the phoenix, neither of which is ever to be seen in Ch'in? The drums in your orchestras are covered with crocodile skin, though as far as I know the crocodile has never lurked in your rivers or lakes.

Answer me, prince—of all the jewels, treasures, and curios with which your storehouses overflow, and which delight your eyes in the high halls of your palaces, is there one, produced in Ch'in itself? And yet their shapes and colors are pleasing to your senses. If you carried your policy through to its logical conclusion, you would have to part with all those precious trifles made of ivory, rhinoceros horn, and jasper; with all the finely decorated lacquers, the soft yet heavy silks, and the warm and fleecy carpets that come from the barbarian khans. You would have nothing around you but what was produced at home.

And, alas, would not the elegant galleries of your harems be barer than landscapes under a winter sky if they were bereft of their finest ornaments—the girls from Cheng and Wei, with their lily-white skin and figures supple as willow? And how empty your stables would look without the strong-legged chargers with powerful rumps and the sprightly fillies champing in their stalls!

If everything that now pleases your eyes and ears had to come from Ch'in itself, could your wives appear before you with their hair dressed high with combs inlaid with pearls from Yüan, the delicate shells of their ears enhanced by heavy coral pendants? Could your eye still delight in the way their hips are sometimes outlined in silk, while another day they conceal their slender limbs in heavy brocades? And would your guests still be diverted by the beauties from Chao, whose graceful and sensual movements add so much to the crystal voices, to the elegant songs they sing?

Yet with men it is different! It seems that you and your people are ready to rid yourselves of hundreds of officials, regardless of their talents and merits, simply because they are not natives of Ch'in!

Does this not mean, master, that you think more of your precious stones, your horses, your wives, and your furniture than of your ministers? But is that the right attitude for a prince who aims to extend his authority over the whole world?

If you now reject men of talent, none of them will ever come again to the West to give you the benefit of their advice. In my view, that is tantamount to arming your enemies and provisioning pirates. You are depriving yourself of what used to be your strength, having stirred up the hatred and resentment of all the princes in the Empire.

———

While Li Ssu sadly took the dusty road to exile, King Ordinance summoned before him the traitor whose incredible machinations had done Ch'in more harm than all the armies of the princes put together.

Sheng Kuo stood before a king whose lips were blue with wrath. With eyes flashing and a voice like thunder, Ordinance flung the incriminating bundles of bamboo in his face. Four years' work for nothing! Mountains had been hollowed out, hills shifted, rock hewn right down to the veins of the earth, valleys uplifted, and forests felled. Out of the millions of men mobilized for the task, hundreds of thousands had died of fever or exhaustion. Picks and shovels had been produced by the thousands; carts had been requisitioned, along with oxen, asses, and horses, to transport supplies and raw materials. And it was all a monstrous trick, a gigantic trap that Ch'in had rushed into! This is what happened when a king was foolish enough to follow the advice of rascally foreigners—base, wicked, unscrupulous, venal wretches. Already he was thinking up a terrible revenge, some refined, horrible, protracted torture that would make the victim's agonized body yearn for death.

He glared at the man whom he had been too furious to examine closely before. The man was tall, with thick lips and a stiff black mustache, and his skin was tanned from working in the open air. The slant of his eyes and the bone structure of his face suggested great energy. Ordinance was disturbed. This countenance, this imperious attitude was not how he had imagined the traitor.

He soon recovered himself: men were to be judged not by their appearance but by their deeds. Nevertheless, instead of throwing him into a cauldron immediately, the king addressed him harshly. "Look at these documents. You are guilty of the worst kind of treachery, the most heinous of crimes. What punishment can fit such a breach of faith? I am good at imagining tortures, but even I cannot think of a torture bad enough."

"Prince," replied the other, "ask me, rather, what reward I should receive for my work." He looked at the king steadily, with a coolness that commanded respect. "The question is not whether I have tried to betray you," he went on, "but whether I have actually been of use to you. I have heard that you judge men according to the tasks they perform and the services they render. Men's motives are murky and obscure. What use is it to you to know whether or not I tried to injure you? Look at my work, judge the result, and base your verdict on the facts! Find out what your engineers think, and your inspectors of public works, your agronomists, your stonemasons. Then you'll see that my efforts have been good for Ch'in's economy. That my calculations are accurate, my figures correct, and all the work well done. What has to be taken into account is reality—the facts and nothing but the facts. Once my great project is completed, no one will be able to boast of having done so much for the greatness of your kingdom. The canal will make it possible to triple the yield of the region between the river Ch'ing and the river Lo. Thousands of once barren and unproductive acres will be rich and fruitful. And you say I have done nothing for Ch'in. Surely you jest!"

The king, perplexed, sent for the ministers of agriculture and public works and their engineers.

"What effect will irrigation have on the lands between the two tributaries of the Yellow River?" he asked them. "How many *mou* will benefit, and what sort of yield will they produce?"

"Prince," said the minister of agriculture, bowing three times, "this man is a—"

"I didn't ask for your opinion of this man. I can judge him for myself. I want you to tell me about what is within your own competence. And if ever I should find out that you're lying, I'll have your tongue cut out and you yourself pickled in brine! Give me a quick summary of the benefits the canal will bring to the northern part of Double Light."

The minister trembled and was speechless.

The superintendent of granaries stepped forward, bowed, apologized for his audacity, and spoke.

"The river water conveyed by the canal will make it possible to irrigate at least a thousand square leagues. And if we manage to drain off the stagnant water and the deposits of saltpeter that now make part of the area useless, we could hope to put another forty thousand *ch'ing* under cultivation. The yields would be more than one *chung* per *mou*. Irrigation would also make yields more regular in a region that is subject to great variations in rainfall. Planting could be done before the first rains, which are often late, and there could be two harvests a year. All the capital's food could be supplied by the surrounding countryside. The strain would be taken off the other waterways—the advantages would be incalculable. That, at least, is the opinion of Your Majesty's humble servant, who deserves a thousand deaths for having dared to speak despite his lack of competence."

The minister of agriculture hung his head. He knew he had just lost his job. The king, impassive, dismissed him and his experts and turned to the minister of public works and the controllers of forced labor.

"I should like to know," he said, "if the project is practicable, what stage it has reached, and whether Sheng Kuo does his work properly."

The minister shook out his sleeves, bowed his head three times, and cried: "He's a spy and a traitor! He ought to be tortured and put to death without further ado! What is the point of this investigation?"

"Answer my question or you'll be the one flogged! You are not the judge of his crimes."

"We have used up thousands of days of forced labor, and hundreds of thousands of convicts and slaves have died of epidemics or exhaustion. Only yesterday, eight hundred people were buried when an embankment collapsed—"

"Stop weeping over your brigands!" roared the king. "What do the deaths of a few thousand scoundrels matter if they serve to strengthen the army and make the country greater? Is the work progressing as planned? Can the canal be built or not?"

But the minister flapped his sleeves like an enormous owl and obstinately predicted misfortune and catastrophe for Ch'in if it continued to employ a spy.

At that point an ambitious secretary in the minister's retinue, after making the suitable obeisances, spoke up loudly: "We have already completed more than three-quarters of the work. The hardest part is over. All we have to do now is dig a few hundred leagues across flat country through soil that is hard but not rocky. It would be madness to abandon the canal just when the end is in sight. If we were to stop, Han would have won and we would have done all that work for nothing. Let's at least not throw away all our efforts!"

"And what is Sheng Kuo like as a technician?"

"He is probably the best hydraulic engineer in the Empire. We could do great things if every engineer were like him. He's indefatigable; nothing escapes him. He knows not only how to manage things but also how to give orders to people. His calculations are always accurate: he never makes a mistake in working out the lie of the land or the resistance of the soil. There hasn't been a more skillful worker since Yü the Great corrected the courses of the great rivers!"

The king sent his experts away and summoned Sheng Kuo again.

"You're free," he told him simply. "Go and finish the work you've begun as quickly as you can!"

Sheng Kuo prostrated himself and touched his forehead to the ground. Then he rose and said humbly: "Prince, it is true I worked for Han. They sent me to ruin your economy and exhaust your strength in some immoderate scheme. That was why I suggested building the canal. I was sure Ch'in would never be able to manage it. But I hadn't reckoned on the perseverance of your people, the efficiency and self-sacrifice of the minor officials, the order and organization of the state. I came to like what I was doing—I fell in love with the work—and soon I had only one fear: that I might not complete the canal, might not take it as far as the river of the North, sweeping aside all obstacles, boring through mountains, gouging a long furrow through the bowels of the earth.

"Prince, I love digging canals, measuring slopes with compass and setsquare, diverting the natural course of rivers, taking advantage of the terrain to impose my will on their turbulent waves. To impose my will on nature herself. I love to uncover the veins of the earth, expose its secret lineaments to the light of day, and decipher the riddles of the dragonlike images hidden in the rock.

"I found it exhilarating to have under me that obedient multitude, who worked so hard and swiftly to the syncopated rhythm set by the overseers. The thud of the rammers, the squeal of ropes and pulleys groaning under cartloads of earth—these gave me greater pleasure than the accents of Cheng or Wei.

"In any other state, the project would have been doomed to failure. But Ch'in is not one of the six kingdoms. The chants of those who set the rhythm may be rough and monotonous, but with their help the earth is banked up twice as fast and as firm as in Han. And the laborers themselves may be squat and coarse, and almost simple-minded, but they are more hard-working, conscientious, and frugal than in any other province.

"I saw myself as Yü the Great, drilling through mountains, changing the course of rivers and linking them to the sea. I forgot to protect myself against the fierceness of the sun or the insults of the rain. Like Yü himself, I wore myself down walking long distances and trekking through mud. I had but one object: to do the job quickly and well, and so hand my name down to posterity. I completely lost sight of my original purpose in coming to Ch'in. Yes, I had betrayed Han now in favor of Ch'in. And what are the few years when I served Han compared with the centuries over which Ch'in will enjoy the benefits of the canal? I am sure that, with the extra wealth it will bring you, you will be able to conquer all the princes: the land I have freed for agriculture will feed hundreds of thousand of men for years!"

Then the king spoke.

"Sheng Kuo," he said, "men should be judged by results and not by intentions. You have performed a worthy task. If we were to leave unfinished what has been begun, we should just be falling into our enemies' trap, squandering our wealth and the strength of our people.

"The canal must go on. I want the work to be speeded up. A new army of conscripts and convicts will be raised. You are the only one who can bring the project to a successful conclusion. You are hereby promoted by three grades in the hierarchy, and your emoluments are doubled. Let it be known to all the world that Ch'in judges only by results!"

The next day the king received Li Ssu's letter. It didn't offend him. "I was on the brink of a big mistake and exposing myself to the mockery of the whole Empire," he said to himself. "I must take less notice of the dignitaries and the princes of blood royal."

So he canceled the expulsion order against foreigners and ordered Li Ssu and the rest to be brought back before they crossed the frontier. The couriers' lives depended upon retrieving them in time.

———

Li Ssu set out again in the pale light of dawn. After the tension of the night, he felt extremely weary, and he looked gloomily at the landscape that had once elated him. The yellow earth shivered in the early sun. The threatening ramparts of the fortifications cast sinister shadows; the muddy waters of the great river spread out into a huge lake like a mirror of cruelly glinting bronze.

As he passed the high walls of the leper houses, Li Ssu felt a deathly chill. He passed bands of convicted prisoners, men and women—"pounders of rice and rammers of earth," as they were called in Ch'in's legal parlance. As prisoners, they wore red tunics and had crimson caps hiding their shaven skulls. Many bore traces of horrible mutilations, with gaping holes for noses, and dark tattoos on forehead or cheeks—marks that branded their brutish, resigned faces with the seal of infamy.

They went in groups of twenty, linked together by heavy bronze chains that ate into the flesh and left open wounds on the ankles. Each group was accompanied by a *ssu kuo*, or former prisoner serving out the end of his term as a guard. Hardened by years of deportation, they were no longer conscious of anything but the thud of cudgel on flesh or of rammer on clay. Suffering, toil, and persecution had reduced them to human beasts, more pitiless and ferocious toward one another than the jailers or the torturers.

Passing through a small town on the second day, Li Ssu witnessed a horrible scene. A leper convicted of theft was being drowned. A large tub eight feet high and two spans wide, with a winch and a weight suspended above, had been set up in the market square, and the man, bound from head to foot, was hoisted into it. Li Ssu's eyes met those of the victim, frantic as a cornered animal. Then from amid a sheaf of spray came a strange hoarse, inhuman shriek, as of a soul in torment: the man's nostrils were so eaten away by disease that he could not breathe properly. Next the weight came down, fitting exactly into the opening of the tub and ruthlessly pushing the man under the water. A few thumps were heard against the sides of the tub; then silence. The tub was removed to a special burial place.

Li Ssu felt terribly depressed. The dying gasp of the leper echoed the mutiny that filled his own heart.

On the third day, he came to the village of the Black Horse on the Han frontier, where a long line of people had formed at the gates. Officials were searching everyone, checking all identities. Some villagers denounced a deserter who had tried to hide among the crowd of foreigners. Just as the guards were going through the list of people who had been banished, a cloud of dust arose along the sun-baked road, and men on post horses appeared galloping toward the custom house, the banners of the king's couriers streaming behind them. Some passers-by were toppled into the dust, and a child's head was crushed by the horses' hoofs.

"Make way, louts!" shouted the guards. "An urgent message from the great king!"

Their leader dismounted by the gate and unrolled the decree canceling the expulsion order.

Li Ssu was borne in a triumphal chariot back to Double Light.

———

The very next day, his seal of office was restored to him. To show how much Li Ssu's services and advice were valued, the king entrusted him with the delicate task of deciding what should be done with the fallen prime minister. Li Ssu very shrewdly asked Lü Pu-wei to withdraw into exile in Honan.

Every day Li Ssu was received in private audience.

"The Empire is about to fall like a ripe fruit," he told the young king. "Seize the opportunity and get it firmly in your grasp, and you will soon be master of the whole world. Use corruption and murder;

break up factions; hand out gold in order to unsettle people; spread disorder and confusion. Compare allegations with one another to see which are true; try out every point of view to arrive at the best decision; be always on your guard. Get into the habit of applying the law. Dig up the past to find out about the future. Argue from the near to the far, from the inside to the outside. Leave false clues in your path; cover your traces. Test people's convictions by contradicting them; preach the false to elicit the true. Have individuals in isolation checked so that they do not escape you. Pretend to be taken in, to see how far people will go. Inspire holy terror by seeming omniscient. Sow discord, stoke up dissension, fan the flames to burn up cliques and factions. Spread false rumors. Keep moving your officials around so that they never have time to breathe; promote minor officials over their superiors. Continually divide your enemies, and set them against one another, so that no other power can ever challenge your own."

They worked out a plan for annexing the Empire, deciding that in order to frighten the princes into submission they would start by conquering Han, the weakest among them.

The Lü Pu-wei case was taking its course. Li Ssu gathered evidence. The former prime minister still enjoyed powerful support, but the acting minister was determined to destroy him.

A clumsy move on the part of the merchant gave Li Ssu an opportunity sooner than he expected, and by the second month of the twelfth year of Ordinance's reign he was writing out the decree sentencing the fallen minister and all his friends to banishment.

———

A year later, thanks to the relevations of Yao Chia, an agent in the pay of Ch'in, he denounced the subversive activities of Mao Ch'iao, the minister attached to the household of the queen mother. Ordinance had conceived an implacable hatred for Mao Ch'iao on the day the man pleaded in the queen's favor, and he now had him summarily executed in public.

Upon the death of her last supporter, the queen mother went out of her mind. During the day she lay prostrate, staring into space, but at nightfall she would become strangely excited and put on powder, perfume, and her best finery, then address sighs and words of love to an imaginary listener. She was thought to be possessed by a fox. Ostensibly to remove her from this diabolical influence, the king sent her away to Yung. There, deserted by everyone, she caught a fever and in a few weeks was dead.

Li Ssu was promoted to the post of minister of the interior, with an exceptionally handsome salary of three thousand *shih* of grain.

CHAPTER VI

_____

DEATH OF A FRIEND

While Li Ssu was making a career for himself in Ch'in, Han Negation
vegetated in Han, a prey to the jealousy of the senior dignitaries there
and to persecution from rapacious civil servants. The king, who was
not very intelligent, obstinately refused to give his relative any appointment. The addresses, speeches, and petitions that poured feverishly from Han Negation's brush had no effect whatever upon his
pusillanimous kinsman.

Embittered, Han Negation withdrew from public life and spent
all his time writing vitriolic, incendiary pamphlets on the cowardice
of kings and the greed of ministers. He condemned the Confucian
scholars whose teachings undermined the foundations of the state,
the knights whose alleged exploits were an offense against the law,

and finally the king himself, blinded by base flatterers who were leading the country to ruin.

He dwelt at length on the problems of rhetoric and the snares of oratory. *The Rage of a Solitary*, *The Five Vermin*, *The Forest of Anecdotes*, *Impossibilities of Discourse*, *Accumulations I*, and *Accumulations II* made him famous without giving him a whit more influence on the king's decisions. His writings were copied and his ideas diffused throughout the Empire; his sayings were on everyone's lips. But his theories received no application at all in his own country.

When the king of Han learned through his spies that Ch'in was preparing a major offensive against him, he remembered that Han Negation had once been Li Ssu's fellow pupil and at last gave him a post. Then, as the situation grew critical, he summoned him to a secret interview.

A few days later, Han Negation left for Ch'in at the head of an embassy. He was received immediately by King Ordinance, who had longed to meet the philosopher since reading *The Rage of a Solitary* and *The Five Vermin* by the dusky light of his oil lamp.

Han Negation made a speech that pleased the king greatly, though Li Ssu, with some amusement, recognized it as a student exercise written when they were both in Ch'u. The subject of the dissertation was: "Shang I has a first interview with the king of Ch'in." Was his former comrade running out of ideas? Or had he merely been taken by surprise at being received so soon, and lacked the time to compose something more suitable?

The king, however, was dazzled. The limpid style, the balanced phrases, and the energetic tone all delighted him. The ideas that Han Negation expounded were novel to him, and he summoned the philosopher often, and listened to his advice. Han Negation's influence began to mount, and Li Ssu, who at first had been proud of his friend and basked in his reflected glory, began to feel the gnawings of jealousy.

Ch'in's threat against Han became increasingly evident. The king of Han sent one letter after another urging his envoy to persuade the insatiable Ordinance to direct his territorial ambitions elsewhere. Han Negation hesitated. He wanted to show himself worthy of his king's confidence and to win his friendship by some outstanding achievement, in the hope of seeing his theories applied to his own people. But his political sense told him that the country he served was doomed. Between Ch'in and Han, history had made its choice. To continue serving his prince was to go against the course of events and to betray himself. And yet to opt for Ch'in was to betray his blood. He spent long, sleepless nights. But after he had made his decision, fidelity to his own nation seemed a kind of cowardice, and he despised himself for it.

He had to declare himself sooner than he might have wished. A certain Yao Chia, who had worked for all the princes before finally selling himself to Ch'in, knew what part the king of Han wanted the philosopher to play.

To protect himself against Yao Chia, Han Negation spoke ill of him to the king. Ordinance, shaken by these allegations, sent for the man and accused him to his face.

"You have used my money to flaunt yourself among the princes!" he cried.

"Naturally!" replied the other coolly.

"And you still have the effrontery to stand there before me?"

"Prince," said the sly man, bowing, "I have been a model of fidelity. Had I not shown myself loyal to you, what prince would have agreed to employ me? Yet there isn't one who wouldn't welcome me with open arms if I was ever expelled from Ch'in."

"But aren't you a porter's son, convicted of theft, and a minister banished from the country you served?"

"Wasn't Duke Lü Wang, who founded the Chou dynasty, expelled from Ch'in by his wife? Wasn't he a bankrupt butcher whose rotten meat no one would buy, a runaway minister, a fisherman who never caught a fish, a laborer who could never get a job? But that didn't stop Ching Wen from taking him as his adviser and unifying the Empire. And wasn't Kuan Chung a small-town draper in Pi Jen, mocked by all the villagers and thrown into jail in Lu? But Duke Huan of Ch'in didn't mind that—he made him his minister and, thanks to him, won dominance over the Empire. And Pai Li-hsi was a beggar from Yü who sold himself for five sheepskins, but Duke Mu didn't hesitate to make him his minister. All these men either had a murky past or were of low extraction, but each of them contributed to the glory of the prince who appointed him to high office. An enlightened ruler doesn't listen to gossip—all he cares about is ability. I'm astonished that Han Negation should have said such things about me. No doubt he fears that I know too much about *him*!"

"What?"

"I suspect he plays a double game."

"Can you prove this?"

"Not yet, but I may be able to sooner than you think."

The king told Li Ssu. At first Li Ssu was incredulous, but after a moment he said: "We must go by the evidence: his theories ought to make him choose in favor of Ch'in. But I mustn't let myself be swayed by personal considerations. Han Negation was my friend, and perhaps I'm partial. Pretend to attack Han and watch how he reacts. Then we'll see."

Soon a rumor spread that an offensive against Han was imminent, and Han Negation wrote a letter to the king that Ordinance passed on to his adviser for an opinion. Li Ssu's answer was not slow in coming. He wrote:

I am bound to accept the cruel truth. The shades of my ancestors know how much it costs me. Han Negation is only here to win prestige in Han for defending its interests. Do not be misled by his eloquence. I know how clever he is at decking the most specious arguments in the disguise of truth. Do not be ensnared by his sophistries. Analyze the problem coolly and thoroughly.

If you deign to follow my advice, this is what you must do. Raise an army but do not name its objective. The government of Han, afraid that you will launch it against them, will have no alternative but to submit. Meanwhile, send me to the Han court to persuade their king to come to Ch'in. Then hold him hostage as you negotiate with Han. That way you'll obtain part of his territory and his own absolute obedience without striking a blow. This easy victory will disappoint the hopes of Chao and make Ch'u hesitate, and the princes will vie with one another in servility.

Pray study these suggestions carefully, prince, and beware of acting hastily.

So Li Ssu was sent as an ambassador to Han, where he asked to be received in audience by the king. The king refused. Li Ssu was kept under strict surveillance, and one of his agents let him know that there was talk of his being arrested and held hostage. A clever plot on the part of his former friend, he thought. Han Negation must have reasoned that his own king valued him less than the king of Ch'in valued Li Ssu. But that did not take Ordinance's obstinacy into account. At all events, Negation had shown his hand in luring him, Li Ssu, to Han. Li Ssu had been outwitted by the very person he tried to trick! A fine mess he'd got himself into! The thought that the head of his former fellow student would fall at the same time as his own was small comfort.

But Li Ssu himself was not blameless. It had been rash of him to assume that Ch'in's armies would intimidate the feudatory princes so easily. He had forgotten how stupid and unrealistic they were, and how much intriguing still went on at the Ch'in court. He realized now that others might be cleverer than he at that complicated game. He cursed conspiracy and faction. There was no watertight stratagem. The best-laid schemes could go wrong. He consoled himself with the thought that this was probably one of the last compromises with the old order before the law was established in all its purity. Calculation, guile, and trickery would be done away with then, but meanwhile he must extricate himself.

Deciding to brazen it out, he sent the king of Han a threatening letter designed to convey that he expected to obtain through intimidation the interview which he had not received from a weak and impressionable king through courtesy. Without waiting for a reply—he could guess only too well what it would be—he exchanged clothes with a servant of his whom he could trust and escaped, returning to Ch'in in the guise of a peddler.

This journey taught him much. Han was trying to deceive Ch'in, and Negation was party to the plot. It was probably he who had guessed Li Ssu's plan and warned the king of Han. Li Ssu seethed with rage. The hatred he felt was made up of jealousy, hurt feelings, fear, and calculation.

When, still dressed in rags and turning these thoughts over in his mind, Li Ssu crossed the frontier and passed the inn for foreign ambassadors, he suddenly came face to face with Han Negation, just back from the capital itself and about to put his chariot away. Negation let out a gasp on recognizing the minister of the interior, and, without asking any questions, invited him into his apartments. He sat him down in the place of honor and ordered drinks and sweetmeats. Li Ssu could not help recalling that it was in this very inn that Hsü Chia had entertained Fan Sui disguised as a porter.

But there the parallel ended. He and Han Negation had been friends, and his host knew very well what his rank was. But could one still talk of friendship with a man who had tried to lure him into a trap, perhaps even to kill him? As he ate the sticky millet gruel that served to remove the roughness from the palate, he studied his companion's face. Twenty years had gone by since they first met, and age had extinguished the flame that once shone from the man's eyes. The delicate, almost finical features now sagged, giving the face an expression of weariness and resignation. Its thickened lines, the rather weak chin, and small, full lips suggested an anxious and irresolute nature. Suddenly overcome by foolish nostalgia, Li Ssu slowly put down his bowl and said wistfully: "Do you remember what you said to me just before you left Hsün Tzu?"

His companion's glance hesitated a moment and seemed to seek something distant in space and time. He had forgotten. Then the minister of the interior realized that in the old days he had meant less to Negation than Negation had meant to him. This one-sidedness wounded him and revived his resentment.

"You said there had to be a Li Ssu to get the ideas of a Han Negation put into practice!"

A gleam came into his former comrade's eye. Now he remembered. Li Ssu was grateful, and at the same time angry with himself for being grateful.

"Yes, I remember—you had just said, 'Why, after creating a Li Ssu, did heaven have to go and produce a Han Negation!' But now I ought to say, 'If only Li Ssu had never crossed Han Negation's path!'"

"And *I* ought to say that Han Negation does all he can to *prevent* Li Ssu's ideas from being put into practice!"

"I don't see how I've stood in their way."

"By scheming to dispatch me to the Yellow Springs."

"Ah, so that's it. I knew we'd get around to that. What happened in Han to make you come back in that curious getup and with such a grudge against me?"

"I just barely escaped with my life! But you know all about that. It was cleverly done. The letter you sent to the king, pretending to give yourself away so as to lure me to Han!"

"I don't know what you're talking about. I did no such thing. It would have been stupid to try. All I've done is attempt to help Ch'in by pointing out that it would do better to turn its attention to Chao rather than persecute Han, which is already subdued. Otherwise Ordinance will alienate all the feudatory princes."

"Do you think you can make me believe that a man can serve two masters? If you work for Han, you can only be against Ch'in. For Ch'in, Han is like an angina—as long the patient stays quiet, he doesn't feel it, but the slightest exertion and he gets a heart attack."

"But Ch'in and Han are like lips and teeth—take away the lips and the teeth are cold."

"Empty phrases! Ch'in's true greatness requires the subjugation of all the princes."

"I can't see why the triumph of the law requires the destruction of Han. But I don't have to justify my behavior to someone who's only looking for an excuse to get rid of a friend he now considers a rival. As the popular proverb says, 'Say a dog is mad and drown him.'"

"And who else but you would profit from my death? Not that I blame you: all's fair in love and war."

"But I'm not working for—" cried Negation.

Then he stopped. A strange gleam came into his eye. He'd nearly fallen into the trap. Li Ssu wanted him to admit that he had been working—and would continue to work—for Han, and thus that he was in the pay of the enemy. He began again.

"Am I the only person in Ch'in who would like to see the last of you?" he almost hissed.

"Who else but you is in communication with Han?"

"Your naïveté amazes me."

Now it was Li Ssu's turn to blush.

"I was right when I said you'd always be ahead of me!" he said angrily, and left, dissatisfied with the interview. As he made his way to the palace, he thought over the various elements in the affair. It might well be that it was not Negation but Yao Chia who had advised the king of Han to give him a hostile reception. Yao Chia knew more about his intentions than Negation did. He was vexed with himself for not having thought of this before. Yao Chia was dangerous. But did that mean that Negation was to be trusted? He'd nearly admitted he was working for Han! He was either a potential rival or a double agent. He must be got rid of.

But in the remote little room where it was the king's habit to discuss his secret affairs, the minister, after reporting on his mission, gave a more equivocal account of his conclusions.

"Han Negation," he said, "whom I took to be my friend, is plotting against Ch'in. I know he does so for perfectly understandable reasons. He's of Han blood and is defending his family—what could be more natural? And I wouldn't be so petty as to hate him for having deceived me. But we have to act in terms of politics, and, however great our admiration for him as a person and for his writings, we must put the national interest first. It might well be more of a compliment to him to put his theories into practice and punish him as he deserves than to deny his principles and spare him.

"Han Negation cannot serve Ch'in, for no one can be loyal to two princes at once. Yet, if you send him back to Han, you will be preparing a rod for your own back—a mistake a wise prince tries to avoid. On the other hand, I cannot advise you to put him to death, first because it would seem like jealousy on my part, and second because to kill the person whose teachings have inspired one's whole system of politics is to put oneself in a very awkward position. If you did that, everyone would say you were ungrateful. For the moment I can see only one solution, and that is to put him in prison on some pretext or other while you consider your final decision."

Yao Chia, who was present at this interview, now intervened. "It seems to me," he said, "that Li Ssu is being unpardonably tolerant. A minister ought to put the welfare of the state before his own inclinations. Shang Yang had no qualms about betraying his best friend to buttress the reputation of his prince. Han Negation is a threat to the state and ought to be eliminated, and any minister, any subject whatsoever, who disagrees is not a truly devoted servant. Prince, do not be carried away by your sympathies, or allow flatterers to encourage your weaknesses!"

Li Ssu cast a venomous glance at Yao Chia, an unyouthful young man whose slimy elegance and affectation of moral severity produced in Li Ssu the same sort of disgust as a centipede. "Yao Chia, my friend," he said to himself, "your teeth have grown long of late, but even a jackal, though it borrows a wolf's fangs, won't last long against a tiger."

Bowing to the king, he said sarcastically to Yao Chia: "I can understand why you're in such a hurry to get rid of him. He knows too much about you, doesn't he?"

King Ordinance, feeling a sudden headache come on, asked both of them to withdraw.

He was suffering from one of the nausea attacks that accompanied the making of any unpleasant decision. He had been quite shattered by Li Ssu's and Yao Chia's revelations. That the man he admired so much, whom he practically revered, should have been plotting against him! But it wasn't exactly that. It was, rather, that he had been serving another master. Ordinance sighed. Could you expect people to be devoted to you when all they cared for was advancing their own interests and satisfying their own thirst for glory? Wasn't this the very foundation of Negation's teaching? But if so, wouldn't it have been better for him to betray Han for Ch'in? Yet he persisted in serving a half-witted princeling already written off by history. In theory Negation was a pragmatist who maintained that men were motivated by self-interest alone, but in practice he was an idealist, one of those staunch and disinterested individuals whom he denounced in his writings as the most dangerous trouble-makers.

Human beings were strange bundles of contradictions.

And the king himself—what line of conduct was he to adopt? Should he do as Yao Chia suggested? It was the most prudent course, but Yao Chia had spoken only out of envy. Ordinance was more inclined to follow Li Ssu's advice. He wouldn't be happy putting to death someone who had given him such pleasure, such pure joy. Oh, if only he could render Negation harmless, reduce him to the status of a slave—a slave whose task it would be to elevate his—Ordinance's—soul and widen his horizons with his writings. If he could merely cripple him, for example, so that the man was no longer any use for anything else; or keep him shut up in a cell with ink, brush, and writing tablets, on a meager diet but with no ill-treatment, so that his intellectual faculties wouldn't be impaired.

As the minister of the interior left the palace in Double Light, his thin, predatory lips wore an enigmatic smile. He was about to eliminate both his rivals by pitting them one against the other.

"Yao Chia, you little rat," he thought to himself, "I will pulverize you as if you were a praying mantis raising its feelers to stop a war chariot!"

A shadow briefly darkened his brow: the ghost of an old friendship, the smell of a bare little room whose walls had witnessed so many passionate debates. For a moment the bitter taste of treachery was in his mouth, but he quickly dismissed the thought. It was the other person who was guilty of betrayal. He felt sorry for himself, thinking how heavy was the burden of ambition.

Han Negation lay in a small dark cell. His letters remained unanswered. The magic of words no longer had any effect on the king of Ch'in. Han Negation was desperate. He couldn't face the humiliation of being chastised in public and dying mutilated after slow and horrible tortures. His overheated imagination made him feel his bones already crunching under the saw, his flesh shrinking from the scalpel that sought the most painful places in his nerves and muscles.

He heard the sound of footsteps in the passage, the clink of metal, the key turning in the lock. He trembled: they were coming to fetch him. But the guard let Li Ssu into the cell—a friendly Li Ssu, his eyes brimming with compassion.

Li Ssu bowed to the ambassador from Han, clasped him to his bosom, and could not restrain his tears.

"Do you remember the conversations we used to have, Han Negation," he said, "in the little house in Han Tan, after we'd attended the master's lectures? Who could have foreseen then that fate would bring us face to face like this, in a cell, you a prisoner and I your judge! But no. I don't want to be your tormentor, Han Negation.

I am here without the king's knowledge, to do everything in my power to make things easier for you."

"Won't the king take notice of my petitions?"

"Petitions?" exclaimed Li Ssu.

"I sent two appeals to the king. He didn't mention them to you?"

"He never received them. They must have been intercepted by Yao Chia. Yao Chia has acquired a great influence over the king and has his own spies in the palace. He hates you like poison: you know too much about him."

"I exposed him!"

"That confirms my suspicions. My poor fellow, I'm afraid it's all over for you. They say you're going to be put to death. I'll try once more to see what I can do with the king. But he's so obstinate, he hardly ever changes his mind."

He wiped a tear away with his sleeve as his friend wrung his hands and begged the favor of being allowed to kill himself.

"That's why I'm here," said Li Ssu, and took from his belt a little bag of embroidered silk containing a small flask carved out of agate.

"Take this," he murmured. "But do not be rash. Remember, nothing can bring the dead back to life."

And he practically fled, his shoulders shaking with sobs.

Two days later, Li Ssu wrote the king a moving letter interceding for his friend Han Negation and accusing Yao Chia of trying to get rid of a compromising witness.

The king, worried, ordered the prisoner to be brought before him. But when the messenger arrived, Han Negation's body was already cold. The news of his favorite author's death upset the king and made him feel guilty. Li Ssu denounced Yao Chia's intrigues and proved that he had intercepted two letters sent by the prisoner. The king's guilt turned to anger and vented itself on Yao Chia, who was thrown into prison, where he committed suicide rather than face an ignominious death.

CHAPTER VII

AN ANACHRONISM

Li Ssu could see law and order growing stronger every day, and Ch'in's borders extending farther and farther. The nobles no longer dared oppose him; they bowed before him like mere provincial governors. In Ch'in itself, the ferocity of the punishments handed out ensured a unanimity unbroken by any murmur of resistance. Stocks that had been built up through the labors of the peasants were squandered in an instant on wars of conquest, leaving no surpluses to fatten any parasite. Thus orators, scholars, and sophists no longer scoured the land, and the inhabitants of sleepy country towns could now go on living their peaceful, stultifying lives without having their brains troubled by cranks or charlatans. Nature itself yielded to the rule of law. No vapors, comets, or star showers disturbed the regular procession of the heavenly bodies; day followed night undisturbed, and the seasons of the year pursued the even tenor of their cycle.

It was in the midst of this happy period, when Li Ssu thought he had mastered the course of events, that a wretched adventurer named Ching K'o cropped up to remind him that history does not easily allow itself to be put into the straitjacket of absolute predictability. The fortress of pure necessity had only to be invaded by one anachronism and the whole edifice immediately crumbled into confusion, chaos, and potential annihilation.

––––

Master Ching loved books and was an expert fencer, but he had tried in vain to talk to Prince Yüan of Wei about the importance of his art. So he went from town to town with his sword at his side and his books on his back, and was received by princes and welcomed by nobles who prided themselves on entertaining such adventurers. The days of the great patrons were over. The prince of Meng Ch'ang was dead, and so were the prince of P'ing Yüan and the duke of Wei, Bulwark of the Faith. Ching K'o stayed for a while at the court of a country squire, then set off at random, righting wrongs, avenging injuries, punishing local tyrants, robbing the rich to give to the poor. He helped village folk by putting down brigands and won a reputation for generosity and disinterestedness. It was said that he always kept his word, finished what he started, saved lives, and restored family happiness, and that everywhere he went the good rejoiced and the wicked trembled.

Sitting erect in his shabby chariot, the tall cap of a scholar perched on his topknot, he went to and fro across the Empire. At Yü Tz'u in the province of Ping, he had an argument about swordsmanship with another swashbuckler, named Ko Nieh, with whose theories he refused to agree. Ko Nieh went pale with rage and glared fiercely, whereupon Ching K'o got up and left.

To the host of the palace where both of them were staying Ko Nieh boasted: "He contradicted me, I gave him a black look, and he took fright. You may be sure he's still running! Ha ha! He didn't dare stay! No one contradicts me about the martial arts!"

The host sent for Ching K'o. But Ching K'o had already harnessed his horses and left town. When the servant returned with this news, Ko Nieh gave a guffaw and said: "What did I tell you? Naturally he's run away. How could he have stayed after the look I gave him? I terrorized him!"

Ching K'o went to Han Tan, where he was received by Prince Spring Quiet, whose house was open to both sophists and bravos. But the retainers of this marquis were not as wise or as virtuous as their predecessors, and the style of the young patron was not to be compared with the splendor of the prince of P'ing Yüan in Han Tan's heyday.

One day when they were all drinking and playing *liu po* and tempers were heated with gambling and alcohol, Ching K'o got into an argument with Lu Kou-chien about how the game should be played. Lu Kou-chien, with bloodshot eyes, his hand on the hilt of his sword and his mustache bristling, maintained that five pawns were not equal to one owl. Ching K'o replied calmly that this sort of argument was pointless, because an owl was nothing without the pawns. The pawns gave the owl its strength, and, on the other hand, all you had to do to win was take out the owl with a pawn.

Lu Kou-chien, mad with rage, let fly a volley of insults and blew in Ching K'o's face. Ching K'o bowed his head in silence, then rose and went out of the room. After that he did all he could to avoid Lu Kou-chien.

The other bravos began to whisper that Ching K'o was a coward and frightened of Ko Nieh and Lu Kou-chien. The princes and nobles treated him with less consideration.

Chao was being ravaged by war. In the space of a few years, the Ch'in generals Huan Ch'i and Meng Ao had seized Yü Yü, P'ing Yang, and I An. And after the murder of his envoy Han Negation, the king of Han had acknowledged himself Ch'in's vassal. Yet the princes went on with their ceaseless struggles, Chao against Yen, Wei and Ch'in allied against Ch'u. Money for entertaining and maintaining knights was scarce, and Master Ching, led by destiny to seek new pastures in the North, fetched up one day in the kingdom of Yen. There he settled in the capital, Ching Ch'eng.

He spent his time wandering through the lanes and exploring the outskirts of the town, strolling around the market places, visiting country squires, and making a name for himself amongst eccentrics and unknown sages—all those who prided themselves on their uselessness or their poverty. He met men who lived for their art, humble as that art might be. And his tall, angular form, a rapier at its side, became a popular sight in the streets of the capital.

He made friends with a dog butcher, formerly a high official, who had fled from Ch'in, and with a talented musician named Kao Chien-li.

When Master K'o met Shuo the dog butcher for the first time in the market, Shuo was drunk. His cap was crooked and his leather apron, spattered with blood, gave off a horrible smell. His thin legs were encased in ragged trousers, with strips of cloth of an indefinable color wrapped around them to the knees. But our wandering philosopher could see he was a good man by the way he cut up the meat. His knife moved easily and in harmony with the music of the dynasties, the rhythm of the cosmos. Ching K'o felt as if he were witnessing a religious ceremony. Shuo's hands took hold of the animal skillfully; the knife seemed to beat time as it went to and fro, light and smooth, like the flapping of wings or the gestures of a dancer. Shuo's whole body was full of grace, without a flaw, in tune with the heavenly notes of the Dance of the Mulberry Bushes—a unique and silent mime perceived only by him, Ching K'o. He felt as purified watching this fellow slice and split, twist and cut, as when he himself poured libations to the ancestors or attended a funeral ceremony.

He waited reverently for Shuo to finish, then bowed three times and asked to be his friend. The other burst into raucous guffaws, followed by obscene gestures and a stream of insults. "A plague on the lousy philosophers who want to change the world and think life has a meaning! What's the good of all that rubbish? What's the good of all your bowing and scraping? I'm dry—I'd rather have a jug of wine than any of your compliments."

The knight errant stood his ground.

"How do you manage to divide a carcass like that?" he asked. "It looks as if your knife had no substance, as if the blade were shearing through nothing."

"It's because I love the Tao," the butcher replied. "I wasn't always like this. At first all I saw was the animal. Then, after three years' meditation, I forgot the form I had to cut up. And now it's my spiritual intuition that guides my hand, not my eyes. I know the form of the beast so well that I can concentrate just on the interstices. I never touch the veins or the arteries, the muscles or the tendons— not to mention the bones! A good butcher wears down one knife a year because he cuts only the flesh, whereas a bad one, always chipping the blade on the bones, needs a new knife every month. I've been using the knife you see here for nineteen years—it's cut up thousands of animals—and the edge is as keen as if just whetted.

"The joints have empty spaces in them, and the blade is very thin. If you can manage to introduce it into the spaces, the knife virtually wields itself, because it moves through the void. Every time I have to dissect a joint, I examine it closely, hold my breath, concentrate, then insert the blade carefully—and the bones separate easily."

"Tell me, Master Butcher, isn't that a quotation from Master Chuang?"

"I see you're a scholar," sneered the other. "This calls for a drink. Come, I'll let you buy me one in the tavern."

It was in the tavern that they met Kao Chien-li the lute player, half drunk and playing a tune to himself. It was a moving, wistful air, expressing proud detachment, scorn for honors, and condemnation of an age in which the base and the grasping triumphed.

The three became boon companions. All of them loved wine, and they would go from tavern to tavern downing cups of millet or yellow wine and millet beer and talking about the meaning of the arts they practiced.

Kao Chien-li maintained that sounds in themselves meant nothing, containing neither joy nor sorrow. But the harmonies of the musical scale could touch the chords of human feeling just as skillful fingers plucked the strings of a lute, stirring the fibers of the heart and making them vibrate with the joy, anger or despair within us. Music was never understood unless the souls of player and listener were in mysterious accord. So it was wrong to call some music depraved, or some tunes lascivious, or certain songs chaste and pure, for lust, virtue, regret, and gaiety were subjective impressions, not objective qualities. They derived from ephemeral impulses within the souls of player and listener, not from any physical phenomenon.

Ching K'o thought music was cheerful or sad in itself, and that tunes reflected the state of society. Shuo, between drinks, would mumble that perfect music expressed itself not in sounds but in colors, and that the greatest lute players didn't need strings on their instruments to move men's hearts because they drew their melodies from the music of the spheres.

They spent night after night like this, talking about anything and everything, sometimes cheerful, often sad. As it grew late, the butcher would begin to praise uselessness and declaim passages from Master Chuang: "As Nan-p'o Tzu-ch'i went over a wooded hill, he saw a huge tree. A thousand four-horse chariots could have been sheltered in the shade of its branches. 'What sort of a tree is this?' exclaimed Nan-p'o Tzu-ch'i, 'and what is it good for? If you look at it from below, you can see that its branches cannot be made into beams because they are too crooked. If you look at it from above, you can see that its great trunk, all knotty and cracked, is fit only for coffins. If you lick its leaves, you get ulcers and abscesses in your mouth. If you smell it, you go mad.' And he concluded: 'It is of no use at all; that is why it has grown so large.' A philosopher is like this tree."

And the butcher would go on in comical tones, like a master

addressing his students: "The ancient exorcists say that a white-faced ox, a pig with a turned-up snout, and a man with piles are all unfit to be thrown as offerings into the Yellow River. The sacrificers say they are bad luck. But to a holy man they symbolize the greatest happiness. . . .

"Mountain trees that are tall and straight attract the ax. Combustible fat is burned, the cinnamon tree is stripped of its bark, the lacquer tree is cut. Everyone knows the usefulness of the useful, but no one knows the usefulness of the useless."

And he would proceed to tell the story of the man whose chin reached down to his navel, shoulders rose higher than his skull, buttocks were level with his ribs, and innards bulged out of his chest. He escaped all conscription, forced labor, and war, received help and assistance from the state, and lived out his natural term of life.

"So," Shuo would conclude with a hiccup, "if a man with a physical deformity can get enough to eat and die of old age, it should be even easier for anyone who can assume the monstrous appearance of perfect virtue!"

The other two would sigh with relief: at least they'd been spared the anecdote about T'o the Hideous! But they weren't to be let off so lightly: they still had to listen to Shuo's prophecies.

"One day Hui Tzu said to Chuang Tzu: 'The king of Wei left me the seeds of a huge variety of gourd. I planted them, and the plant bore a fruit with a rind that had a capacity of more than fifty bushels. But it couldn't be used to hold water because the rind wasn't strong enough, and it couldn't be cut up to make bowls because the rind was too flat. So, not knowing what to do with it, I chopped it to bits!'

"Chuang Tzu replied, 'How unimaginative! Why did it have to be used to hold things? You should have had it made into a ship to sail the seas.'

"My friends, you are two enormous squashes waiting for someone to find a use for you. But remember, once someone does use you, I'm afraid *you* may be made to sail to the Yellow Springs! Ah, Ching K'o, Ching K'o—you're dying to find a use for yourself! Why can't you just enjoy being useless?"

Late at night they would emerge from the last tavern and stagger through the deserted streets, singing and dancing in the public squares. Kao Chien-li played the lute and Ching K'o sang an accompaniment. Moonlight struck tawny reflections from the varnished tiles of the palace roofs against the deep crystal of the northern sky. And beneath the starry firmament the two musicians would summon up sad songs of knights betrayed, ministers cast off, and wives abandoned. Life seemed bitter, their own existence empty. They clung together sobbing, while the third member of the party tried to catch his own shadow by the calm light of the moon. Then they would burst out laughing, strike up some gay or martial music, and end by rolling around in the gutter, dead drunk.

Thus the days and nights passed beneath the ever-clear sky of the capital of Yen with its pink surrounding hills. Master Ching made other acquaintances among the patricians of Ching Ch'en, who knew of his reputation as a righter of wrongs and admired him for his virtue. He became a friend of Master T'ien Kuang, famous among the princes for his wiliness and daring.

In the fifth year of the reign of King Ordinance of Ch'in, Cinnabar, the crown prince of Yen, whom his father had sent to Ch'in as a hostage, escaped and returned to the capital. Previously, throughout his childhood, he had been a prisoner in Chao, where he and Ordinance had played together in the women's quarters of the palace of the prince of P'ing Yüan. Cinnabar imagined that something of this early friendship would still survive.

But by the time he arrived at the Ch'in court, his former companion had become ruler of the most powerful kingdom in the land, and instead of the warm welcome he had hoped for, Cinnabar met with nothing but rebuffs, insults, and disdain.

Ordinance took every opportunity of humiliating and belittling him, and the hostage, as the son of a ruler who was weak and without influence, could only choke back his tears and brood over his resentment. The last straw came when, during one of the great banquets lasting ten days and nights and known as "carousals of the long night," Ordinance, slightly tipsy, flung his arms around him and said earnestly, "Brother, don't think I have forgotten our former friendship. I remember very well how we used to play together in Han Tan. True, you were proud then, and I was only a poor refugee. But I haven't discarded the past. I've decided to give you a partner, a marvelous partner. No, don't object—I'm sure she'll be just right for you. I know the tastes of your people, and I don't think their ruler can be different, for it is kings who determine customs."

At a sign from him, the orchestra broke into a martial air and, to the rattle of tambourines, in bounded a huge white goat, bleating loudly. It was decked in red ribbons; from its lacquered horns hung pendants set with jade and pearls; its hoofs were painted; on its head it wore a long plume of peacock and kingfisher feathers interwoven with gold.

"There she is!" yelled the king, roaring with laughter. "I've never seen a better-matched couple! Don't your people live and copulate with goats as their favorite wives?"

Cinnabar started up, reaching instinctively for his sword, but it wasn't there: no one was allowed to come into the banqueting or audience chambers armed. He moved to strike the man who had insulted him, but the guards intervened. So he rose and left, amid the laughter of the dancing girls, the servile smiles of the courtiers, and the disapproving looks of ministers, offended by the vulgarity of the proceedings.

Reprimanded by the more virtuous of his advisers, who thought such behavior unworthy of a great king, Ordinance made a few vague excuses to the mortified hostage, blaming his pleasantry on drink. But he refused to make a public apology. Cinnabar asked to be allowed to leave the court, for after such an insult it was impossible for him to remain in the same city as the king, but Ordinance only guffawed and said, "I'll let you go when hens are cocks and crows are white!" And then he dismissed him.

The prince of Yen, transported with rage, resolved to brave the king's anger. He outwitted the guards, arranged for the city gates to be opened two hours early, and, crowing like a cock, escaped his pursuers and returned home.

There he wandered about the east wing of the palace, meditating revenge. Food had lost its savor; music had no power to distract him. Ch'in had unleashed its armies against Ch'i, Ch'u, Chao, and Wei, and they were gobbling up the princes as a silkworm gobbles mulberry leaves. Soon the headsmen from the West would be at his own frontiers. They would make short work of his meager forces. Han Tan, the capital of Chao, had fallen to General Wang; the king of Chao had been taken prisoner, and his son, who managed to escape, established the kingdom of Tai in the northern part of his territories. And now the Ch'in armies were sweeping northward like a pack of wolves.

Cinnabar turned over all kinds of ruses in his mind and worked out all sorts of plans, but all that emerged from his mental contortions was a sense of his own helplessness. He confided in his tutor, Chü Wu, who found himself hard put for an answer.

"Ch'in now includes more than half the Empire," he said. "Its power intimidates Wei and makes Chao tremble. In the North it's protected by the strong natural defenses of the Sweet Springs and the Mouth of the Valley. In the South it controls the fertile plains of the King and Wei rivers. It has captured the natural wealth of Shu and Pa. It is bordered on the right by the great ranges of Lung and Shu, while to the left there are impassable mountains. Its population is large, its soldiers well trained, its arsenals full of carefully sharpened weapons, armor, and helmets tough as bronze. If Ch'in should take it into its head to send troops to the south of your walls and north of Wei, I don't see what you could do. And because of an insult, you would rub the dragon the wrong way and arouse its terrible wrath!"

Some time after this, the Ch'in general, Fan the Opportune, incurred the enmity of the king and fled to seek asylum in Yen. Cinnabar welcomed him, giving him a wing in his palace to live in.

Then Chü Wu asked for an audience and remonstrated with the heir presumptive.

"Prince," he said, "you cannot keep this fugitive under your roof! Doesn't your blood run cold when you think how you are stoking up against yourself the hatred of the most powerful monarch in the world? Wasn't it enough to defy him by fleeing his court? Must you take in one of his enemies as well?"

"Should I have stayed and let myself be insulted?"

"Couldn't you have won your way back into his favor?"

"Can one cajole a wild beast? If he had granted me his friendship, it would only have been to devour me the more easily. No, the only way I could have satisfied him was by letting myself be flayed so that he could wrap himself in my skin. The sole reason for his hatred is that I knew him when he was poor. Hasn't he threatened that when he conquers Chao he'll bury alive there every witness to his exile in Han Tan? You confuse prudence and cowardice. What's the point of living if saving your head means to lose your honor?"

"Very well. But, leaving aside the fact that you drew down Ch'in's wrath by escaping, don't tell me you don't take a perverse pleasure in tweaking the tiger's whiskers by sheltering his enemy! But this is like sitting on a hunk of raw meat in front of a ravening wolf! Even though you have ministers as wise as Kuan Tzu and Yen Tzu, you have no alternative but to submit. Banish the general to the land of the Huns as soon as possible, to avoid giving Ch'in an excuse to attack you!"

"Your policy is for me to be a doormat to my enemy."

"Listen before you take offense. What I am suggesting is a long-term policy."

" 'Long-term'! My rage will consume me!"

"Be sensible and hear me out! Make an alliance vertically with Wei, and reconstruct the horizontal axis with Ch'i and Ch'u. Then you'll be able to put an end to Ch'in's supremacy. Han and Wei are subject to the tyrant of the West only in appearance: in their hearts they loathe him and are restrained only by fear. If war breaks out again and sets all the princes against the Kingdom of the West, Ch'u has only to come to the help of the alliance, and circumstances will turn in our favor. Then—and then alone—can you avenge yourself. Adopt what I still venture to call this long-term scheme, and you will not only receive satisfaction for your wrong but also leave a name to posterity. Fu Ch'ai, who raised his country out of its own ashes, waited twenty years to avenge the insult inflicted on him by Wu. Meanwhile, in his own territory he radiated virtue, winning the respect of the nobles and the love of the people. Rule benevolently and your sufferings will find their recompense."

"That takes time—too much time!" answered Cinnabar irritably. "By then we might be corpses. But it's not so much that that bothers me as the compassion I owe my guest. What, I should drive him out of his place of safety and hand him over to the brutal Huns? No, I'd sooner kill myself!"

Chü Wu bowed stiffly.

"So you are prepared to sacrifice your family altars to your personal animosities. Alas, what can I do for you in that case? You'll soon be like the down of a duck in the flame of a furnace."

He paused for a moment, then added, as if it hurt him to speak: "There's a certain Master T'ien Kuang in Yen who is said to be intelligent, upright, and brave. Perhaps he could advise you on the sort of thing you're contemplating."

"Would you be so kind as to introduce me to him?" said the prince, bowing.

Chü Wu went to Master T'ien Kuang's house and, after the traditional salutations, whispered in his ear: "The crown prince would like to talk to you. It's an affair of state. Would you agree to accept his invitation?"

"I am at his disposal," was the reply.

———

A tall, thin old man with a hooked nose presented himself at the gates of the crown prince's palace. He wore a simple robe lined with gray fox fur.

Cinnabar took him to his own apartments and, after making him many low obeisances, swept the dust off a mat and begged him to be seated. When he was sure the old man was comfortable, he sat down, too. Then, looking furtively around to make certain that they were not overheard, he rose and prostrated himself yet again before his guest.

"Master!" he cried. "Yen and Ch'in cannot both live under the same sky! Help me!"

T'ien Kuang settled his robe and said in a faint voice: "A mettlesome steed of the steppes can cover a thousand leagues in a day, but when age has made his legs heavy he can be overtaken by plow horses. The years have used up my vitality. My arm no longer has the strength to hold a sword, and my hoary head is worthless, incapable of inventing the brilliant stratagems for which I was famous in my youth."

"Nevertheless, master, tell me what to do!" The prince suddenly burst into tears and clutched imploringly at the visitor's gown. "When I was a hostage there," he explained, "the king of Ch'in humiliated me horribly. As a result, I cannot sleep and am obsessed always by the same thoughts. If anyone could tell me how I might take my enemy's life, even at the cost of my own, my heart would burn with joy again, like embers rekindled or a skeleton raised from the dead."

T'ien Kuang bowed his head.

"A difficult matter," he said. "It could involve the destruction of a whole country. Permit your humble servant to reflect."

They adjourned into a lofty chamber where a banquet had been set out. The prince served his guest with the utmost reverence, refusing to eat until the other had finished.

Then T'ien Kuang half-closed his eyes and murmured: "I know the people you have around you. None of them is suitable for what you have in mind. But, if I may make a suggestion, I have a friend called Master King. He's the man you need."

"Will you arrange for me to meet him?"

T'ien Kuang nodded, rose slowly to his feet, and took his leave. The young prince conducted him down the steps, and there, before they parted, he couldn't help saying, "This is a matter of the utmost importance. Please don't speak of it to anyone."

T'ien Kuang gave his solemn promise.

Then he went straight to Ching K'o and said: "Everyone in Yen knows we are great friends. The crown prince, having heard of my achievements in the past, has sent for me to help him in a matter in which his dignity is involved, together with the survival of his kingdom. I am old and of no use to him, and that is why I took the liberty of suggesting you. Could you oblige me by going to see him?"

Ching K'o bowed.

"Master, I am at your service," he said.

Then T'ien Kuang took his arm and confided sadly: "I was taught that the loyalty of honorable men was never called in question. But just now the prince saw fit to ask me to hold my tongue. That means he does not trust me. And when a man of integrity no longer inspires confidence, it is time for him to die."

He drew his sword. Before proceeding, he asked his companion to go and tell the crown prince that T'ien Kuang had taken his own life and would be sure to speak no more. Then, without further ado, he slit his throat.

The knight errant bowed to Cinnabar in the lofty audience chamber with its painted beams, then took a head from the box he carried under his arm and held it out in both hands to the young man.

"T'ien Kuang cut his throat in my presence," he said. "Do not worry—he revealed nothing."

The crown prince took the head reverently in both hands, put it down with care, and bowed before it, touching his forehead to the ground. Then he dragged himself on his knees to where Ching K'o stood, and burst into tears.

"May I be accursed," he lamented. "May the wandering spirits of T'ien Kuang bring misfortune down upon my head! I let my tongue run away with me, but I call heaven and earth to witness that I never meant him to take his life! I only wanted to impress on him that he'd been entrusted with important secrets that had to be kept dark if my plans were to succeed."

Ching K'o said nothing. When the prince offered him a mat, he sat down. Cinnabar rose from his own mat to come and bow before the sage.

"Master T'ien Kuang did me the honor of accepting my invitation," he said, "in spite of my unworthiness. I told him of my troubles. Isn't that a proof that heaven pities the orphan of Yen and hasn't abandoned him in his distress?

"Until that bloodthirsty monster Ch'in swallows all the riches of the world, it will be like a hungry wolf. It wants to subject all the princes to its rule. It has already thrown the king of Han into prison and wiped his country off the map. It is raising vast new armies to invade Ch'u, and in the North it watches Chao like a cat watching a mouse, ready to pounce. Wang Ch'ien, at the head of three hundred thousand men, is at the gates of Shang and Te. Li Hsin has advanced to T'ai Yüan and Yün Chung. Chao is already exhausted and can't hold out much longer. Once Chao is annexed, woe betide Yen. My princedom is small and weak and ravaged by constant war. Even if I mobilized the whole male population, I couldn't stand up to Ch'in's terrific strength. All the other princes have given way, and no one dares enter into a defensive alliance.

"Faced with this danger, my poor head has come up with the

stupid idea of winning the friendship of some very valiant knight and sending him to Ch'in laden with gifts. The king of Ch'in, tempted by these treasures, will grant him an audience. And so I shall achieve my object, with either the capture of the tyrant or his death. All the princes, freed from his yoke, will rebel and attack his provinces. And I shall almost die of joy.

"If my envoy cannot capture the king of Ch'in alive, he'll stab him in the chest. The Ch'in generals will take advantage of the resulting power vacuum to carve out fiefs for themselves and form independent kingdoms. The court, bereft of its leader, will disintegrate. Ministers and princes will tear one another apart like hyenas fighting over a dead tiger. Then the princes will exploit the void left by the tyrant's death, revive the league, and annihilate Ch'in completely!

"This, then, is my fondest wish—the plan I have been meditating in my heart for years. But, alas, I do not know into whose hands to put my fate. All I ask of you now is to give the utmost consideration to the idea."

Ching K'o remained silent for a long while. Then he said, "Yes, it is an important matter. The fate of the world depends upon it. I don't know if I am up to such a task."

Cinnabar went over to him on his knees, banged his forehead on the ground, and begged him to think his offer over and not reject it out of hand. The other finally agreed to his request.

Ching K'o was made an acting minister and lived with the prince in the east wing of the palace. Cinnabar visited him every day and arranged banquets in his honor, at which he was presented with three huge cauldrons containing an ox, a sheep, and a pig. Cinnabar lavished gifts, attentions, and care upon his guest, sending him silks and lacquers and ancient jades looted by Yen troops from the palace in Ch'i. He gave him a chariot that was covered in leopard skin and had wheels of sandalwood, drawn by horses from Ferghana. Ching K'o was entertained by singers and dancers from the royal ballet troop, damsels dressed in fine silks and wearing headdresses of feathers and pearls.

The prince himself did not care for the girls, with their teeth of jade and slanting brows like moths' antennae, cooing and twittering in the private apartments. He preferred the deep voices and masculine smells of men. At the great feasts that the crown prince gave in honor of his friend, men and women were enjoyed and interchanged freely, but to the soft perfumed flesh of concubines Cinnabar preferred the muscular body of a knight. He shared both his women and his pleasures with Ching K'o, and they slept on the same couch.

Day by day, Ching K'o exercised a greater influence over the fainthearted prince and, like a cruel and tyrannical wife, developed increasingly extravagant demands as the other grew more and more yielding. Cinnabar agreed to everything without a murmur, as if this were the most natural thing in the world. He hastened to satisfy his imperious guest's most trivial wish, treating it as a kind of test. The service he himself was asking deserved every possible return.

One day the two of them were in a pavilion by the lake that surrounded the palace, watching the huge gray turtles at play in the greenish mirror of the water. The knight expressed the desire to beat the creatures with gold ingots and put them into a panic, so that he could contemplate the mixture of white foam and red blood while the rich gold glinted beneath the rippling bronze surface. Wouldn't that make a delightful picture? And he wanted to see those great animals, still as primeval rocks, roused from their slumber and plunged into destruction and nothingness.

The prince had chests of ingots brought up from his coffers, and the knight, exultant, as if intoxicated, began hurling the bars of gold with all his might. The turtles' shells could be heard cracking; streaks of crimson sullied the limpid water. Thin, scaly heads writhed on wrinkled necks. In their vain efforts to escape, those perfect symbols of the universe swam here and there and tried to submerge. But their carapaces, at last, floated upside down: the dome of the sky and the square of the earth unnaturally reversed in death. Several chests of ingots had been swallowed up in the lake when Ching K'o, panting and sweating, suddenly stopped.

"Don't think I'm worried about your gold, prince," he guffawed. "It's just that my arm is tired!"

His whims now knew no bounds.

In his stud farm the prince had a horse from the northwestern steppes, a gift to his father from the khans. It was a splendid beast, with solid hindquarters, strong legs, and a fine, thin muzzle. It had hollow cheeks and deepset eyes, and its ears stood up like bamboo shoots in the spring. After a gallop, its sweat looked red against its ash-blond coat. The prince made a present of it to his friend.

The two often rode side by side across a wide plain that smelled of the steppes and was surrounded by violet hills against a deep-blue sky. The lacquered hoofs of their mounts scarcely touched the ground as they flew over the turf and past the white and gray trunks of the trees and their dark-green plumes overhead. The riders flushed out all kinds of quarry, hunted gazelles and long-haired wild asses, hurtled up hill and down dale, skirting marshes that bristled with coarse rushes, marshes dotted with bright-gold flags and stirred by the supple branches of willows.

Then they were on firm ground once more, the earth sounding like a drum under the horses' hoofs, and they would gallop madly, as if to overtake the chariot of the sun.

Once they dismounted near a little cottage, their cheeks flushed from the keen air, and rested in the grass. While their horses grazed the bright-green turf, they drank from a spring that gushed from a shiny black rock.

Still short of breath, Ching K'o took advantage of the halt to say to the prince, "I've been told the liver of a thoroughbred is the most exquisite dish in the world."

He instantly leaped into the saddle and galloped back to Ching Ch'eng.

That same evening, at dinner with his host, he was served a soup made from the liver of the horse in question.

But that was not the worst. Cinnabar's gynaeceum included a female lutist given him by the prince of Chao. She was pretty, with a fair complexion, sloping shoulders, and a figure as graceful as a willow tree. Her teeth gleamed like Yüan pearls, and her long-lobed ears were hung with jewels bright as dew. The perfect arch of her brows and her crimson lips were vivid against her white makeup. When she played the lute, her fingers, light as milkweed, seemed to have a life of their own.

One day, after gazing at her for a long time, Ching K'o, the knight errant said, "What beautiful hands!"

"If you want her, she is yours," the infatuated prince hastened to assure him.

"No," came the reply. "All I want is her hands."

Next morning, a young page brought him a pepper-plant box inlaid with jade and fastened with a copper clasp. Ching K'o opened it. On a pale-green silk lining lay two slender white hands with pearly nails and wrists encircled by a thin ring of blood, which brought out their dazzling brightness. Ching K'o smiled and closed the box.

Time flew like an arrow. Ch'in's armies conquered cities, overthrew the forces of the princes, beleaguered their fortresses, massacred their troops. The prince of Yen grew gloomy and wandered from room to room silently, with furrowed brow. Ching K'o often thought that he looked at him with bitter reproach.

But the knight still wallowed in pleasure. Sometimes, when he was alone, he would go and lie on the roof of the tallest tower in the palace and hum wistful songs about knighthood and valor as he gazed up at the stars.

One day he appeared before the king, dressed once more in the ordinary clothes of a knight errant, bowed, and said: "Your hatred must be deep indeed, and your trust infinite, to have put up with all my caprices," he said. "I will try your patience no longer. Give your orders. I am ready."

"When do you mean to set out?"

"Not just yet. I have not yet reached inner perfection. As you must know, the key to success lies within oneself. The Yellow Emperor told us to quiet our lymph, calm our blood, and curb our anger. When I have emptied my heart; when I have reached the degree of elevation from which death seems like a return, and life and death but two aspects of one thing; when the endless cycle of universal transformations no longer frightens me—then I shall set out. The armies of Ch'in are still distant. Armies fight best with their backs to the river. Wait a bit longer."

The days went by, and the water clock measured out its crystal notes. Ching K'o wallowed in debauchery night and day in a sort of frenzy for living, frequenting the lowest kinds of taverns and carousing with his two friends until all three rolled dead drunk in the mud. But this life was beginning to taste of dust and ashes; he was wearying of dissipation. He spent hours doing nothing but staring at the sky, clear as a diamond in those latitudes, and at the complex and fateful motions of the stars.

One night, in the midst of their revels, the butcher said with a grimace: "I told you two that you were a couple of squashes waiting to find a use. You think you've found one, Ching K'o? But you'll see, your use will turn out to be no different from your uselessness! We do not belong to the age we live in. We should lie low. We are parasites. Don't you see, Ching K'o—and you, too, Kao Chien-li—that history has left you far behind?"

Ching K'o was disturbed by Shuo's words. He knew he was embarking on a desperate venture, but he seemed to have been specially selected by fate for such enterprises. What did it matter whether he succeeded or failed? His name would go down to posterity; he would leave his mark on history.

The Ch'in armies were now on Yen's southern border. Chao was vacillating, its kings cutting one another's throats at court.

Every day Cinnabar grew more worried and morose. He was tormented by doubt. Had he been duped? He heard how Ching K'o had knuckled under shamefully to Lu Kou-chien and Ko Nieh. Suppose he wasn't a real knight? But Cinnabar said nothing for fear of offending him. He had already been responsible for one man's death.

Finally he could bear it no longer, and sent for Master Ching. "The Ch'in army is on our southern frontier," he said, "and will cross the river Ying any day. Even if I wanted to, I couldn't keep you here any longer."

Ching K'o answered as if he could read the other's mind. "My behavior, I know, has aroused suspicion," he said. "People told you that I was afraid of those two wretches. I did not expect to have to justify myself, but I do not want your confidence in me to be undermined. If I declined to avenge the insults of a couple of braggarts and bullies, it was because I did not want to risk death for nothing. It would have been doing those scoundrels too much honor to endanger, in some low brawl, a life destined for higher and nobler things. I knew that I had been marked out by fate. I was biding my time. It has now come. But everything still depends on you. And I fear that, although you suspect me of holding back, it is really *you* who are not ready. If we do not give the king of Ch'in sufficient inducements, do you think that he will let me near him? As you know, he has offered ten thousand pieces of gold and an estate of ten thousand families in exchange for General Fan's head. Give me the general's head and a map of the prefecture of Tu K'ang, one of the key strategic areas in Yen. If I have them, the king of Ch'in will agree to grant me an audience."

"General Fan asked me to take him in when he needed shelter," answered Cinnabar. "He is my guest. I cannot abandon my sacred duty in order to avenge a personal grudge. What you ask is impossible. Think of something else."

———

Ching K'o went straight to General Fan. "You have suffered much from Ch'in," he said. "Your whole family—father, mother, wife, children, and cousins—have been murdered. None of your line is left. Ordinance is offering a reward of a thousand gold ingots and an estate of ten thousand families to anyone who brings him your head. How do you mean to avenge yourself?"

Fan the Opportune gnashed his teeth and heaved a deep sigh; tears ran down his black beard. "Whenever I think of the king of Ch'in's treachery," he said, "I am racked to the marrow of my bones. I ponder stratagems and plans of vengeance, but can think of nothing that will work."

"One word from you can avenge the insult inflicted on you, and save Yen from the threat incurred by your presence here."

The general, surprised, came closer to Ching K'o and asked tremulously, "What is that magic word?"

"I want your head to give to King Ordinance. When he knows that I'm bringing it, he'll grant me an audience, and I'll grab his sleeve with my left hand and stab him in the chest with my right. I will thus avenge you and Yen at the same time."

Fan the Opportune bared himself to the waist, gripped his left wrist with his right hand, and cried out in a voice cracked with hatred: "I have worn down my teeth from grinding them with rage, and resentment has eaten my heart and liver like gangrene. The thought of vengeance tortures me night and day. I am only too happy to do as you wish!"

He seized his long sword of shining steel and cut his throat.

As soon as he heard the news, the crown prince rushed to the general's palace and knelt before the still-warm body, sobbing and wringing his hands. He tore at his face with his hands; his disheveled hair trailed in the dark blood oozing from the gaping wound. Then he rose, carefully detached the head from the trunk with his dagger, and had it placed in a box. The box was made of magnolia wood with a veneer of black currant and wild-pepper bark and set with pearls and jade from K'un Shan. It was lined with rose petals, kingfisher feathers, and pheasant plumes woven together with gold thread and silk.

Then he ordered one of his entourage to find him a fine steel dagger, the sharpest in the Empire, sharp enough to cut in two a hair laid on the blade. Thus he came to acquire, for a hundred pieces of gold, a dagger Lady Ch'ing had forged with her own hands in her workshops in Ssuchuan. His doctors were ordered to prepare a very strong poison, which was tried out on condemned prisoners: one scratch brought instant death. Cinnabar put it away carefully in a box inlaid with mother-of-pearl and gave it to Ching K'o.

Master Ching needed someone to go with him and help him in his task. There was a man in Yen named Ch'in Wu-yang, seven feet tall and tremendously strong. At the age of eight he had killed his first man with a blow from his fist. No one dared look him in the face for fear of incurring his anger. He agreed to go with Ching K'o.

On the day of their departure, Ching K'o waited for his friend the butcher to come to say goodbye. Shuo lived in a hovel in the suburbs, far from the palace, and he was late. The knight waited. The sun sank on the horizon, and as the tops of the hills blocked the slanting rays, the slopes disappeared in shadow.

The king grew anxious: it was getting dark, and the knight showed no sign of going. "The sun sets," he said. "If you still have something left to do, or some engagement, I can get Ch'in Wu-yang to see to it for you."

Ching K'o drew himself up and shouted angrily: "Are you the one going? No—it is I who depart on this one-way journey! Armed with nothing but a dagger, I will enter the terrible kingdom of Ch'in, whose armies have never been vanquished. If I delay, it is because I wait for a friend. I would have liked to say goodbye to him. But never mind—since you're in so much of a hurry, I'll go."

He leaped into his chariot and whipped the horses. The prince, with those of his intimates who had been let into the secret, accompanied Ching K'o, dressed in white as a sign of mourning. When they reached the river I, on the southern outskirts of the city, the travelers offered up a sacrifice to the gods of the roads before setting out along the highway.

Kao Chien-li played his lute, and Ching K'o sang sad songs in the sober *pien lü* mode, which made everyone weep:

> *The wind blows over the cold plain.*
> *The waters of the frozen river flow.*
> *A brave sets out*
> *On a journey with no return,*
> *A brave sets out*
> *On a desperate mission.*

Then they went on to martial airs in the *ya* mode, and every breast swelled with epic pride. Eyes rolled fiercely, fists were clenched. Their hair stood on end.

Ching K'o saluted all his friends. Then, a tall black shape in the dim light of sunset, he vanished without a backward glance.

In a ditch halfway between the palace and the northern outskirts of Ching Ch'eng, a drunkard dressed in rags and a leather butcher's apron lay dying, in the last stage of alcoholism. His jacket was covered with vomit and his trousers with excrement, but he sang the lament of the madman of Ch'u passing Confucius's gate:

> *O phoenix, phoenix!*
> *Destroyer of prejudice!*
> *The future is no more,*
> *The past is no more.*
> *In a world at peace,*
> *The sage emerges.*
> *In a world at war,*
> *The sage conceals himself.*
> *Oh, in this filth,*
> *There is nothing but torture!*
> *Happiness is a feather*
> *For him who catches at it.*
> *Misery is lead*

For him beset with care.
Farewell, farewell!
The diligent sages are dead.
Danger, danger
Threatens their devoted servants!
Thorny, thorny
Is the path of the student.
Will I, avoiding ruts,
End up in a quagmire?

As soon as he arrived in Ch'in, Ching K'o sent sumptuous presents to Meng Chia, the palace secretary and a favorite of the king, asking him to tell his master the great news. Meng Chia, delighted to be the first with this intelligence, hurried to see Ordinance.

"Yen must be trembling at your power," he told the king, "if he offers no resistance to your generals. He lays his kingdom at your feet and begs to be your servant. The only favor he asks is that, seeing as he was formerly one of the feudatory princes, he be appointed prefect or governor, so that he may still have charge of the temple of his ancestors. The fear you inspire in him is so great, he does not dare appear before you in person to present his request and ask your pardon. But, in order to please you and show how much he respects your slightest wish, he has had General Fan's head cut off and has sent you a map of the key strategic positions in Tu K'ang. He asks you to accept these gifts as a mark of his respectful submission. An ambassador awaits your orders to come and lay before you the presents and his master's humble greetings."

Ordinance was overjoyed. A broad smile spread over his wolf-like countenance. He was victorious; the princes were terrorized; everything was coming under his sway. He conquered kingdoms without a battle, like the great monarchs of antiquity.

———

Ordinance was dressed in his finest clothes beneath his long silk mantle with its white sable collar and dragons and phoenixes embroidered in gold on a vermilion ground. Hangings of bright wool and painted silk stood out against the dark frescoes of the great audience chamber. Gaudy banners and streamers hung from long lacquered poles. As the most powerful ruler under the sun took his place on a dais at the top of a flight of jasper-and-topaz steps, Ching K'o, escorted by the brawny Ch'in Wu-yang, climbed other stairs. These led into the palace and were ornamented with zigzag stripes and carved serpentine dragons. The weighty awning that sheltered them was supported by bronze columns topped with capitals of enameled silver shaped like gourds.

Ching K'o and his companion handed their swords to the palace guards, removed their shoes in a huge antechamber paved with terracotta tiles that depicted hunting scenes, and entered another room, which was lined with black pillars. Aromatic herbs burned and crackled in brass cressets fixed to these columns, and all around were heavy greenish bronze cauldrons ornamented with the heads of tigers and dragons: protectors of the kings and guardians of the virtues of the nation. Rumor said that it was in these cauldrons that the king had recalcitrant ministers boiled.

A double row of men wearing leopard-trimmed caps and embroidered tunics stood motionless, as if they, too, were cast in bronze; they held the royal standards and other insignia.

The two visitors entered the huge audience chamber through the north door, with Ching K'o carrying the head in its box and Ch'in Wu-yang bearing the map in a cylindrical case. They advanced along an avenue formed by courtiers brightly decked with sashes, cords, and other symbols of office. When they reached the bottom of the steps, Ch'in Wu-yang looked up. He saw a man sitting cross-legged, impassive, resting his elbow on a table. The man was like a sleepy tiger.

Ch'in Wu-yang was afraid. His legs gave way under him, sweat broke out on his ashen forehead, and he could barely stand. A murmur arose. The king knitted a suspicious eyebrow.

Ching K'o turned toward his companion, laughed, then bowed to the king and apologized. "Prince," he said, "this poor lout knows only the goats and horses in our meadows. He has never left Yen before. Do not be surprised if the sight of a son of heaven puts him in such a state. Your terrible majesty makes him tremble. Be good enough to forgive him, and allow me to bring you the map he carries."

The king let out a laugh that was more like a roar. "Very well," he said. "Relieve Ch'in Wu-yang of the map, since the poor fellow cannot bear the sight of the dragon."

Ching K'o took the cylindrical case and hurried up the steps. He bowed to the king and with both hands proffered the head and the map. The king opened the case and swiftly unrolled its contents. There was a flash of blue, and Ching K'o seized the dagger hidden in the map, gripped the king's sleeve with his left hand, and with his right stabbed at the king's chest. But before the blade struck home, Ordinance pulled back and the fine silk of his sleeve gave way. He tried to draw his sword, but it stuck in its scabbard. Though he struggled with it in panic, the long steel blade hung straight from his belt, and his arms were not long enough to free it.

Ching K'o leaped at him again like a tiger, and the terrified Ordinance took flight. The knight now chased the king, and after the first stupefaction, the room became a scene of indescribable confusion. Ministers, secretaries, courtiers, and scholars all broke ranks, jostling one another and waving their arms. No one was armed, because weapons were forbidden in there. The guards were below, outside the antechamber, and could not enter the audience chamber without orders from the king, and in his extremity the king didn't think to send for them. Even if he had, they would have arrived too late.

Completely at a loss, his mind a blank, the king dodged around a column. But his assailant caught up with him. Ordinance was putting out his hands to ward off the blow, when Hsia Wu-chüeh, the physician on duty, threw his heavy bag at the murderer and knocked him off balance. The king still ran around and around the large bronze pillar, flapping his sleeves like a blind vulture. His hat was all askew, his hair beginning to come down. But he kept on circling wildly, in a daze.

Then Li Ssu shouted: "The sword! Behind! The sword! Behind!" The king, as if wakened from a dream, pulled his belt around so that his sword was at his back. Now holding the sheath in his left hand, he was able to grasp the gold-encrusted bronze pommel in his right and draw the long blue steel blade.

He turned on his pursuer and pierced him through the right thigh. As Ching K'o fell, he hurled the dagger at the king, but it missed. The blade hit the bronze pillar, striking a spark, then dropped to the tiles. Now the king fell upon Ching K'o, until the blood flowed from eight deep wounds. Realizing that it was all up with him, the knight mustered his strength for one last effort, propped himself against the pillar, and laughed in the king's face.

"Hell!" he said. "I failed because I wanted to take you alive, so that you would sign a treaty that would satisfy the honor of the crown prince of Yen. But someone else will take over and wash out the insult."

Then the guards finished him off.

It took Ordinance a long time to recover from his fright. He had nightmares, dreaming sometimes that he was a wolf pursued by hounds with the snouts of pigs. Or he dreamt that he was a tiger chasing sheep through a desert strewn with steep, glittering mauve rocks: just as he was about to devour the flesh of one of his victims, he realized that it was his own. He screamed so loudly in his sleep that he roused the whole palace. He surrounded himself with guards, then dismissed them, afraid they might strangle him while he slept.

Li Ssu was worried. The guards were made to search the palace. The sound of boots echoed through the galleries; running footsteps caused panic among the eunuchs. Doors slammed. The women were terrified.

Sometimes the king dreamt that he was being hunted by a huge she-bear who had taken his sword. He ran between blocks of basalt, through mud that was soft and sticky.

He wasted away. His skin was green, and his nose jutted out like the beak of a bird of prey. The soothsayers advised him to offer sacrifices to the gods of the mountains and rivers.

Gradually the nightmares lessened. He recovered. Fear was succeeded by anger, and by the giving of credit where credit was due. In a tearful voice Ordinance declared: "My doctor loves me—he threw his bag at my assailant. And my minister gives excellent advice."

News of the affair spread throughout the Empire. All the bravos and swashbucklers praised Ching K'o. Ko Nieh, afraid of becoming an object of scorn and opprobrium for having insulted him, cut his own throat.

———

The king's armies were unleashed upon the princes. Millions of men from the West swept over the eastern provinces. General Wang Ch'ien carried all before him like a raging torrent.

In the tenth month of the twenty-first year of Ordinance's reign, the city of Ching Ch'eng was taken and the southern part of Yen annexed by Ch'in. King Yen the Cheerful, together with his son Cinnabar, his generals, and the last remnants of their crack troops, withdrew to Liao Tung to organize resistance.

But Li Confidence, who had taken command of a column, followed close on their heels, and the king of Chao's son wrote a letter to King Yen advising him to hand over the head of his son Cinnabar to appease Ordinance's wrath.

The Ch'in generals continued to harass what was left of the vanquished army, and the Yen soldiers, hungry and exhausted, hid in the marshes along the river Yen, hoping for an opportunity to break out. But the net tightened on them inexorably. Finally the king ordered his son killed and the head delivered to the king of Ch'in as a token of surrender.

Five years later, the king of Yen was brought as a captive to Ch'in and thrown into prison. His kingdom was turned into a province of Ch'in.

After the failed assassination attempt, the intimates of the crown prince and the friends of the knight errant were tracked down. Those who managed to elude the Ch'in bloodhounds were scattered all over the land lying low.

Kao Chien-li, changing his name, worked as an odd-job man for a minor nobleman in the town of Sung Tzu. Time passed. He led a hard life and found it difficult to endure his low position. Whenever he heard one of the guests in his master's banquet hall playing the lute, he paced the antechamber, unable to tear himself away and muttering comments on the performance. Word of his strange behavior came to his master's ears, and he was asked to come in and play. When he did so, the audience, astonished, burst into applause. He was offered wine, but he fled in tears. Back in his hut, he took out his own lute and his long sheepskin-lined cloak, went back to his master in the banquet hall, and played. The audience rose and bowed low before him; he was fêted and honored like a distinguished guest.

Soon he was being invited by all the noblemen in the town, and his reputation as a lute player spread throughout the Empire. Ordinance heard of him, and being a music lover, summoned him to the court. One of the courtiers recognized Kao Chien-li. But Ordinance could not bring himself to have him put to death—he did not want to lose such a fine musician. So he merely had his eyes put out. "That will make him play even better," he said.

Ordinance often had Kao Chien-li play to him in private, so pleasing did he find the sad strains. Every day he listened to him with more enjoyment. He would send for him when he couldn't sleep:

he liked being lulled by the soft vibrations of the strings in the clear light of a starry night.

Every day Kao Chien-li placed a small piece of lead inside his instrument, to make it heavier. He played softly, hardly touching the strings, and the music was like a breath, barely more than a silence. The Emperor had to come near to listen, and every day Kao Chien-li played more softly, and every day he put another piece of lead inside his lute. One day the Emperor came so close that the blind man could feel his breath on his cheek. He lifted his lute and struck. But he missed, and was put to death, and his body was thrown to the dogs.

A few months later, a tall man with a face like a dragon stood in the market place in Double Light and cried: "Listen to the sad story of Ching K'o, who tried to kill a tyrant so that his name might be famous forever and his exploits always fresh in your memories!"

In the hum of astonishment that followed, he sat down and sang a wild and tragic song, accompanying himself on the lute:

> *I shall keep you, Cinnabar,*
> *Said the wicked king,*
> *Till the cock cries at night*
> *And crows turn white.*
>
> *That summer it snowed.*
> *The crows turned white,*
> *The cock cried at night,*
> *And Cinnabar escaped from Ch'in.*

An awed silence fell upon the audience as he sang. Even the guards listened, petrified, and did not think to arrest the singer. When he finished, Lu Kou Kien the bravo, for it was he, swept his fingers across the strings with an ironic twang, bowed, made off down a narrow lane, and disappeared.

Then, as if a spell had been broken, everyone shouted, policemen ran in all directions, local officials took down names. Houses were searched, people interrogated. Lu Kou-Chien was found and subjected to the five tortures before being executed in the market place. The guards involved were found guilty of negligence and put to death; the local officials were deported to Ssuchuan. An edict was issued threatening the death penalty for anyone who mentioned Ching K'o. And Li Ssu took even more radical precautions. Itinerant bards were banned and replaced by authorized troupes of singers and musicians. Their repertory had to be approved by the music bureau, which was part of the Ministry of the Interior.

BOOK THREE

*The August
Emperor and
Eternity*

CHAPTER I

BLACK IS
THE WINTER

Ordinance was neither surprised nor particularly pleased to hear that the king of Ch'i had been captured. In fact, he was disappointed. Perhaps he had expected his final victory over the feudatory princes to be accompanied by some portent: the sun standing still in the sky, the appearance of a new star, an unknown plant suddenly blooming in the palace courtyard—anything to mark the event. But there was nothing. No prodigy revealed itself either to his astrologers or to his soothsayers.

It was a gloomy spring day. A thin, raw drizzle streamed in silver droplets over the downy leaves. A mist blurred the outlines of the hills, and at his feet the waters of the river were leaden.

He was in a drawing room in the palace of Chao. He had had copies of the palaces of all the princes he conquered built on the hills north of the river Wei, so that, by traveling twenty leagues along the river, he could remind himself of the extent of his annexations. It was because of the mood he was in that he had come to the palace of Chao: he always came here when he felt melancholy.

To the left of the building, a huge rectangle of flattened earth awaited the erection of yet another replica: a copy of the palace of the last of the six princes.

Suddenly struck by the cold air, Ordinance moved away from the window and went to sit at a low table placed over an arrangement of bricks that were heated by coals. A comforting warmth from the ducts of this apparatus permeated the space under the table and the mat on which he sat.

He began to wonder why he felt so low-spirited. Were all his victories making him blasé? He had eaten kingdoms as a silkworm ate mulberry leaves—slowly, surely, ceaselessly, and in secret. But his domination over the Empire was the result of a long process begun before he was born. He had inherited Ch'in's political and administrative organization from Shang Yang; the diplomatic policy had been determined by Shang I and developed by Lü Pu-wei; and General Peace of Arms had established the military strategy. He himself merely reaped what others sowed.

Li Ssu would have approved of all this, seeing it as proof that Ordinance was moving with the current of history. But Ordinance couldn't help thinking that it was hard for a prince to be the incarnation of history. He felt as if he'd been cheated: his victory lacked splendor; there was something shabby about it. The Yellow Emperor conquered the Empire in a single battle, and a single battle had sufficed for the founders of the Yin and Chou dynasties to overthrow the tyrants. Whereas he, Ordinance, could not have said where and when his own triumph began.

The decisive struggles, he now realized, had taken place in the reign of Ch'in the Resplendent. The kingdoms of Han, Wei, Chao, and Yen were crumbling now under the weight of their own weakness. The capture of a few towns, a show of force here and there on the frontiers, some skillful infiltration of spies—these had been enough to bring them down like autumn leaves at the first frost. Then each king was brought to the capital, Double Light, with a yoke around his neck, chained hand and foot like a convict, and sent into exile in Yung or Ssuchuan.

The resistance put up by Ch'u had given Ordinance a bit of excitement. He was kept in suspense by the ups and downs of the campaign, with its troop movements, offensives, and counteroffensives. But, now that he thought about it, he could see that this had been due mainly to the recklessness of the general in command. He had been rash enough to appoint the impetuous Li Confidence to the post, who, carried away by his successes against Yen, undertook to defeat the formidable Ch'u with two hundred thousand men. But the recent victory over Ch'i was really only the culmination of an inexorable trend.

"Conquer without bloodying the sword," Hsün Tzu used to say.

"If an enlightened monarch defeats the enemy as easily as a man breaks a rotten plank, it is thanks to the divine web," Ordinance's best captains maintained. And wasn't he a past master in the use of double agents? Was there anything in the kingdom as perfect as his spy network?

That was what he had thought until he was able to look at the secret archives of the kings he conquered. The Han secret service had nothing to learn from his. Chao's spies had infiltrated everywhere. Ordinance, considering himself a virtuoso in manipulating the divine web, had to admit that all the princes—even the dullest—had been skillful at weaving it around their enemies.

When he asked Li Ssu about this, the minister shrugged scornfully and said: "Only a minor factor! Espionage won't work unless backed up by political organization. Our secret service was no better than those of our rivals, but our social system was stronger. Our sabotage against them was effective because their officials were vulnerable to slander. Countries like that are easily undermined. But in a country such as ours, the divine web catches nothing in its toils, as the Cheng Kuo affair clearly shows. Even if your enemies had managed to bribe your whole court, they wouldn't have been able to control your policy or your government. The law is not to be bought, and that's why I say that, while the use of agents may decide the outcome of a war, the successful use of agents depends upon political organization. Our enemies led their countries to ruin because they neglected this truth."

Ordinance began to think that no king under the sun, since antiquity, ever set up a system as good as his. The unostentatiousness of his victories was perhaps the best proof of his greatness. His progress toward world dominion had been all the more irresistible because he had acted, quietly and unseen, in conformity with the same principle that made the sea hurl itself at the cliffs or the river erode the mountains. He possessed the same peaceful strength as the ocean.

He inhaled deeply and felt calmer. He was now master of the universe. And since heaven was slow to recognize the fact, he would announce it to the world himself. He summoned one of his secretaries and dictated the following proclamation:

Because I am but one poor, weak individual, I had to raise an army to inflict a just punishment on the cruel and depraved kings, and by the grace of my ancestors I have visited on all six of them the penalty their evil deeds deserved, pacifying their kingdoms and conquering their lands.

Today the Empire enjoys law and order. But I fear that if the title I bear, with the other appellations appended to it, is not changed, the Name will no longer correspond to the Form. And it would be a great pity if my achievements did not go down to posterity, and my deeds were not an example to succeeding generations! So I would be glad if you, my ministers and advisers, would consult together to find a title appropriate to the imperial mission I have just completed.

The council met in the great debating chamber in the old palace. Wang Kuan, the prime minister, Feng Kieh, the chief secretary, and Li Ssu, minister of the interior, spent hours discussing the matter before they could agree. Wang Kuan did not want to change any of the titles of the Chou kings. Li Ssu thought that there should be new marks of distinction to correspond to the new facts, but the only title he could suggest was that of "Emperor." Feng Kieh agreed with Li Ssu but thought his suggestion very tame. Finally they agreed on a statement, each privately resolving to put all the blame on the others if it was unlucky enough not to please the master of the universe.

> After lengthy consultations with the Scholars of Vast Learning, we have come to the following conclusion: in ancient times there was a Lord August Heaven, a Lord August Earth, and a Lord August Supreme. The glory of the latter was unsurpassed until you came. Your humble servants therefore risk incurring your wrath by suggesting that you adopt the honorific of "August Supreme." Your orders will be known as "mandates" and your decrees as "proclamations." When you assume this title you will abandon the epithet of "orphan" for the more imposing one of "impenetrable."

After much reflection, the Emperor sent for his ministers. "I don't care for 'Supreme,'" he said, "but I will keep the title of 'August' and add to it that of 'Emperor.' I wield over the earth the same power that the gods of the directions exert over the sky. So henceforward I shall be known as August Emperor, and for the rest I shall follow your advice."

A decree was issued conferring on his father the posthumous title of "August First Ancestor," while another proclamation set out the rules governing imperial appellations:

The habit has grown, of giving the dead posthumous titles that correspond to their behavior when they were alive. This deplorable practice allowed a son to criticize his father and a subject to judge the conduct of his master. It was a harmful and inept custom, and I shall not observe it. From today, posthumous titles are abolished forever.

As the first Emperor of a new and glorious dynasty, I add to my honorific title the phrase "the First," and my descendants will number themselves likewise through succeeding generations, so that there will be a Second August Emperor, and a Third, and a Thousandth, and a Ten Thousandth, and so on, until time ends and numbers are exhausted!

He derived great satisfaction from composing this decree. Now, even if he died, he would give birth to a line that would last as long as the world. And his strong vegetable spirits, nourished with rich meats by his descendants, would haunt the earth and rejoice in their underground dwellings for thousands of years. He vowed to make his tomb the largest monument ever.

But a few days later his elation faded, succeeded by vague apprehension. He had attempted to have names correspond to forms, yet the new era dawning ought really to be reflected in every symbol. The whole range of signs needed to be changed, not just a few titles; if he did not take the necessary steps, he would leave an opening for disorder to re-establish itself in his possessions.

He sent for Li Ssu and told him of his fears, ordering him to seek out emblems appropriate to the spirit of his reign. Li Ssu applauded his master's intentions but said that he was not competent to help: it was a matter of cosmology, and he confessed that he had neglected the subject. The astrologists and historians, and the college of Scholars of Vast Learning, were much better qualified than he to solve the problem.

———

So, in the great hall devoted to the promulgation of the calendar and the observation of signs in the heavens, Ordinance gathered seventy-two of the most learned men in the Empire—from Ch'i, home of scholars; from Chou, land of cosmologists; and from Yen, country of soothsayers and seers. They wore rough homespun robes and tall shiny hats of brown linen. The long strings of their broad leather belts hung down to the upturned tips of their straw slippers. They were constantly bowing. The gravity of their demeanor tempered the exaggeration of their gestures.

The Emperor gazed at them curiously: this was an unfamiliar species of humanity. He knew the generals, with their vigorous movements and deep, brusque voices; he knew the changeable and wily sophists and the stiff and circumspect officials. But he was bewildered by this flapping of sleeves like the wings of huge birds, this significant wagging of heads, and all these meaning looks.

A venerable graybeard stepped forward, bowed twice, flapped his sleeves, and said: "Master Ch'ung has explained the laws governing the alternation of yin and yang. The spring brings birth and presides over charity. The summer brings growth and stands for virtue. Autumn brings fulfillment and represents justice. Winter preserves, and stands for seemliness. Such is the round of seasons upon which a wise man models himself. There is no need to change the calendar. Revive the rules of the early kings, return to the rites of the Chou, and your reign will be glorious."

He went on, prostrating himself as he spoke: "The sun is yang. The nature of yang is resplendent. The moon is yin. The nature of yin is dark. The relationship between the two symbolizes the superiority of a prince over a minister. Any lack of balance in government or education results in flood, drought, or swarms of harmful insects. That is the only cause of strange apparitions and disasters. Men reflect the regular round of the seasons and are ruled by the ordered motions of the stars."

Then an even more aged scholar advanced and made the customary obeisances. "Since someone has already made bold to discourse about the nature of things and the round of the elements," said he, "allow me, prince, to speak of them, too. The *Book of Changes* leaves no room for doubt about the laws governing the alternation of yin and yang, and the *Annals of the Kingdoms* provide ample information on the Theory of the Five Elements. The four seasons and the five elements all prosper and decline in their turn. Yin and yang are different by nature. Spring and summer are the seasons of procreation and the bearing of fruit, and the period during which one should practice charity. Autumn and winter are times of seclusion and death, during which punishments and tortures are inflicted. If you do not plant at the right time, the shoots do not mature, for, just as when you practice charity in winter, you flout the natural cycle. But this person does not know the difference between the seasons. He confuses yin and yang, venerating charity and ostracizing punishment. If he were right, the cormorant would never make the first sacrifice, nor would wild beasts kill their first victim. There would be no hunting in autumn, no great shooting parties in winter."

"Nature cherishes life," retorted the first old man, "and has a horror of death. It likes to reward and hates to punish. That is why yang is fullness, lavishing good on the world. Yin is emptiness, but it helps yang in its task. Yang is firmness, yin flexibility. Heaven scorns winter and reveres spring; it exalts yang and abases yin. Have you never wondered, dear colleague, why kings exact obedience by turning toward the south? By facing yang and turning their backs on yin, they show in their very posture that they give precedence to virtue over punishment!"

The Emperor was disconcerted by this incomprehensible debate, and gazed at the speakers in bewilderment. He had the vague impression that one of them defended ritual while the other advocated punishment, but he could not see the connection between this and the question he had put forward. He shook off his torpor and thundered: "Enough talk! Kindly choose the signs appropriate to my reign and never mind boring arguments about the seasons!"

A murmur ran through the crowd and the scholars hung their

heads in embarrassment. The Emperor did not know about the quarrel between the two schools, one maintaining that the elements were engendered and the other that they came into being through mutual destruction. But the choice of signs depended upon which of the theories was adopted.

Another man came forward. "Only Tzu Yen," he asserted, "has ever understood the laws governing the evolution of the five elements; he also discovered the stages leading from condensation to dispersal. The virtues take turns triumphing over and succeeding one another, and every dynastic cycle is under the influence of one or another of them. The five elements correspond to the five directions, and the latter rule over the seasons, each of which is under the influence of a special part of the heavens."

Then the quavering voice of a scholar from Wei intervened. "This part of the world is governed by wood, and its divinity is the Green Emperor. The South is governed by fire and its god is the Red Emperor. The West, ruled by metal, has the White Emperor for its divinity. The North is governed by water and its divinity is the Black Emperor. . . ."

"No," interrupted a learned man from Chao, "heaven has six parts and is offered nine sacrifices a year. The first is called *yü*, and—"

But the scholar with the quavery voice went on imperturbably. "Just as every direction has a corresponding season, color, note in the scale, type of government, as well as a particular god in the sky and his assistant on earth, so every dynastic age is governed by a principle that depends on a direction, an element, and a color. All we need to do to find the signs suitable to your reign, therefore, is work out the laws that govern the succession of the elements."

At this a gaunt-faced character flapped his sleeves frantically and cried: "In his treatise on war, Sun Tzu says: The Yellow Emperor chastised the Red Emperor in the South. He fought in the plain of Fan Tan with his back to the mountains and in accordance with the arts of war, and he vanquished the enemy. For three years he gave his people peace, cultivated cereals, and did good works. Then he made himself master of the Green, the Black, and the White Emperors. The Yellow Emperor punished the rebels from the four directions, put down sedition by introducing just laws and institutions, and gave all his peoples peace and prosperity. Your own victories are the equal of his, your laws as wise as his. The Yellow Emperor reigned by virtue of earth, and made plants and animals flourish. He ruled in mercy, having conquered by force. You should adopt the color yellow, the number five, the note . . ."

But another sage was already advancing to refute that theory.

"In the struggle between the Yellow and Red Emperors, the Yellow Emperor used water and his enemy fire. The water overcame the fire. Water is the sign of darkness, severity, and punishment. You should rule through the laws and honor the color black."

A scholar from Lu waved his embroidered cuffs in agreement. "Every virtue is reflected in a sign," he said. "The Yellow Emperor ruled by virtue of earth. A dragon appeared when he came to the throne. And as the elements triumph in turn, in infinite succession, earth beaten by wood, wood beaten by metal, metal beaten by fire, fire beaten by water, water beaten by earth, the Yellow Emperor, the first founder of a dynasty, ruled by virtue of earth. The Hsia ruled by virtue of wood. A green dragon appeared when Yü, the founder of the dynasty, offered up a sacrifice to heaven. The Yin ruled through metal, and molten copper and tin flowed forth from a mountain. The Chou reigned by fire, and a red crow appeared when they came to power. The Ch'in dynasty now succeeds the Chou, and can reign only by virtue of water. All the proof I need is that one day, when your illustrious ancestor Duke Wen went out hunting, he caught a black dragon. Is that not a guarantee of the virtue of water?"

He was interrupted by the indignant protests of a sage from Chou. "The first trigram corresponding to the beginning of spring is a flash of lightning, which stirs the earth and fertilizes it. It is associated with wood. And through the lightning's impregnation of the earth everything is born. So it is through wood that the imperial principle is established. And just as an infant comes forth from his mother's womb, so the elements succeed one another according to the laws of birth, not those of destruction. The Yellow Emperor was not the first ruler to enjoy imperial dignity. Long before him came the August of Great Brightness, who ruled by virtue of wood, for the origin of the year lies in the spring. Grass and vegetation of all kinds flourished under him. Then K'ung K'ung, his minister of works, usurped power and ruled over the nine provinces. But since he had no right to do so, he could not really embody the imperial dignity. Next came the ardent Emperor whose name was Divine Plowman, who succeeded Great Brightness by virtue of fire, for fire is engendered by wood. He taught men to plow and sow. When the dynastic virtue of his race declined, the Yellow Emperor appeared. As fire engenders earth, he ruled through earth. Four emperors followed him, the first being Small Brightness, who reigned through metal, since earth engenders that element. And so on, down to the Chou, who ruled by virtue of fire. And since fire is not destroyed by water but engenders earth, you can reign only through earth. If you choose water, I fear you may be another K'ung K'ung."

The Emperor felt dizzy. His head was awhirl with colors—black, yellow, white, green. . . . And the elements cavorted in a wheel of generation and destruction, dispersal and succession. . . . The idea of destruction was attractive. But yellow was the color of the center. . . .

Then a very determined voice spoke up: "What nonsense!" he said. "The signs are clear. Your ancestor caught a black dragon. Ch'in's first month begins at the tenth moon, the last of the winter. Your government is one of laws and punishments. Your reign can be only that of water, for water corresponds to winter, the season of punishments!"

"And its number is the numerical emblem of the sky, too," added a courtier.

"True," agreed the Emperor wearily.

So it was decided that the tenth month should be the beginning of the year throughout the Empire. Everything would start with the first day of the tenth moon. On that day, delegations from the Empire would come to the capital to deliver their greetings, give account of their administration, and receive new directives. Black was to be the main color for jackets, robes, trousers, tunics, and so on, as well as for standards, pennants, and horses. Six being the number that corresponded to winter, it was taken as a standard of measurement. Official hats were six inches high, chariot wheels had to be six feet apart, and a pace was henceforth to be six feet, too. The royal coach was drawn by six or a multiple of six black horses.

The Yellow River was renamed "Virtue of Water." Punishment was to be more strict than ever; the government was to be inflexible; and no one was to expect any mercy from the Emperor.

Thousands of convicts painted the pillars of palaces and temples black. The brightly colored frescoes with their splashes of vermilion and pink were covered with gloomy pictures dark as ebony.

————

While the Emperor and his cosmologists were deciding the signs that would best convey the character of the new era, Li Ssu dealt with the law.

He had a census taken of all the male population in the conquered territories. Anyone who failed to register was severely punished. The idea was that no one should escape administrative surveillance.

With his own hand he wrote out a model circular to be sent to all the prefects and had it distributed to the provincial governors:

From Governor So-and-So to all his prefects, subprefects, and heads of subdepartments. The purpose of the criminal law is to guide and educate the people and to restrain their baser instincts and love of money. Now, even though the laws are clear and precise, and the code lists all possible crimes along with the appropriate punishments, I hear that certain officials still carry out their duties in an individualistic manner. They refuse to reform and prefer to continue in the old ways. Village heads, district leaders, and even assistants at the departmental and sub-departmental levels are acting with undesirable indulgence, allowing citizens to flout with impunity the decrees and prohibitions of our sovereign lord, the August First Emperor. Thus a part of our administration nurtures parasites and is in league with antisocial elements.

So, from today, that the rules may be clearly understood and the laws respected, we give notice to the regional and local offices working under every provincial administration that inspectors are being sent out to investigate the country. Their task is to make known every unpunished crime or abuse that comes to their attention, and to send to the central administration of every province the names of any prefects, subprefects, and heads or assistant heads of subdepartments who are tolerating practices contrary to the new decrees. The guilty parties will be brought before special courts and sentenced according to the legislation now in force. We wish to make it clear to all officials that no one, whatever his rank, will be spared. If it appears that some prefectures have a particularly large number of crimes left unpunished, the prefects concerned and their assistants will be brought before a special tribunal—and let them not expect any mercy!

Every province is to send to every prefecture a copy of a circular based on the present text. Each prefecture is to make copies of the circular and send one to every subdepartment and district within its jurisdiction. Copies of this edict have been posted on the walls in the capital.

This proposal was submitted to the August First Emperor, who approved it wholeheartedly. He encouraged Li Ssu to write, also, a handbook for the perfect civil servant, to be sent to every prefecture throughout the Empire.

It seemed to them that a reprehensible laxness prevailed in many of the conquered territories, and that the provincial civil servants needed taking in hand. Li Ssu's tireless brush flew over the silk once more.

It is the duty of every official to publish laws and decrees without delay, so that the business of the state may be conducted speedily and without procrastination. The perfect civil servant is honest and open. He serves his superiors diligently, is frank, cordial, and cooperative. He knows that he cannot settle public matters to suit himself and is careful not to be influenced by his own inclinations. One never hears him questioning government policy or criticizing his superiors.

A bad civil servant, on the other hand, does not do his best to promulgate edicts and prohibitions and explain them to the public. He is venal. He neglects urgent business. He likes to discuss general political principles and does not shrink from denigrating the decisions of his superiors. He puts his own concerns before the public interest. He is individualistic and resists orders sent from the capital. He hides his incompetence with bluster, talking loudly about what needs to be done and how the administrative system could be improved, thinking to demonstrate his zeal with as little effort as possible. He rolls his eyes, puts on a determined expression, and clutches his left wrist with his right hand—an easy way of showing one's courage! He is a fluent talker and makes long flowery speeches in order to pass himself off as a politician. He says "white" when he means "black." He seems humble but is as vain as a peacock. He is self-effacing, but in a way that suggests that he is a neglected genius.

Thus he sometimes manages to win the esteem of his superiors. But such behavior must be ruthlessly punished.

From now on, reports will be made to each provincial center on the behavior of higher officials. Their work will be appraised under prescribed headings, and those who are given negative marks will be reprimanded. Their files will be flagged "unsatisfactory," and they will be denied promotion.

———

The court buzzed like a beehive. Delegations from the conquered provinces arrived one after another. The air was full of offers of help, suggestions of reform, requests for explanations of the new edicts, petitions, and plans for reorganization. The August Emperor made a point of reading everything, hearing everyone, and deciding everything for himself. But he was soon overwhelmed by the flood of conflicting ideas and suggestions.

He decided to fix the administrative form of his Empire once and for all, so as to silence objections and establish everything correctly. The Empire must speak with one voice and live by one heartbeat. Right thinking could have but one center: himself. But as long as the center remained undecided, the Empire would suffer from the cacophony with which it was afflicted at present. He summoned his council to resolve the matter.

Wang Kuan, the prime minister, was, like most court dignitaries, still attached to the old regime, and pleaded with the Emperor: "The princes have just been annihilated. But Yen, Ch'i, Chao, Han, and Wei are a long way from your capital, and we fear that if you do not delegate some of your authority, you will be unable to maintain order in all the provinces. We suggest, therefore, that you create fiefdoms and bestow them on members of the imperial family."

The council agreed.

Then Li Ssu reared up like a viper and hissed: "Today, thanks to the shrewdness and foresight of the First August Emperor, all the territory within the four seas is regularly divided into provinces and prefectures. It seems to me that the titles and dignities he has conferred on his sons and trusty servants are quite adequate marks of his esteem, and that their emoluments and shares in the taxes are more than sufficient to support them in a suitable manner. The

Empire must have a single center, where all decisions are made and all thoughts and opinions originate. If everything radiates from one point, it will be easy to keep the peace in all your territories. What must be avoided at all costs is the creation of several sources of authority. That would mean the destruction of your Empire and the end of its unity."

The Emperor gave a sly laugh. "I shall take the advice of my minister of the interior," he said.

He ordered Li Ssu to prepare a plan for the reorganization of the Empire. The two men found themselves sitting up late, as they had done earlier in Ordinance's reign, discussing fundamental principles. Every evening the son of heaven summoned his minister to a different room in his palace, which, like his kingdom, had grown to an inordinate size. He would move from east to west like the sun, through pavilions, towers, and terraces, all linked by hanging bridges, ornate balustrades, and galleries lined with pillars. And as the pale-silver rays of the moon touched the muddy waters of the Wei, Li Ssu set before the Emperor the results of his labors.

The Empire was divided into thirty-six provinces. Since six was the number corresponding to water, the administrative divisions of the Empire were bound to be the sacred number multiplied by itself— a number that was doubly yin, just as the capital was doubly yang. The numerical symbols balanced and merged in a subtle harmony. The yin began to ascend when the yang was at its apogee, and similarly, at the winter solstice, when days were shortest, the yang was concentrated and at the height of its potential.

At the head of each province Li Ssu placed a governor, a commander, and a political instructor. The latter's task was to spy on the governor and supply the court with secret reports on him. No official, whatever his position and however far removed he was from the central authority, was to think himself safe from the Emperor's all-seeing eye. But, lest the political instructor himself should become too powerful, Li Ssu arranged for him, too, to be spied upon, by one of his subordinates, whose identity was not revealed.

In the vast offices where he worked from dawn on, ruling over a multitude of scribes, secretaries, archivists, and legal officials, Li Ssu came and went, supervising everyone's work, sending for archives and accounts from the provinces, comparing the various legislative systems, going through trial records and court sentences and noting down precedents. He examined every subdepartment's annual account of income and expenditure. The object of all this toil was to prepare new regulations concerning slave workers and convicts.

So that there would be no room for misunderstanding anywhere in the Empire, the Great Emperor ordered the standardization of all weights and measures. Officials visited every office to examine and adjust the former standards, and every new measure had to bear the following inscription, composed by the Emperor himself:

> In the twenty-sixth year of his reign, the August First Emperor completed his unification of the world, and the princes and the black-haired people knew peace and happiness. He introduced new titles and assumed that of "August Emperor." He issued a decree ordering his ministers Wei Chuang and Wang Kuan to unify standards of measurement. All the rules are clear, and nothing disturbs the tranquillity of his subjects or the universal application of the norms.

On the Emperor's orders Li Ssu then undertook the standardization of writing, abolishing the variants that existed in the other kingdoms. He required that all official documents be written in the style used by the government in Ch'in.

It was said among the people that a hermit named Wang found the old form of the Ch'in style too complicated and, pitying the scribes who had to toil and waste precious time over it, simplified it by inventing the cursive mode. It was this form, so the story went, that the August Emperor now brought into general use. He wished to reward the hermit, who at present lived on wild berries alone in the mountains, but Wang declined his invitation. The Emperor flew into a passion: "The Impenetrable has foiled the policy of the league and pacified the world! Who is this Wang that dares disobey my orders?" And he sent an official to seize him, bring him back to the capital, and put him to death by way of example.

Just as they were about to throw him into the wagon that was to take him to prison, Wang turned into a bird and flew, circling over the heads of the guards. The official prostrated himself. "The Great Emperor will have me chopped to pieces if I go back empty-handed!" he wailed. "Have pity on me and give me a token to appease his wrath!"

The bird dropped two marvelous fans made of feathers. But when the Emperor took them in his hands, they flapped furiously and flew away. "Alas," sighed the Emperor, "I have offended an immortal. Will I ever be able to speak with a sage again?"

And, as a sign of repentance, he named the mountain where Wang had taken refuge the Mountain of Fans and built a temple to him there.

This story spread first in the streets of Double Light and then throughout the Empire. The Great Emperor did not like it and tried to find out who had started it. In vain. But there was a scribe named Wang Tz'u-chung who lived in retirement in Fan Ch'eng, and he was executed. Then a decree was issued forbidding anyone to mention the story on pain of death. So it disappeared from the lips of the children and of all the inhabitants of the Empire.

———

Ordinance spent sleepless nights going through the maps of his Empire. His long fingers, strong as an eagle's talons, scratched the surface of the silk as he undid the scrolls, smiling savagely and drinking in with his eyes the veins and lineaments of the rocks, the straight lines of the roads and canals, the squares and circles denoting cities, towns, and villages. If he laid all the maps end to end, he would obtain a picture of the whole of the territory in his power. But there were too many of them—thousands and thousands of maps, some folded away in lacquer boxes, others rolled up in cylinders of carved wood. So he ordered painters to depict his Empire on the four walls of a huge, especially built pavilion.

His cartographers told him that in the east his Empire stretched as far as the Bay of Po Hai, then plunged like the prow of a ship in the ocean. It extended through the provinces of Wu and Yüeh to border the lands of strange beings that lived in houses with windows facing north, for it was in the north that the midday sun appeared in those parts. This was a murky and water-logged region inhabited by people with hollow chests, black teeth, pierced ears, and pigeon toes: deformed gnomes with skins darker than ebony. Its western borders reached Ling Yao and Chiang Chung, stopping short at the foothills of Ch'ing Hai, the home of mountain folk who live off the sour cheese produced by their goats and bushy-tailed yaks. To the north the Empire was bounded by the bend of the Yellow River and skirted the Ying Mountains, beyond which lay the vast grassy plains of the steppes, the harsh and inhospitable lair of the Huns, with their swift steeds and deadly arrows.

It was not until the frescoes on the walls of the pavilion were complete that the Emperor realized the vastness of his domains.

To celebrate his victory and announce to gods and men the advent of a new era, he ordered celebrations lasting more than thirty days in every province. When they were over, he issued a proclamation saying that the war was over and peace restored. Under him the world was to enjoy rest and concord. War was banished, and all weapons were confiscated and sent to the capital: spears, halberds, javelins, arrows, and swords piled up in the Emperor's palace and overflowed from his storehouses. To impress the people, he had all these gathered together and melted down in enormous stone molds, to make two gigantic bells mounted on bronze frames. When they were rung at full strength, they shook the tiles off the roofs in Double Light and could be heard for a thousand leagues around.

Ordinance had dreams about a tall man with half-closed eyes, a dragon's nose, and a tiger's mustache. He ordered twelve huge statues cast in bronze in this man's likeness. Weighing two hundred and forty thousand pounds, they were arranged in two rows on the six steps at the main entrance of the palace.

In an alley in the capital, a child sang a song predicting that the Ch'in dynasty would be overthrown by one who looked like the men of bronze. The child, tortured, would not reveal where these subversive ideas came from. The residents of the entire neighborhood were put to death.

CHAPTER II

THE SACRIFICE ON MOUNT T'AI

The blue veins and dark meanderings against the fawn background of the map of the Empire, which was dotted with red to mark the cities and fortresses, made the August Emperor want to explore his possessions. He knew only a few places in it: the city in Chao where he had spent his childhood, Double Light, the palaces by the river Wei, and Yung in the Northwest. He had also looked upon the ruins of Big Bridge, in the wake of his generals, and the remains of Yin and Yeh in Ch'u. But he had never seen the great black expanse on his western borders.

It was spring when he started out on his expedition, accompanied by his ministers, counselors, wives, and eunuchs. Hundreds of wagons carrying food and clothing, tableware, weapons, and armor followed the black-lacquered imperial chariot drawn by twelve black horses.

On either side of the procession streamed somber pennants borne by horsemen wearing black silk trousers.

An inspection carried out by the Emperor in Lung Hsi and Pei Ti, on the edge of the steppes, left him disappointed. He found nothing different from what he had already seen in other landscapes. Even the feel of the desert wind burning his cheek was familiar. So he gave up the idea of imitating King Mu of Chou by crossing the western deserts to meet the queen mother of the West in the K'un Lun Mountains and drink a cup of sweet wine with her on the shores of the Jade Lake.

After a detour to the North, the Emperor's train arrived in Tzu, where he saw a high mountain that was said to be holy. He climbed to the top and raised a stele there praising his achievements.

When he descended from that height, a scholar in a shiny black silk hat and a robe cinched by a broad sash with long dangling ends suggested that he perform the *feng* and *shan* sacrifices to show that he was the equal of heaven.

Ordinance, impressed, asked Li Ssu for his opinion. But Li Ssu said he knew nothing about such things. He was not really interested in ritual. On the other hand, he did not want to offend the Emperor. And who knows—he thought—perhaps such ceremonies were useful as manifestations of royal power. They began to discuss the meaning of the rite and how it should be performed, but the debate went on and on. Finally the Emperor, impatient, summoned the seventy-two sages. They met in the great audience chamber in the palace at Lin Tzu, formerly the home of the prince of Ch'i and now the Emperor's temporary residence.

The learned men prostrated themselves toward the north, between two rows of dignitaries whose dark robes sparkled with their badges of office.

One sage said, "These ceremonies take place at intervals of more than a thousand years. How could the memory of such ancient matters be preserved intact? Do not perform a sacrifice grown dim in the mists of time!"

Another protested: "The *feng* sacrifice is described in the *Book of Documents*. Chün went up into the holy mountains to perform the appropriate ceremony at an auspicious time, honoring the highest and most ancient peak in all the five directions. The *feng* ceremony is the same as that for the inspection of fiefs."

Another venerable sage added his word: "The son of heaven sacrifices to famous mountains and great rivers. The five peaks are like the Three Kings. The rivers symbolize the nobles. The sacrifice of the Eastern Peak is not an investiture rite!"

Another sage waved his sleeves and bowed. "The *feng* and *chan* sacrfices are ordinary sacrifices only when addressed to ordinary mountains. But when the *feng* sacrifice is performed on the Eastern Peak, it manifests the divinity of the reigning monarch.

"Out of all sixty-two kings who performed it, only the Yellow Emperor was able to carry out all the rites perfectly. The sacrifice on T'ai Shan ratifies the gaining of divine authority. The Yellow Emperor would go up into the eight holy mountains to meet the gods and spirits. After conquering all the peoples in the world, he began studying the arts of immortality. Skeptics were chopped to pieces and pickled in brine.

"Meditating for three years, he entered into communion with the forces that are invisible. He forged himself a three-legged cauldron and discovered the philosopher's stone. A dragon came down from heaven and carried him off, along with his seventy-two ministers. Your merit, August Emperor, is no less than the Yellow Emperor's. You must perform the *feng* and *shan* sacrifices in order to perfect your virtue. Sacrifice to Mount T'ai, and you will take your place among the immortals!"

The crowd of scholars heaved a sigh, waved their sleeves, and gazed at one another in disapproval. But when they saw the king's expression, no one dared protest. Confused and terrifying images were coming back to him, reawakening the old dread—that the round of the seasons, the alternation of day and night, the joys and sorrows of men—even of his poorest and lowliest subjects—would go on without him, as if he had never been. A slight tremor of the earth, the collapse of a mountain, and the world, after a faint quiver at its disappearance, would continue on its way like a cart that has dropped a bit of dung.

He who molded his people as he willed would be swallowed up in the great universal mold—to be ground up, kneaded, and shaped in accordance with a will that was blind, impartial.

To sit up on his mat and know, unseen, the slightest thoughts and deeds of all his subjects, merely by reading the reports of his informers; to be able to tell, without going out of doors, the exact positions of the sun and the moon in their cycle, merely by consulting the metal arrow on the water clock—wasn't that already a kind of divinity? But he shuddered at the thought of the black bag into which he would be put one day—and decided to attempt the sacrifice.

He asked the Scholars of Vast Learning to work out the order of the ceremony. The result was pandemonium. None of them could agree. The old sage who presented the Emperor with the petition when he came down from Mount Tzu had withdrawn to an inaccessible peak after uttering some cryptic phrases to the effect that Ordinance must go live as a hermit for three years on Mount T'ai. Ordinance wouldn't even consider that. What was the point of immortality without power? Someone would take the opportunity to murder him, a poor, defenseless mortal in a hut on the Eastern Peak!

Some of the scholars argued that, as with all other sacrifices to mountains, the offerings ought to be buried. Others maintained that the ritual was the same as the sacrifice to the sky, which was performed at the winter solstice in the south. The *chan* sacrifice was merely an oblation, to the earth and then to the sky. But some objected that first one had to perform the *feng*, the sacrifice to the sky, and only then salute the earth with the *chan*.

Prudent scholars advised offering a *feng* sacrifice first at the foot of the mountain, to test the gods' intentions. If the answer was favorable, a second offering could be made at the top. One sage thought he could remember that in the olden days the wagon wheels were wrapped in straw in order not to wound the sacred soil of the venerable peak. The ground was carefully swept beforehand with brooms made of rushes, and wands of peeled hemp were used to burn the sacrifice. The scholars agreed on only one point: that that part of the ceremony was secret.

The Emperor dismissed them all and decided for himself. As some of the soothsayers had advised, he would perform two *feng* sacrifices. One would be at the foot of the mountain, in the presence of all the dignitaries. There would be torches, so many that their light would make the sun seem pale. This first ceremony would confirm his legitimacy. The second would take place at the top of the mountain, and there he would enter into mystic communion with the transcendental forces. This time, no one else would be present.

They set out. On reaching the foot of the mountain, the Emperor took a ritual bath and was fumed with aromatic herbs, then went into retreat for three days in a humble hermitage. Meanwhile, a circular mound was built out of five different colors of earth, a color for each of the five directions. The raised path leading to it was covered with three layers of grass matting, a tribute which the Huai barbarians had paid the ancient kings. The victims, chosen because they were fat and without blemish, were shot with arrows and roasted over fire. The meat was portioned out to be eaten; there was no dried meat or jujubes, as in the great royal sacrifices.

When the first ceremony was over, Ordinance retired to his hut. But he could not sleep. His heart thumped madly in his chest, and shudders shook his body. In the morning, after what seemed an endless night, he began to climb the southern side of the mountain.

He wore a plain robe of white silk, and his black cap of closely woven silk shone like lacquer. The sun had only just risen, and the spring air was still quite chilly. The slanting yellow rays revealed a landscape wet with dew, and the rocky slopes loomed gray behind rainbow-tinted clouds. Tall pines cast dark shadows over the opalescent veins in the mountainside. Specks of mica and yellow orpiment made bright spangles on the granite in the morning light.

The Emperor did not follow the road that he had had hollowed out of the side of the mountain for the wagons, but took a little path that wound upward through the forest. He felt lighthearted now, purified by the beauty of the day. He walked quickly, the soft leather of his boots swishing against the stiff material of his robe. He took care not to crush the moss and grass growing between the stones: the whole mountain was holy—grass, flowers, trees, soil, and rocks.

He was now engulfed by a strange silence, as if the mountain were sealing up the trees behind him as he went along. The stillness of nature was intensified by the flutter of a bird's wing, the cry of a pheasant, the snap of a branch. Ordinance suddenly had a feeling of immense solitude.

Even when alone in his apartments, he could sense the presence of the guards outside the painted doors of the antechamber and knew that he was surrounded by thousands of men on the alert against any attack. He was protected, also, by a series of high-walled courtyards.

Now, for the first time in his life, he was entirely on his own. What if someone took the opportunity to make an attempt on his life? Perhaps there were brigands or rebels lurking in the thickets, ready to slay him with a crossbow or a dagger in the throat? He shuddered and instinctively grasped the hilt of his long sword. Then he tried to be sensible. The mountain had been searched thoroughly by the minister of the interior's security officers. All the approaches were guarded, and his route had been kept secret. Apart from a few trustworthy men in his own entourage, no one knew about the rite he was about to perform. Besides, his person inspired too much awe for anyone to dare raise a sacrilegious hand against him! Who would be so mad as to risk the wrath of a son of heaven?

But, despite all his efforts at self-control, he found himself walking faster and faster. Finally he ran, pursued by the harsh cries of wild animals. The howling of monkeys echoed the dread in his own heart. He clutched at his magic mirror carved with protective symbols, to ward off the demons of fear troubling his mind. But in the mirror he saw a little hopping monkey with long black whiskers and a human face. Then the mirror reflected only the green grass.

Sweat streamed down his face. He fought for breath; he had pains in his legs. He was not accustomed to exerting himself like this. His foot became tangled in the strings of his sash and he tripped, grazing his hand on the rough bark of a tree. He felt like kicking the tree but restrained himself. One could not strike the flora of a holy mountain and hope to get away with it. This was all part of the test. He forced himself to be calmer, to breathe and walk more slowly.

How beautiful and terrible the mountain was! The veins in the rocks showed gleaming black facets, and streams dropped from the cliffs like threads of silver. You could hear the gurgle of brooks, the sound of water shifting dark-blue pebbles speckled with gray, like children's marbles made of agate. Clear rivulets whispered along like smooth-skinned snakes between the black shale cliffs; their granules of quartz flashed blue and purple.

He climbed higher, enjoying the infinite variety of greens. The peaks were almost blue, with the gray glint of kingfisher feathers. The dark green of the forest was dotted with crimson clumps of red myrtle and the white sprays of magnolias. Everything seemed to have been planted by a divine gardener. Tall pine trunks soared up purple and black. The mountain pear stretched its slender branches toward the sky; the downy-leafed plum and the flowering cherry threw patches of mauve on the pale-green background of the catalpas.

Ordinance lost all sense of time. Being on the mountain lifted his spirits. Although he climbed higher, the summit did not seem any nearer. He walked between tall cliffs rent by chasms, their walls covered with strange marks that resembled bands of lightning, clouds on sacred urns, and the open jaws of wild beasts of basalt grinning horribly. Occasional spots of cinnabar and pink jade glittered in the black rock like bloodshot eyes.

It seemed to Ordinance that the overhanging boulders might crush him. His heart began to thump again, and he could hardly breathe.

247

There was a sudden gust of wind, and it grew quite dark. He was enveloped in a dense cloud. The tortured pines seemed to be uttering warnings with their broken limbs. He was not on any path now, and his robe kept catching in the briars. He wandered in the thick mist, his head reeling, his heart scarcely beating. He had a presentiment that he would die here, struck down by the gods for trying to equal them.

No birds sang now, and in the silence the rain could be heard drumming on the leaves. The sound swelled into a roar as the rain became a deluge. The clouds dashed against one another in terrible tumult, as if they were furious dragons fighting. The downpour broke the young shoots, crushed the tender grasses, shattered the fragile petals of spring flowers. The air was cleft by a streak of mauve lightning; the swiftly rising wind shook the branches; the trees set up a mournful groan.

The Emperor ran as fast as his legs would carry him. The mirror dropped out of his sleeve and clattered down the slope. A root shot out a clawed hand and tripped him. He staggered to his feet, his clothes in tatters, the white silk of his tunic stained with earth and grass, his chin bleeding. His hand hurt. His jade ring had slipped off somewhere. Then there was another flash, followed by a clap of thunder. Ordinance lost consciousness. He lay on the ground, thinking that he was dead, and a river of mud swept down the steep slope and covered him with debris torn from the mountainside. He managed to summon the strength to drag himself to a tall pine. Flinging his arms around it, he sobbed, rubbed himself against its gnarled trunk, and begged the tree to save him.

He promised it kingdoms, fiefs, titles, and untold wealth if it would come to his aid, if it would spread its protecting shade over his head and preserve him from the anger of the elements. All around him, nature bent under the violence of the storm, shuddering in horrible spasms. Boulders crashed; muddy cataracts broke against shining fangs of rock. Bottomless gulfs opened to swallow murky torrents.

He felt helpless, as helpless as when he was a little boy in the palace of the prince of P'ing Yüan in Han Tan. Fragments from his childhood sped past like flying clouds—the humiliations and the night terrors he had suffered after fleeing his father's house, the fear of death, the hostility of everyone around him. He clung tightly to the trunk, his only friend. A tree! A tree was all he had in the world to defend him! He saw Ching K'o again, the unspeakable Ching K'o, hunting him down, his wolf eyes shining with hate. Why should men hate him, the great, magnanimous king? Why were gods and humans so malicious? He sobbed. Everything seemed to whirl around and around.

———

While his master climbed Mount T'ai to perform mysterious rites, Li Ssu at last had a few hours free in which to write down the new rules on slaves' and convicts' rations, which were to be attached to the instructions about granaries.

All slaves, male and female, are to be fed as follows: two *shih* of grain per month for men, one and a half *shih* for women.

Those not performing a particular task lose their right to a share. Children doing forced labor will get a *shih* and a half per month. Small slaves and girls employed in pounding will get a *shih* and two thirds of a bushel per month. If they are unable to carry out all the work assigned to them, their share falls to one *shih*.

Male convicts and slaves under four feet, six inches, and female slaves and huskers under four feet, two inches, belong to the category of "small slaves."

Anyone over three feet, six inches is hereby declared fit for forced labor.

Small slaves, male and female, are registered as adults in the eighth month of the year. If their growth causes them to be moved into another category, they will receive a ration corresponding to their new status in the tenth month.

Convicts who dig or ram earth, or perform similar tasks, shall be given the following daily rations: half a bushel of grain in the morning and a third of a bushel at night.

Those employed in supervisory or other light work are to be given one-quarter of a bushel per meal.

The sick are to be fed according to their particular case and at the discretion of those responsible.

Rammers, women employed in pounding or sorting, warders, and anyone else doing relatively demanding work will receive one-third of a bushel per meal.

Any official taking it upon himself to give extra rations to slaves or convicts doing light work will be punished with the utmost severity.

Diggers and female pounders serving a sentence of less than a month are to be docked one-tenth of the normal ration.

Slaves over sixty years old are to be fed as if they were doing demanding work.

And so on.

Li Ssu laid down his brush with satisfaction. He had finished an important piece of work.

————

When the Emperor, still clinging to the tree, opened his eyes, there were ants running across his numbed limbs. The storm had passed. Mists smelling of fresh grass and wild mint swirled up from the damp earth and wreathed the treetops with a bluish halo. The sun shone high in the pale-blue sky, and the leaves, washed by the storm, had the rich luster of jade. Soaked, Ordinance shivered with cold. After conferring on the tree the title of "marquis," he resumed his journey. All his fears had disappeared with the tempest, and he felt cleansed like the rest of nature. Rays of gold played in the branches. The birds twittered, the monkeys whooped merrily.

He was saved. The Great Emperor, calm and serene, had come through his ordeal without weakening. Heaven had given him its backing and he would soon accede to immortality. He walked slowly and with dignity to the summit. The area where the sacrifice was to take place had been prepared according to his instructions. Men were waiting with the victims to be offered up. It was so high here, you felt you could reach out and touch the sky. The Emperor, muddy but imperious, gestured to the escort to withdraw.

He then carried out a series of complex, mysterious rites.

He ate and spent the night in a specially constructed pavilion. Though tired after his long walk, he did not sleep well. He dreamt that he was fighting a hairy one-legged giant with pointed teeth. He uprooted a huge pine tree and dealt the giant a terrific blow. The monster's brain burst, covering him with blood. He drew back in horror, but then saw that the blood had turned into a wonderful salve redolent of cinnamon. Birds with human heads bore him on their wings to a palace with floors of jade and gates of solid gold. The pillars had capitals like daffodils with petals of mother-of-pearl, and supported beams of rare wood carved with tigers and dragons intertwined. A crowd of dignitaries bowed as he passed, and he could see from their feather robes that they were immortals.

He went up a flight of ten steps of marquetry inlaid with all the jewels in creation and sat on a mat woven from kingfisher feathers, gold thread, and soft reeds. He realized that the monster's blood was cinnabar, and that he had become king of heaven and earth and the ten thousand beings.

Next morning he went down the mountain on its northern side, calm, majestic, and sure of himself. He proceeded to Mount Liang Fu, a small, rounded hill, and there performed the *shan* sacrifice in accordance with the rites which he himself had chosen. Then, on the Eastern Peak, he raised a stone bearing an inscription, to celebrate his achievements and perpetuate his name:

The Great Emperor, when he ascended the throne,
Promulgated laws and rules
To make his subjects docile and obedient.
In the twenty-sixth year of his reign
All the people in the world came to do him homage.
He went into barbarous countries
To inspect his peoples and climb Mount T'ai.
He embraced the eastern borders of his kingdom,
And prompted his ministers
To do diligently and well
What was needful.
Luminous is his goodness, inexhaustible his justice.
Dispensing happiness and prosperity,
And protecting his posterity,
His dynasty will last forever!
The wise precepts of the August Emperor
Will be handed down to future generations.
His teaching will never be forgotten.
Follow the instructions he bequeaths to you,
Pass on his heritage, obey his prohibitions!

The Scholars of Vast Learning, vexed at not having been able to take part in organizing the liturgy, made fun of the Emperor and told everyone that he had failed miserably: heaven had disavowed him, raising a terrible storm.

Li Ssu got wind of this and had the slanderers secretly executed.

To impress the people and spread fear in that rebellious region, he had carved in the rock gigantic footprints, four feet long and two feet wide, and let it be known that these had been made by the August Emperor's shoes. In the temple built on the summit of the Eastern Peak he placed a set of *liu po* pieces made of cypress wood. The long ones measured five feet and the pawns were eight inches in diameter. The rumor was started that the Emperor, after ascending the sacred mountain, had played there with the gods.

CHAPTER III

TRAVELS THROUGH
THE EMPIRE

The Emperor continued eastward and reached the coast of Shan Tung, where he climbed Mount Ch'en, on the tip of the peninsula, in order to survey the eastern limits of his Empire. But he was disappointed, because the landscape was shrouded in mist. So he came down from the mountain and went on along the coast. He stopped and beheld the vast sea before him, thinking how fine it was to rule by virtue of water, and murmured verses to himself from the *Book of the Way and of Virtue* as he watched the waves breaking on the shore.

> *The spirit of the vale never dies;*
> *It is the mysterious feminine,*
> *The gateway to the dark female,*
> *Root of earth and heaven.*

Then, falling silent before the boundless horizons that merged into the gray-tinged sky, he went on:

> Back and forth like the sea
> I come, I go ceaselessly.
> Everyone has something to do.
> But I alone forbear,
> Stubborn and surly.
> Why so unlike everyone?
> I still am not weaned from my mother.
>
> Learn the masculine,
> Retain the feminine.
> Make yourself the vale of the world,
> Keep to immutable virtue,
> Go back to being a child.
> Nothing is weaker than water,
> Nothing stronger in undermining.

Was not the model he should follow here in front of him—limitless, changing, and yet unchangeable; low and yet infinitely venerable; soft and malleable and yet unyielding; cloudy and confused like the world in its earliest days? The origin of all things?

He remained for days gazing at the surface of the water, now dark, now pale green tinged with lilac. Sometimes it was blue, reflecting the utmost abyss; sometimes streaked with crimson by the rays of the rising sun. He listened to the watery hills breaking in fringes of spray upon the rocks; was lulled by the motions of the tides beneath the starry sky—slow, strong, and deep, like a pulse from the very entrails of the world. It was the heartbeat of the universe. Here was the equivalent of his own power, dark, mysterious, and unbounded.

While the Emperor leaned over the coral balustrade of a palace by the sea, gazing pensively and in wonder at the waves as they moved and yet did not move under the cerulean heaven, Li Ssu toiled away at edicts and regulations. He was glad that the mother and father of the people had momentarily turned aside from the business of the Empire. It didn't seem right to him that a son of heaven should himself keep watch over everything that went on in the most remote government offices. It was fitting, of course, for a monarch to have his ministers spied upon. To make sure that they did not conspire against him, he needed to know everything there was to know about his executives, the very arms and legs of his rule. But it was unseemly for a great prince to interest himself personally in the matters of humble farmers. What were civil servants and a centralized administration for, if not to spare the master of men unnecessary exertion?

On the advice of the scholars of the East, the August Emperor offered up sacrifices to the eight gods of the peninsula in the land of Ch'i, the name of which means "navel." The inhabitants of Ch'i prided themselves on being the navel of the world, and Navel of the Sky was the name of the lake in the center of Shan Tun. Its waters had the deep, dark look of a divine eye, and on its dark shores the Emperor offered up sacrifices to the master of the sky. Then he returned to the foot of Mount T'ai and worshipped the master of the earth.

He also went on a pilgrimage to the tomb of Ch'e yu, where, in a bleak landscape of stunted pines, he prayed to the master of war. He offered sacrifices to the principle of yin on the Three Mountains, and to the principle of yang in Shih Fu. Likewise to the master of the moon and the master of the sun on Mount Ch'en, which is like the Great Bear, sticking its sinuous tongue into the sea and toward the sun in the extreme northwest of Ch'i. Then he turned south and offered sacrifices to the master of the four seasons in Lang Ya.

There the coast formed a natural balcony facing south over the sea. Enchanted by the beauty of the place, the Emperor decided to build a palace and a city there. He had a pavilion made, with galleries and a terrace, below which the town was to be constructed. When all the building was completed, by convicts, he had thirty thousand families transported to live there. They were exempted from forced labor for twelve years by way of compensation.

On the huge terrace, with its balustrade of green-and-white marble, he raised a tall stele celebrating his own virtues.

> In the twenty-sixth year of the Great Emperor
> A bright new era began.
> The laws were centralized,
> Weights and measures standardized.
> Everyone must observe the norm.
> Each has an occupation
> Matching his abilities.
> All men under the sun
> Work with one heart.
> Morals, also, were standardized,
> And the characters used in writing.
> In every corner of the land
> Visited by the heavenly bodies.
> In every busy province,
> Men live happily
> And die in their beds.
> The virtues of the August Emperor
> Strengthen the bounds of the universe,
> Exterminate rebellion,
> Put down sedition.
> Everything obeys the cycle of the seasons.
> He promises all a glowing future.
> Plants and animals prosper,
> And weapons are silent.
> Neighbors keep watch on one another,
> Relatives inform on relatives,
> And thieves lie low!
> Everywhere, shouts of joy and delight.

Everyone follows the law.
In all the eight points of the rose of the winds
There is no land
That does not belong to the Great Emperor.
In the West his empire includes the quicksands,
In the South it is bounded by the Pei Hu Mountains,
In the East it is lapped by the eastern sea,
In the North it borders on Ta Hsia.
Wherever man has set foot,
The soil bears the Great Emperor's subjects.
His glory eclipses that of the Five Emperors.
His benevolence extends even to oxen—
Everything knows his kindness.
The August Emperor has unified the world.
He has divided it into provinces and prefectures
In which harmony and peace reign.
His line shines with a dazzling brightness.
He is one with reason.
He follows the path of virtue.
His glory will be immortal!

All the ministers, seeking to add still further to the greatness of the Great Emperor, as a mark of their admiration and enthusiasm for both his deeds and his person, sent a petition requesting that their praises be engraved on the stele, "that their attitude might serve as a model and guide to the masses."

The Emperor ordered the sages of Ch'i to show him the direction in which lay the three isles of immortality. The sages pointed to a misty speck on the horizon. For a moment he thought of setting sail for it, but was afraid to trust his august person to the hazards of the waves. He had time, yet.

The Emperor continued his journey through ancient P'eng Ch'eng, watered by the river Ssu. He was told that in the forty-second year of the reign of King Hsien, as the dynasty was declining, the cauldron of the Chou flew out of the palace and plunged into the river. And recently something shiny and green had been glimpsed a few leagues downstream from the city. Ordinance was delighted; yet another auspicious sign! Heaven was bestowing upon him the talismans of the dead dynasty! He had soundings taken. A thousand convicts from south of the Blue River, tattooed with stripes, tortoises, and dragons, were set to work locating the treasure. A wooden bridge was constructed to support a crane and winch, then divers attached a bronze cable to the ring of the cauldron.

The Emperor watched and gave orders from the riverbank. Men tugged at the cable until it almost snapped, but to no avail. Another cable was added, and each was pulled by five hundred men and some powerful horses. Then something moved beneath the smooth surface of the water. With unbearable slowness it began to rise. The men streamed with sweat; a few of the horses fell. The *sseu ku* flogged the exhausted convicts. New shifts of men and horses were brought. Gradually, with a horrible stench, an enormous urn emerged, like a marine monster that had been decomposing for thousands of years. Suddenly there was a loud crack, and the bridge collapsed, carrying away with it men and beasts. Not one escaped alive.

Ordinance decided to send for Cheng Kuo to retrieve the cauldron. He prepared to raise an army of conscripts. The search began again. But the relic had been swallowed up by the waters of the Sseu.

The August Emperor spent a restless night, plagued by bad dreams. He dreamt that he was pulling up the Chou cauldron by means of a smooth, warm, flexible rope—which he suddenly realized was Lao Ai's penis. The cauldron emerged, and in it sat his mother. She beckoned invitingly to him, then vanished beneath the seething waters. Next the face of Piebald Cloud appeared and gave a silvery laugh. Ordinance felt foolishly moved. But the laugh ended in a death rattle, and the little girl's bloody head whirled around for a moment in the cauldron and then disappeared. The cauldron of the Chou fell back into muddy water, and the sticky organ of the false eunuch became a snake and grew wings. Clawed feet sprouted from its sides, and a dragon's jaws gaped wide to devour the Emperor. He shot an arrow into its eye, and a great flood of red splashed over earth and sky. In a dying spasm the dragon clawed open his enemy's breast, and the heart of the August Emperor flew out through the wound, bounced across the landscape, and plunged into the Ssu. Ordinance stood on the riverbank and called to it, in mourning clothes and with his hair loose, but his heart stayed hidden and refused to emerge from the murky waters.

He awoke breathless, covered with sweat, feeling that there was a lead weight on his chest. He had the auguries read, and was advised to sacrifice a bull to the god of the river.

This he did, and was about to resume his journey when he noticed a strange mist rising from the subprefecture of the river Ssu—orange-colored, swift, and volatile. His eagle eye recognized it as the mystic aura belonging to the founder of a dynasty. He decided to challenge it.

As he passed through the main town of the district on his way to the mist, he noticed two bold young men standing straight at the back of a bowing crowd—bowing out of either admiration or fear. Ordinance overheard the younger of the two speak to his companion.

"Is there anything more unbearable," he said, "than the presence of a great man?"

The other clapped a hand over his friend's mouth and hissed, "Idiot! Do you want us all slaughtered?"

Then, without the least sign from the Emperor, members of the neighborhood committee pointed the youths out to security men who mingled in the crowd, and the youths were surrounded, brought before the imperial procession, and sawed in half, with all their relatives. The August First Emperor chuckled with satisfaction. He was seeing Li Ssu's system of universal mutual surveillance at work, and it was extraordinarily efficient!

Meanwhile, the exhalation moved westward, and the imperial train swung around after it. When the Emperor and his retinue reached a small town in the northwest of the subprefecture, Ordinance began to have difficulty breathing, as if the air itself were offering resistance. Terrible effluvia rose from nearby. His enemy must be there. He scanned the crowd that bowed to him and encountered a hostile glance half hidden around a corner. He shuddered, recognizing the man who had appeared to him in a dream and whose face he had given to the twelve giants that guarded his palace. He signaled to his soldiers to seize him, but the man vanished. Houses were searched, people questioned, arrests made, but no one knew him.

The Emperor set up camp on high ground, hoping to locate the aura more precisely after dark. From his observation post he saw it hesitate, then disappear behind hills covered with heath and marshes. After having the hills surrounded and ordering the provincial troops to kill anyone they found there, he abandoned the search and continued on his journey.

When he reached the south bank of the Blue River, he was affected by strong emanations coming from eastern Wu. He summoned his geomancers, who predicted that in five hundred years an imperial cloud would arise in Wu. They also noted a great deal of energy in the configuration of the earth in the prefecture of Golden Hill. The August Emperor frowned. Was it possible that his own line would die out, that his descendants would not go on worshipping his shade until the end of time? He must repress the chthonic forces lurking in this wild and fertile earth. The prefecture was renamed Hill of Cows, and deep excavations were made in the Bell Mountains, which bordered it in the north, in order to destroy its underground contours. The district of Big River, where the mystic vapors had been seen, was crisscrossed with canals by a hundred thousand prisoners, and given the ignominious name of Convict Gang.

Somewhat reassured by these severe measures, the Emperor and his party embarked on Lake Tung T'ing in sandalwood boats filled with white-skinned singing girls and musicians. The rowers were men tattooed with multicolored dragons.

As they moved over the water, the Emperor admired the lush vegetation and the bright colors of the trees reflected in the quiet mirror of the lake. Rhinoceroses and buffalos disported themselves on its shores, and he heard the trumpeting of elephants tall as gray hills. Then the boats turned and followed the river Hsiang as far as a temple in the hills, at which point a violent storm came up, nearly wrecking the Emperor's boat and making him very seasick. He had to stay in bed several days to recover from the shock.

Once on dry land again, he called together the Scholars of Vast Learning.

"Who is the god of this river?" he thundered.

For once the sages were unanimous.

"We have heard," they said, "that the goddesses of the river Hsiang are the two daughters of Yao, wives to King Chün, whose tomb is not far from here. The *Book of Mountains and Seas* says quite specifically: 'The hills around Lake T'ung T'ing are the home of the Emperor's two daughters. There are storms whenever they go forth and frolic on the slopes.' On the promontory where the river flows into the lake is a cave that leads into the mountains of Wu. The spirits of the river Hsiang often use this passage to travel from one place to the other."

The Emperor paled. "How dare two unimportant spirits thwart the August Emperor's journey! The insolent creatures shall be punished as they deserve! It is not to be endured that the daughters of a bad king and the wives of an impious son should raise the waves against the holiest Emperor of all time!"

He harbored a secret grudge against Chün and Yao. Was this due to the fact that Li Ssu and Han Negation, had always quoted them as models of the justice and humanity which they themselves argued against? Or was Ordinance jealous of Chün and Yao for always being depicted as perfect? But perhaps, deeper down still, he was irked by the sentence in the *Book of Documents* that read: "Chün offered up sacrifices on Mount T'ai, paying no attention to the storm."

It may have seemed to him that Chün was praised at his, the Emperor's, expense.

Three thousand convicts were sent to cut down all the trees on the mountain. Then the mountain was painted red as a mark of infamy. All its temples were destroyed, and sacrifices to the goddesses of the Hsiang forbidden. Anyone found worshipping them was put to death.

The Emperor returned to Ch'in through the Wu Pass, in time to proclaim the new-year edicts in the capital, Double Light, and to receive the officials from the provinces.

There was much rejoicing—banquets and dances, music and acrobatics. Jugglers from Bactria kept more than a hundred black and white balls in the air with their hands and feet. Two tightrope walkers approached and retreated from each other, swaying and tilting their shoulders, on a thin silk cord more than twenty feet above the ground. Two children did somersaults and pirouettes while juggling lighted torches on a beam supported on swords. A magician from the Far West made an elephant disappear, turned a fierce tiger into a tabby cat, and divided himself into pieces and put himself together again. A hairy, half-naked giant balanced on his forehead a pole with a bunch of children perched on it.

There were trained animals, and wrestlers male and female. All the tumblers, dancers, and acrobats in the world were there. The audience was amazed by the variety of the entertainments and the skill of performers from countries whose names they had never even heard of. The celebration concluded with a procession of dragons and fishes dancing and changing shape, all in a long scintillating caterpillar that wound its fantastic way through the fumes of wine and the heavy scent of myrtle.

The dignitaries, tipsy, followed the dragon, wishing their beloved sovereign long life and infinite happiness. This was the custom in the Southwest, to avert calamity in the new year.

As soon as the festivities were over, Ordinance resumed his travels through the Empire, making for the East. Once across the mountains, he went along the Yellow River toward the eastern peninsula. The long black procession curved like a somber snake across a marshy plain filled with pools and sandbars.

Two men stood waiting behind a tree. One, a dark-skinned giant seven feet tall, had the coarse, broad face typical of the natives of Pa. He held in his hand a metal mace. The other, white-skinned and elegant, was named Shang Liang, and his family had served Han and provided it with prime ministers for generations. When Han was annexed and its prince hauled away into captivity, Shang Liang took this barbarous treatment as a personal insult and swore to have his revenge on Ch'in, even if it cost him his life. He sold the hundreds of slaves his family owned, neglected his brother's tombs, and reduced his style of living in order to raise enough money to maintain an army of mercenaries.

He meant to follow in the footsteps of Ching K'o, but the constant searches and close surveillance to which the families of the nobility were subjected forced him to give up this idea. He dismissed his militia and kept only one man, Hu Fu, the giant now leaning against the tree and nonchalantly toying with the metal club. They had met when, as a student of the rites in Cheng, Shang Liang led a delegation to the barbarians on the coast.

Shang Liang heard that the king was on an expedition to the East. The road to Shan Tung, after a bend at Yang Wu, turned north across a desolate plain broken only by swamps and an occasional tree. It was the least suitable place imaginable for an ambush. That was why Shang Liang chose it: he hoped the guards would relax their vigilance there.

The long procession advanced, shining bright as lacquer under a sweltering sun. One imposing coach, drawn by twelve black horses, was surrounded by guards with banners depicting water dragons and followed by a large detachment of crack palace cavalry. Then came other chariots, sumptuously decorated with patterns in red and black. The main chariot had to be the Emperor's.

Hu Fu whirled his mace over his head and hurled it at the

imperial coach. Whistling through the air, it hit its target. The fretted wooden windows were smashed; there was a thud as of flesh being struck, a piercing scream, and a spurt of blood that splashed the guards on either side of the vehicle. The horses reared, and the chariot swerved into a ditch.

The two men, with a wild whoop of satisfaction, leaped on their horses and vanished into the landscape. Rapid orders were issued and horsemen swift as thunderbolts rode forth from the imperial procession and cordoned off the plain. But the fugitives were gone.

Ordinance, whose carriage was actually creaking along in the middle of the column, felt a mixture of fury and jubilation. The idiots! Did they think the August Emperor would risk his life by making his own vehicle so obvious? Since the two assassination attempts, he had taken care to have decoys included in all his processions. The passengers in the large black coach had been only eunuchs.

The whole region was searched with a fine-tooth comb; the villagers were interrogated. But in vain. The army scoured the countryside over a radius of fifty leagues; then the search was extended to the whole Empire. Thousands of vagabonds, thieves, smugglers, anchorites, and beggars were transported in order to intimidate the people and make them hate the rebels.

Then the August Emperor went on with his journey. When he reached Shan Tung, he climbed Mount Shih Fu and had a stele erected to proclaim his glory.

> *In the twenty-ninth year of his reign,*
> *In the middle of spring,*
> *Emanations of the budding yang*
> *Spread their soothing scent,*
> *And the August Emperor,*
> *Reaching the coast,*
> *climbed the great Mount Shih Fu.*
> *His brightness lit up the ocean.*
> *Gazing at the sea below,*

His ministers remembered his successes
And sang of his past exploits.
His military prowess
Made the whole world tremble.
Into steaming cauldrons he threw
Noisome insects and stinking beasts.
He came to the rescue of the oppressed,
Restoring order and security.
Sublime is the Emperor's virtue!
His vigilance never fails!
Ears and eyes ever alert,
He introduced an age of peace.
He strengthened government
With just institutions,
Fixed regulations, unified measures,
And added to the weight of the law.
He shed light on the Way.
His teaching spreads through provinces
Formerly ruled by unworthy princes.
The torch of his benevolence
Steadfastly illuminates the world.
Each has his place in the hierarchy.
People do as they ought,
Accurately and completely.
Everything is as it should be.
From north to south, east to west,
He offers a constant example.
How great he is!
In every land his wise teaching
Is obeyed with joy!

And all his dignitaries, unanimously proclaiming that there has
never been a glory to match the glory of the First August Emperor,
insisted that these praises be set down in stone!

Having left this token of his visit and his greatness at the eastern extremity of his Empire, he set out for Lang Ya, where he spent several months gazing in admiration at the sea from the terraces and pavilions built by the convicts. Then business summoned him back to the capital, and he left that delightful spot, where the soft sea breeze had caressed his sad and heavy heart.

The black column retraced its steps through the mountains back to Double Light.

CHAPTER IV

THE IMMORTALS

By the orange-yellow light of a whale-oil lamp in the shape of a sea serpent belching flames, the August Emperor was enjoying the works of his favorite author. As he read, he murmured the great philosopher Negation's sibylline yet lucid verses aloud.

> *Heaven has its destiny,*
> *The body has its woes.*
> *Savory smells and well-cooked meats,*
> *Thick wine and crisp viands*
> *Please the palate but ruin the health.*
> *Beautiful girls with white teeth*
> *Rejoice the sense but destroy the essence.*
> *Never reveal your ever-inactive powers.*

Whatever happens in the world,
The main thing is to keep to the center.
A wise man sees what is important.
Calm and alert, he waits to be served.
Every being in the universe
Reveals its light to his darkness.
Officials of the left, officials of the right,
To your posts!
He opens his door and stands before you.
He neither changes nor alters
While moving with the two ceaselessly.
Follow the reason of things.
Every object is in its proper place.
Everything is where it ought to be.

Then he began to think about the old commentary in the *Book of the Way and of Virtue*:

Virtue is the great workman,
Principle the entrepreneur.
The master of the world is the sound,
The Empire the echo.
The master of the world is the form,
Man and beast the reflection.

As always when he couldn't sleep at night, Ordinance was tortured by the thought of eternity. The sacrifice on Mount T'ai had not soothed his fears. He was more afraid than ever to shut his eyes, for fear of never being able to open them again. As usual, he had several boxes of documents brought up, to distract himself from his anxiety.

When the water clock marked the fifth part of the night and he had finished the work he had set himself, he continued to sit, gazing into the incense burner. Amid the swirls of smoke, against a background of gilded bronze mountains, lost paradises surrounded by a mystic circle, he wondered if the world would go on existing after his death. Since ruling over an empire encompassing everything under the sun was a work of continual creation, he was an incarnation of the principle of the universe, a cause and an origin at once immanent and transcendent of all things. He told himself this many times, but still was afraid of dying. But was not sleep a foretaste, an antechamber, of death?

It made him relax his vigilance. When his eyelids lowered their curtain of yellow flesh over his piercing eyes, things happened independently of him, people went on acting without his knowledge. Yet his sleep was troubled by violent dreams, dreams full of pursuits and bloody fights with faceless monsters or gods in the shape of birds. He often seemed to be submerged in a sticky liquid. He would be seized with palpitations; his heart would seem to stop; he couldn't breathe; there would be a buzzing in his ears. Was it possible that he who ruled over the largest Empire in the memory of man, who had laid down the cruelest and most implacable laws in the world, who was the head of a state in which everyone occupied a position in accordance with his merits—was it possible that such a one could suffer such sleepless nights and troubled dreams?

It was true that he would hand down a name to posterity, that he would live forever. His powerful and hungry shades would haunt the earth for a long time before melting into the anonymity of the souls of humanity itself. Who could tell, even, if his *hun*s and his *p'o*s would ever really dissolve, glutted as they would be with the sacrifices of an empire whose confines were those of heaven and earth? But, with these attempts to reassure himself, he had to admit that an immortality which depended on the charity of his descendants was somewhat degrading for a prince who had seized the entire world in his mighty grip.

In the quiet of the meditation room he thought these gloomy thoughts. Staring absently into the clouds of yellow smoke, his eyes began to notice the twisted shapes and precipitous gorges depicted on the black-and-gold walls. Panthers, deer, and gods with bulging skulls lurked on the side of the mountain, at the base of which was a round pool where lotuses displayed their silver petals and pistils of jade.

He had long wondered about the isles of immortality and whether they really existed. He possessed many representations of them and they were mentioned in the ancient books. Nor had he forgotten his encounter with the sage on the terrace at Lang Ya, who pointed to the gray line of the horizon and said, "Yonder lie the isles of immortality. They are called P'eng Lai, Fang Shang, and Ying Chou, and on their grassy slopes grows the plant of immortality."

Questioning other sages on the matter, he had been told that the islands of the immortals were in the middle of the Po Hai Sea, several thousand leagues from the coast. Whenever a ship attempted to land there, it was driven back by a contrary wind or current. The harder one tried to approach, the farther away one was swept. But in the most ancient times a few men with pure hearts had seen emerald-green meadows where pure-white animals and birds frolicked with silver-haired men having the faces of young virgins. In the distance one could make out palace gates of solid gold set off with jade and emeralds.

Some said that from a distance the islands looked like a white cloud on the horizon. As one drew nearer, they turned into an inverted cone, like the clear reflection of a mountain in the deep, smooth mirror of a lake.

And so Ordinance's days and nights went by, divided between the delights of power and the fear of death. In the thirty-first year of his reign, he received a report from the prefect of Yüan Hu. That region had for some time been ravaged by a plague. Corpses lay scattered all over the countryside. But recently white crows had been laying strange plants on the faces of the dead, and the dead were revived.

The August Emperor sent for specimens of the herb in question and had it examined by his soothsayers. None of them recognized it. They advised him to consult the master of the Valley of Demons. This anchorite was pleased to reply that the plant was the herb of immortality, which grew on the Original Continent in fields of emerald. A single stem was enough to resuscitate a thousand dead men. Ground up, sifted, distilled, and made into a pill, it conferred eternal life.

The Original Continent was one of the mystical names of P'eng Lai.

The Emperor was enchanted, and a certain Master Shang, catering to his passion for longevity, wrote him out a passage from the *Chuang Tzu* on the isles of immortality.

At court and among the Emperor's intimates, the only topics now were alchemy and the elixir of life. He set sail for the islands during one of his journeys along the East Coast, but he was subject to seasickness. Vomiting much and thinking that his last hour had come, he turned back to the mainland. Then a seer called Hsü the Blessed offered to go there for him.

The Emperor watched anxiously as the heavy barks disappeared into the mist one quiet summer evening.

Several months went by, and there was no news of Hsü. The Emperor had a worrying dream. He was climbing the Tsung Nan Mountains, a small range to the north of the capital, to honor the temple dedicated to Lao Tzu, and offered up the following prayer:

> *The Great Tao includes all.*
> *It bestows immortality.*
> *Lao Tzu departed to the west,*
> *The Tao knows when he will return.*
> *Master, I have so many things to ask you;*
> *I seek P'eng Lai, but cannot find it.*

When he set down his offerings and saluted the egg-shaped stone that represented the immortal, the latter appeared in human form in a blaze of white light, holding a pearl between thumb and forefinger.

He nodded, laughed softly without speaking, and drew a book and some talismans from his sleeve. The talismans turned into a pair of red sandals, then joined together like wings and flew into the blue sky, changed into magpies. The Emperor looked at the book. But as fast as his eyes ran over the mysterious signs written on the scroll, they disappeared; soon he was left holding a blank piece of silk. The sage gave a fierce, sneering laugh and rubbed his face with his right hand. The face immediately became as smooth as an egg, without eyes, nose, or mouth, and the sage began to declaim in a grotesque nasal voice:

> Beings are born of the moving principle
> Though it is not their creator.
> It is the cosmic egg
> That let a mystic fart.
> The world was born of indigestion.

Then Lao Tzu disintegrated into an evil-smelling mist, and the Great Emperor found himself immersed and gradually sinking in a thick yellowish substance that reeked of excrement.

He awoke covered with sweat and gasping for breath. His limbs were weak and his head ached. His dream seemed so ridiculous, he dared not speak of it to his soothsayers.

Shortly afterward, Hsü the Blessed appeared at the morning audience to give an account of his mission. He bowed twice to the August Emperor, mumbled a lot of excuses, and began.

"Prince," he said, "I was not able to bring back the drug of immortality. On my way I met a sea god, an enormous, scaly brown dragon who asked, 'Are you the messenger of the Western Emperor?'

" 'I am,' I said, bowing.

" 'Why are you here on the eastern sea?'

" 'I look for the herb that prolongs life.'

" 'Your Emperor's offerings are not enough,' the sea god said politely. 'You will be allowed to see the herb of immortality but not to pick it.'

"We continued our voyage, cleaving the green waves in the direction of the rising sun. After a month at sea we reached P'eng Lai. I could see the gates of the palace of the immortals, woven entirely of agaric. A messenger appeared, with a face of bronze and the body of a dragon, and giving off a radiance that lit up the sky. I bowed twice and asked humbly, 'What might the prince of the West send that would please you?' He answered: 'Send us young pages and virgins, and many workmen. If your master agrees to that, he will find what he seeks.' "

So that was the meaning of his dream, thought Ordinance. He had not yet attained the way, but heaven was on his side. He sent three thousand boys and girls from his palace to sail with Hsü to the islands of P'eng Lai and Ying Chou. He was careful to send plenty of food and wine also, together with valuable trinkets and skilled craftsmen.

A year went by, and Hsü did not return. Then the Emperor's spies reported that children were singing a curious song in the streets of Double Light.

> Clever Mao has become immortal.
> He went to heaven on the back of a swallow,
> Came down again to have some fun,
> And went back up again.
> If the August Emperor would learn from him,
> Let him call the first month
> Peaceful Perfection.

Ordinance had inquiries made, and his advisers studied reports from the provinces about certain strange phenomena. In the ninth moon of the thirty-first year of his reign, the peasants of K'uei Chi told local officials that a man known as Master Mao had found the elixir of life and been borne up to heaven by a dragon. That was a good sign. The Emperor named the first month of the year Peaceful Perfection. But still Hsü the Blessed did not come back.

The Emperor suddenly decided to go to the coast himself and build a bridge to where the sun rises. In this way, he thought, he would be able to reach the isles of the immortals and meet the gods and spirits. Cheng Kuo was put in charge of the project. But, taking soundings of the sea, he declared the task impossible. When the Emperor insisted, however, he gave in. Twenty thousand conscripts were raised, and thirty thousand convicts. Huge stone pillars stood above the waves. But as the water got deeper, the work progressed more slowly. Eventually a stone platform reached out a few leagues into the sea. Then a terrible storm blew up and swept it all away, drowning seven thousand men.

That night the Emperor dreamt that a spirit that could move mountains offered him his services. The black-faced spirit whipped the cliffs until they streamed with blood and plunged into the sea with a sound of thunder. The Emperor said that he wished to meet this spirit on the stone bridge that now stretched over the waves. The spirit agreed, on the condition that no one make any picture or other representation of its appearance, of which it was ashamed.

Ordinance advanced over the bridge, his face stung by the sea air, accompanied by an escort of dignitaries all in black. The sky was low and threatening, and there was a dark and heavy swell. When they reached the end of the causeway and met the god, a mischievous young page drew a picture of it on his hand. The spirit noticed.

"You have broken your promise!" it shrieked. "Go back before it is too late!"

Ordinance turned and fled like lightning. The sea roared, the waves hurled themselves on the bridge, stones flew in all directions. He reached dry land just as the bridge was engulfed. Through the howling storm he could hear the cries of his entourage as they were crushed among the rocks.

He told this dream to his soothsayers, and they advised him to make expiatory sacrifices to the gods of the sea and of the Yung Ch'eng Mountains.

Li Ssu said thoughtfully: "The red rocks advancing leagues into the sea near Yung Ch'eng . . . One could make a good legend out of that. I'll have the officials in charge of propaganda spread it throughout the Empire."

Poets were paid to sing about how the red rocks of Yung Ch'eng, which advanced in a line toward the East, were the remains of a bridge built by a powerful spirit at the behest of the Great Emperor but unfortunately destroyed through an error on the part of one of his retinue.

Ordinance abandoned his idea of the bridge and made for the Bay of Shih Li. In Chieh Chu he met Master Lu, a magician from Yen, who said that he was looking for the immortals' Gate of the Grave and Obscure Speech. The Emperor gave him a job in the astrology department and, since Master Hsü had evidently failed in his mission, sent Lu off to to P'eng Lai, along with Masters Han Chung, Hou, and Shih.

At the gates of the city, Ordinance erected a stele commemorating his exploits:

> The August Emperor raised an army,
> Punished the troublemakers, put down sedition.
> His military skill wiped out the lustful vipers.
> His good people rejoiced in his desire for peace.
> Even horses and oxen were objects of his care,
> And the earth brought forth fruits at his hands.
> The face of the earth was changed by his uprightness.
> The people are no longer oppressed by forced labor.
> In his wise rule dissension is stilled.
> Men dig, women have only to weave.
> Everything is in its place.
> His goodness protects every living creature.

The peasant works his bit of land
And lives contentedly in his village.

Thus, with one voice did all his ministers praise him, begging that
this stone be set up to serve as an example forever.

Before returning to the capital, Ordinance went to the northwest borders of his realm. There, he breathed the keen air of the steppes and wondered at the tents and strange customs of the nomads. Meanwhile, Master Lu and the other sages were caught in a terrible storm in the Bay of Po Hai. Part of their fleet was lost, and they had to return to the shores of the Western Kingdom.

Often the August Emperor was visited in his sleep by fabulous characters. Just before Master Lu's return he dreamt that a man from distant Yuan Kieu came to his court in a boat shaped like a snail. He woke with a start. He had fallen asleep by the incense burner and his sleeve had caught fire. What could all this mean? he wondered. The king of Yüan Chiu was not mentioned in any book. He no longer told the soothsayers about his dreams—all they ever did was suggest sacrifices to river and mountain gods, uninteresting divinities who had no influence over his fate.

After the failure of his expedition, Master Lu returned to court and related the strange adventures that had befallen him. At the height of the hurricane he encountered in the East—just as his ship was about to capsize—a god with a shining halo, who said, "Your master has not yet attained the ultimate perfection of virtue. He must build a terrace in order to please the gods."

Then the sea abated and Lu landed on an island. There he met the immortal An Ch'i-sheng, who gave him jujubes as large as gourds. Master Lu paused at this point in his narrative and produced some enormous dried dates, which the Emperor found delicious. Lu went on to tell how An Ch'i-cheng said: "Master Lu, you have the bones of immortality. Your name is in the celestial records. Your virtues would allow you to perform the great work of alchemy here and now, but heaven has entrusted you with the task of guiding the August Emperor along the right Way. His name, too, is written in the books of the immortals, and he can even become the supreme guide of the gods if he will only practice inner meditation." Here An Ch'i-sheng drew from his sleeve a scroll containing the secret recipe for long life and fecundity.

Ordinance installed Master Lu in a wing of his palace. Every day he was summoned to speak to the Emperor about the arts of longevity. Master Lu revealed the hidden meaning of the sacrifice on Mount T'ai.

Hitherto Ordinance had considered Negation's commentaries the subtlest exposition of the secret teachings of Lao Tzu, but now the sages maintained that this was merely the external, superficial aspect of the doctrine!

True, there was a passage in the *Book of the Yellow Emperor* where the monarch's counselor said: "Begin by governing your own body. When that is at peace, then you may rule your Empire. Let the internal and the external agree, and the government will be perfect." The Yellow Emperor renounced his throne to go into retreat on Mount Po Wang, where he meditated for three years and found himself.

Ordinance had taken this to be a parable: a monarch ought not to be transparent—he should remain obscure and hide his likes and dislikes from others. But the Taoist masters understood it differently: a ruler was not an emanation of the law, but the universal law itself. His own body was the norm. He escaped from the Tao by becoming the Tao personified. The *Book of the Way and of Virtue* assumed a new dimension. Ordinance dimly perceived a way in which he might free himself from death and the dread of it, from inevitability and the cycle of becoming.

The lines "The sage empties hearts and fills bellies, weakens wills and strengthens bones," which he had interpreted politically, was seen by the Taoist commentators as a prescription for long life, meaning: "The sage husbands his seed in order to keep his vigor intact and his bones strong. The seed is related to the kidneys, which govern the bones and strength. Lust harms the spermatic essence and causes loss of light. For essence engenders breath, breath spirit, and spirit light."

Though some points remained unclear, Ordinance now saw unsuspected, new horizons open up before him, new lands to conquer in himself. There was a third meaning in Lao Tzu even more mysterious than the one revealed by Negation. Negation had spoken only of the external, of the kingdom, but the masters of the Tao concentrated on what lay within. The external interpretation was the way of ministers. The internal interpretation was the way of kings. That was the one that he himself must follow. He must become one with the Great Tao, in which all beings were created. Great sovereigns became gods. The Yellow Emperor went up to heaven on a dragon. The perfection of the Empire was a visible, tangible sign of the monarch's inner fulfillment, the irrefutable proof of his divinity. He had overcome the external, and must therefore now be master of himself.

Ordinance fell asleep and dreamt that An Ch'i-sheng came to him and said, "A thousand years from now we shall meet again on P'eng Lai." He left him a pair of red sandals with wings, which he put on. They were magpies, and flew up with him into the air, giving him an enormous feeling of pleasure.

When he told his dream to Master Lu, Lu said: "An Ch'i-sheng asks you to seek the gods. You are making progress, but are not quite ready yet to receive the gods in yourself."

———

Li Ssu was uneasy. The Empire was growing too rich. Surpluses piled up in people's courtyards, and granaries groaned beneath the weight of cereals. Trade had revived in the provinces, and he noticed that ordinary folk were acquiring a taste for luxury and dissipation. Even the peasants in Ch'in had grown soft. The country was full of speechmakers and sophists. Discussions about the law were common in the market places. Despite constant vigilance and the terrible punishments inflicted for the slightest crime, there were still thieves.

One evening, when the Emperor, accompanied by four guards, went incognito on a tour of inspection of the streets of the capital, he was attacked by brigands at the banks of Orchid Lake. The assailants were repulsed, and paid for their audacity with their lives. Not one survived. The incident gave the Emperor a certain amount of pleasure. It had a tang of adventure. During the brief skirmish the agreeable sensation of hacking at his enemies' flesh had for the moment prevailed over every other feeling. But, once back in the palace, he gave vent to his fury. In spite of all his efforts, absolute order was still not established! Evildoers still committed crimes right outside the palace walls.

For ten days the police searched people's houses and checked their movements and identities. Weapons were confiscated, twenty thousand people were sent to prison, and fifteen thousand deported for various offenses. But Li Ssu knew that this was only a palliative.

The destruction of the Hsiang temple, the attempt to build a bridge across the sea, the construction of new roads and canals— these were not enough to employ the Empire's total manpower or harness all its resources. Li Ssu dreamt of a great military expedition involving millions of men, swallowing up the surpluses and galvanizing all spare energy. The present peace left Li Ssu in a quandary: he had lost one of the best means of manipulating the masses. He knew that there were vast areas in the West where the people's customs were quite different from those of the central provinces. But it would not be a good idea for the Emperor to attack them and try to extend his sway even farther toward the limits of the universe. Some of these people were little more than animals. There were also differences in language. How were such disparities to be reconciled? No, another approach had to be found, a plan whose requirements would correspond exactly to the excesses that needed to be used.

He sent for Master Lu.

"I am in charge of what is external," he said to the sage, after the other had bowed twice. "You are master of what is internal. The inner affects the outer. But the Emperor pays less and less attention to my advice: he prefers that of the gods. I wish that they would tell him to do a thing that would be of use to his country."

"I understand," said Master Lu, bowing low. "What do you have in mind?"

"What we need is an expedition against the barbarians," answered Li Ssu. "The Emperor takes pleasure in his possessions and looks toward the East. Have him look to the West instead. But by way of defense rather than attack."

A few days later, Master Lu sent the August Emperor a text composed of cryptic characters that Ordinance's quick eye soon recognized as a rebus. If one paired off the radicals, one obtained a series of ideograms that read: "The Hu will be the downfall of Ch'in."

Ordinance now feared that the Hu, the barbarians to the North, might disturb the peace that he had established in his provinces. He sent for his maps and was appalled by the huge void of the steppes. A little while later, the ingenious Li Ssu sent him a present: a silver coin stamped with the profile of a man with a hooked nose and the eyes of a bird of prey. Ordinance was informed that the medal came from the kingdom of Great Ch'in in the Far West, a country as vast as his own Empire, where wise rulers had established perfect order and inferiors obeyed their superiors like shadows or echoes. One could leave bars of gold by the roadside and no one would steal them. Men walked on the left side of the street and women on the right, like wild geese. He must be very sure of himself, this king with a head like a vulture's, to expose his face to his empire like that, letting it be handled by the meanest of his subjects! Ordinance found the profile irksome. He had the coin melted down, and the silver mixed with the metal in his own mint.

He decided to take precautions against the West, that counterpart of himself, and stem the furious tide of barbarians beating at the borders of his realm. He must protect established order against the reckless savagery of unruly and elusive outsiders. The Empire would have to shut itself in, build a wall against irrationality. This was the only answer.

An army of three hundred thousand men was raised to repel the Huns on the northern border. Ch'in seized all the territory south of the Yellow River and built a high wall on the land thus taken from the barbarians. Meng T'ien, who had led the military operations, was put in charge of the engineering works that followed. Yen, Chao, and Ch'in had already built fortifications in the North against nomad incursions, and these were strengthened and linked together. Then a million men were sent to lengthen this rampart. Long files of convicts in red caps could be seen swarming up the roads to the North and Northwest, and soon an earthen wall like a monstrous worm rose and fell across the landscape, its smooth brown back shimmering beneath the burning summer sun. The earth was banked up, pounded in time to the chant of the leaders, whose job it was to set the rhythm. The ground echoed dully, and animals fled in all directions, panic-stricken at the ceaseless vibration.

The men of the South died by the thousands from exhaustion and the drought of arid plains that were swept by winds now scorching, now freezing. The dead were buried in the Wall, their bones serving as struts, for lumber supplies were irregular. Sometimes a cloud of dust would rise in the still air: a barbarian attack. Hundreds of men fell to the nomads' treacherous arrows.

They learned to be constantly on the alert. Punitive expeditions were mounted, but the Huns just melted away into the tall grass of the plains or into the desert dunes. Nevertheless, whether in the sweltering summer heat or the icy cold of winter, the Wall continued to take shape, creeping like a brown dragon bristling with battlements and towers across valleys, hills, and plains, leaving its gigantic trail now on wooded, now on barren country, and hungrily devouring convicts, slaves, and conscripts, whose corpses were left to rot within it.

To cope with the resulting labor shortage, vagabonds, idlers, loafers, and peddlers were transported to the site. Cheng Kuo, whom Meng T'ien had taken on his staff, was in his glory. Meng T'ien himself and his brother Meng I tried to pursue the barbarians.

It was like fighting a shadow. But they acquired a taste for this warfare of ambush, incursion, surprise attack, looting, and lying in wait. They also came to love the Great Wall and the way it swallowed up both men and space. They struck deep into Kansu, as far as Lan Chou, and along the Yellow River eastward from Yü Shang, joining the wall to the Yin Mountains in the desolate steppes. They erected a triple barrier of fortifications on the upper bend of the Yellow River. Forts were spaced out along the Wall, and markets grew up around them, in which people of many and various origins rubbed shoulders. Caravans came and went, trading in exotic goods that included merchandise from the most distant lands of the West. Strange men with magic powers, deepset eyes, and hair the color of cinnabar or gold came to live in the new towns.

The great brown coil snaked farther and farther east, leaving behind garrisons, watchtowers, and beacons. Pei Chiu, and High Portico in the Ordos desert, were taken and turned into fortresses. Outposts successfully defended the colonies that grew up behind the Wall. The population was made up of convicts.

One day the Huns would trade with the settlers, selling them horses, bright-colored rugs, and blankets made from yak tails. The next day they would steal their cattle, burn their houses, kill the men, and rape the women. Meng T'ien decided to strike a decisive blow that would deal with them once and for all. He ordered taxes to be paid directly to the army commissariat, to speed up the distribution of pay and rations. He took great pains to see that the troops were comfortable and well fed. His men were taught to fight like the barbarians, shooting backward from the saddle at a gallop. He improved the system of beacons and signals so the outposts of the army could inform the general staff of all enemy movements. Strict orders were issued that whenever a horde of nomads attacked, the troops were to shut themselves up in their fortresses. The slightest departure from these instructions was punished severely.

Every time the bonfires signaled an attack, the men rushed back to their fortified positions, and for a year the barbarians did not inflict a single casualty. As a result, the Huns became scornful and insolent.

Meng T'ien's troops grew tired of watching and waiting, of always retiring at the first sign of attack. Judging that the right moment had come, Meng T'ien assembled three thousand horsemen, three hundred war chariots, fifty thousand armored infantry, and ten thousand crack bowmen, and subjected them all to intensive training. He then sent a huge herd of cattle out into the steppes.

When the Huns attacked, the detachment of troops guarding the cattle withdrew. The khan, seeing an easy prey, unleashed the whole of his force, whereupon the troops which General Meng T'ien had concealed behind neighboring slopes emerged to cut off the force's rear, encircle it and annihilate it to the last man.

Taking advantage of the irresolution this produced among the other tribes, Meng T'ien penetrated deep into nomad territory, where he took several encampments by surprise and exterminated all the male population. The women and girls were taken into captivity. The Tan Lan, the eastern Hu, and the Hu Lin were wiped out, and the rest of the tribes either fled westward in terror or surrendered. There were no more raids: barbarians and border people now engaged in trade with one another instead of battle. The markets flourished, and many of the Huns adopted the Ch'in way of life.

Five hundred thousand convicts sentenced to forced labor were sent to cultivate the land won from the Huns, and Meng T'ien complained of being short of manpower for the Wall. Li Ssu, in a move designed also to rid the Central States of their riffraff, sever family ties, isolate individuals, and terrorize the people at large, deported all officials whose accounts were not in good order or of whom inspectors had given unfavorable reports. But the Wall needed still more workers, and soon it was the turn of the merchants and skilled craftsmen.

Despite all his efforts, Li Ssu did not succeed in eradicating trade altogether. Indeed, such parasitical activity now flourished better than ever, stimulated by the security of the Wall and the defeats inflicted on the khans.

It was impossible to hold back the flood of wealth spreading over the Empire. Instead of depleting the surpluses, the expeditions against the Huns had increased them. The only good things the war accomplished were to frighten the people, wipe out factions, and break up families.

———

Protected by his wall, the August Emperor was happy, and in his six palaces he devoted himself to the search for immortality. For a moment he thought that he had found the secret in the esoteric treatises of the Yellow Emperor. These writings were given him by a seer named Realization of the Self, who claimed that they pointed out the true way to eternal life—through the art of the bedchamber.

"Know the masculine, retain the feminine" meant nothing more or less than complementing, reinforcing one's seed with female emanations. The secret was to take without giving. Ordinance now regretted the ignorance that had allowed him to deposit his august sperm in a woman, strengthening thereby her vital force at the expense of his own. Fortunately, he was not much attracted by white teeth and arched eyebrows, and had always restricted such contacts to the minimum required for the performace of his royal duty and the perpetuation of his line.

Among the thirty-six hundred women now in his palaces, he sought out those who were fittest to nourish his vital force. Horoscopes were drawn up, and Realization of the Self went through all the imperial concubines—the "chosen maids," "splendid beauties," and "blooming flowers"—and selected seventy-two. He discarded the prettiest ones, in order not to arouse the Emperor's desire—it would not do for the means to become the ends. The women were all tall, with large rectangular heads, big mouths, strong white teeth, and noses not too flat. Above all, they had to have a fine skin and an extremely fair complexion.

Ordinance delved eagerly into his esoteric handbooks on the arts of the alcove, shuddering at the words of the Pure Young Girl in the *Secret Book of the Yellow Emperor:*

> The queen mother of the West achieved the Tao by nurturing her feminine forces. She had only to have intercourse with a man once, and he fell ill with exhaustion and died in a decline. But she, by this means, acquired such a wonderful complexion that she had no need of cosmetics. Know, then, that the divine mother who rules over the paradise of the West and loves to couple with young men is a ravening tigress. Do not forget that every woman's nature is like hers!

Shivering with fear, he read on:

> In the act of intercourse think of your adversary as a clay pot, but of yourself as a valuable vase. When the seminal fluid begins to stir, withdraw! Sleeping with a woman is like riding an unbroken filly without reins, or like standing on the brink of a precipice full of swords.

He sighed as his feverish hands tore open the scrolls and his eyes scanned the dark ideograms. He had now come to the dialogue between the Pure Young Girl and the Yellow Emperor. "My heart is sad. I pine. My breathing is irregular. I am overwhelmed by vague apprehensions," the Emperor told the woman who was to initiate him.

Ordinance's own symptoms! He read on avidly.

"Any weakness in man," answered the Pure Young Girl, "is to be attributed to an imperfect performance of the sexual act. Woman is superior to man as water is superior to fire. . . ."

True, thought Ordinance. But didn't he reign by fire?

"A king must never lose sight of the fact that a fundamental part of his royal duty concerns his relations with his wives. He must be familiar, therefore, with the techniques of sexual intercourse. The principle is simple. It consists in sleeping with one's partner without emitting semen—or emitting it only on rare occasions. This method makes the body light and evanescent. Soon one can fly in the air at the whim of wind and cloud. One becomes immortal. . . ."

Ordinance's fingers impatiently traced the final ideograms of the conclusion:

Ordinary men have only one wife, and this is fatal to them. The Yellow Emperor coupled with a thousand girls in one night and so lengthened his life. That is the gulf that separates the initiate from an ordinary mortal. The initiate's only difficulty is to find enough women.

With the aid of the young women chosen by the soothsayer, the August Emperor set about practicing the various positions designed to bring immortality: the spooling silk, the coiling dragon, the four-eyed fish, the pair of swallows, the butterflies, the up-tailed ducks, the moaning monkey embracing a tree, and so on. First came purification through fasting, through fuming with sweet-smelling herbs, then the choice of a propitious day, then the careful placing of his partners at the eight points of the rose of the winds. He circulated among them in a complicated pattern based on the motions of the stars and the symbols of his reign. Even in his bodily movements he scrupulously observed the right rhythms, 3-7-9 being the male series and 2-6-8 the female. Alternating the two rhythms—now slowly, now quickly, in six cycles of six numbers, so as to arrive at a perfect form of the number of water—he breathed deeply, eyes half closed, mind concentrated, tongue tight against the roof of his mouth. With his lips pressed together, his neck taut, his penis stiff, he arched his back and squared his shoulders. Sweat poured from him as he put into practice the movements in the *Secret Book of the Yellow Emperor* and the postures prescribed in the *Secret Book of the Girl of Jet.* His seed went up through his spine to feed his brain and strengthen his bones. Soon he was able to hold in his sperm for a very long time.

But after several months of this, he was short of breath and began having dizzy spells again. He suffered from violent headaches, and his penis often remained obstinately soft and limp. He could not stand the sight of women. Realization of the Self made a swift departure from court.

The Emperor then sent for Master Lu, who denounced Realization as a fraud. The true method of retaining the One did not consist in nurturing one's yang at the expense of the woman's yin. On the contrary, one had to realize one's femininity. "Retain the feminine. Be the valley of the world," as Lao Tzu said. Also: "Essence of the supreme Tao: confusion! darkness! Height of the supreme Tao: chaos! opaqueness!"

Lu went on to quote sententiously: " 'In silence embrace the spirit and your body will be healthy! Be calm, be pure, do not torture your senses or disturb your essence, and you will enjoy eternal life! Retain the One in order to preserve harmony; sublimate your desires so as not to be dominated by the outside world.'

"Such was the teaching of the saint. How could it be just a matter of not ejaculating? At that rate, Chao Kao, your eunuch, would have ascended to heaven long ago! You must bring about the mystical fusion of yin and yang by making the heavenly maidens descend into your body. It is within you that the sacred intercourse will take place, and from that union will be born a divine embryo. It will develop in the hollow void of the womb and replace your fleshy envelope with a body of immortality. Lao Tzu has said, 'The spirit of the valley does not die. It is called the dark female.' The female is the earth, quiet and inert. Woman is all passivity. Man must model himself on her. Concentrate his seed. Do you remember the saying 'The vale of the world: return to childhood'? He who can become the vale of the universe will make himself master of the Tao. He will return to the fetal state—or, rather, be everything at once, mother and child, man and woman, inner and outer, fulfilling in himself the plenitude of nonbeing.

"You must know, august master, that in the beginning Lao Tzu created a female body in which to be incarnated. Then he changed himself into a lustrous pearl, which came down from heaven and lodged in the mother's womb. It germinated, grew, and became a little child, who for nine months sang sacred hymns in his warm nest. And when he had lived thus for eighty-one years in his mother's body, he emerged through her left armpit. He had white hair from birth; he possessed all the wisdom in the world the moment he entered it. That is why he is called Lao Tzu, the 'aged child.'

"Thus did Lao Tzu change his own body from emptiness into female form. He was his own mother, and he was born of himself. Each one of us can become the mother of the Tao. Concentrate. Visualize the gods who live in you. The whole of the universe is within us—mountains, peaks, seas, rivers, gods, and spirits all have their counterparts in the microcosm of the human body. Between our eyebrows the True Lord of the Tao darts forth his nine heads on one body, clad in a scarlet coat studded with jewels. Son of the Great One without ever having been born, the spontaneous materialization of the original breath, he resides in the head, in the midst of a rubescent cloud. . . .

"The left eye is the abode of the duke of the East; in the left lives the queen mother of the West. The duke is action, the queen nature. She reigns on the sacred peak in the K'un Lun Mountains and is sometimes called Mysterious Jade. Dressed in crimson, she is nineteen inches high. The queen of the West and the duke of the East meet in the Yellow Court and make love, and from their coupling a child is born named True Cinnabar of the North. The seed of immortality is none other than our own true self."

———

Seated by his incense burner, breathing in the heady scents of gum, myrrh, and cardamom, and half-hallucinating from the drugs of arsenic, the Emperor entered into a state of meditation, hoping to come face to face with his true self. The great primeval gods took shape in a whirling kaleidoscope, dissolving in an ever-changing prism. His internal organs burst into sprays of brightness, incarnadine or yellow. Flashes revealed pearly stipples of living flesh, and green cascades empurpled by the gleam of pulsing entrails. Then the organs re-formed into hieratic divinities stiffly bound in broad-belted crimson robes, into bowing human heads surrounded by diadems of light, although their bodies were those of phoenixes.

But Ordinance soon tired of the phantasmagoria of his own viscera as mythological beasts. Perhaps he was afraid of what he saw. The palpitation of the living flesh, the writhings and howlings of his innards, filled him with disgust. He felt weary, weak, and longed to see once more his dancing girls, his female orchestra, his horses.

The idea of making himself pregnant and nourishing a fetus within his masculine body was repugnant. The whole thing was absurd. That could not be the right way. At least not for him.

One day he told Master Lu outright: "I don't want to turn myself into a woman. I have pacified the whole world and established order in it—why are the gods so slow to react? I find visual images wearisome, and gymnastics tire me out. What's the point in doing backward somersaults like a howler monkey, flapping my arms like an owl, hopping on one leg like a crane, twisting my neck around like a tiger, or loping along like a bear? Meditation bores me; contemplating my own insides makes me ill. My stomach is half destroyed with pills—I'm full of resin and arsenic, cinnabar and mica, and my body is like a furnace. Since I stopped eating cereals and replaced solid food with dried meat and jujubes, I've suffered terrible stomach pains. Breathing exercises give me dizzy spells and buzzing in the ears. And, in spite of my very strict diet, I still haven't excreted the three corpses of cereals. Master, I need something different!"

The Taoist realized then that he could not force a regime suitable for a saint upon a man as ardent and eager as the Emperor. "Everyone finds the Tao in his own way," he answered soothingly. "One must never do violence to one's own nature—that is another of the Master's fundamental lessons. I know of great saints who have achieved immortality by wallowing in the mud and staying drunk day and night. Amuse yourself with your wives, gorge yourself on roasts and venison, give yourself up to hunting and other distractions. But do not forget to purify yourself with sacrifices and offerings. Send embassies laden with gifts to the gods of the Eastern Sea and the oceans of the Far West. Build towers and pavilions and terraces to receive the mystic forces and auspicious influences that fill the universe. In short, be respectful and attentive to the gods, and I am sure that they will grant you immortality."

Ordinance gave up fasting and exercising and immediately felt better. He had a pleasant dream in which he climbed a ladder to the sky and licked the nipples of heaven. The taste was sweeter than honey—a sure sign that he would soon attain eternal life.

CHAPTER V

THE MECHANICAL MEN

The people were restive under the severity of the law and the burden of inhuman labor. A ballad spread through the Empire and came to be sung in the streets and market places of the capital, telling of the quest of Meng Chiang, a spirited young woman whose husband had been sent to help build the Great Wall. When, after two years, there was no sign of his return, she braved the winter's cold and the sultry heat of summer and set out to look for him. After many trials and tribulations she came to the vast deserts where the dread Wall cast its menacing shadow. There, at the foot of the Wall, she learned that her husband, like millions of his companions, had died of cold and hunger, and that his corpse was buried inside the man-eating dragon.

She wept, cursing both the Wall and its builder, the terrible and pitiless August First Emperor. She wept so much that the Wall crumbled away, revealing her husband's body, and the bittersweet rain of her tears immediately brought him back to life.

The bards who sang this song were sentenced to death, and anyone who listened to them was deported for life or reduced to slavery. But people could still be heard humming it in the streets.

Li Ssu ordered the propaganda service to produce an ode praising the charity of the Great Emperor's daughters, who assuaged the thirst of convicts working on extensions to the royal palaces. The ode met with little success.

The Empire was ruled with an iron hand. But the string of a bow perpetually drawn would eventually snap. Perhaps the government's grip should be—or, rather, seem to be—relaxed, as in the fable in the *Chuang Tzu*. A monkey tamer had to ration his animals because of a food shortage. To make them accept the reduction, he told them, "From now on I will give you only three taros every morning and four every night. Does that suit you?" Cries of outrage. "Very well," he said. "I yield to your wishes. Four taros every morning and three every night. Are you satisfied now?" The monkeys were so pleased that their objections had been taken into account, they lay down quietly in their cages and went to sleep.

Li Ssu suggested proclaiming a general amnesty and arranging festivities to celebrate the occasion. The Emperor agreed. At the end of the rejoicing, when the Scholars of Vast Learning came forward to wish their beloved sovereign long life, Chou Ch'in-cheng, master of the palace guards, recited a eulogy on the achievements of the august monarch:

"In the past, the land of Ch'in measured no more than a thousand leagues. But now, thanks to the supernatural perspicacity and transcendent wisdom of our most enlightened sovereign, the whole world has been pacified and brought under his sway. He has repelled the Man and the I barbarians. All the countries beneath the moon and beneath the sun obey him. He has transformed the feudal states into prefectures. His subjects live in peace and happiness, free from foreign wars and internal strife. His achievements will go down in posterity."

Ordinance preened himself. He raised his goblet and was about to signal to his female orchestra to begin when a scholar by the name of Sun Yü-yüeh spoiled his pleasure by presenting him with a protest.

The Emperor was shocked by the virulence of the learned man's petition, but passed it along to his privy council as a matter of form. Li Ssu, furious to see that he still had not succeeded in silencing the vile Confucians, decided to gag them now once and for all.

The Emperor had ceased worrying about immortality. This was a good thing in itself. The law was strong enough for the Empire to survive any whims on the part of its ruler, but the law must not be subjected to criticism. Different opinions must be banned. That was the only way the inexorability of the law could be maintained, whatever the vagaries of the monarch.

The minister sent the August Emperor a petition proposing the eradication of all thought. The petition was favorably received: it was no more than Ordinance expected. He, the Emperor, must be the sole criterion of truth. A law that was the subject of debate ceased to be a law at all: it was no longer natural or necessary. Did people discuss the validity of hunger or thirst?

His edicts must be like night and day, autumn and spring, bringing life or death, plenty or devastation. He must stultify his people: or, as Lao Tzu put it, "fill bellies and empty hearts." That had been his own teacher's doctrine, too. He must never forget it.

He read with renewed pleasure Negation's commentary on the *Book of the Way and of Virtue:*

Wang Fu was walking with books on his back when he met Hsü Feng. Feng said: "Government is action. Action arises from the historical moment. Anyone who cannot recognize the historical moment cannot follow a steady path. Books are a repository of discourse, a by-product of intelligence. A truly wise man has no need of books. Why bother with a useless burden?" Wang Fu burned his books and danced around the bonfire.

A holy man needs no words to teach, and a sensible man does not burden himself with writings. Our age disapproves of this attitude, but Wang Fu returned to the right path. That is what Lao Tzu meant by "learning to unlearn." Hence the saying "To learn to unlearn is to do what the common run of people decry."

Heaven required Ordinance to strengthen his bones for the sake of his inner perfection, but it also wanted him to empty his subjects' hearts. Negation himself knew that to establish the law a ruler had to cultivate his own inner perfection—though Negation had done no more than glimpse the practical consequences of this axiom. Ordinance had excluded desire from his own heart; now he must banish thought from the minds of his people. Every fresh stage in his internal fulfillment must be matched externally, in the government of the Empire, by a new step in the direction of absolute order.

The body and the country were linked together, like inner and outer, name and form, shadow and substance, sound and echo. He wrote "Approved" on the back of Li Ssu's petition.

Li Ssu was enormously relieved. His plans were working out. The center would at last stand alone, and soon perfect order would reign. To abolish guileful intelligence, suppress thought, empty the heads of the people, and make the legal code as unquestioned as natural law—wasn't this the policy of any statesman worthy of the name? He had been wrong to think of relaxing the pressure. On the contrary, what was needed was to make the law even more implacable. But he had soon seen his error and was back on the right course.

One morning the inhabitants of town and country alike found copies of a stern proclamation posted on all their public buildings:

Anyone owning classical books or treatises on philosophy, history, or religion must hand them in within thirty days. After thirty days, anyone found in possession of such writings will be branded on the cheek and sent to work as a laborer on the Great Wall or some other government project. The only exceptions are books on medicine, drugs, astrology, and agronomy.

Private schools wil be forbidden. Those who wish to study law will do so under government officials.

Anyone indulging in political or philosophical discussion will be put to death, and his body exposed in public.

Scholars who use examples from antiquity to criticize the present, or who praise early dynasties in order to throw doubt on the policies of our own, most enlightened sovereign, will be executed, they and their families!

Government officials who turn a blind eye to the above-mentioned crimes will be deemed guilty by virtue of the principle of collective responsibility, and will incur the same punishment as that inflicted for the offense itself.

Police inspectors were sent throughout the provinces to see that the new directives were carried out. Thousands of volumes were brought, either voluntarily or under pressure from neighbors, to local government offices. Scholars committed suicide. Prefectures were lit by the flames from burning books. There were denunciations, house searches, deportations. Many were detected trying to evade the law. The roads heading north and northwest were crammed with long lines of prisoners wearing red convict caps, their faces branded with the black stamp of infamy. Three million men were sent to live near the Wall and populate the new territories.

The Wall was finished, and the forces assembled to build it must now, in accordance with the sage precepts of Shang Yang, be directed and neutralized. At Li Ssu's suggestion, the August Emperor began to translate the principles guiding his government into the physical form of the Empire itself. The capital was to be the hub from which all roads radiated—"the central emptiness that makes the chariot move." The road network was extended. Every highway was sixty paces wide, with a plot down the middle planted with a pine tree every three *chang*, and a wall on either side with steel spikes on top. Staging posts at regular intervals provided fresh horses, food and shelter, and the protection of garrisons.

New palaces were built. The August Emperor found the old ones too small now to suit the present state of the Empire. At one of his audiences he proclaimed: "King Wen of Chou had his capital in Feng, and King Wu had his in Hao. It is the land between these two cities, south of the river Wei, that is the most fitting site for the residence of a son of heaven."

So a palace was built in the middle of the park at Shang Lin, a region of tigers, gazelles, and sweet-scented trees. An imposing edifice soon took shape, measuring five hundred paces from east to west and four hundred from north to south. Its terraces could easily have accommodated ten thousand men. The ceiling of the great hall was forty feet high. A raised bridle path surrounded the whole, and a triumphal arch looked down on it from a hill. A covered way led from the nothern façade across the river to the old palaces in Double Light, like the bridge that joins the Milky Way to the constellation of Ying Shih.

Five hundred thousand prisoners helped build the enormous palace. It gave an impression of colossal and sinister strength, with its endless galleries supported on black lacquer columns, and its lofty dark-tiled roofs. All around it, tiered pavilions carved with red-and-black tigers and dragons intertwined reached to the sky. The gleaming inlays of mica, jasper, jade, gold, and amethyst were muted, cruel.

The Emperor had promised himself that he would enlarge his tomb. The tomb, begun at his accession to the throne, became too modest for his subsequent glory. The Wall had delayed this project, but now that the Wall was finished some of the labor used there could be redeployed on the monument. Blocks of marble were hewn from the mountains in the northeast for the sarcophagus and the funeral chamber. Whole forests were felled in the southern marches, and the tall trunks floated down from Shu and Han to the capital. The earth trembled with the pounding of rammers. Special roads were built through the mountains, but the weight of the materials carried along them ruined the surfaces. Thousands of men and draft animals died of exhaustion. Wagonload after wagonload of earth was emptied, valleys were filled in, hills flattened.

Thirty thousand families were moved from their homes and resettled at the foot of the funeral mound on Mount Li, so that a whole city might look after the Great Emperor's tomb and keep up the ceremonies due his shade. Fifty thousand families were similarly transplanted to Yün Yang, to populate the town created near the new palace and see to the August Emperor's comfort during his earthly sojourn.

Three hundred new palaces were built in the mountains, to provide pleasant halting places for the court when it traveled. Renovation work was done on four hundred existing palaces in the eastern part of Ch'in. And, as the Emperor had defined the western border of his possessions by means of a wall bristling with towers and fortresses, so in the east he erected a huge stone, like a gate, on the tip of the Shan Tung peninsula. The whole of the Empire had become his dwelling, with covered walks linking all seven hundred palaces and converging on Double Light, his main great audience chamber.

But the work being done visibly did not make him forget his spiritual quest. The men he sent to P'eng Lai never came back. Probably they perished in a storm—unless, failing in their mission, they ran away. He had sent people to seek the drug of immortality in every corner of the Empire. Some had crossed the icy wildernesses of the Northwest and climbed the K'un Lun Mountains. In vain.

With a pang he saw the tumulus of his final resting place rise ominously in the distance. If only just his garments could be buried there, while his body went straight up to heaven!

He had sought, in the K'un Lun mountains, the gods who were to be found within each one of us, but his quest had been fruitless. All he found were threatening shadows.

He consulted his magicians. They were at a loss. Finally Master Lu spoke.

"The gods may be troubled by some malign influence. In the esoteric books it says: 'The master of men must be unknown by all in order to ward off the powers of evil. Once these disturbing spirits have been driven away, true men may descend. True men can enter water without getting wet and jump into a brazier without being burned. They can ride on the clouds, and they live as long as the earth and the sky.'

"Prince, you rule the Empire ceaselessly and never rest. You need a period of calm and quiet meditation to acquire the concentration necessary for the descent of the gods."

The Emperor was silent. He was thinking of the lines from the *Book of the Way and of Virtue:*

> *Troubled and confused.*
> *Others are brilliant,*
> *But I am as impenetrable as the void.*

"Yes," he thought. "It is probably because I am still visible that the gods cannot come to me. No one knows where the true gods dwell; they are everywhere and nowhere. But my slightest gesture is known to everyone. Other men guess my most secret intentions. The gods do not like this. I must make myself impenetrable. If I could move about without anyone's knowledge, I am sure the gods would give me the elixir of immortality."

And he chanted under his breath:

> *Looking at him, you see him not.*
> *He is a form that is formless,*
> *An image that is imageless,*
> *He is ephemeral, elusive.*

Ordinance, too, must see without being seen, must present to others the smooth mirror of nothingness.

He issued a new decree: "The August Emperor, venerating and

loving the immortals, is himself to be known henceforth as the True Man."

He gave orders that all two hundred and sixty-four palaces, towers, terraces, and belvederes within a radius of three hundred leagues from Double Light should be joined by covered ways protected by walls. Each palace was stocked with concubines, eunuchs, servants, and all necessary articles and ornaments, so that Ordinance no longer needed to take them with him when he traveled. Any member of his entourage who revealed the place which the Emperor had honored with his presence was punished by death. In order to mislead his courtiers and subjects, replicas of his coaches and carriages went back and forth constantly in the labyrinthine network he set up among his palaces. His guards were not informed of his destination until the last moment; his arrival was always a surprise. Sometimes he made detours or backtracked, pretending to go to one place but really going to another. At one point, he thought of using doubles, but he feared that a double might pretend to be the real Emperor and murder him. Instead, he had wooden dummies sit in the coaches and chariots that constantly traveled the covered roads.

One day, as he was going to a residence of his that stood on a grassy hill north of the capital, he noticed that the carriages belonging to his prime minister's train were grander than his own. He mentioned this to his retinue. Later, he noticed that the prime minister's style was more modest.

"A member of my escort has repeated my words!" he bellowed. "I want the name of the traitor!"

All the people near him were questioned, but no one confessed. He therefore had everyone who had been with him on the journey in question put to death.

Because he was afraid his concubines or eunuchs might talk and give him away, he decided to terrorize them. He had made an oblong mirror of bronze, four feet wide, five feet nine inches high, and framed by a double row of mysterious talismans and hexagrammatic symbols from the *Book of Changes*, together with decimal and duodecimal signs from the celestial trunks and the terrestrial branches. He had the word spread that the front of the mirror reflected the shape of things but the back revealed the inner truth about them, showing a man's heart and veins, viscera and meridians as if the flesh were transparent. He called the mirror "the mirror of truth."

To demonstrate its powers to his harem, he summoned a rather simple-minded young favorite of his and told her he wanted her to help him play a joke on the others. She was to walk toward him carrying a dish, with a dagger hidden in her sleeve. He would turn the mirror on her and shout, "Her intentions are evil! I see her heart trembling in her breast!" She would be searched, the dagger would be found, and he would pretend to have her put to death. Of course, it would be only a pretense: in fact he would install her in another palace, where she would live in the lap of luxury. She agreed. Everything went according to plan, and the young woman was arrested. It was only when she felt the cold steel of the executioner's sword on her neck that she realized that the end of the story was not part of the joke.

The incident made a strong impression on all the women. Terror reigned throughout the royal palaces. The Emperor used the mirror several times, and such was the fear it inspired that no one who had done anything wrong could look onto it without betraying himself. Ordinance had several concubines and a few eunuchs executed in this way. And no one knew where the Emperor was or where he intended to go next.

All human contact, all dealings with anything made of flesh and blood, was now a source of irritation to him. He wanted everything to be exactly according to his wishes, for every action to be performed at exactly the prescribed moment, just as the water clock sounded its silvery note precisely when expected. But his dancing girls, his female orchestra, his horses, graceful and skilled as they all were, were subject to slight hesitations and unevennesses. This now struck him as an offense against the principle of inevitability. He had the impression that he was being defied or mocked. Anything unexpected, the slightest discrepancy between what was foreseen and what was done, felt like a wound. The human machine did not lend itself to the demands of the absolute as well as a water clock.

In the royal workshops in Double Light there was a Ch'in craftsman of surpassing skill. He once thought to win the Emperor's favor by presenting him with panels of transparent lacquer. At first there seemed to be nothing extraordinary about the panels, but when they were fitted into window frames and the golden light of sunset shone through them, the animals painted on them moved about. Tigers pounced on deer, dragons breathed out rainbow fountains, and cranes flew off to paradise. At first the Emperor was dazzled, and for three years the inventor busily provided panels for all six of the palaces. Then Ordinance wearied of the novelty: it seemed a lot of time to spend on a thing that produced the same effect as an ordinary window.

So the craftsman stopped producing panels and turned to the making of mechanical figures. He tried to rediscover the secret of Lu Pan, who had managed to reproduce natural movement. After two years of unsuccessful experiments, the man gave the Emperor a jade flute with horses and chariots carved on it. When one blew into the mouthpiece, the horses tossed their heads, their legs began to move, the wheels turned, and the whole procession seemed to drive off. The Emperor, fascinated, wanted a whole mechanical orchestra.

The artisan cast twelve men in bronze seated cross-legged on a mat. Their faces were painted in such minute detail that they looked alive. He dressed them in embroidered clothes and gave them musical instruments—lutes, flutes, zithers, and tambourines—studded with semiprecious stones and inlaid with ivory and mother-of-pearl. Two tubes ran under the dais they sat on, which served as a base, and connected, branching, to each of the players. One of the tubes was empty; the other contained a bundle of wires. Two men sat behind a screen that concealed the ends of the tubes: the first man manipulated the wires, the second blew into the other opening, and the bronze marionettes came to life, moving their fingers and rolling their eyes. One could hear the sound of stringed and wind instruments just as if it were a real orchestra.

The slighty jerky movements of the metal dolls gave Ordinance a kind of voluptuous pleasure. It was as if at last these men were obeying an immutable law. Yet he noticed certain irregularities. The rhythm of the musicians' hands occasionally varied: this was because the man working the wires and his companion blowing down the other tube sometimes became tired. Since the Emperor was dissatisfied, the artisan improved his invention, arranging to have the sound produced hydraulically and the wires to be connected to a water wheel.

The Emperor was soothed by the mechanical repetitions of his bronze dolls, that invariably produced their inexorable notes. He ceased to be offended by the involuntary twitchings of flesh or the imperfections of human breathing and circulation.

He wanted more puppets. The artisan produced scenes in which hounds chased a stag among the mountains, tigers devoured oxen in a forest, and a distant line of royal wagons moved across a landscape by the sea. The figures worked by a system of pulleys, ratchets, cogwheels, gears, and converters circling on bronze rails against a painted screen.

Soon servants made of lacquered wood were offering the August Emperor wine and dishes of food. The Emperor had the controls within easy reach and could regulate the speed of his manikins' movements, making each one do his bidding. He was as happy as a little boy. They were his creatures, and they obeyed him. They had no desires, no thoughts, no movements other than those dictated by the master of machines.

The craftsman never stopped trying to improve his handiwork, wanting to create the same element of surprise that existed in real life. By using cogwheels of different sizes, he almost managed to reproduce genuine human movement. He proudly presented two maidservants dancing and offering cups of wine. At first the Emperor suspected a trick—they looked so alive. He had them broken open. Inside, behind the organs made of precious stones, he found nothing but metal springs and wheels of bamboo.

He was worried: wouldn't chance reappear, even in machines? The engineer reassured him, showing him that the number of combinations and permutations possible with all the wheels was finite. It was possible to predict the mechanical men's movements, because once the cycle was complete they could only repeat the pattern.

The Emperor was delighted. "Perhaps it's the same with human beings," he thought. "If one could figure out the periodicity of their moods, one would become absolute master of their fates!"

The concubines languished in the harems, the singing girls lost their voices, and the Emperor's acrobats grew fat. Some of his dancing girls tried to pass for puppets, imitating their jerky movements, parading themselves thus in front of the master of men in the hope of winning back his favor. But they were immediately unmasked and decapitated.

The artisan also produced nautical scenes. Sandalwood boats sailed on a circular river under a roof supported by columns of porphyry; they carried courtiers, singing girls, and musicians. Mythological tableaux sailed by on floating islands: Yü the Great went through the Dragon Pass; the mother of Hou Chi, ancestor of the Chou, put her foot in the giant footprint that was to make her pregnant; King Mu drank wine on the jade lake with the queen mother of the West or, huge and terrible, met the sea god on the isles of immortality; Chün fished in the Pool of Thunder. Islands and boats floated slowly past as the characters on them performed their mechanical gestures. They passed, again and again, like the changing yet immutable round of the hours, spanning eternity itself. It seemed to Ordinance that the universe was one huge machine and he its driving force.

The workers toiled away without interruption; the royal factories, foundries, sawmills, saddleries, and potteries were devoted entirely to the production of the manikins. Men cast, carved, engraved, hammered, fashioned in every possible way puppets of bronze, wood, bamboo, and leather, containing metal wheels of all shapes and sizes, ratchets, springs, counterweights, and pulleys. Steel hearts were made, coral lungs, livers of cornelian, enamel eyes, and porcelain teeth, while the women wove wigs from the hair of executed prisoners.

The Emperor gave a show depicting all his ministers and wives life-size, in which puppets imitated the morning audience. His own image rolled its eyes fiercely and received the stiff, admiring obeisances of a crowd of courtiers, while assembled dignitaries genuflected in the background.

Ordinance clapped his hands with delight.

He had a river made in a field, with a covered terrace running along it, to entertain his guests on special occasions. The guests would be seated at the various bends in the stream. Orchestras playing lutes, bells, and gongs rode on the water in boats of sweet-smelling wood ten feet long by six feet wide. Some puppets did cartwheels; others performed balancing acts. Concubines of incomparable beauty opened cherry lips in mechanical smiles, showing teeth more dazzling than pearls. Waving hands as graceful as milkweed shoots, they made their long sleeves whirl rhythmically about their wrists of painted wood.

Nearer the bank were smaller boats, each steered by an oarsman in the stern. In the bow stood a puppet serving cups of wine. Behind it another ladled the wine from a cauldron, which two more puppets busily heated. Whenever a boat drew level with a guest, it stopped and the puppet in the prow offered him a cup of wine. When the guest emptied it, he handed it back to the puppet, which turned toward the puppet with the ladle, which then bent over the cauldron, dipped its ladle in the amber liquid, and refilled the goblet to the brim. It handed the goblet back to the puppet in the prow, and the boat moved on to another guest.

Everyone was astounded and said it was a miracle.

Ordinance began to think of populating the entire Empire with these puppets.

He started with his tomb.

Seven hundred thousand convicts had already dug an enormous pit down to the third level of the earth. Bronze had been poured into the hole, to anchor the building safely in the underground strata and appease the chthonic spirits. The laborers built a spacious, vaulted funeral chamber lined with gray marble.

Clay replicas were now made of the Emperor's palaces, terraces, and belvederes, with their mullioned windows and carved balustrades, their galleries and peristyles. The administrative buildings were reproduced, too. Great reception rooms were luxuriously furnished, and rare and curious objects brought and buried in them.

Then the Emperor ordered his artisans to make figurines with automatic crossbows, and to provide them, moreover, with traps and snares, to ward off tomb robbers. The rivers of the Empire were reproduced in mercury, and the silvery liquid was made to flow gently toward a sparkling sea by means of a hydraulic mechanism. Mountains also were represented, with their irregular rocks and crooked trees. A crystal vault painted with stars revolved overhead.

Thus the whole universe was simulated—the square earth studded with mountains, the round sky dotted with stars.

Long torches in the shape of fantastic serpents and fed by seal oil spewed eternal flame. Hydraulically powered robots stood ready to dance and sing, and at a given signal metal carousels would unfold processions of princely steeds or wild beasts.

All this, so that the Great Emperor, should he ever die (though this was most unlikely), might enjoy the sight of his figurines, beneath the twinkling dome that turned above the silver rivers, going through the same motions over and over again forever.

———

Li Ssu sat on the dais with Yu, his eldest son, beside him on his left. He was celebrating his appointment to the post of prime minister, and Yu, who was prefect of Three Rivers, had obtained a month's leave to join in the festivities. All the dignitaries in the capital had come to offer their congratulations, and thousands of chariots crammed Li Ssu's courtyard and overflowed into the adjoining streets.

The shimmering garments, the perfect service, the luxurious food set before his guests, and the adulation addressed to himself brought tears to Li Ssu's eyes.

"Alas," he sighed, "my master, Hsün Tzu, used to say that whatever reaches its peak must fall, because nature abhors extremes. And have not I, Li Ssu, a humble bourgeois from the subprefecture of Shang Ts'ai, been raised to the highest of dignitaries by a master who in his infinite goodness did not scorn my modest talents? I have climbed to the summit of honor and glory, higher than any subject in the Empire. Now there remains for me to do but await the moment of my downfall."

Everyone protested: he still had years of happiness before him, and his fame would shine forever in the clear skies of Ch'in.

But when the last notes of music died away in the mists of night, together with the wishes for long life and everlasting happiness proffered by the dignitaries who hated him and the courtiers who feared him, and when the fish oil sputtered out in the tall cressets of gilded bronze—then Li Ssu felt a great emptiness.

He thought about his relationship with the Great Emperor. And he was afraid. Until now he had guided and influenced the monarch's acts, but the man himself eluded him. And the man was growing more and more distant. The quest for the absolute which the Emperor had translated into politics now cut him off completely from the world of men. Li Ssu thought of the ceremony in honor of one's ancestors: their spirit was incarnated in the living grandson, and often, by means of a trance, it spoke through his lips. The grandson thus became the head of the family line, but really was only the mouthpiece of the spirit speaking through him—nothing more than a puppet being manipulated.

Li Ssu had imagined himself to be the mysterious spirit that breathed power into the Emperor. Invisible, formless, faceless, it was he who set the sacred image in motion. Without his minister, would not Ordinance be like a child—empty, exhausted, weak, and practically lifeless, once the god ceased to inhabit him?

But now the minister began to harbor a horrible suspicion. Suppose it was the other way around? Then he, Li Ssu, would be the visible face of a superior spirit embodied in the August First Emperor—a mere exteriorization of the mystic impulses of the great king. An object. An indispensable object, certainly, for Li Ssu was still the Emperor's sole link with reality, and without him Ordinance would probably sink into madness—but still only an object. An inert and amorphous thing that owed its semblance of solidity to the divine power of history as reified in his master.

Unless they were, both of them, the two aspects of the imperial Tao, as inseparable as a garment and its lining, as the internal and the external. . . .

But what did it matter which was the "body"? Whether he, Li Ssu, collapsed like the bag of a bellows when someone stopped blowing into it, or came to a halt like a puppet when its strings were severed, or faded into the air like a spirit whose funeral tablet was destroyed—in any case, he would probably not survive the death of his master.

He had forebodings that the end was near. The Emperor was ill. Drugs, and a diet based on the ethereal spirits, with arsenic and pine kernels, had finally ruined an already delicate constitution. Ordinance had always complained of flashes of heat that affected his brain and the marrow of his bones. The doctors whispered together and shook their heads.

Li Ssu shrugged. He was getting old. What was the point of dwelling on morbid fears? Had he not set up a legal system that rewarded talent and efficiency? Had he not done his duty responsibly and well? There was no reason for him to worry.

He dismissed all disagreeable thoughts, went to bed, and fell into a calm and dreamless sleep.

CHAPTER VI

HERRING FOR
A CORPSE

The Emperor became gloomier every day. He did not sleep, afraid that death might take him by surprise or that he might miss a visit from some god. Horrible battles took place in his body between the vital spirits and the cereal demons. He was consumed by an inner fire.

His soothsayers were certain that deliverance was near and that he would soon shed his earthly envelope: his immortal body would ascend to heaven and his subjects would worship the empty shell left in his tomb.

Still he had not found the herb of everlasting life. And no god appeared to him—not in the labyrinth of paths where fake copies of himself went ceaselessly to and fro, nor in the lofty chambers whose dark-painted ceilings depicted the battles between the Yellow Emperor and the god of war, nor in the theaters where he gazed with a disillusioned eye on the jerky movements of his bronze and wooden figurines. Heaven had deserted him.

He felt ill and alone. He distrusted everyone. His marionettes made him doubt his own power. Perhaps he, too, walked upon a stage, a brilliant semblance toward which all eyes turned, not seeing the water wheel that made it move? Who knew what man or what obscure force pulled the strings? At one point he had even feared Li Ssu. He carefully reread *Ten Mistakes, On Regicide* and *The Three Parapets: Precautions to Be Taken Against One's Intimates*. Han Negation's writings seemed to sound a warning:

> When ministers become too influential, the life of the sovereign is in danger. The power of the nobles is the ruin of kings. So an enlightened sovereign avoids at all costs letting his ministers meddle in matters that should remain his own preserve. Once their fame eclipses his own, once their image is popular in the provinces, his throne is in peril. Nothing should be held in greater reverence than the person of the prince. No position may be higher than his, no authority more absolute, no glory more dazzling. These are advantages he must be careful neither to acquire nor to maintain by means of external aids. For a prince should not rely on the help of any of his subjects. The only way for him to keep his position is to obey political necessity.

With some apprehension he went through the long list of kings assassinated by their ministers. Not degenerate rulers like the tyrants Chieh and Chou, but monarchs whose reigns were glorious. He thought of Negation's remark: "Kings are more to be pitied than lepers." King Shu Fu died of hunger, shut up in his drawing room by his prime minister. Chao Ch'e, elevated to the highest dignity in Ch'i, lost no time in hanging his prince by the heels from the ridge pole of the ancestral temple. The unfortunate king took a whole day to die. After the demise of Kuan Chung, loyal minister of the haughty prince of Ch'i, his other ministers—Li Hsi and Li Ya—fomented unrest, and the duke, imprisoned in his palace in T'ang I, died of starvation. No one thought of burying him until the worms crawled out from under the doors and invaded the whole palace.

But these were mere ramblings: he, Ordinance, would certainly not meet with so tragic a fate. Thanks to the techniques he used, he was able to control his subjects and restrain their ambitions. But he must never relax his vigilance, for the least sign of weakness would be exploited to deprive him of his power. In this respect Li Ssu was no different from the rest. But Ordinance knew that he was too shrewd a politician not to realize that his master's end would spell his own. He was hated by the court, and only the Great Emperor stood between him and death. Li Ssu really was his creature.

Li Ssu always said that the Emperor should leave his officials to take care of the business of government and concern himself only with supervising the most senior executives, who were an indispensable link between the ruler and his people. But it seemed to Ordinance that they formed a barrier rather than a link. He set up a network of spies and informers—children, pages, young palace eunuchs—who provided him with reports on the government and on the sayings and doings of his own entourage. Children were not such liars as adults. Still, they were not to be relied on implicitly. So he instituted a dual system of surveillance, having his young informers spy upon one another.

In order to keep his retinue and all his subjects safely under his thumb, he sought to alarm them with his perspicacity: that they would think that nothing that happened anywhere in the Empire escaped him. He read all the reports, those submitted by his officials and those submitted by his secret police. Every evening there was a ceremonial weighing. He would heap up documents until the scale indicated a hundred and twenty pounds—his evening ration—and did not sleep until he had read them all. Every decision rested with him: the form that written characters should take, the size of weights and measures, the amount of prisoners' rations, the cut of the civil servants' uniforms.

He uncovered all the tricks played by his servants and courtiers. Only a few days before, he had had the assistant cook beheaded for putting a hair in his soup in order to throw the blame on the chief cook and take his place. Ordinance even scolded market officials about the stray cows that ate the peasants' grass on the outskirts of the capital.

Sometimes his omniscience was a burden. He wished he could shut his eagle eyes and go meditate in some country retreat. But he mustn't relax. The father and mother of the people had to be always on the alert.

Master Lu and Master Hou presented him with an extract from the *Chuang Tzu* about the Yellow Emperor's retreat, but the August Emperor took it as a criticism, or even an attempt to make fun of him: they were trying to belittle him and make themselves look important. He was vexed with his Taoist advisers. Soon they had other reasons for anxiety. Rumor had it that Hsü the Blessed, who had vanished years ago, had settled on an island a few leagues from the coast and founded a flourishing colony. Some enemies of the soothsayers asked the Emperor to mount an expedition to go see if this story was true.

Masters Lu and Hou arranged to meet at a lonely spot. After looking around to make sure that they were not being spied on, they discussed what they should do.

"The Emperor has always been violent and tyrannical," said one, "but now he goes too far."

"He thinks he is better than all the saints," answered the other, "past, present, and to come."

"There are more than three hundred astrologers in his palace, all excellent scientists and great scholars. But none of them dares tell him what heaven thinks of his government."

"Ominous signs occur more and more often."

"Is it normal for an Emperor to poke his nose into what goes on in small towns and villages?"

"And for no one else to be allowed any say?"

"He's so full of himself, he thinks he's the Tao in person."

"And if he doesn't find what he's looking for, heaven help us!"

"He'll never find the elixir of eternal life."

"And we'll have to pay!"

"You know, don't you, what we should do?"

"Only too well," answered Master Lu.

The next day the Emperor felt dizzy and sent for his two magicians. But they had disappeared. That night he dreamt that he was climbing a steep mountain accompanied by Master Lu, and when they reached the top they met An Ch'i-sheng, a handsome old man with white hair and the face of a child. A dragon crouched beside him, and the two sages climbed onto its back. The Emperor was about to mount behind them when they gave him a nasty kick and he fell to the ground. The dragon rose into the clouds amid the irreverent chuckles of the immortals, and the Emperor was left alone among weird boulders and cliffs.

Soon after the news of Master Lu and Master Hou's defection, Hsü the Blessed's head arrived, with a detailed report on the trick that he had played.

The Emperor, beside himself with rage, paced his palace like a caged tiger.

"I gathered all the books in the Empire," he fumed. "Since some of them were too full of pernicious doctrine to be left in general circulation, I wisely decided that literature and science would benefit from their removal from private collections.

"I welcomed with open arms all the world's scholars, scientists, and sages, and I fostered letters and the arts, hoping that the magicians would find me the elixir of immortality. But those on whom I founded my hopes betrayed me. Han Chung, Master Lu, and Master Hou all ran away. Hsü the Blessed received enormous sums of money from me so he could go live quietly on an island. They all thought of nothing but their own basest interests. Their theories and speeches were only a veil concealing their greed. I lavished wealth and honors on Hou and Lu, and tortured myself to follow their inhuman disciplines. All in vain. My stomach heaves, my heart fills with bitterness at the thought of such guile and wickedness! I should like to wipe every sage and scholar and philosopher off the face of the earth. Li Ssu was right. The time for talk is over!"

He was told about the latest song the little girls in the capital were singing as they skipped outside their houses. The words were the same as those some criminal had written on Confucius's tomb after the burning of the books. It was said among the common people that the Emperor had desecrated the holy man's grave. That was ridiculous—he had the greatest admiration for the master. But it made him furious to know that the little girls in the city were making fun of him.

> Oh, the great king is naughty!
> He has gutted my house.
> He sits on my roof
> And steals my clothes.
> He eats my rice
> And borrows my bow,
> And bang! bang! bang!
> Watch out for Sandy Mount,
> For death awaits you there.

The Emperor had inquiries made and the scholars' houses searched. Subjected to severe interrogation, the scholars vied with one another in making damning accusations against their colleagues. The interrogators, taken aback, referred these to the Emperor, who cross-examined the scholars himself and exposed the contradictions in their evidence. He obtained four hundred and sixty-three confessions. The accused all admitted they were guilty of insult and slander against the Sovereign Emperor, of conspiracy, sabotage, and attempted murder. That they had tried to overthrow the dynasty and restore the hateful old regime of feudalism.

The entire population of Double Light was ordered to be present at a show designed to intimidate the citizens and terrorize the opposition. Pits were dug and the scholars buried alive in them after suffering the five tortures: bastinado, amputation of the nose, branding of the cheek, amputation of the feet, and castration.

Punishments rained down like hail. There were countless deportations. Every suspect was pronounced guilty and sent either to the freezing marches in the Northwest or to the fever-ridden South. Most perished.

Ordinance's eldest son, Fu Su, uneasy about the murmurs of protest, remonstrated with him.

"Father," he said, "we have scarcely finished pacifying the Empire, and the loyalty of the people on our borders is far from sure. Yet here you make enemies of the scholars, displeasing your subjects by enacting harsh laws. I am afraid that eventually this policy will be fatal to you."

Ordinance made him superintendent general of the army on the northern frontier, thus exiling him to the province of Shang.

The Emperor now felt that the ground trembled constantly beneath his feet. He was dizzy, his head ached, everything was repellent. Food left him with the taste of dust and ashes. Even his puppets bored him.

When the planet Mars was in the constellation Hsin—an unfavorable omen—a shooting star fell in the province of Tung and turned into a reddish stone. The astrologers saw this as a bad sign. The planet Mars was a principle of contrariety, presiding over military matters abroad and government upheavals at home. But, then, the Great Emperor's life had been punctuated by sinister apparitions. In the fifteenth year of his reign, a comet had occupied half the sky for a hundred and twenty days.

A report came in from the Tung prefecture. The following words had been found carved on the stone fallen from heaven: "On the death of the First Great Emperor, the Empire will disintegrate."

The king, already in a melancholy mood, became very angry. The whole of the local population in Tung was arrested and questioned. No one confessed. The peasants were tortured. Without result. All the inhabitants within a radius of thirty leagues were put to death, and the stone was melted in a furnace.

To raise the morale of his subjects, official bards were dispersed among the provinces to laud the great sovereign's exploits. Many mysteriously disappeared. Some were stoned to death.

In the autumn of the thirty-sixth year of his reign, Ordinance had a dream that affected him deeply. He dreamt that an envoy from the East, walking at night along the road from P'ing Shu to Shan Hsi, was stopped by a man who held out a jade ring and said, "Give this to the prince of Lake Hao." Then the man added, "This year the Great Dragon, venerable founder of the race, will die." Before the envoy could reply, the man melted into the darkness, and he was left holding the green ring. The envoy, who resembled the Great Emperor in appearance, noticed that the jade ring was the same as one the Great Emperor had lost in a storm on Lake Tung T'ing many years before.

The Emperor awoke bathed in sweat. He pondered this portent. "River spirits cannot see more than a year into the future," he thought. "The dragon and founder of the race can only be me, the master of men. The ring is a token, and the gods chose to give it to me after it had been in the water, the symbol of my power.

"Doesn't this mean my reign is about to end?"

He recalled the predictions in Master Lu's text, which had been interpreted to mean: "Hu will be the downfall of Ch'in." So he deported more than three hundred thousand families to the Northwest, to form a defense against the Huns. He attempted to conciliate the families by raising them one degree in the hierarchy.

Then he had the auguries read. A journey would be a good thing for him, said his soothsayers. But Li Ssu advised against it and made him read the *Ten Mistakes* of Negation, of which the two most to be avoided were traveling too much and failing to name an heir in time. The Emperor was silent for a while, then scowled at his prime minister—who decided not to pursue the matter.

In the thirty-seventh year of his reign, on the K'uei Ch'u day of the tenth month, Ordinance left his capital and set out on a journey to the East. Li Ssu, his minister of the left, went with him. Feng Ward-Off-Evil, his minister of the right, remained in the capital. Hu Hai, a eunuch, Ordinance's youngest son, asked to be allowed to go with him, and the request was granted. First they headed south. In the eleventh moon they arrived in Yün Meng, where the Emperor offered up a sacrifice at Chün's grave at the foot of Mount Nine Doubts.

He went down the Blue River by boat, admiring once more the reflections of the lush forests in its quiet waters. After Tung Yang he reached T'ien Tang and entered the estuary of the ever-turbulent river Shuo. He tried to cross it but could not, and ordered a bridge to be built. After a fortnight's work, however, the piles were swept away by a tidal wave, so he turned back and crossed the river Yü Hang a hundred leagues to the west, where the banks were narrow. Then he climbed Mount K'uei Chi, offered up a sacrifice in honor of Yü the Great, and raised a stele in praise of his own exploits.

> *In the thirty-seventh year of his reign*
> *The August Emperor inspected his Empire.*
> *When he reached its eastern border,*
> *He climbed Mount K'uei Chi.*
> *He understood the workings of history,*
> *He put the art of politics into practice.*
> *He separated the wheat from the chaff,*
> *And nothing remained hidden from him.*

His inspired rule purifies morals.
People live in peace, working diligently.
The obedient citizens delight in uniformity.

Thus do the ministers of the August Emperor celebrate his virtues,
and with one voice ask that their praises be carved on this stone.

Ill at ease, the Emperor decided to return along the coast. He passed through the ancient land of Wu, intersected by rivers and lakes and scarred with canals; he crossed back over the Blue River at Chiang Ch'eng, then followed its banks to his seaside residence at Lang Ya. It was from there that boats had been sent out in search of the immortals, and he sighed as he thought of the swift passage of time, his lost youth, his present solitude. Despite his immense power, he was weaker and more helpless than a newborn babe.

He slept badly, with the sea breaking over the rocks below. An immortal appeared to him in a dream and said cryptically: "The weed of immortality is still within your grasp. It is guarded by a huge fish that prevents anyone from reaching the islands of P'eng Lai. But if a skillful archer could ambush and shoot it, the way would be clear."

Then he found himself suddenly alone in the middle of a lonely moor, holding a crossbow. An enormous fish rose from the water, its ravenous jaws agape. He loosed an arrow and hit it in the eye. The sea went red, and the fish turned into a bronze giant. The Emperor dived into the water, and he and the fish engaged in a fierce struggle. The sea god had a human face and a dragon's tail. The Emperor squeezed the monster's neck tight in his arms, and the god wound his tail around the Emperor's waist. The sea was covered with crimson foam, and as darkness fell over the two adversaries the Emperor realized that he was fighting against himself.

He questioned his soothsayers, and they told him that the sea gods were guarded by sea monsters. If, after all his sacrifices and precautions, his dreams were still haunted by these beasts, he must eliminate them at all costs in order to gain access to the true gods.

He had a huge net spread, to head the monster toward the shore. Then, holding a crossbow at the ready as he walked the deserted strand, which was sparsely dotted with sickly shrubs and weatherbeaten rocks, he waited for the fish to appear. The sea wind stung his cheeks and plucked at his sleeves as he went from Lang Ya to Mount Yung Ch'eng along the rocky promontory. But he saw nothing. The waves were calm and green, merging into gray sky. He pressed on as far as Shih Fu, walking fast and resting in his chariot whenever the terrain allowed, bow always poised and eye alert for the slightest movement.

At last, on a dreary, flat beach, he saw the silvery back of a huge fish break the surface of the water, and he shot. The fish thrashed, and the sea was tinged with crimson; then the beast was swallowed by the waves. Ordinance had got the better of the recalcitrant gods.

Next day, however, he was struck down with violent nausea and unbearable pains in the head. Still, he walked along the sea front, watching the changing yet motionless surface of the dark water. Finally, reluctantly, he headed west.

Now scarcely able to stand, he realized that he was going to die. But no one dared refer to his condition: illness and death were forbidden subjects. Soon he was in the last extremity, vomiting bile. The people around him anxiously observed his livid pallor, hollow eyes, and gaze already turned inward. They reached the palace at Sandy Mount and stopped there for him to rest from the fatigues of the journey. He asked to be left alone, and wrote a letter to his eldest son, whom he had exiled in the northern marches. Just as he appended his seal to what he had written, death seized him, in the tower of Deep Repose. It was Ching Yin day in the seventh month.

Li Ssu feared that if the dignitaries in the capital learned that the Emperor had died while away on a journey, they would conspire to overthrow the dynasty. No heir had yet been named, and the death had taken place a great distance from Double Light—two very dangerous factors. Li Ssu decided, therefore, to keep the matter secret. Only three intimates knew besides Li Ssu, Chao Kao, the eunuch in the Emperor's personal suite, and Prince Hu Hai. The body was put in one of the carriages used for resting, with the slatted shutters and gauze curtains designed to retain heat in winter and provide ventilation in summer.

Officials still came to the carriage for their orders, and servants brought food there as before. The eunuch spoke in place of the corpse, and also dealt with the meals. No one suspected.

As the black cortège continued westward, Chao Kao approached Hu Hai and said, "The king is dead. He would never give any of his family a fiefdom or other estate, and all that he left is a letter addressed to Fu Su. It has been passed on to me as the officer responsible for the dispatch of decrees and sealed orders, but I have not yet sent it. Read it—it is tantamount to an investiture."

He handed the young man the following lines, written in his father's shaky hand: "Fu Su, my son, bring Meng T'ien's armies to the capital immediately, perform the funeral ceremonies, then bury me in my tomb at Li Shan."

"As soon as Fu Su reaches the capital, he'll proclaim himself Emperor!" cried Chao Kao. "You won't have anything—not even an inch of land!"

"What do you want me to do? If my father died without leaving me anything . . ."

"At this moment power lies in the hands of three people—you, me, and the prime minister. And you don't even put up a fight! The Empire will not obey a prince whose only claim to legitimacy rests on a fortunate combination of circumstances.

"King T'ang the Victorious and King Wu killed their masters and stole their thrones, and the Empire made no objections. On the contrary! No one who wants to do great things balks at such details. Fortune smiles on the bold. Shrink from no crime or felony, and the gods will bow before you. Come, do as I say—you won't regret it."

"The king's death has not even been announced, the date of the funeral has not even been fixed, and you want us to confer with the prime minister!"

"Time! Time! He who delays will never achieve anything! Strike while the iron is hot!"

Hu Hai let himself be won over.

"Of course," said the eunuch with a sly smile, "if we don't get the prime minister on our side, we're sunk. But leave it to me—I'll persuade him."

Chao Kao went to Li Ssu and, after looking around to make sure that no one could hear, said: "The king is dead. He wrote a letter to his eldest son, asking him to take charge of the mourning ceremonies. The letter is in my possession, as are the imperial seals. No one knows about all this. The choice of a successor, therefore, depends on you and me."

"I refuse to listen to any more," cried Li Ssu. "Such thoughts shouldn't even enter your head!"

"Answer these questions, then. Who has done more for the Empire, you or Meng T'ien? Who is the better politician, you or Meng T'ien? Who is more popular? In whom has the king's eldest son more confidence—you or Meng T'ien?"

Li Ssu was silent.

"I have worked in the inner palaces for more than twenty years," said the other, "and never have the lands of a fallen minister been passed on to his descendants. On the contrary—their families have been exterminated and their altars razed to the ground. The Emperor had ten sons. The eldest is inflexible in character and interested only in military exploits. If he comes to the throne, he will strip you of your badges of office and send you back to your village.

"But I have had the honor of being in charge of the youngest son, Hu Hai. For years I have been his tutor, with plenty of opportunity to get to know him. He is a diligent student, with a kind heart and a great sense of justice. He is the best of all the Emperor's sons, and it would be both wise and realistic to choose him as his father's successor. Think well before you decide anything rash."

The two men stood facing each other. Li Ssu looked Chao Kao up and down scornfully: with his close-set eyes, the man was just like a rat. "You hate Meng T'ien implacably," he said, "because his brother wanted to put you to death for embezzlement!"

"I wouldn't take that tone if I were you. The highest positions are not the safest at the moment."

"Am I supposed to consult with a wretched eunuch whose mother was reduced to slavery after her husband was put to death, and then went and fornicated with another slave?"

"Your origins are not so noble that I need blush for mine!"

"I'm not talking about blood but about nobility of soul. Not another word, now, or you'll regret it!"

"A wise man conforms to the necessities of the moment—or that's what you and your friend Negation once maintained. Leaves that have turned yellow by autumn fall at the first frost; nature awakes at the sound of the oriole. These are inexorable and necessary laws, and politics, too, must obey them. It so happens that power is now in the hands of Hu Hai, and I shall do all I can to help him realize his ambitions. Let me also remind you that I belong to the inner palace and am therefore senior to civic officials. Hu Hai is your prince. Do you mean to flout the orders of your superior? Really, I'm astonished that you refuse to hear reason, preferring to hide behind notions that are so out of date!"

"Ch'in suffered unrest for three generations for having dispossessed the legitimate heir. The sons of King Huan of Ch'i were beheaded for fighting over the throne. I still have enough self-respect to refuse to lend myself to such schemes."

"Don't you know that the strength of a nation lies in the solidarity between inferiors and superiors? Nothing can shake a country where the ruler's own officials and the ordinary civil servants act as one. Come around to my way of thinking, and you will enjoy the fief of a marquis for many long years. Refuse to do so, and woe betide your family! If I were you, my heart would freeze at the mere thought. But I believe you're a shrewd enough politician to adjust to circumstances and profit by them. You only hesitate because you haven't yet assessed the situation properly."

Li Ssu pondered. The guard was made up almost exclusively of eunuchs and courtiers who supported Chao Kao. Hu Hai had his own men, too. Li Ssu himself could not count on the loyalty of the officials and dignitaries—not all of them were his friends. Even if he managed to oppose the eunuch and eliminate him, he would get no thanks for it. Meng T'ien was very close to Prince Fu Su, and there was no love lost between Li Ssu and the general. If the Emperor's eldest son came to the throne, the best Li Ssu could expect was dismissal and the loss of his seals as marquis and of his position as prime minister. The worst did not bear thinking of. . . .

The awful thing was that the eunuch was right. Li Ssu looked up at the sky, sighed, wiped away a tear with his sleeve, and said wearily: "Is it because we live in troubled times that I haven't the courage to sacrifice my life on the altar of duty? Although, now that I've lost my master, for whom would I be shedding my blood?"

Chao Kao went back to Hu Hai's chariot triumphantly. "I delivered the enlightened order of His Majesty the crown prince," he said, "and the prime minister had no alternative but to obey."

The three men conferred and decided to destroy the August First Emperor's letter, which they replaced with another:

I have traveled all over the Empire offering up sacrifices to the gods and the spirits of the mountains, in the hope of winning their favor and obtaining the herb of immortality.

To you, my son, and to General Meng T'ien, I entrusted the command of several hundred thousand men. But you have had no success. You have conquered no territory, yet have lost thousands of soldiers in battles. Still, despite your unworthiness, you have had the audacity to remonstrate with me, criticizing my decisions and tarnishing my glory. Your heart is full of resentment and hatred because I would not make you heir presumptive. Fu Su, you have never behaved as a dutiful son. You have been disloyal. So I beg you to importune me no more with your presence.

As for General Meng T'ien, throughout all the years that he has lived away from our court he has failed to follow the right path. He has always supported your plots and schemes. He is not a good servant of the state. Let him, too, kill himself! His second in command, General Wang I, will replace him as head of the armies in the Northwest.

They sealed the letter with the imperial seal, and one of Hu Hai's followers was instructed to deliver it to Fu Su.

———

The young prince went out to meet the messenger, unrolled the letter, and burst into a flood of tears. Then he re-entered his tent, and was about to cut his throat with the sword the envoy had handed him when Meng T'ien stayed his arm. "The Emperor is on a journey," he said. "He hasn't yet designated a successor. He entrusted us with the command of a force of three hundred thousand men on the frontier. You are superintendent general of the army—a very distinguished position. And yet you would let a mere note end your life! Make sure first that it's not a trick. Ask for confirmation before you do anything irreversible."

Outside, the messenger grew impatient. "You've read your father and Emperor's order!" he called.

Fu Su was dutiful. "When a father orders his son to kill himself," he told Meng T'ien, "it's unheard of for the son to have the impudence to demand explanations!"

And he seized the sword and cut his throat. But Meng T'ien

refused to obey the orders, so the attendants of Hu Hai's follower rushed into the tent and arrested him, and he was thrown into Yang Chou prison.

———

The black cortège moved on toward the capital. Until now the weather had been cool, and the litter on which the dead man lay was packed with ice. But once they left the Yellow River and T'ai Yüan behind and crossed the Eternal Mountains, it became terribly hot. Despite all the mineral drugs inside it, the body began to decompose, giving off a horrible smell. The eunuchs guarding the coach fainted. It was impossible for the stench to go unnoticed.

So Chao Kao and Li Ssu ordered a load of herring to be carried alongside the king's coach, to mask the smell. The procession arrived in Double Light in a strong stench of fish tinged with the sickly reek of corruption.

EPILOGUE

A rat retreated furtively into its hole on hearing the sigh Li Ssu heaved as he gazed gloomily at the moldy walls of his cell.

"What a world!" muttered the former prime minister. "How can an utterly worthless prince be expected to listen to the advice of a man of integrity?"

The tyrant Chieh put Pan-lung P'eng to death, Chou killed Wang-su Pi-kan, and Fu Ch'ai, king of Wu, had his minister Wu Su-hsü sewn up in a sack and thrown to the fishes in the Blue River. And history repeated itself. He, Li Ssu, had not the talent of those famous victims, nor did the prince he had served possess a quarter of the greatness of any of those three tyrants. It was only natural that he should die for the services he had rendered.

The government of the Second Emperor was about to fall into chaos. Besides putting all his brothers to death to seize the throne, the Second Emperor had eliminated the faithful servants of the state and raised the lowliest creatures to honors in their place.

It was comical, really, thought Li Ssu. The prediction that he and Master Wu had concocted was coming true. Hu the downfall of Ch'in—but it was not the Hu barbarians, as expected, it was Hu Hai, Ordinance's son! As if heaven were taking its revenge for Li Ssu's skepticism and impiety. That his prediction should have brought about Ch'in's downfall!

But he was growing as superstitious and peevish as a Confucian! He gritted his teeth. Feng Ward-Off-Evil and Feng Ch'ieh had preferred suicide to the disgrace of imprisonment, but he, Li Ssu, refused to give in and leave the reins of government in the hands of the vile Chao Kao. He must stay alive in order to make the young prince listen to him, and to denounce the eunuch's schemes. Admittedly, he was also afraid of death and couldn't bring himself to take his own life.

The rat stuck its nose from its hiding place and took a few steps in his direction. Li Ssu was too deep in thought to notice. He went on listing the new ruler's follies, staring into space.

"He enlarged the next-door palace, as the people call it, that horrible great barn on the south bank of the river, as if his subjects weren't burdened enough by forced labor and taxes! The gods know I didn't spare him my protests. But what could I do if he wouldn't listen? He has no human feelings. A bloodthirsty madman. He kills his brothers without the least remorse and eliminates his most faithful servants without batting an eyelid. The only thing he thinks about is building palaces, towers, and terraces, for which he squeezes his people and squanders his wealth. All the country east of the mountains has raised the standard of revolt. But he is deaf to heaven's warnings and obstinately follows the advice of a criminal!

"Perhaps I shall have the painful pleasure of seeing the rebels at the gates of Double Light, and even sacking the proud capital!

Yes, soon wild animals will browse on the grass that grows up between the broken stones of the palace courtyards."

Chao Kao, entrusted with the matter by the Second Emperor, had his predecessor indicted. The main charge was "conspiracy to overthrow the state."

It was a clever move. In the course of their march on the capital, the leaders of the insurgents had led their ragged army through the prefecture of Three Rivers without encountering any resistance. It was not until they reached the Hung Mountains that they were defeated by Shang Tan. The latter, in charge of the convicts building the First Emperor's tomb, armed those convicts and promised them remission of their sentences if he was victorious. The prisoners fought well and forced the rebel army to retreat. After Shang Tan's great victory, an inquiry was held into the attitude of the administration in Three Rivers. There was talk of connivance with the rebels. But the prefect of Three Rivers was none other than Yu, Li Ssu's elder son. This was excuse enough for the eunuch to have Li Ssu executed—seeing as Li Ssu was too much of a coward to rid the Emperor of his presence himself.

The former minister's soliloquy was interrupted by a clatter of boots and the clang of the door opening. Five guards rushed in, seized him, kicked in his teeth, stuck slivers of wood under his nails, and cut him with knives to make him confess. Overwhelmed with pain, Li Ssu admitted he was guilty of treason, of aiding and abetting the rebels.

When his torturers left, Li Ssu wept. Was it possible that, having known such glory, he should fall so low? Then he cheered up. He would fight to the end. The game wasn't lost yet. By the magic of the word, he would succeed in opening the eyes of a prince led astray by an unscrupulous adviser.

He asked the guards to bring him writing materials, and soon his brush was flying once more over the silk.

———

Li Ssu was full of hope when he heard the door open. Ten men in the uniform of palace officials came in and questioned him. He felt quite confident that the king had liked his petition. He revoked his confession, insisted that he was innocent, and made accusations against the eunuch Chao Kao. The men then drew clubs from their sleeves and beat him senseless.

Leaving the prison, they removed their uniforms and went to Chao Kao's house, to report what had happened. "He's not likely to try that trick again," they boasted.

A cruel smile lit up the eunuch's face. Soon he would be rid of the last obstacle to his ambitions. He arranged for Li Ssu's petition to King Hu Hai, which he had intercepted, to be delivered. Impressed by the vehemence of the letter, Hu Hai sent an official to interrogate Li Ssu further. But when the real officers entered his cell, the prisoner was too terrified to withdraw his confession.

When he read their report, the Second Emperor exclaimed, with tears in his eyes, "To think that I almost believed the accusations of that scoundrel Li Ssu!"

———

Meanwhile, the officials in charge of the inquiry into Yu's role in the rebel invasion of Three Rivers discovered, arriving there, that Yu had been murdered by one of the leaders of the insurrection. When they heard, back in Double Light, that Li Ssu had been arrested and charged with treason, they falsified their findings and accused You, to avoid incurring the wrath of Chao Kao, the new power in the land.

In the seventh month of the second year of the reign of the Second Emperor, former Prime Minister Li Ssu was pronounced guilty of high treason and sentenced to death and the five punishments. The execution was to be carried out in the main square of Double Light. Li Ssu was taken from his cell and tied to his younger son, Hsieh. As they were driven through the streets, Li Ssu turned to his companion and said, weeping bitterly: "Do you remember when we both went out through the Shang Ts'ai gate, with our big brown dog on a leash, to hunt hare? We didn't know how lucky we were then!" Father and son burst into sobs.

———

After Li Ssu's execution, Chao Kao was made prime minister of the left, and his decisions prevailed in everything. To demonstrate that he was the one who wielded power, he gave young Hu Hai a stag, saying, "Be good enough to accept this horse."

"But it's a stag, isn't it?" asked the Emperor in astonishment.

"No, a horse," all his entourage insisted.

Chao Kao had learned what he wanted to know: that he could call things by whatever names he pleased.

The Emperor was frightened, thinking that something must be wrong with his eyes. He consulted his soothsayers, but they had been bribed by the eunuch and told him: "The great sacrifices you offered up at the equinoxes and the solstices did not purify you completely. You must perform an expiatory fast."

He was sent to the estate at Shang Lin, where he spent his whole time hunting. Chao Kao let a prisoner loose in the grounds and shot him down with arrows. The he went and rebuked Hu Hai. "You have killed an innocent man," he told him. "That is a great sin in the eyes of the gods, and calamities will rain down on you. You had better go into retreat as a sign of contrition."

Hu Hai withdrew to his country palace at View of the Barbarians, but he had not been there three days when the eunuch ordered a section of the guard to put on clothes of mourning and march across the land brandishing arms. Chao Kao himself rushed in to the Emperor shouting, "The rebels are coming! The rebels are coming! We're surrounded!"

Hu Hai went to the top of a tower. When he saw all the armed men dressed in white and advancing on his palace, he fainted. Chao Kao forced a sword into his hand, made him cut his own throat, and took the imperial seals.

He wanted to have himself proclaimed Emperor, but the court dignitaries objected. The ground trembled beneath his feet as he approached the dais, and he realized that heaven was against his plan. So he resigned himself to appointing an Emperor—Tzu Ying, one of Ordinance's nephews. Tzu Ying, afraid of suffering the fate of his cousin, cut the eunuch's throat and murdered all his supporters.

Tzu Ying had not been on the throne three months when one of the rebel chiefs seized the capital. The government surrendered without a fight.

Tzu Ying and his wife came before the victor clad in mourning garments and with ropes around their necks. The rebel leader, from whom there emanated a bright-yellow light, had them imprisoned while he decided their fate. He affixed seals to all the official buildings and withdrew outside the walls of the city. A month later, an army of nobles led by King Hsiang entered the capital in their turn. Tzu Ying and all the members of the imperial family were put to death, and the entire population of Double Light was massacred. The concubines and treasures in the royal palaces were carried off, and the tomb of the First August Emperor was sacked. The city burned for three months before the fires died out.

MAIN CHARACTERS

LÜ PU-WEI, merchant, protector of White Crow and possibly the true father of the future First Emperor.

LI SSU, minor civil servant in Ch'u, retainer of Lü Pu-wei, later prime minister to the First Emperor.

FIRST EMPEROR (Ch'in Shih Huang Ti), known as Ordinance, son of White Crow and of Lü Pu-wei's former concubine.

WHITE CROW, son of Family Peace, held as a hostage in Chao, father of Ordinance. Also known as Boy from Ch'u.

FAMILY PEACE, crown prince, son of King Ch'in the Resplendent.

CH'IN THE RESPLENDENT, king of Ch'in.

LADY OF HUA YANG, favorite of Family Peace, adoptive mother of White Crow.

THE QUEEN MOTHER, former concubine of Lü Pu-wei, wife of White Crow, mother of the First Emperor.

FAN SUI, Wei orator, later prime minister to Ch'in the Resplendent under the name of Shang Gratification.

TZU HSI, eldest son of Family Peace, legitimate heir to the throne of Ch'in.

TU TS'AN, adviser to Prince Tzu Hsi.

WEI THE ASSEMBLER, prime minister of Wei, prince of the blood, sworn enemy of Fan Sui.

BULWARK OF FAITH, prince of the blood in Wei, brother of the wife of the prince of P'ing Yüan.

SPRING AWAKENING, ex-bourgeois prime minister of Ch'u.

CHAO THE PANTHER, prince belonging to the Chao royal family, hostile to Lü Pu-wei.

PURITY OF JADE, spy in the pay of Lü Pu-wei.

PEACE OF ARMS, also called Pai Ts'i
WANG CH'IEN
LI CONFIDENCE   } Ch'in generals
MENG T'IEN

CHAO KUO   } Chao generals
LIEN PO

THE CRIPPLE, spy in the pay of Ch'in.

Piebald Cloud, the Cripple's daughter.
Han Negation, philosopher, fellow student of Li Ssu.

Hsün Tzu, Li Ssu's teacher.

Yao Chia, orator and double agent.

Lao Ai, lover of the First Emperor's mother.

Cheng Kuo, engineer and double agent.

Su Tai
Ts'ai the Benefactor } sophists

Cinnabar, crown prince of Yen, enemy of the First Emperor.

Ching K'o, swashbuckler in the pay of Cinnabar.

Kao Chien-li
Shuo the Butcher } Ching K'o's friends

Hsü the Blessed
Master Lu
Master Shih } Taoist sages
Master Hou
Han Chung

Chao Kao, eunuch, enemy of Li Ssu.

Hu Hai, successor to the First Emperor.

Fu Su, First Emperor's eldest son.

Tzu Ying, successor to the Second Emperor (Hu Hai).

AFTERWORD

The events described in *The Chinese Emperor* are true, or at least were regarded as true by the official chroniclers and historians of the period. With the exception of Purity of Jade and Piebald Cloud, all the characters are "historical"—they are mentioned in documents contemporary with or immediately subsequent to the relevant events. The second half of the third century B.C. really did see the creation and fall of the first centralized empire. The political organization set up by the First Emperor (Ch'in Shih Huang Ti) and his minister Li Ssu endured for more than twenty centuries in various avatars—of which the present regime is the latest.

The main lines of my narrative derive from the *Annals of Ch'in* and the *Chronicle of the Reign of Ch'in Shih Huang*, along with histories of noble families, genealogical tables, and biographies of Li

Ssu, Lü Pu-wei, Fan Sui Ching K'o, Meng T'ien, and so on, by the famous Han historian Ssu-ma Ch'ien. These sources were supplemented by narratives and anecdotes from *Stratagems of the Warring States*, a miscellany of documents (sophists' speeches and letters, politicians' ruses, diplomats' and secret agents' reports, rhetorical exercises, etc.) compiled by the bibliographer Lü Hsiang in the first century A.D. Other historical material is from encyclopedias and philosophical treatises dating from the end of the Warring States and the beginning of the Han dynasty.

But, although it follows the main historical facts, this is not a history book, or even a historical novel. I sought to create an atmosphere, and suggest certain ways of looking at human and political relationships, rather than revive or reconstruct a bygone age. Quite apart from its events and its social history, the world of Ch'in fascinated me as a mirror of the present day. The legal system concocted by Negation and put into practice by his fellow student and murderer, Li Ssu, exemplifies the way all bureaucratic states operate. This does not mean that it is modern. On the contrary, Ch'in is an archaic, a very archaic society, into which the Lie has not yet been incorporated. Ch'in's leaders are not afraid to say what they are doing, and what they are doing is strangely like what all present-day politicians do, except—a large exception—that the latter either say nothing about what they are up to or dress it up in ideology.

Over and above the political fable, *The Chinese Emperor* tells the stories of several curious lives or quests—quests in which people with an absolute thirst for power become divested of their personal characteristics and cease to exist as individuals. They merge into their office to become Great Men, the very opposite of characters in a novel. In this respect it is a book without characters, like a history, for its only "characters" are not really involved in the action. Ching K'o, Shuo the butcher, and so on are people lost in a world that rejects them and from which they stand apart.

Since I was not writing a history of the First Emperor, I allowed myself a certain amount of freedom in the use of sources—the same sort of freedom a novelist enjoys, though I kept it in tight rein. The society I wanted to describe is not an imaginary one. To characters genuinely (or reputedly) historical I often ascribed words and deeds spoken or done by others—but preferably by their contemporaries.

Here are a few examples.

Lü Pu-wei's petition, Li Ssu's letter, and the dossier compiled by the acting minister are invented, but they have a point of departure in fact. An inquiry really was held into the part played by Lü Pu-wei in the palace revolution fomented by Lao Ai, and into his relations with the First Emperor's mother. Li Ssu really was Lü Pu-wei's retainer, and his rise to power did coincide with—and therefore was ascribed a role in—his former protector's downfall.

The letters in the book are modeled on the many stylistic exercises of the period showing how to write an epistle or petition to a prince.

Lü Pu-wei never wrote an autobiography. I made use of some of the speeches in his encyclopedia, the biographies of merchants in the *Historical Memoirs* (Chapter 129, "Huo Chih Lieh Chuan"), the monograph on human and economic geography in the *Han Shu* (Chapter 28, "Ti Li Chih") and the argument for the defense put forward by the chief secretary in the dispute over salt and iron, a merchant who became a head of state.

Li Ssu did not write the rules concerning rations for convicts and slaves, and the circular on the perfect civil servant is not by him, either. We do not know if he ever saw the inventories and reports at the beginning of Chapter 1 of Part Two, but they are authentic documents that he might have read or written. The circular on the perfect civil servant and the regulations about rations are instructions sent by the governor of the province of Nan Chün, in modern Hupei, to the various administrative areas under him. They were discovered in 1975 in a tomb at Yün Meng. In the same tomb were found various legal records, parts of which I made use of in relevant places.

The idea of the robots was suggested to me by one of the anecdotes in the *Lieh Tzu*, a Taoist work. It tells how Lu Pan, a mechanic, made robots so perfect that the prince he served had them opened up to see whether deceit was involved. The Chinese of antiquity seem to have been fascinated by the myth of animated dolls. The *T'ai P'ing Kuang Chi*, a collection of *mirabilia*, devotes three sections to technical marvels in this field. One example it mentions is a series of nautical exercises performed by robots in the presence of Emperor Yen Ti of the Sui (the *Shui Shih T'u Ching*). That particular account belongs to a later period (fourth century A.D.), but refers to a very ancient phenomenon. Ch'in Shih Huang, the First Emperor, also had robots made. The *Hsi Ching Tsa Chi* (*Various Notes on the Capital of the West*), attributed to Ke Hsüan (third century A.D.), says that Lü Pang, founder of the Han dynasty, discovered robots and a magic mirror in Ch'in Shih Huang's palaces.

The information contained in the "Various notes" is not entirely imaginary. One of the sets of armor it describes in detail, made of plates of jade sewn together with gold thread, was recently exhumed from a tomb. But its way of looking at and describing things is different from ours.

The *Historical Memoirs* mention the presence of robots in the tomb of the First Emperor. Recent excavations revealing that absurd and terrible terra-cotta army suggest that the information in Ssu-ma Ch'ien is correct. All the great emperors were obsessed by robots: Yen Ti of the Sui was only following a tradition. In the same way the palaces, canals, and roads he built were directly descended from the public works of the First Emperor.

The legends and fables, Taoist or otherwise, that quickly grew up around the figure of Ordinance were of great help in re-creating his dream world. And while the descriptions of palaces and landscapes owe much to iconography and archaeology, they owe even more to the poetic prose of the Han period (the *fu* of Ssu-ma Hsiang-ju; the *fu* of the capital of the East and of the capital of the West; the *tz'u* of Sung Yü) and to the descriptions in the ancient encyclopedias (mainly the *Ch'u Hsüeh Chi* of the T'ang and the *Fa Yüan Shu Lin* of the Sui). These passages show us how nature and the city were perceived.

It is not possible to cite the methods I used and the liberties I took with my sources in the case of every episode in the book. For any reader interested in history or in separating fact from fiction, I list my main sources as follows.

Shih Chi (Historical Memoirs). I used Chavannes's French translation of these annals of reigns, genealogies, tables, and monographs, but not the biographies.

Han Shu (Annals of the Han Dynasty). I consulted these for the monographs on punishments and penal legislation, the five elements, canals, the calendar, sacrifices, the balance of trade, and natural and economic geography.

Chan Kuo Ts'e (Stratagems of the Warring States) and *Chan Kuo Tsung Heng Shu (Texts from the School for Politicians)* often provide a different version of the facts from that in the *Shih Chi.*

Mongraphs in the *Hou Han Shu (Annals of the Later Han Dynasty),* the *Ch'in Shu (Annals of the Tsin,* third to fifth centuries A.D.), and the *Sung Shu (Annals of the Liang Sung,* fifth century A.D.) provide information on omens, miracles, fashions in clothes, carriages, etc.

Aristocratic life and ceremonies are minutely described in the *Rituals (Li Chi, I Li, Ta Tai Li Chi*—the first two of these translated into French by S. Couvreur, the third by B. Grympas). Interesting information is also provided by the Confucian classics: the *Kuo Yü (Discourse on Kingdoms),* the *Shih Ching (Book of Odes),* the *Shu Ching (Book of Documents),* the *Ch'un Ch'iu Tso Chuan (Annals of the Principality of Lu,* and the anecdotes appended by way of commentary), the *Mencius* and the *Analects* of Confucius.

The mental universe of the period can be reconstructed completely thanks to the many philosophical works that have come down to us. These also give valuable details of daily life, especially the *Han Fei Tzu.*

The *Hsün Tzu* brings together the lectures given by the teacher of Han Negation (Han Fei) and Li Ssu. It contains a discussion between the elderly Confucian and his legalist disciple.

The *Han Fei Tzu* contains the various writings of the philosopher Han Negation, whose theories were put into practice in Ch'in.

There are a number of other works of this school, such as the *Kuan Tzu* by Shang Yang, prime minister of Ch'in, according Ch'in pre-eminence over other princedoms. The *Shen Tzu* provides a link with Taoism—or, rather, certain schools of it—as do even more clearly the *Fa Ching, Shih Ta Ching, Ch'eng*, and *Tao Yüan* (respectively the *Norm*, the *Ten Essential Principles*, the *Scales*, and the *Source of the Tao*). These texts belong to the Yellow Emperor school and form an appendix to the manuscript of the early Han *Lao Tzu* discovered in a tomb in 1973.

The encyclopedia commissioned by Lü Pu-wei has come down to us, and the text seems authentic. It is called the *Lü Shih Ch'un Ch'iu—The Springs and Autumns of Mr. Lü*.

Taoism is present throughout the book, since the legalism of Li Ssu and Han Negation derives from a certain interpretation of the *Lao Tzu*, and the Great Emperor's mystic quest is also Taoist. In addition to the treatises of the "Father of the Taoist system"—the *Chuang Tzu*, the *Lieh Tzu* and the *Lao Tzu*—I have used archaeological discoveries relating to gymnastic, dietetic, and respiratory practices. These provide a link between early Taoism and later texts.

In this connection I consulted texts contained in the *Tao Tsang*, a compendium of Taoist writings compiled and printed in 1442—for example, the *Lao Tzu Chung Ching (The Central Canon of Lao Tzu)*, the *Wu Fu Hsü* (The preface to the canon of the Five Talismans), the *Huang T'ing Ching*, Ho Shang Kung's commentaries on the *Lao Tzu*, the *Pao P'u Tzu* (the master who embraces the simplicity of Ko Hung), and the *Huai Nan Tzu* (not strictly Taoist, though strongly influenced by Taoism).

Lastly, as regards war and espionage, which figure largely in the book, I have drawn a great deal on Sun Tzu's masterpiece, *The Art of War*. But there are other treatises on the same subject: Mo Tzu devotes several paragraphs to it, and *The Book of Prince Shang* four sections, and a new book on strategy belonging to the fifth century and written by Sun Ping, a descendant of the great strategist Sun Tzu himself, was exhumed in 1974. The *Huai Nan Tzu* contains many paragraphs on the subject, and the appendices to the *Lao Tzu* also attach great importance to it.

There are innumerable collections of *mirabilia* containing anecdotes or curious facts about the August First Emperor: for example, the *Shui Ching Chu*, the *Shih Chou Chi*, the *Sou Shen Chi*, the *Yu Ming Lu*, the *Shu I Chi*, and the *Shuo I Chi*, to name but a few.

There are now a fair number of translations into Western languages of philosophical and historical works concerning the end of the Warring States period. However, I have always worked from the original texts, not wanting to be imprisoned in a version that gives only one of several possible interpretations. A translation can never be anything but a single reading of a text that contains multiple readings. Spared the necessity of transcribing a message as such from one language into another, I was able to apply factual material directly to fictional purposes. This permitted me, with a clear conscience, to use the original texts with considerable freedom—more freedom than translation as currently understood can ever allow.

ABOUT THE AUTHOR

Jean Lévi was born in 1948 in Paris. After receiving his doctorate in France, he studied in China at the University at Peking, the University of Fudan, and in Shanghai from 1973 to 1975, during the Cultural Revolution. A sinologist of note, Lévi has published numerous articles on the totalitarian systems and mythology of ancient China. *The Chinese Emperor* won the Goncourt Prize for historical fiction.